WINDS OF SUCCESS

Author, Richard Jan

Library of Congress registration number: TXu 1-688-624.

Published by Richard Jan Hoekstra

Last Edited, 7/15/2024.

ISBN:
Hardcover: 978-1-964289-68-7
Paperback: 978-1-964289-67-0

Winds of Success is the title of the first book in a series titled **Dying to Succeed**.

To date, twelve books make up this series, written first and foremost for your entertainment. In the future, God willing, additional books will be added.

The books in this series include:

Book 2, Living with Death

Book 3, Pretending to be Alive

Book 4, Presumption of Sanity

Book 5, Running with Regret

Book 6, Longing to go Home

Book 7, Afraid to Hope

Book 8, Waiting in Infinity

Book 9, Chasing after Time

Book 10, Casualties of Words

Book 11, Traveling into Chaos

Book 12, Snows of Fear

Please Note: My books do not have chapters. Instead, they have episodes like journal entries which are identified by place, date, and time. The speaker is also identified. Where only the time has changed from a previous episode, the date and place may not be repeated, but the speaker is always known. Please forgive me if this is initially confusing. I am confident it will become easier to understand once you have read a few pages.

Richard Jan

Music may best exemplify the internal workings of the mind. Not logic as is commonly thought. If logic ruled the world, we would live in a different world. Perhaps the problem is that we believe we live by logic when in fact our minds are governed by an operating system far more elusive. As I wrote these books, I often played music. May I suggest that as you read these books, you listen to music in the background. I cannot pretend to instruct you concerning what music to play. We all come to music, as we do to words, from different backgrounds. Play the music you love, something that moves you deeply in your soul.

RJ

Deep calls to deep.

I hear your voice in the roar of a waterfall.

And in the rush of breaking waves washing over my soul.

You send your love with the light of a new day.

And in the dark night, your song is still with me,

Like a prayer on my lips to you, the God of my life.

Contents

ACKNOWLEDGMENTS

It is only fair that I acknowledge the help and encouragement which I received from New York Book Publishers. I went to them initially looking for guidance in editing, cover design, marketing, and distribution. They promised me that they could fulfill my needs. I accepted their proposal and began working with them virtually while living in the Midwest with their company's resources located in New York City. Our journey together has been an adventure; one not taken lightly, but traveled with some trepidation and concerns. Special thanks goes to Victor Hughes, who guaranteed me they would not let me down. And thanks to my daily contact, Serena Hoffman for understanding my concerns and assuring me that everything was progressing as it should. And to Jim Bannister who took the time to talk to me when I needed a conversation. And to the many editors and artists who have contributed greatly to the final product. Thanks to them all for helping me achieve what I had hoped for when I first contacted this New York Book Publishers.

AUTHOR'S NOTE

Although I am familiar with the colored gemstone industry from having worked in it for ten years, I don't pretend to be an expert on any level. My knowledge can best be described as that of a man traveling through a city without ever stopping for an extended period of time to experience the living conditions up close. And yet, as I contemplated my journey after it came to an end, I thought it was interesting and perhaps worthy of being a wonderful subject for a book.

But what I discovered as I wrote was that the real story was not the gemstone industry, but how the cast of characters reacted to the challenges they faced, challenges similar to what we daily endure. And it is my hope that knowledge gained from existing for a time in their shoes as you read this book; may encourage you to live a fuller, more purposeful life.

-   Richard Jan

CHARLOTTESVILLE, VIRGINIA, USA, HEADQUARTERS OF GEMSTONE INTERNATIONAL INC., WEDNESDAY, OCTOBER 15, 2:55 A.M

Moonlight crept into the executive's vacant office through large floor-to-ceiling windows, spreading vague gray shadows over a modern chrome and glass top desk before falling gently on a silent phone.

During the day, this communication device came alive. The phone's console buttons were constantly blinking with urgency, seeking prompt attention, demanding to be heard immediately, revealing the urgent need for action. Calls came in from all over the world, conveying voices that demanded the attention of the phone's owner. More than anything, this modern technological innovation offered ample evidence of its owner's success. A business had been built using this phone, a very successful business.

But at this time in the dark night, the phone displayed nothing, no evidence it was anything more than a meaningless object without purpose; a silent sentinel, a watchman waiting for the morning; hoping to avoid calls which spoke of tragedy, problems which could not be easily solved... disasters that a brilliant strategic business plan could never have anticipated.

A CAMBODIAN SAPPHIRE MINE,
WEDNESDAY, OCTOBER 15, 1996, 11:05 A.M.

A distant, malevolent rumbling traveled ominously through the treetops before the source of the caustic noise thundered into view.

Jet-powered helicopters, hovering and loud, dotted the sky, their deafening energy transforming a serene landscape of miners who only moments before had been peacefully digging gemstones from a muddy stream. Fireballs erupted in rapid succession from their whirling rocket turrets, raining down on helpless victims looking up in horror, screaming and running for cover. With no time to comprehend the murderous intent of their airborne attackers, explosions surrounded them. Dirt and rocks flew into the air, filled with pulverized bloody limbs. A miner's eyes narrowed as a fireball headed towards him with only time for a brief prayer, desperate and pleading as the weapon of terror tore into his body; ash, bones, and torn flesh remaining in its wake.

Thankfully, mercifully, the lethal scene quickly became obscured by clouds of dust rising from the force of the blasts, covering the massacre like a veil, hiding the murderous deeds from sight; too gruesome to be observed by innocent eyes. Only fate determined who died and who lived in the first minutes of the attack. Lucky victims died instantly, gone before they understood that the last seconds of their lives had passed, while unlucky innocents lived longer; bodies torn by flying shrapnel, blinded and dumb from lethal explosions; their remaining minutes on this earth filled with excruciating pain. Those who still had time and hope ran for safety, their feet crashing through the forest as they scurried and fled the deadly aerial assault, desperate to avoid the lethal missiles as the earth shook relentlessly from the constant barrage, rebelling against the violent explosions.

BANGKOK, THAILAND, OLD FAMILY MANSION, 3:25 P.M. LUANG NUE

'Violence should not be necessary,' Luang stated as forcefully as he dared, his tone firm, not wanting to appear either too emotional or defensive.

He had heard enough. It was time to speak.

Searching the faces of his family members for their reaction to his words; they returned his silent question with rigid, unforgiving faces; waiting and perhaps wondering if he had overstepped his welcome this time and would be asked to leave.

From time to time, under no given schedule, the ranking members of Luang's family were invited to gather around a long conference table in the old family mansion to discuss issues important to the family. Although attending these meetings was not compulsory, willfully disregarding an invitation was a sure method of being demoted in the family hierarchy. It was an act that could inevitably lead to reduced privileges and monetary compensation afforded to those who were loyal.

As acting patriarch of his family, Luang was permitted to sit at one end of the long conference table. From his angle, he could see his entire family gathered together. And while they still respected him, they had begun to place less value on his opinions. Sensing this change, the old man had come to this meeting hoping to avoid an open confrontation, but he could not remain silent. Regardless of the consequences, he felt compelled to speak.

'Plans we make in the future should not include violence,' Luang repeated for emphasis, referring to the Cambodian operation that had taken many innocent lives. 'Surely our family no longer needs to resort to violence. These methods are from our past. Not now. Now, we are civilized. Better methods are available to accomplish our goals: law-abiding solutions, peaceful solutions with less risk,' his words pleading, hoping for reason to prevail.

The room fell silent; all eyes turned towards him. Luang sat back in his chair, attempting to look unconcerned, masking his true feelings, hoping the other men seated around the table could not sense his inner tension. The inability to control one's emotions was considered a sign of weakness in his culture and he did not want to appear weak to the younger members of his family. His goal had been to express his opinion with authority, nothing more.

The long, heavy table around which Luang and the other family members sat had been fashioned from dark wood. It was finely polished and adorned with gold embossed corners. Only a few papers marred its glassy surface; each was neatly positioned and aligned with the edge of the table and the other sheets to ensure symmetry. The men at the table, with the exception of the old patriarch, sat rigidly upright, waiting patiently for the conversation to continue. All were dressed neatly in Western-style suits, white shirts, and ties: the uniform of successful businessmen. They knew Luang was free to express his opinion, as were the other members of his family, but only one man at the table had the power to decide, and the old patriarch had taken a significant risk in challenging him.

At the opposite end of the long conference table sat this man, Luang's nephew. His chair was considered the seat of power, occupied by the man who governed the family's affairs.

The chair had once belonged to the old patriarch until very recently. Luang had given up his right to sit in the chair, not because he had been pressured to resign but by his own decision, but because he had decided it was time to enjoy what remained of his life without the constant responsibility and work that came with being the head of his family. And even though his opinions no longer ruled, Luang was still invited to sit at the table, but only in an advisory role, a role that depended completely on the will of and was given through the grace of his nephew- Sarawong Nue.

Sarawong was named after an ancient relative of great importance. Having that given name was a sign that he would be a great warrior. But he did not favor his given name, and he did not use it. Instead, he chose to be addressed simply as 'Nue, the family's last name, a mighty name which he felt suited him perfectly.

Luang was aware of his nephew's desire to be called Nue. But despite this knowledge, Luang always called his nephew by his first name, a small measure of disrespect which made any dispute between himself and his nephew more challenging to resolve.

Silence was Nue's initial response to the Luang's comment and in accordance, the room remained quiet. No one sitting at the long table dared to speak, clearly aware it would not be wise to take sides in a dispute between two high-ranking family members.

Finally, after a measured time, Nue answered, his voice cool and controlled, measured and firm. 'Our plans must be fluid. They must be allowed to flow along a path of least resistance. Like the waters of a river flowing to the sea, we cannot put obstacles in front of our plans. Our plans must move swiftly and without obstruction. Our work here is to facilitate our family's success, nothing more. Our efforts should be directed to allow our plans to flow with ease. If the path of least resistance is like a gentle river that can be navigated through business alliances and contracts, then we will use peaceful methods,' he stated, his tone bordering on condescending. 'However, if the waters of our plans flow through raging rapids over large hindering rocks, then violence may be required to overcome our problems,' his voice rising. 'We cannot be concerned with what method we choose. Our only concern must be to meet our goals. We cannot fail.'

The old patriarch's eyes swept the room as he listened to his nephew's monologue. Knowing now that his nephew would not heed his advice, Luang wondered if he had gone too far in disagreeing. Perhaps this would be the last time he would be invited to sit at this grand table in this elegant room.

For him, this would be a tragedy. He loved this room. It was magnificent, filled with a richness that hundreds of years of glorious family history had bestowed upon it. Its walls were covered with grand paintings depicting the history of his family. Portraits of all the great patriarchs, their descendants, and the organization's original founders stood stoically, lining the walls of the grand room. Placed in gold embossed frames, the images on the walls told stories of conquests on battlefields painted with the red blood of conquered foes. Luang's eyes wandered, glancing at proud horses rearing over the broken, bleeding bodies of slain soldiers, conquering warriors holding swords high in victorious salutes, screaming maidens, and rich treasures. The bounties of war.

When viewing these majestic old pictures, the old patriarch felt admiration pass through his body. But he also sensed that these scenes from battles of ancient generations were no longer exemplary. Now, the spoils of war were captured on a different kind of battlefield, a battlefield where computers and phones were weapons, where a modern battle plan was a strategic business plan.

Arriving at the family mansion for today's meeting, Luang had slowly ascended the marble steps leading to the grand old wooden doors. The main entrance was commanding, massive, and magnificent. Each step was like a journey through time. He remembered the first time he climbed these stairs as a young boy. Over the years, he rose in the ranks to become the head of the clan. Now, his heart wept when the old doors were opened for him not as the man who lived in this mansion but simply as a visitor. He remembered better times, times when these doors were opened by him to welcome others.

He loved this old house. He missed it terribly.

The family mansion was constructed during a time when Bangkok ruled a vast area of Southeast Asia. According to legend, the mansion was once nothing more than a simple hut on the banks of a river: the humble home of an ancient ancestor. But when the king noticed this ancestor's fearless deeds and proficiency on a battlefield, his ancestor had been gifted land and a grand title. From a simple, poor beginning, this house had become the headquarters for one of Thailand's most powerful family dynasties. Rebuilt and remodeled many times, first from mud and wood, then with stone and stucco, this mansion had been continually expanded and renovated until it now stood on the land given to the family by the king as the home of the Nue clan. With its tall spires, carvings of elegant design, and great columns, the mansion served as a symbol of the family's wealth and power. The surrounding lush, landscaped gardens were a means of separating the space from the outside world.

In accordance with tradition, the head of his dynasty always lived in this house. Luang had once been this man. He had lived in this mansion for many years. Because he had no son, his nephew became his natural heir. When Luang decided it was time to relinquish his position of power, he had to abandon his right to live in this house. He was required to move. This was very difficult for him. He now enjoyed returning to his ancestral home for visits. He especially liked sitting in this grand conference room. And some days, like this day, he regretted his decision to retire. He had been successful during his time, successful without the use of violence. The family's empire had grown in wealth primarily because of his ability to negotiate alliances, treaties, and deals. For the last forty years, the family's fortune had increased significantly due to his ability to make decisions based on peaceful strategies. He introduced the use of modern communication machines and became an expert in international laws governing business and finance.

His work had served his family well. He saw no reason to return to the old ways. He regretted his nephew's recent retreat into the past. It saddened him. The cost was the loss of innocent lives. But he also knew his nephew faced a challenge that was nothing like anything he had ever faced. A foreign company headed by an American had come into existence and this company had quickly ate into the very core of his family's business, operating on a global scale.

Thousands of countrymen's jobs were lost as a consequence; jobs lost to gem cutters in countries such as Sri Lanka and India; money lost to gemstone sales in Hong Kong. The economic losses were profound. They dealt a staggering blow to his nation's economy and his family's business. Something needed to be done. The Thai government demanded it.

It was expected that his family deal with this issue as had been their responsibility in the past, employing all means at their disposal, including murder if required.

CHARLOTTESVILLE, VIRGINIA, 7:10 A.M., JOHN VAN LAAN, CEO OF GEMSTONE INTERNATIONAL, INC.

'John.' Helen's stern voice interrupted my concentration, erupting out of the black plastic intercom on my desk, immediately demanding my attention.

I had been comfortably sitting at my office desk reviewing a resume from an applicant for the job of my personal secretary when Helen buzzed me. She was the office secretary and I was her boss, but there were times when Helen acted more like my mother than my secretary.

The applicants I had interviewed to date were primarily female. Some were very talented and some pretty, but something was missing in each of them, some spark which said, 'Hire Me.' And to be honest, even though many of the applicants were very attractive, their interviews made me weary. I hated sitting at my desk with a fake smile on my face, listening to them tell me a bit about themselves. I did not care what their aspirations were; I just needed to know if they were willing to work for me the way I required.

Thankfully, I had only one more application to review that morning before returning to my normal tasks, such as reading a mining report which had come in from Montana.

The mine was an important source of income for my company. It was a great cash cow mainly because its supply of gemstones was constant and secure. It was not subject to local political uprising which, unfortunately, was a problem for mines in many third world countries. And although the percentage of high-quality stones was not great, the Montana mine could be very profitable if operated efficiently. Even though most of the stones did not exhibit the deep red color of a genuine ruby, some pink sapphires that came from Montana, were in my opinion, wonderful gemstones of exquisite beauty.

It is not widely known that a ruby is a red sapphire. Corundum is the technical name for sapphires. In its pure form, it is a clear crystalline stone; its hardness exceeded only by diamonds. Its vibrant color comes from trace amounts of iron, titanium, or chromium found in its crystals. Sapphires are commonly assumed to be blue, but they occur naturally in many colors, including gold, green, and purple. It is my opinion that red rubies and blue sapphires are far more beautiful than diamonds. And they are rarer.

'John.' Helen's voice interrupted again, insistent and unyielding.

I pushed a button on the intercom. 'Yes, Helen,' I replied, wondering why she had come into the office early. But then she often arrived early, knowing that calls came in from around the globe. Time was no constraint when doing business on an international basis. And Helen liked being in control, which she accomplished by managing the incoming calls.

'Vidu is on the phone,' she replied.

Vidu Warnapura owned factories in Sri Lanka that cut and polished most of the sapphires and rubies my company purchased from across the globe. Thousands of sparkling, colored gemstones were graded and sized under his supervision in preparation to be mailed directly to clients. Stones that did not fulfill an existing order were sent to distribution Houses in London, New York, and Hong Kong for later sales.

He was a vital resource, not only for the work his factories supplied but also because Vidu was my mentor in the business. I owed him big time. Without Vidu's help, I would never have been able to build my company.

'Vidu?' I answered my phone while calculating the time in Sri Lanka. It had to be late afternoon on his island home, and he seldom called at this hour. I immediately became concerned.

'Sorry, John,' he replied over the phone. 'I hope I'm not interrupting something important.'

A small man by Western standards, Vidu had dark skin and black wavy hair. He was very handsome, almost pretty, with the black eyes that typified his island nation. His normal manner of speaking was extremely calm. This, combined with a unique English accent softened by a naturally happy Indian dialect, made for pleasant conversation.

'Don't ever be sorry, Vidu. You can call me anytime. You know that.'

I liked Vidu, and I hoped he felt the same way about me. In the beginning our relationship had not been easy to establish in a world separated by thousands of miles of distance and hundreds of years of cultural differences. However, according to Vidu, we had a common bond, a common legacy. Dutch sailors had settled on his island of Sri Lanka during the Colonial Era. He said he understood and liked Dutch people from having lived comfortably with them for generations. And given that my genetic background was Dutch, he assumed he would like me as well.

I had laughed, explaining that if he had the unfortunate experience of becoming acquainted with my Dutch ancestors, the strict religious folk who settled Western Michigan, he might have a completely different opinion, one which was far less complimentary. He had knowingly smiled and I believe my honesty helped us to get off to a good start.

'I know, John, and thank you,' he replied. 'But I am afraid I am the bearer of bad news today.'

Now, I was even more concerned. Vidu was a tough and experienced man. He almost never overestimated the importance of anything.

'I have just now received a terrible phone call,' he continued. 'I am sorry to have to tell you this, John, but I was informed...' his voice trailed off. 'One of our Cambodian mines has been raided.

Many miners have lost their lives today, John. It's possible our friend, Loc Tran, is among the dead. It was a massacre, John. So many dead, and the villager's gemstones were stolen.'

I took a deep breath. The news was bad, very bad.

I tried to somehow process it, given that our relationship with the miners in Cambodia had been going so well. Vidu's company was our contact in the region. Gemstones we purchased from this area were first-rate. The loss of product from the mine would be a significant economic blow to my company. But that was nothing compared to suffering of the villagers.

'How many miners were killed?' I asked, fearing his answer.

'I don't know the details. I have only now just received a preliminary report. Helicopters, soldiers in uniforms, details are not clear,' Vidu replied. 'I only thought you would want to know.'

'I'm so sorry, Vidu.'

'It is not your fault, John.'

'Do you know who is responsible?' I asked

'I'm guessing it was a regional dispute over mining rights. Unfortunately, these things happen.'

COLUMBO, SRI LANKA, SAPPHIRE CUTTING FACILITY, 6:40 P.M. VIDU

Vidu put down his phone.

A call had come in immediately after his conversation with John. The call was not pleasant, nothing to calm his already disturbed state of mind after receiving news of the tragedy in Cambodia.

Vidu prided himself on maintaining control in difficult situations, but he had difficulty keeping his composure that afternoon, his mind deep into imagined dead bodies lying on a river bank.

The man had called to complain.

Why, Vidu wondered, was someone always complaining, complaining to him, no one else. Why not someone else? Was it his fault an American had accomplished what no one else in the business had been able to do for hundreds of years? Wasn't it better this way? Everyone made more money, a lot more money, especially miners in Africa and Southeast Asia. Workers in cutting factories in India and in his country, Sri Lanka, now had jobs, stable jobs. Thousands of jobs around the world have been created with help from the American company. Yet, despite the progress, someone was always complaining, complaining to him.

He knew why.

Because it was in their nature to complain. He answered his own question. Still, he was tired of their constant grumbling, sick of being the middleman. All because John was his friend.

Suddenly, he had an urgent desire to get away from his phone for a few minutes, time to clear his mind from the dense drivel of small minds. He did what he always did when he needed a break. He headed for his factory. Exiting his sparsely furnished, air-conditioned office, he walked down a long hall and opened a door into a large warehouse. Compressed, hot, humid air immediately assaulted his senses. Sweat beaded on his forehead despite humming metal fans tucked into walls, providing a measure of relief. A hot, pungent smell permeated every corner of the building filled with workers and machines everywhere.

Rows of young Sri Lankan women could be seen hunched over metal tables. In the center of each table was a small revolving wheel covered with highly abrasive material. A mechanical arm above the wheel held a rough sapphire. As the wheel turned, the mechanical arm was lowered, causing the rough gemstone to grind against the revolving serrated surface. The stone touched the rough surface of the wheel for only a short time, enough to create a highly polished facet on the stone's hard surface. Then the arm lifted and the stone was turned a fraction before once again being lowered to the surface. Each contact with the wheel created another smoothly polished facet until the whole surface of the stone was fashioned into a perfectly shaped gemstone.

Vidu casually reached over to pick up a particularly clear blue sapphire from a pile of newly cut and polished gemstones lying on one of the tables. Holding the gem up to an overhead fluorescent lamp, he gazed in the heart of the beautiful stone. A myriad of sparkling blue flashes reflected in his eye as he rotated the stone with his fingers. He took a deep breath, sighed, and returned the stone to the pile.

The gemstones always gave him pleasure. When everything else in his world seemed to be heavy on his mind, Vidu could always count on his gemstones to revive his diminished spirits. The gemstones were so magnificent that it was almost unbelievable that they were found on this earth. In a way, they seemed divine. Peace could be found inside the soul of a gemstone. The light shining from the dark inner core of these wonderful stones originated from somewhere close to the hot flowing center of the earth where the gemstone was formed. Imprisoned for millions of years, its light was now allowed to escape in flashes of brilliant color; as if the gemstone was gratefully sighing, its light once again allowed to freely rove the universe, lingering in space with its sisters, the stars.

Proceeding down long aisles of women toiling over gemstones, Vidu was pleased with what he saw. All of them were hard at work. A few of his workers turned to smile at him. They were mostly young and worked long hours by U.S. standards. Their work was repetitive and difficult, but they were happy to have a job. The money they earned freed their families from poverty.

Stopping at one of the tables, he observed a pile of rough stones ready for polishing. To the untrained eye, they looked like nothing more than dull blue gravel. But Vidu knew what was hidden within the dull, unremarkable exterior. Fascination and beauty dwelled there.

Rough stones prior to cutting and polishing are larger than the finished product. Gem weight is lost in cutting and polishing, but this cannot be helped. A stone's true value cannot be realized until after it is properly cut. Only then can it be sold for a good price.

This factory was the oldest factory Vidu owned. It was devoted to cutting only sapphires. Sapphires were Vidu's favorite gemstones. Sapphires were the reason his company existed. They were a natural resource of Sri Lanka, found in the streams and on the hillsides of the island nation. The stones didn't look very pretty in their natural state: gray, white, and opaque with only a hint of blue. Only after they were color-enhanced in special ovens was their natural beauty realized.

In the past, his island's raw sapphires had been cheaply sold to Thailand where the gemstones were color-enhanced, cut, and marketed. While Thailand grew wealthy from the sale of these gemstones, Sri Lanka languished in poverty.

Vidu's company had changed that. After starting small, cutting a few local stones which had managed to evade the Thai buyers, Vidu gained some outside contracts. The first came from African gemstones. Then, he secured contracts to cut diamonds from Russian mines. But it wasn't until after he partnered with his friend from America that he achieved real success. With loans from John, he built two factories. In time, his company grew to eight factories in six years. Two more were on a drawing board.

When people wanted to complain, he wondered why they didn't call his friend, John, in America. But he knew why. They called Vidu because he grew up in their world; he knew their struggles. He knew what they were facing. He was like them, from a small, impoverished country. They assumed he would understand. And he did understand.

He understood everything was different now, better. There was no more bartering, no haggling, only good prices for rough stones, far more than was received seven years ago.

Sapphires from his home country of Sri Lanka now being cut in his factories, benefiting Sri Lanka, not Thailand. His country's economy was growing. He employed hundreds of employees working two shifts, and he was hiring more every day.

However, he did worry sometimes.

Success had come quickly, perhaps too quickly. While he and his country prospered, other countries suffered.

Unfortunately, Thailand was one of the countries which was negatively affected. He wondered if they would retaliate. Would a price be paid for his success?

Was the massacre in Cambodia only the beginning?

CHARLOTTESVILLE, VIRGINIA, LATER THAT AFTERNOON, 4:00 P.M, MONICA SORENSEN

Her resume felt heavy in her hand- guilty, slightly dishonest.

When it was finally time for an interview, Monica Sorensen wished she had included everything and been honest about her life. Honesty was a quality she valued. It would have been far better to have written all her accomplishments on this application, not just the ones from her most recent employment history.

Why not include them all, she thought? If she didn't get this job, she didn't get it. She could find another job. But this job sounded interesting, and she wanted an interesting job after her horrible experiences in the job market.

Washington, DC, had done this to her.

Government bureaucracy had chewed her up and spit her out. DC was a city without conscience, without pity, nothing more than an unabated, uninhibited rush to power. Having long ago become an expert in the art of ignoring reality, this city lacked heart, filled with unbridled delusions of grandeur.

When she couldn't tolerate working in DC anymore, she moved to Charlottesville, Virginia, about a two-and-a-half-hour drive from DC. She had decided to return to a better world filled with good memories: the location of the University of Virginia, where she had previously received her law degree. She took the first job she landed as a waitress and rented an apartment, spending most of her free time reading books and chilling out. It had been relaxing, but after a while, she became bored and decided to look for a job with more challenge. She read the help-wanted ads. One ad in particular caught her attention. The job was personal secretary to a CEO, with full benefits, excellent pay, and the opportunity to travel.

She applied, purposely not including everything on the pages of the application. She was worried that if she listed all her accomplishments, she wouldn't get the job because she would be considered overqualified. Most of her impressive credentials were omitted, such as her law degree and work record from DC.

Now, as she sat waiting patiently in a spacious lobby filled with comfortable leather seating, spotless granite floors, and modern artwork gracing the walls accompanied by tinted, floor-to-ceiling windows, she wondered if her decision to exclude all of her accomplishments in her resume had been wise. The interior of the building, which housed Gemstone International, was impressive, nothing like what she expected when she drove into the parking lot. The exterior of the building didn't indicate that this company was anything more than an ordinary business. The interior, however, presented a completely different face, one of wealth and success.

She felt small sitting in the lobby. Felt like even with all her actual accomplishments, she would not be considered qualified for the job. But it was too late. Her application could not be changed at this late hour. Her only hope was to receive the job based on her attributes. She just needed to present herself as the perfect candidate in the interview, and in this respect, she did not lack confidence. Dressed in her best business suit, she looked put together and professional, like she was a woman who would take no nonsense. And she was also exceptionally beautiful. Her beauty had attracted many admirers. But being attractive was not something that made her proud, grateful perhaps, but her accomplishments in school and her career gave her the most satisfaction. These she had earned through hard work and discipline. They gave her the confidence she needed. They were why she had no reason to be nervous. Her previous job had put her into situations far more stressful than any this job could possibly create.

And yet... perhaps it would not be wise to act too confident during her interview. Maybe it would be better to put on a nervous face and act more like the person her resume described- a lowly waitress who wished to secure a better position.

4:15 P.M, JOHN VAN LAAN

Helen's voice, loud and demanding, sounded through the intercom, impossible to ignore. 'John, your last applicant is here.'

Unfortunately, my ability to concentrate was gone by this time in the afternoon, buried deep in imagined images of a massacre in a faraway country; images of pain and suffering roaming freely through my brain. The village in Cambodia was well known to me. I had visited there. The miners had been friendly and gracious. A foundation funded by my company had built a medical clinic for their families near the village. It was financed by my company. A new school was on the drawing boards.

I couldn't remember how many families lived in this village, but I did remember seeing the children, their happy faces playing in the village. I wondered how many children were crying for their fathers and mothers now. I badly wanted to do something to end their sorrow, but Vidu had warned me that it would be next to impossible to accomplish quickly. We would have to be patient.

As a result I had no real interest in conducting another interview, and I was severely tempted to tell Helen to send the applicant home. But thinking it would be impolite to cancel at this late date, I wearily said, 'Okay.'

'Why so blue?' Helen teased, knowing most of the applicants were young women, some very pretty. Helen naturally assumed I liked interviewing them.

Quickly clicking off my intercom to avoid Helen's taunting, I had a job to do. It was time to get it done. I glanced at the folder on my desk marked 'Monica Sorensen.' Sighing, I skimmed her application, trying to remember what I had read in the morning. Nothing special had captured my attention.

These initial job interviews required professionalism. Therefore, I conducted them while sitting at my desk. And despite what Helen assumed, I was less than fond of the process. I suppose I could have avoided them completely by having Helen hire the secretary, but that didn't seem right. The successful applicant would report directly to me.

The door to my office opened. The applicant followed Helen inside. I came out from behind my desk to greet her.

Her hand felt soft and warm.

'This is Mr. John Van Laan. He will be conducting your interview. John, this is Ms. Monica Sorensen.' Helen introduced us, waiting to see my reaction.

The applicant was tall with long red hair. Her demeanor appeared initially confident despite a shy look on her face. She wore a tailored brown suit, which fit perfectly, the shade complimenting her big brown eyes. The neck of the suit was open, revealing a nice tan, a long neck, and beautiful clear skin.

She stood for a moment, still holding my hand, saying nothing, waiting, I assumed, for me to speak.

I was stunned, temporarily immobilized, still holding her hand.

She was a picture from a fashion magazine: red lips, shiny flowing hair, and eyes that instantly bore deep into my pathetic soul. Fortunately for me, she had the presence of mind to break the awkward silence while releasing my hand. 'My name is Monica,' she said with an irresistible smile. 'Most of my friends call me M.'

'Okay, M, it is,' I half apologized even though an apology wasn't necessary. 'It's a pleasure to meet you. Let's sit over here where it's comfortable.' I pointed to the couch in my office, immediately recognizing that I had broken one of my rules of conduct. My intention was to act professionally, but I continued as if this was what I had planned all along.

'That will be all, Helen.' I motioned for her to leave without looking at her, fearing she was preparing to give me a 'I told you so' smirk.

She just smiled knowingly and closed the door.

The area in my office, where I indicated we should sit, was used mostly for informal business conversations and brainstorming with partners or employees. I found it sometimes productive to work in a less formal setting. Creative solutions often flow better when the atmosphere is relaxed.

When designing my office, I took a different approach than most CEOs. The cushioned gray leather couches and matching chairs were my personal touch. In the middle of the room was a low, circular, glass-top table. The base for the table was an old driftwood log sculpted by the waters of Lake Michigan. I had dragged it off the beach when I was a young man. It was my connection to my hometown- Grand Haven, Michigan.

One wall in my office, the one closest to the couches, was covered with smoky glass. Behind them was a large-screen TV, a bar, and a small kitchen. The opposite wall had a more business-formal look, with a conference table placed below a bookcase that held my personal library. Books lined each and every shelf there; books on business, personal development, professional development and gemstones filled the shelves. Two tall oak doors with silver handles dominated the far wall. The doors separated my office from a corridor. The corridor was filled with offices and led to the lobby. Helen's office was immediately outside my door.

The desk in my office had a glass top and a chrome metal frame. A computer and a telephone system were placed on it. Floor-to-ceiling windows lined the walls behind my desk, displaying a view of a forest valley stretching to the southwest horizon and beyond to hills in the distance. It was a gorgeous view and I loved to gaze at it while drinking my morning coffee in mental preparation for day of work.

As Monica sat down on one of the soft leather couches, I struggled not to stare. Her legs were long and strong, like those of a dancer, moving with obvious grace.

'May I get you something to drink?' I asked, opening the smoky glass doors in a wall disguising a bar.

'Maybe a Coke,' she replied politely.

I was tired. The Cambodian massacre sat heavy on my mind. I badly needed something strong to ease the weight of tragedy.

'It's been a long day. I just received a difficult call... A man I know died. I'm going to have a glass of wine,' I explained hesitantly, breaking yet another of my personally devised rules of professional conduct. 'Would you like to join me?'

'I'm sorry,' she replied. 'Was he a friend?'

'No, not really, a business associate. He lived in Southeast Asia.'

'How did he die?' she asked politely.

'I'd rather not talk about him if you don't mind.'

'Oh, okay, Sorry.'

'So, what will it be, wine or a Coke?'

'I would prefer a beer if you have one... Is that okay?'

'Of course,' I smiled. 'Beer it is.'

I was beginning to like this woman. Her choice of beer over wine was a clue to her mind. It was a small thing, I know, but it demonstrated she was a woman who was not afraid to express herself, an attribute I preferred in my employees.

I found a couple of Coors in my refrigerator and offered one to her with a glass. Okay, it was time to get my concentration back and get on with the interview. However, before I could say a word, she surprised me by taking over the conversation, perhaps because we were sitting in an informal atmosphere having a beer.

'Do you mind if I ask you a question before we begin?'

'Of course.' I replied.

'Is being beautiful important to this job?' Monica smiled.

Her question was most unusual. I couldn't ever remember an applicant broaching this subject. In a business setting, it was usually considered taboo, less than professional, and even sexist to discuss the physical attributes of the opposite gender. I was both amazed and stumped simultaneously.

'It is,' I finally replied because instinctively, I knew any other answer would sound like a lie and be one.

'Thank you,' Monica said, 'I find it's always better to have this issue out in the open.'

'Why?'

'Well, it just seems people pretend looks are not important even when they know this is not true.'

'So.'

'So, I think it's good to discuss issues openly,' she smiled.

'Okay.'

'So, looking good is important to you?' she pressed the issue while continuing to smile.

'Yes, of course. If you are hired for this job, you will represent me as well as my company. And making a good first impression depends, in part, on your appearance.'

'That's true,' she acknowledged.

'Okay, so does this mean I can tell you that you are beautiful?' I countered, beginning to enjoy our verbal joust.

'You can tell me I'm qualified for this job.'

'You are in this respect,' I returned her smile. 'Let's see how you do in some other areas.'

I think she knew she had me. And, of course, she did. But we still had a game to play, so we played. We drank our beers and talked.

'Do you know what the job requires?' I asked.

'Yes. Your receptionist gave me a quick overview.'

'Let's go over a few items to be certain nothing was missed.'

'If you wish.'

'Good. If hired, you will be a full-time employee on twenty-four-hour call,' I began. 'As my personal secretary, you may be required to travel with me on business trips. You will need to be prepared to travel at any time because sometimes I leave on very short notice. Occasionally, I'm out of the country for as long as a month. These trips are often a combination of business meetings and social events. If an obligatory social reception or dinner is required, I may ask you to attend it with me.'

I explained this to her because it was important that she understood the toll this job could take on her and her personal life. As the Chief Executive Officer of my company, I was often invited to social functions. I tried to avoid these dull occasions whenever I could conjure a lame excuse. I didn't like cocktail parties, and I didn't enjoy small talk. However, sometimes, it's unavoidable, and the thought of going alone to these events was even more distasteful.

I paused to see if she had a reaction, perhaps wondering if I was asking for a date on a business trip. Or requesting for more from her than simply a business relationship. This was the typical reaction from an applicant when I raised this subject in interviews. However, she didn't respond negatively. She simply nodded her head and agreed to go with me when it was necessary.

I was happy with her response, but to be certain everything was on the table, I continued. 'Just so there's no confusion about my intentions, I want you to know you will always be provided separate sleeping accommodations wherever we travel. Our relationship is purely professional, nothing more.'

She smiled.

'If hired, you will be considered an 'at will' employee under a six-month contract.' I continued, 'This means you can be released before your six-month contract expires. However, if you are released, the remainder of the first six months will be paid, including health insurance which is guaranteed regardless of what happens for one year. Any questions?'

'Is that it?' she asked.

'Yes, it's all in the contract you will be asked to sign if you are hired. Please be sure to review it before signing. Should you require an attorney to help you understand the contract, I will pay for one.'

'I can read the contract myself,' she smiled, a twinkle in her eye.

I had a distinct feeling she could do much more. And for some unknown reason, I instinctively knew that hiring her was a mistake, but it was too late.

I had already made up my mind.

LONDON, ENGLAND, HEATHROW AIRPORT, OCTOBER 16, THURSDAY, 7:55 P.M.

A small brown cardboard box moved slowly down a wet conveyor belt exiting the belly of a 747 commercial jet at London's Heathrow Airport. The box featured an unimpressive name and apartment address label, indicating its destination.

However, the unsuspecting address did not deter the Indian baggage handler. Suspecting what was inside, he quickly lifted the carton off the belt and held it in his hands, measuring its weight. It was not large but heavy for a package of its size; he noted the origin was Sri Lanka. This was all the information he needed.

Casually glancing around to see if anyone was looking his way, he tucked the carton under his yellow raincoat. It was time for a break.

Slowly crossing a gray, rain-swept tarmac, he made his way toward the terminal building while holding the carton tightly under his arm where no one could see it. He took it to his locker and placed it in a satchel he carried to work every day specifically for this purpose. Most days, it contained only his lunch and a change of clothes. But today, he would leave work with a stolen box hidden inside.

Several weeks before, a man had approached him at work and told him what to search for. The man explained he would be richly rewarded if he could deliver these packages to him. The offer was enticing, and he needed the money. He wondered how much money he might receive for this carton. It felt heavier than some of the others. That was promising.

He knew it was risky. He was committing a crime. But he wasn't stealing simply for himself. He had been saving his money for something important. With any luck, the cash he received for this parcel would give him enough money to buy an airline ticket for his brother. He was looking forward to having his younger brother join him in England. He wanted his brother to have an opportunity to live in the West, to start a new life, and to have a chance to become rich. With this package, it was possible his brother would be coming very soon. This thought gave him joy as he headed for a washroom before returning to work.

Today was just another day; one day closer to achieving his goal. His work was hard, but he didn't mind it. It meant he got to live in the West and reap its benefits. Opportunities were available here that were not available to him in India.

His only complaint was the confoundingly cold rain. He hoped it would let up soon.

He did not like the cold rain in this cloudy country.

CHARLOTTESVILLE, VIRGINIA, OCTOBER 17, FRIDAY, 6:01 P.M. JOHN

'John.'

Helen's stern voice bellowed from deep inside my intercom, startling me as she normally did when I was trying to concentrate.

It was almost like she had a camera rigged in my office for the express purpose of bothering me whenever I was deep into doing work that required more than normal concentration. At the time, I had been reviewing copy for a new ad campaign. I was lost in a different world when her stern voice interrupted.

'Yes,' I replied, knowing I had no choice except to answer her.

'Telephone call, line four, London,' Helen demanded, 'I wouldn't bother you at this hour except it's Arthur on the line.'

'Why are you still here, Helen? It's past six o'clock?' I was mildly frustrated. I had hoped to avoid being disturbed for the rest of the evening. Only a few tasks remained, but they required total concentration.

'I'm leaving now,' Helen replied apologetically. 'Have a nice evening, boss.'

I quickly picked up my phone, assuming any call from Arthur at eleven o'clock p.m., London time, was not necessarily good news. And I really did not need any more bad news.

'John speaking.'

The late afternoon sun cast long, soft shadows across my office as we talked, the rays reflecting off the chrome frame of my glass-top desk. In some light, the desk appeared to be a work of art. Five computer screens blinked off to one side of the desk, displaying impassive data from remote locations worldwide.

'It's Arthur, old boy.'

'Yes, Arthur, lovely to hear your voice again.' I mimicked his accent.

Arthur was the head of our London Distribution House. It was tasked with marketing gemstones to European, African, and Near Eastern clients. London was one of three distribution houses employed by my company. The other two were located in New York and Hong Kong. The New York House handled North and South American sales and was run by Bob Anderson. The Hong Kong House sold gemstones to Far Eastern clients and was run by Lin Hung-Chao. Each house, my word for them, functioned as an independent business, but I considered the men who ran these businesses my partners. I had set them up. Even though they were legally separate entities, I was still their boss because I controlled the products they sold. Without me, they wouldn't have a business.

'Right, John. Sorry to call you at this late hour, but bad news waits for no man,'

Arthur's rather high nasal tone, combined with his naturally snobbish aristocratic accent, always sounded rather comical to me. Still, at that moment, I was far more concerned with what he had to say than how he said it.

He continued, 'I've spent all evening attempting to track a shipment from Sri Lanka. It disappeared upon arrival at Heathrow Airport sometime late yesterday. When I didn't receive it today, I tried tracking it. No luck.'

'You sure?' It can't just disappear?

'Quite sure,' Arthur stated.

I paused. If true, this was the third shipment lost in the last month.

'What is your estimate of the value?' I asked.

Arthur could be heard shifting some papers, finally coming back on the line. 'According to the shipping manifest, I would guess the retail value to be approximately one hundred thousand US dollars. Unfortunately, some rather expensive gemstones were in this parcel.'

The gemstone business demands constant transportation of stones for treating, cutting, inspection, and sales. Moving these packages around the globe by insured couriers can be expensive and not necessarily secure because couriers are easy targets for criminals. As a result, gems are commonly transported by everyday carriers in unmarked and uninsured packages to unsuspecting addresses. This method normally works well because it offers few clues to what is inside the package. But not always. Occasionally, a shipment gets lost. This doesn't happen often, but when it does, the parcel is usually recovered after a short time; normally, the result of having been accidentally diverted for a few hours is some glitch in the transportation system. However, our last two lost shipments were not recovered. And in cases such as this, it can be assumed they have been stolen, usually by someone who has infiltrated the system, someone who knows how our methods work and what to look for; someone who is a business insider.

'Have any of the lost gems come up for sale on the market?' I asked.

'No,' Arthur replied, 'I have sent out inquiries throughout Europe. Nothing has been reported to date.'

'Nothing in North America either,' I commented. 'I've been checking.'

All gemstones can be traced. Microscopic differences in gemstones are markers indicating where they were originally mined. Color, size, and cut are also good indicators. When crooks try to sell the gemstones, the stones can often be traced back to their seller after appearing on the market.

Arthur was silent.

'Not good.' I stated.

'I agree, John. If ordinary blokes were to blame, we would have seen the stolen gems on the market by now.'

'But that hasn't happened.'

'Right,' Arthur replied. 'Quite out of the ordinary. Why steal something if you are not going to sell it? Makes no sense.'

'Do you think someone has infiltrated our routes?'

'I don't know how?' Arthur replied.

'Yes, but what other explanation is there?'

'Could be pure coincidence, just a bit of bad luck,' Arthur commented flippantly.

'Seems highly unlikely to me,' I countered. 'But even if you are right, we can't afford to wait around for another shipment to get lost without doing something. Don't you agree?'

'I suppose,' Arthur sounded unconvinced.

'Good. I suggest using alternative shipping routes. Maybe that will cross up the buggers.'

Arthur was silent.

I continued, not waiting for him to object. 'I was planning to visit London next week to meet with Vidu. Why don't I move up my itinerary so we can discuss new routes in person rather than by phone or fax? Hopefully, that will make the routes more secure.' I paused, reviewing my schedule in my head. 'I can be in London by, say, Monday. Does that work for you?'

'I'll make it work.' He sounded defeated, more concerned than he let on.

'Thanks; I'll call Vidu and ask him to hold all shipments until we have established new routes.'

'Good.'

'Now go home, Arthur. Get some rest. And say hello to Elizabeth for me.'

'As you wish,' sighed Arthur, obviously tired.

'Look, Arthur, don't get discouraged. We have solved bigger problems than this. We can get through this.'

He hesitated as if he wanted to say more. I knew him. He liked to disagree. He wasn't always comfortable with me having authority over him. However, this time, he didn't bother,

'Evening, John.'

'Evening, Arthur.'

I put down the phone while glancing briefly at the ad layout I had been reviewing. My concentration was gone. I turned to the small bar in my office and poured a drink.

Before my company was formed, gemstones, such as pristine green emeralds, sky blue topaz, and blood-red rubies were sold for fractions of their true value. That was my opinion, of course, and it was not shared by the more conventional forces in the industry. But I thought it was true, and it was what I used as the basis for forming a company. Under my direction, Gemstone International Inc. changed the gemstone industry.

Taking control of the market in one colored gemstone was the first step. It all started with sapphires. These were chosen for several reasons: first, because they were very durable- a nine on the Mohs scale of hardness compared to 10 for a diamond; second, because they were scarce; and third, because they were very beautiful.

Building a successful business took time, a lot of work, and an abundance of patience. The last few years have brought us success. We are now the dominant force in the world of sapphires. My company controls over sixty percent of the market. Some even called us 'a cartel.' I personally didn't like the term, but it isn't far from the truth.

Reaching for the intercom, I buzzed Jason, my boy wonder in accounting.

'Go home, Jason,' I said when he answered his phone, knowing he would still be in his office. This interaction between us was normal. It was our private joke. Jason was a workaholic like me. He seldom went home early. Most days, he outlasted me.

'Yes sir,' he replied.

I knew he was smiling even though I could not see him. And he knew I appreciated his work ethic. In a way, he reminded me of me when I was his age. He just needed some direction and experience, and I was more than happy to provide him with both.

'But before you leave, please reschedule my London trip to leave New York on Sunday, arriving Monday morning.'

'Yes, sir.'

'And find the personnel folder for Monica Sorensen. It should be on Helen's desk.'

'The redhead, sir?' Jason asked.

'Right,' I almost blushed, glad no one was in the room. 'Give her a call first thing tomorrow morning. Ask her to come in and sign an employment contract. Then inform her she will be traveling with me to London on Sunday afternoon.'

'Yes sir. Good choice sir.'

'Thanks Jason,' I put the phone down and smiled.

7:05 P.M. JOHN

I didn't need a house.

Although living in Charlottesville was enjoyable, the traffic was terrible. Stoplights are timed for delay. It was always a slow commute to work. My house was big and comfortable, but I spent more time in my office than at home. After working too many late nights and sleeping on a couch in my office, I decided to sell the house and build an apartment attached to my office building. It was simply a matter of efficiency and economics. Why waste time and money commuting back and forth between a house and an office every day? Made no sense.

My apartment is small by conventional standards, but my needs are few. Besides, no one can live in more than one room at a time. So, it doesn't matter how big the apartment is. It's the size of its rooms which are important, and they are spacious with high ceilings and white walls. Woven rugs cover tile and wood floors. A one-and-a-half-story fieldstone fireplace is set between sliding glass windows in the living room. Modern in appearance, the apartment is furnished with comfortable, casual furniture made of wood and leather. My favorite room is the den. It is a small library with bookshelves on three walls. And like every other room in the apartment except the kitchen and the bathrooms, it has a wall of windows that view a valley to the west.

Hidden in one of the bookshelves in the den is a small door that opens into my office, allowing me an easy escape from work. However, physically leaving my office is more easily accomplished than mentally leaving. It is often difficult to put aside thoughts of my company. My work is my life.

However, as was the case today, a time comes, usually around seven p.m., when food and sleep eventually force me to abandon my office for my apartment.

Arny was humming in my apartment's kitchen when I entered. He is my housekeeper, my valet, my chef, and my confidant, and most of all, he is my friend.

Prior to working for me, he moved around, job to job, always looking for that elusive stability that Southern culture seldom offered a black man. Or perhaps drinking was a past problem, I didn't know, and it wasn't my business to ask. Rumors said women were a contributing factor. Apparently, he knew a few, or so he has informed me.

One day, a bit down on his luck, he took a janitorial job at my office. And, as was my habit, I liked checking out the office building in the evening to ensure it was secure and locked down. After Arny was hired, I often found him working late on some project when I went on my rounds. When asked why he was still on the job, he often shrugged his shoulders and said he had nothing better to do. Seemed odd to me, but I saw no harm in his diligence.

Eventually, I began to look for him after work, and usually, he could be found. Our chance meetings eventually became more or less routine. Occasionally, I invited him into my office to share a few beers, which soon became a habit. He helped me unwind at the end of the day after I discovered he liked to talk. And he could talk, believe me. He could talk about anything and everything for hours, which was great. I learned about his life through his stories. Occasionally, he even listened to a couple of my tales, although I had to admit, my life was not nearly as interesting as his. Plus, I couldn't tell a story like he could. Most of the time, I simply listened.

Slowly, unceremoniously over time, we put aside our roles as boss and employee and became friends. That's why building an apartment for him next to mine seemed only natural when I built one for myself. And when I discovered he liked to cook, having learned skills in the fast-food industry, I assigned him a new job title: personal housekeeper and chef. But in reality, we were simply friends in a slightly unconventional relationship. Through an unspoken agreement, we assumed our roles, roles which made both of our lives better.

'I suppose you want something to eat at this late hour?' he asked.

'I still consider eating something of a priority,' I replied.

'Tell me why you can't eat at regular hours like everyone else.'

'Because it would make your life too easy.'

He groaned and asked, 'Had a tough day?'

'I've had better,' I replied. 'Say. Isn't this your poker night? Don't you need to go?'

'Yes, want to tell me what ya want first.' he sighed.

'Steak.'

'Shoulda known. Don't you ever want something easy like soup?'

'Sure, soup's fine.'

'Right, soup.'

I sat at a bar in my kitchen while he cooked steak on an indoor grill. He had a beer as he worked. I sipped a whiskey. This was always the best part of my day; relaxing with a drink and pleasant conversation with my friend.

I knew he liked working for me even though he always tried to make me feel he was doing me a favor. Sometimes, I think he was. He could have retired. He was old enough, but income from a job made his life better.

And in some small way, I think he knew I needed him more than he needed me.

11:15 P.M. JOHN

I had a small desk in my bedroom for late-night work.

This evening, it was covered with papers in preparation for talking to Vidu. I knew he would be in his office when I called, morning his time, night for me.

I glanced over the papers, hoping to have everything straight in my head, before carefully dialing his twelve-digit international number. Phone systems in Sri Lanka are notoriously unreliable. Recently, Vidu switched to a cell phone, making contacting him easier.

'Good morning,' he answered carefully in his crafted Indian dialect.

'Vidu, it's John.'

'Evening John.'

'Evening Vidu.' I paused before saying, 'Unfortunately, I have some bad news. We've lost another shipment in transit to London.'

'Heathrow?' he asked. The tempo of his voice was slow, and his words were spoken clearly.

'Yes.'

'John, I have cautioned you before about using this airport,' he continued. 'The Indian baggage handlers at this airport are much too clever.'

'Yes, I know, but Arthur was confident, and it's his territory.'

Vidu didn't immediately respond. I sensed he didn't like Arthur. It probably had something to do with Arthur being a Brit and England being a colonial power in the past, lording over lowly countries like his Sri Lanka.

'Vidu, the numbers are starting to become a problem,' I continued. 'A serious problem. We can't stand to lose many more shipments.'

'I agree, John. How can I help?'

'I've decided to put a hold on all shipments. I want to establish new routes before more stones are shipped.'

'Very good, John. May I offer some suggestions?'

'Please do, but first, could I ask a favor? I'm moving up my trip to London, arriving Monday to discuss the new routes with Arthur in person because there's less chance of someone overhearing our discussion. So, can I ask you to come early, say be in London by Tuesday? I think Arthur should hear your input on this matter. Afterwards, you and I can discuss a loan for your new factories.'

'I will change my flights today if this is what you wish,' he replied without complaining.

'I know it's short notice, but yes, it would be a great help. I don't want the board to think I'm taking these losses lightly.'

'I understand,' Vidu stated.

'Any more news out of Cambodia?'

'Details are still arriving.'

'How many dead?'

'Hundreds.'

'Who would have a reason to kill this many people?' I asked, still having a difficult time making any sense out of the catastrophe.

'Yes, it would not seem necessary.'

'So, why?'

'I don't have an answer, John.'

We continued, arriving at no conclusions. More facts were needed. As we talked, I sensed a deep frustration burning beneath the surface in my friend. Vidu sounded even more distressed than I felt. He had worked with some of the murdered men and knew them personally. Eventually, we had no more words to say except goodbye.

After turning out my lights and settling in bed, anxious thoughts greeted any attempt to sleep. Why? I wondered. Why did I always have an uneasy feeling my life was out of control? And why did the cold gray nights of fall always feel edgy in anticipation of winter's harsh, unrelenting disaster? I said a prayer, asking God for strength and grace.

Eventually, I fell into a fitful sleep.

ATLANTIC OCEAN, OCTOBER 20, SUNDAY, 10:15 P.M. JOHN

The anxious concerns that had dominated my dreams lifted from my mind like a spider web in the wind; quickly lost in the sunlit activities of a busy Friday morning.

The wheels of business took precedence. I had places to go and people to see. Friday was demanding, filled with last-minute instructions to Helen. Saturday was spent on paperwork and other company tasks, which could not wait. Then, all too soon, it was Sunday morning, time to pack and hurry to the airport. A quick helicopter ride to La Guardia and a plane bound for England awaited me. I breathed a sigh of relief as our British Airways 747 took to the sky, pushing me back into a first-class leather seat as the plane accelerated.

Monica, my new personal secretary, was seated beside me, holding a glass of wine. I assumed her drink was to quiet her anxiety. Her hand was steady as she held her drink, her gaze focused on the view outside the window. Dressed in a light brown suit which showed off her slim figure, she looked good; hair up in a bun and her nails done in a French manicure style. Extremely put together as if she had planned her outfit in advance.

From experience I knew that the first few days on a job were always the hardest for a new employee, especially a job like hers where she had to spend considerable time traveling in close proximity to a new boss. I assumed she would be a little nervous and I hoped to make her first day on the job not too stressful.

My trip held no formal obligations, and I hoped it would prove to be a good opportunity to help her feel more at ease in the future. I always gave my secretaries plenty of space in the first few weeks. I wanted to assure them that their duties were exactly as stated in the job description, nothing more. However, some of them had other ideas. Some even thought the job would be easy money. They soon discovered the truth. I was a very busy boss. They would have to work for their money.

Opening my laptop, I began formulating new shipping schedules in my head in preparation for discussing them with Arthur after arriving in London. While typing a general outline, I paused. Nothing coherent was coming together. I closed my laptop. It was late, and I was tired.

Monica was reading a magazine, looking for content.

'Miss Sorensen, mind if we talk?' I asked.

She looked up at me and smiled. 'Yes, but please call me M.'

'Oh, sorry, sure.'

'My younger brother couldn't pronounce Monica, so he called me M, and the name kind of stuck,' she explained, placing her magazine on the table beside her.

'I'll try to remember.'

'Thanks.'

'Look. I have no social functions planned for London, only company meetings. I will need you for some typing, shipping schedules, and last-minute memos. Nothing extremely difficult. I'm hoping this trip will serve as a good orientation.'

I paused, wondering if I should invite her to dinner with Arthur. It's what we usually did when I was in London. But... I didn't want her to think her primary duty were to be my date... Still... it could be fun and educational.

'I normally have dinner with my London partner and his wife,' I hesitated. 'But please understand, you're not obligated to come... although, I think you might enjoy the experience. We usually eat at his fancy club. Going there is like a walk back in time.'

'I'll come,' she replied simply.

'Okay, good. I shouldn't be too busy on this trip. Hopefully it should give me some time to provide you with more background on my company.'

M silently took in the information.

'Sound okay?'

'Mr. Van Laan,' she replied, 'I have no experience with a job like this. I will try to follow your instructions very carefully. I ask only one thing.'

'What?'

'If I do something wrong, please inform me. I won't let it happen again.'

'Of course, although I don't think you will find me too critical. And please call me, John.'

'If you wish,' she replied casually, very self-assured and polite, almost to the point of formality.

'Okay, let's get started on your orientation,' I continued. 'I'm meeting with Arthur Wilson in London. He heads up our sales office for Europe.'

She listened attentively while staring straight at me with her big brown eyes, making it difficult to stay focused.

I continued. 'Let me give you a little of Arthur's background. He graduated from Oxford Law. Then, for some unknown reason, he proceeded to get a post-graduate degree in marketing from Southern Cal, probably because he didn't want to start a job. He comes from money, so he had choices. Personally, I like Arthur. We speak the same language when it comes to business. And I'm quite sure he's smarter than I am.' I grinned. 'But I don't mind. I like to work with smart people. They make me look good.'

She smiled but said nothing.

I paused. I was never sure how long a new assistant secretary would last. For some, the stress of long hours and constant travel was difficult. They quit after a month or two. In these cases, I had simply wasted my time giving them a thorough understanding of the inner workings of my company. However, I sensed this might not be true for M. Or perhaps I just hoped it wouldn't happen.

I briefly considered how much to tell her. I didn't want to waste my time or sound too pompous. My company was very complex and very successful. However, despite its recent achievements, I also knew that its existence was fragile. It depended on the continued trust of a very diverse group of people from all over the globe.

I sat back and rested for a minute, encased in the constant low rumbling vibrations inside the plane, evidence that our big bird was lumbering across the North Atlantic sky with us tucked safely inside its great belly. Thoughts of my associates in the business swirled through my mind. Miners, and cutters; partners and employees; all the people who had helped make my company successful. However, it wouldn't take much for the company to fail. If they lost trust in the company or in me, it could easily crumble. Once the trust was gone, the company would die. Trust was the key factor in its success.

She turned to me. 'Did you have something more to say? Or...'

I looked back at her, feeling a bit embarrassed. 'Sorry, I guess I'm daydreaming. I didn't mean to ignore you. It's just that sometimes I find my company very remarkable. But I'm getting ahead of myself. Maybe we should do this some other time. We'll be in London before you know it. Tomorrow will be a busy day for me. I think I would like to get some rest before we land. I have an extra sleeping pill if you'd like one.'

'No,' she said, 'I'll be fine.'

'I'll be occupied most of the day. Check your messages from time to time. I'll have some typing for you, shipping schedules mostly. If Arthur asks me to dinner, as I expect, I'll have his secretary call your hotel room. She will leave you with very specific information concerning the time and place of the dinner. A car will be provided. Otherwise, relax and enjoy your day. And don't worry; you'll like Arthur and his wife, Elizabeth. She usually dines with us. She is very pleasant.'

'Okay,' she picked up her magazine and continued reading.

A picture of Arthur's wife came to my mind. She was a rather plain-looking, typical English woman who considered my hiring young, beautiful female secretaries to be thoroughly disgusting. Arthur, on the other hand, enjoyed meeting them. He liked to flirt. Elizabeth knew this all too well. Occasionally, it made her irritable. But it didn't really matter because deep down, Elizabeth knew she was the best thing to ever happen to Arthur. She brought him social position and, most importantly, stability. Arthur tended, despite his intelligence, to flit from one idea to another.

Elizabeth always managed to put him back on track.

BANGKOK, THAILAND, OCTOBER 21, MONDAY, 1: 20 P.M. LUANG

No longer able to ignore the sealed envelope which had been delivered to him by a courier from his nephew's office; Luang slit it open and read slowly. It explained in detail how his nephew's plans were progressing. Despite Luang's pointed objections; materials, and personnel were moving into position in the United States, Europe, and Hong Kong, just as Nue had promised.

The report detailed a London operation- stealing gemstones in transit. The operation has been successful to date. But it was only a small measure, more a nuisance factor than anything. The Cambodian operation was different. It sent a clear message. It said in big letters, BEWARE of cooperating with this American Company.

Luang frowned.

Cambodia was not a message in his mind. Cambodia was a tragedy, an ugly, messy tragedy. Yes, it accomplished its mission, but at what cost, what cost in human life? The report made it increasingly obvious that his nephew was willing to do anything, including mass murder, to disrupt the American's company.

Luang briefly wondered what he could do to stop these tragedies. But he was an old man. He had done what he could and failed. His nephew had rejected his advice at the family council. He could think of nothing more.

The old patriarch filed the report in his desk while allowing his mind to do what old men's minds do. He remembered his past- the times he had spent with his nephew when the young boy was growing up. Luang was particularly frustrated because he thought he had done a better job of teaching his nephew through his stories of how their family had gained its elevated place in society. The stories emphasized honor, duty, and trust. He had used these stories to teach his nephew about the difference between right and wrong.

His nephew should have understood it was not right to take innocent lives.

LONDON, ENGLAND, OCTOBER 21, MONDAY, 10:55 A.M. JOHN

The polished black limo was parked conspicuously in a no-parking zone outside the entrance to the airport terminal building, fumes from its exhaust pipes rising slowly into a misty gray morning as its black-suited, uniformed chauffeur waited inside the building.

I immediately spotted him holding an ostentatious sign with my name written in big black letters, difficult to ignore. Upon seeing the offending sign, I resigned myself to once again being forced to put up with Arthur's obligatory sense of British aristocratic nonsense, whether I liked it or not.

On more than one occasion in the past, I had complained to Arthur, told him I didn't particularly like being carted around in pretentious automobiles like stretch limousines, but he was insistently inclined to send a large chauffeur-driven limo for me every time I came to London. Even though I had specifically asked him to please send a smaller and faster means of transportation- something which could negotiate traffic would be preferred; he had ignored me once again and sent his insufferable limo instead.

I smiled at the chauffeur. Although I knew him, and he knew me, social position and tradition dictated behavior on this island kingdom more than familiarity. Obligations came with money and position. One couldn't just do a thing. One had to do it in a proper fashion.

The chauffeur tipped his hat.

'Good to see you again, Henry,' I said.

'And you, Mr. Van Laan.'

'This is Ms. Sorensen, Henry,' I gestured to M who smiled.

'Very good, Miss,' he responded with a nod.

After negotiating the rigors of collecting our baggage, we somehow survived the perilous journey from Heathrow despite being bogged down in London traffic. I had to admire Monica. She took it all in stride, never complaining, acting as if she had done this sort of work a million times, looking poised and professional.

After what felt like the drive from the airport to the hotel took longer than the flight across the Atlantic; the limo finally delivered us to the entrance of the Ambassador Hotel. A doorman waited at the curb dressed in a dark maroon uniform accented with gold braids. Opening the rear door of the limo, he greeted us with the tip of his hat and offered a white-gloved hand to M.

'May I help you, Miss?' he asked.

Monica took his hand and gracefully exited the limo.

As I said, the British are all about tradition, and they do it better than anyone. To them, America is simply a poor replication of the British approach to life.

We also have doormen at our hotels. And our doormen wear uniforms just as the Brits. But our doormen never seem to do their duties with the same sense of obligation and ease as their British counterparts. Resentment always seems to linger, like a sense of regret, as if no American should ever be required to serve another.

Ignoring customary protocol while exiting the limo, I took a moment to enjoy the simple pleasure of watching Monica elegantly ascend the stairs to the hotel. A breeze tossed her straight red hair in the wind. Each step of her long legs was a thing of grace and strength, a picture worth taking. She stopped when she reached the top of the stairs and turned towards me; sensing I assumed, my illicit scrutiny. Embarrassed, I quickly retrieved my briefcase from the backseat of the limo and followed her into the lobby.

After checking into the hotel at the front desk, I gave Monica her room key and instructed her to check periodically for messages concerning dinner or work. I told her I would be off to meet with Arthur as soon as I settled into my room.

We parted ways. I made my way to my hotel room.

As usual, my suite was elegantly decorated in the noxious British tradition of overstuffed furniture covered in unsightly patterned designs. Although this time, they were a deep mauve floral pattern and I had to admit I favored the red shade, liked it better than the pastel yellow bird designs in the room I had the last time I was in town. After hanging my clothes and taking a quick shower to wash away the dirt and fatigue from long hours of travel, I ordered a simple meal of room-service eggs and toast for breakfast. Soon after, I was ready to go. I wore a casual black long-sleeved polo shirt, gray cashmere sweater, and wool slacks. From experience I knew that my dress habits irritated Arthur. Showing up at his office in something other than business formal- a starched white shirt, suit, and tie- was considered bad form, but I didn't care. I preferred to be comfortable and enjoyed seeing the horrified look on his face when I walked into his office wearing business casual.

1:30 P.M. JOHN

Arthur's office was a beehive of activity when I arrived.

He had previously given me a personal key card so I could go directly up an elevator to his office without having to stop at his company's main reception desk. But as usual, I had forgotten the stupid thing. Always in a rush when packing, I seldom remembered to take the bloody card.

'Welcome, Mr. Van Laan,' the receptionist said as I dutifully signed in. It was the required obligation for visitors who didn't have a key card.

Highly polished marble floors, darkly varnished wood trim; the presumption of elegance greeted my eye as I waited for the brass doors of the elevator to open. It was a smooth ride to the top floor.

The London Distribution House was located in a prestigious high-rise office building. Like the other three Distribution Houses, their space was divided into two distinctly different operations. Marketing, sales, and accounting were conducted on the top floor in large open offices with high ceilings and banks of fluorescent lights. Monotonous long halls led to the doors of the more ornate senior executive offices. Arthur's office occupied a large corner office.

Then there was real work of the Distribution House which was conducted on the floors below. Rooms closely resembling production lines were alive with activity. Client specifications were loaded into the main computer after the newly arrived sapphires were sorted for color, size, and quality. Product was matched to the client's needs. Boxes of gemstones were made ready for shipment before being transferred to the street level, where they were shipped to clients in Europe, Africa, and the Middle East. All unsold gemstones were stored on shelves in a highly secure room. A thick metal vault door served as the only entrance. The presence of security was pervasive. Uniformed men and women watched over every aspect of the operation which was also monitored by an elaborate computer system.

The London Distribution House had two separate elevators. Employees and guests entered through narrow halls of Plexiglas manned by security guards who checked their pictured identification cards. Because I had forgotten my personal ID card, a security guard greeted me when the elevator opened to the top floor and walked me through; a bit of a nuisance, but a necessary measure both for the protection of the gems and the safety of the employees.

Arthur's office was located as far as possible from the elevators. His visitors were required to wade through two or three secretarial stations before being allowed to enter his private office, all very supercilious as far as I was concerned. But because I had been through this routine too many times in the past, I ignored the secretaries, much to their displeasure, and walked right into his office without asking their permission, hoping to surprise Arthur. Unfortunately, someone must have warned him I was in transit.

'John,' he rose from his desk. 'It's a great pleasure to see you again.'

Arthur's office closely resembled a traditional law office decorated by walls of business and law books, which I was quite sure he had never read. The atmosphere was, in my opinion, a bit austere, but it seemed to suit Arthur. I always suspected he may have rather been a lawyer than a businessman, but I never asked him. I could never have operated from an office like this one. Too claustrophobic, too corporate, no hints that this was a room you could sit around and have a causal conversation.

'Good to see you too, Arthur,' I replied.

A large, darkly stained, ornately carved wood desk overpowered his corner office. Large windows on two sides overlooked the glories of Old London architecture. He worked from a traditional high-backed chair with brass tack and tucked and pleated shiny black leather. Strolling around his desk, he offered a firm handshake, which was, in my eyes, just one more English convention. The fact was, I talked with him almost every day. Regardless, every time I saw him, he greeted me like I was a long-lost friend.

A tall man with good posture and a round face, Arthur sported a thin mustache and prematurely graying red hair curled stylishly behind his ears. He was handsome by British standards, but something seemed to be missing in his breed, something slightly peculiar about the Brits; perhaps the result of too many years of inbreeding on a small island.

'Anything I can get for you, John?' he offered.

'Is it time for tea and crumpets yet?' I asked with a wink.

'Whatever you like.' He buzzed Eleanor, his venerable middle-aged and slightly dowdy secretary.

'Tea and crumpets for Mr. Van Laan,' he said, smiling.

Arthur liked entertaining visitors while sitting in his padded executive chair behind his desk. The chair sat slightly higher than the guest chair on the other side of his desk, commanding a certain austere presence. And his power chair leaned back, whereas my humble guest chair across from his eminence remained immobile; something, I'm sure he considered an edge. I preferred the sofas back at my own office. Here, it felt more like I was being interrogated, not meeting with a colleague.

'Anything we need to discuss before we get onto the main topic?' I asked.

'Discussion of the missing shipments?' he responded.

'Yes.'

'No, not really,' he said, 'I have prepared a preliminary quarterly report for your review, but it can wait. You may read at your leisure. It contains no real surprises. Inventory levels are satisfactory, and sales continue to grow above projections,' he smiled proudly.

Increases in sales were anticipated. Our projections were always conservative, and it had become almost second nature in the last few years to expect sales to exceed projections. Regardless, Arthur looked particularly happy and successful today. He was impeccably dressed in a tailored three-piece suit. I'm quite sure he fit in nicely at his club with all his high-powered London buddies dressed in matching business suits. I suspected old

Arthur rather liked showing off his success. This was fine with me. He had put in the long hours required and earned his rank. Although I feared his family had paid a price.

Like most other families of successful executives, they both benefited and sacrificed for his success. Elizabeth, his wife, coped by taking frequent extended holidays which she once described to me as mental rehabilitation retreats. Arthur's son was a less fortunate casualty. Drugs were his problem. He spent time in rehab. Arthur never talked about his boy. He was too proud. It was Elizabeth who shared the family's dirty laundry. She occasionally called me for no reason; said she just wanted to chat. I accommodated her. I'm a good listener. Maybe that's why she liked me, although I wasn't sure. Perhaps she just needed to tell someone her problems, and I was an easy target. She probably felt safe confiding in me because I wasn't a member of her London social scene.

Or perhaps she confided in me because she wanted me to feel guilty for taking too much of Arthur's time. Like I said, I didn't really know the answer. I just knew I wasn't the problem. The problem was Arthur. He liked to work. Or should I say he liked to be at work? I had experienced this character flaw in other men like him. They simply weren't happy anywhere other than at their offices or their clubs.

I had encouraged Arthur to spend more time with his family. However, he ignored me and continued to put in long hours at his office. Eventually, his inattention to his family created a distance between them that he could not bridge, even when his family most needed him. Lately, I sensed my knowledge of the intimate workings of his family life had weakened our relationship. I wondered if Elizabeth had told him she confided in me. Perhaps she did for spite. I didn't really know. All I knew was something had changed between us- evidenced by a slight shift in the tone of our interactions. Perhaps he wasn't happy with me because I saw the real Arthur behind his British reserve.

Fortunately, it didn't seem to materially damage our business dealings. In my mind, Arthur was someone I thought I could trust.

'Good news, Arthur,' I replied, placing his quarterly report in my briefcase.

He smiled.

The next hour was spent discussing new shipping routes while sampling crumpets and tea served dutifully by his lovely secretary. I suggested we avoid going through Heathrow Airport.

'How about using couriers until we are sure we aren't being targeted?' I recommended.

'Too expensive,' Arthur replied curtly.

'Do we have a choice?' I asked. 'The success of our business depends on delivering gemstones on schedule. Fortunately, your inventory is high right now and you can still fulfill your orders, but that could change fast if we continue to lose shipments.'

'Right,' Arthur finally conceded with a sigh.

He always seemed to resent me whenever I trumped his authority. Fortunately, this didn't happen too often because, normally, we agreed on almost everything. But that didn't change the fact I was Arthur's boss, and he knew it. I often wondered if he thought he was a better man than me. In subtle ways, he sometimes insinuated he was accommodating me, evidenced by the casual comments he made about how I dressed, my US Midwestern background, or my education. He once told me his family tree reached royalty. It gave him an air of superiority. I didn't mind, just assumed it was his nature. He had a genetic need to feel superior. Even so, he grudgingly admired what I had accomplished and he had congratulated me on more than one occasion. But always kind of reluctantly, like it was an oddity of sorts, something he didn't completely understand.

'As discussed,' I continued, 'I have put shipments from Sri Lanka on hold. But we need to resume shipping quickly. So, what do you think?'

'Don't know, really. I still believe the routes we have been using should work. Maybe we are just down on our luck.'

'I think it's more.' I argued. 'Three shipments lost in one month is more than simply bad luck. We can't afford to wait and lose two or three more shipments before making changes. Surely you see the logic in changing?'

Arthur was silent.

I took his silence to mean he finally agreed. 'Okay. Can you develop some new schedules by, say, tomorrow when Vidu arrives?' I continued. 'I would like his input before signing off on them.'

'Right,' said Arthur with a hint of disguised resignation.

I sensed Arthur found it difficult to work with Vidu. Probably because Vidu was a native of a colonial third-world country. Meeting with Vidu always appeared to be a difficult assignment for him. I sighed inwardly, wishing things could be different. But it was what it was, and I had neither the time nor the patience to change what I could not.

It was time to wrap up our discussion. 'Look, Arthur, thanks. You know I trust your judgment, but I've seen enough to be convinced this is more than random thievery.'

'Perhaps you're right, John,' Arthur concurred, attempting to sound positive. 'Interpol has told me they have not seen similar patterns in other segments of our industry.'

'Only we are being hit?'

'Right.'

'Ok, let's get this done... Now, if you don't mind, I'd like to make some calls from your spare office.'

'Will you change shipping schedules for Hong Kong and New York as well?' Arthur asked as I prepared to leave.

'Yes, I'm taking no chances.'

'Good,' he stated dismissively as if he had already moved on to another subject. 'Oh, on a more pleasant note,' he interjected, 'Elizabeth expressly asked me to invite you to dinner at my club tonight.'

I looked quizzically at Arthur, 'You sure it was Elizabeth who asked?'

Arthur's eyes brightened, and a slight smirk formed in the corners of his mouth. 'Rumor has it you brought a new assistant with you?'

Of course, he knew about Monica. I wanted to laugh, but I knew better. I kept my voice calm and asked, 'How do you know that?'

'I'm not without my intelligence.' He smiled.

'Okay then, eight o'clock at your club as usual?'

'Say, why did you let Susan go?' he asked, referring to my previous secretary. Obviously, not wanting to move on from the subject just yet.

I smiled. 'Did you fancy her?'

'No,' he sounded serious for a change. 'Although, I did rather like her.' He paused before saying with a smile, 'I asked because I thought she might be the one to settle you down.'

'I don't have time for marriage,' I scoffed. 'You know this as well as anyone.'

'John, do you really think hiring these young ladies is a good idea?'

'It works for me, Arthur.' I replied. 'Anyway, I think you'll enjoy meeting my new assistant. Please have Eleanor call our hotel and leave the usual dinner instructions for her. Her name is Monica Sorensen and her room number at the Ambassador Hotel is 1587.'

Arthur scribbled the information on a piece of paper as I exited his office.

7:10 P.M. JOHN

If the streetlight attached to an old wrought iron post by the sidewalk had not been attending to its duty, shining brightly through a particularly dull and dismal English evening, casting its light over a small inconspicuous sign drenched in drizzle, etched in brass and hung on one of two stone pillars at the entrance to Arthur's club; it would have been almost impossible to find the entrance to Arthur's club. Fortunately, my cabby knew where to drop me.

Built of fine cut-stone masonry, the stodgy old building that housed his club didn't look particularly out of place in historic London town. However, its interior was unique in ornate finery, filled with grand rooms from another era.

I was greeted at the main entrance. Or it might be more accurate to say I was blocked from entering until my true identity and purpose could be established. No one simply entered this crusty old establishment of stuffy snobbery unsolicited. Only members and guests were allowed inside. And even though I had been to Arthur's club numerous times in the past, I always had to follow the same routine and requirements.

The doorman politely asked my business. I told him my name and said I was a guest of Arthur Wilson and his wife for dinner. Once my credentials were satisfactorily established, I took the liberty of asking the man if an attractive young lady with red hair might be waiting inside for me.

"Yes indeed," he replied with a smile after stepping aside.

Immediately upon entering the premises, my attention was captured by the etched sandstone walls which framed a gaping brickwork fireplace where smoldering logs burned, warming the main lobby. A tradition at the club, the fire welcomed visitors during the cool, wet months of winter, providing the cool interior rooms with necessary heat. A stone mantle rose nearly three stories to the ceiling of its grand atrium. A circular stairway bordering the room with intricately carved handrails reaching upward to the floors above. Gold-leaf framed portraits of former members lined the walls. A picture of Winston Churchill scowled solemnly from above the fireplace, cigar in hand.

I found Monica sitting in the lobby in the company of other guests, all presumably waiting for friends to join them. Thickly woven oriental rugs cushioned the tiled floor, muting the sound of their softly controlled conversations. Seemingly demanded by traditional architecture's austere nature, the guests behavior was demure and poised; almost as if ghosts of their forefathers were waiting in the wings, ready and able to strike down anyone who broke the rules.

I assumed Arthur would be late as usual. He was always late. I didn't mind because I thought it would give me an opportunity to show Monica the club before he arrived. Dressed in a striking gray suit, open at her neck, accentuated by a silver necklace that held a small green emerald; a light gray knit sweater covered her shoulders.

'Quite a place,' she said. 'I don't think I've ever been somewhere like this before.'

'This is only the beginning,' I whispered conspiratorially. 'Wait 'til you see the bar.'

I wondered how she was coping, probably working off adrenalin. I assumed jet lag would soon take over. As was my custom, I rested whenever possible while traveling. The back seat of the black London taxi to Arthur's Club had brought some brief shuteye relief while returning to my hotel for a change of clothes. Suit and tie were the required dress code at Arthur's club. I knew I wouldn't be allowed inside this austere establishment of upper-class nonsense without proper attire.

M looked up when we entered the bar as did everyone the first time they entered this storied room. She gazed at its magnificence in awe. The ceiling was almost two stories high. Four marble pillars sculpted in the style of a Greek temple bordered the room, supporting a ceiling painted in a pastoral scene complete with angels and scantily dressed nubile maidens.

To my surprise, Arthur had already arrived, sitting with his wife, Elizabeth, at a table near one of the fireplaces flanking the room. A permanent scowl was the dominant feature of Elizabeth's countenance. Although not an unpleasant-looking woman, she would not normally be considered beautiful. Tall like Arthur with unremarkable brown hair wrapped tightly in a bun, her presence exuded a simplicity that resonated with a quiet charm. Excessive makeup and jewelry had been applied in an obvious attempt to disguise her rather ordinary features. She wore a large ruby necklace with matching earrings. Born to a titled family, she casually assumed an air of tolerance toward me. I was, after all, an American commoner.

Arthur's jaw almost dropped when he saw Monica. If it had not been for his inner English reserve and the fact he was with his wife, I think he would have given in to fumbling adoration. My choice of traveling secretaries never failed to make an impression on Arthur. However, this time, he looked completely stunned as we approached his table. Accustomed as he was to the fact that my secretaries were generally beautiful, M instantly brought out the bumbling idiot in him.

Elizabeth, on the other hand, simply looked more annoyed than usual. She disapproved of my practice of hiring attractive young women, an opinion she had clearly made known in the past. She also knew Arthur would be completely taken by this latest addition to my staff and would proceed to make a complete fool of himself before the evening was over. An inaudible sigh of disgust escaped her throat when she saw us.

Regardless of her considered opinion of my less-than-admiral character, Elizabeth and I had become friends despite our differences. It was an uneasy friendship in the beginning, but in time she actually grew to like me, or at least I think she did. Humor was the bond that first brought us together. That and the fact that we both relished verbal combat. It made for stimulating, if not pleasant, conversation whenever we were together.

'Elizabeth, so good to see you again,' I leaned over and greeted her with a small peck on her cheek. 'You look especially ravishing this evening.'

'I'm sure,' she replied disdainfully. She was on to me. We both knew it.

'Oh Elizabeth, you know I always so look forward to our dinners.'

'Why, so you can harass me?' she replied impolitely.

'Ah, let's call a truce for tonight,' I smiled. 'May I introduce you to Monica Sorensen?'

'Ms. Sorensen, so nice to meet you,' Elizabeth replied icily and held out her hand as if she was the Queen of England.

Monica smiled and took her hand with a slight bow.

Arthur stood, waiting patiently like the English gentleman he considered himself to be.

'Oh, sorry, Arthur. I almost forgot to introduce you,' I smiled.

'Right,' said Arthur with a grin.

'Monica, this is Arthur. You remember I told you all about him.

'All good, I presume,' Arthur smiled.

'Of course,' Monica replied with a genuine smile.

The nearby fire was warm and inviting. A waiter, standing at attention, looking strikingly similar to a penguin in a starched white coat and black pants, took our order with practiced refinement. Arthur ordered me a drink. He knew his liquors, and he knew what labels I liked.

A great attribute of this bar was its chairs. From experience, I knew I would relax completely after sinking into their large, overstuffed cushions while sipping Arthur's expensive booze. Across our table, he was busy accosting M with a thousand prying questions. Elizabeth looked more annoyed than usual. She gave me one of her pointed stares, hoping I would intervene.

I ignored her, content for the moment to sit and relax, knowing what would happen next. Once she could not contain herself anymore, Elizabeth would attempt to distract Arthur from his excessive attention to my assistant. The English are so easy to annoy because they are so predictable. However, for some reason that I didn't immediately understand, she turned her attention to me instead.

'What happened to Susan?' she asked when she could no longer bear to witness Arthur making a fool of himself.

I whispered in her ear. 'She was like royalty, you know, always wanting something more, even while having everything. Fortunately, in America, we can get rid of people who are a nuisance. Not like royalty, I'm sorry to say.'

Elizabeth was a royalist by birth and did not enjoy being taunted about the trials and tribulations of the royal family. Plus, she had come to expect I would find a way to introduce this subject into our conversation before our evening was over. It was only a matter of time.

'Rather like your President Clinton,' she countered. 'Equally hard to get rid of him, don't you think?'

'Yep, he's always hard. That's why almost everyone likes him,' I responded smiling, 'especially the ladies.'

She gazed imperiously at me. I knew she got my joke. I also knew she found this sort of sexual innuendo distasteful. So common, you know.

'You're simply awful, John,' she pronounced in her aristocratic accent.

'You know the smirk Clinton normally has,' I ventured, 'when only one side of his mouth turns up in a smile?'

'I don't think I want to know,' she replied.

'Well, Republicans say it's because he is a two-faced liar. But Democrats say it's because he just had another erection.'

Elizabeth's cheeks burned a rosy shade of distaste. It was possible I had gone too far this time, but she was just too much fun.

I couldn't help myself.

8:05 P.M. JOHN

High-back upholstered armchairs encircled our dining table, adorned with exquisite matching China and crisp white tablecloths. The tables were arranged with luxurious, weighty silverware— the kind typically safeguarded in most households. Attending to the tables were men donned in impeccable black suit-coats complemented by white shirts and black ties. Naturally, our meal was superb.

Occasionally, I observed M looking slightly lost. She was trying to hide it, but I could see she was awed by this place and trying to act suitably. To be truthful, I couldn't blame her; the level of opulence at Arthur's club was beyond this Midwestern boy's ability to appreciate. I remembered my first experience of it. I had been simply blown away by its craftsmanship. Ornately carved handrails, elaborate glass chandeliers, the formality- everything was so proper and refined.

Arthur and Elizabeth, on the other hand, were indulging themselves in the usual British art form of complaining. Nothing was quite right. Their meat was overdone. Service was too slow. The menu too limited, on and on; our dinner progressing like so many others before it.

I always enjoyed coming to Arthur's club. It was a privilege, an experience, a place lost in time, a retreat secure from the uncertainties of modern life. The club never changed. Its stone walls were thick, built to protect members from the noise and bother of the outside world. Its traditions were established long ago to ignore the frivolities of modern times.

I relaxed and enjoyed the experience. My entree was roast beef and scalloped potatoes, very delicious. Arthur's banter was continual, my contribution minimal. Elizabeth and Monica engaged in polite conversation. Nothing was unusual or different about this dinner until the moment Arthur's voice uncharacteristically slowed. I looked up from my meal to see him staring intently across our room. Searching in the direction of his stare, I immediately saw who had captured Arthur's attention.

'He's back,' Arthur growled in a tone he might use to proclaim the return of the black plague.

Personally, I hadn't seen Phillip Palmer in almost five years, but there he was. Tall, skinny Phillip with his distinctive long straight nose, clean-shaven thin face, long curly hair, mostly gray, falling over his shoulders for effect, sitting straight in his chair like a thespian attempting to look dramatic. His most remarkable feature was his eyes, his coal-black impenetrable eyes. It was impossible to mistake him even from across the length of our large dining room. If nothing else, his protruding nose gave him away whenever he turned to offer a rather Cyrano De Bergerac silhouette. Sitting with Phillip was an unexceptionally handsome looking young man, medium height, dressed in a black suit, gray shirt, and dark tie.

'Phillip?' I questioned, my mood crashing.

''Tis indeed,' replied Arthur.

Elizabeth turned, spotting Phillip. She never liked the man and made no pretense of her aversion. 'How is it possible they let that man in here?' she proclaimed. 'Can't you do something, Arthur?'

Elizabeth had previously told me she had a deep, almost intuitive dislike for Phillip from the moment she first met him. She had warned Arthur about him, but Arthur hadn't listened. He should have.

'He belongs to an affiliated club in America,' Arthur replied. 'He has a right to be here.'

'There must be some way to keep him out.' she said, plaintively.

'I could perhaps do something,' Arthur complained. 'But I haven't seen him here for over a year and I didn't think it was necessary.'

'Who is he?' M asked.

'That's a long story. I'll tell you later,' I quickly replied, not wanting to spoil what remained of our evening by talking about Phillip.

'He's history now,' Arthur stated dismissively, reading my mind. 'No need to be concerned.'

I stole one more glance in Phillip's direction as we ate. I wasn't certain, but it almost appeared as if he was smiling while returning my glare. I quickly dismissed that notion as a product of my over active imagination.

Dinner was concluded satisfactorily; the food was good and the conversation pleasant with no further notice of Mr. Phillip Palmer. But that didn't stop me from wondering why Phillip had showed up here now; in Arthur's club when I was here. Was it a coincidence? Or had he come to harass me?

I quickly dismissed the idea because it seemed completely irrational, even for me. As much as I loathed the man, I couldn't bring myself to think he was that devious.

10:00 P.M. JOHN

Overhead lights reflected off the damp pavement as our black limousine weaved its way through London evening traffic under a constant cold drizzle.

Drops of rain dotted the windshield in a mesmerizing dance of shimmering lights. Outside our opulent automobile, less endowed Brits hurried down sidewalks, bent under umbrellas against a heavy wet wind, hopeful of arriving at their destinations before becoming chilled to the bone by the cold, penetrating rain.

London is a legend in its citizen's minds. And in some respects, it is in real life too. The English consider their city to be the once and forever capital of the world. The rest of the world is simply considered London's playground to them. In their opinion, no corner of our globe should be spared England's rightful pedigree to plunder. But in London's defense, it is one of the few places on earth that gives equal consideration to all. Their opinion of their city and its duty towards the world is nothing like the narrowly introverted attitudes of most isolated Americans. Although, I must say that I am personally more at home in the restless activity of New York than the defined destiny of London.

Tired and jet-lagged, I slumped into the soft cushions of our limo, attempting to put Phillip out of my mind. Too many bad memories were stirred by seeing that man, too many dreams lost to his lies, too many nightmares.

The tires of our limo splashed over the uneven cobblestone streets, jarring the lush leather interior of our vehicle, making it difficult to relax. Monica sat quietly beside me, perhaps sensing my growing unease and trying to be polite; waiting for me to break our silence. When she had asked about Phillip at dinner, I had heard her, but a part of me did not want to answer her question. Discussing him would return him to life. Personally, I had spent considerable effort trying to bury the man's memory. But unfortunately, it didn't look like that was not going to be possible.

'Still want to know about Phillip? I asked.

She smiled. 'Only if you want to tell me.'

'It's a long story,' I replied with a sigh 'Tell you what. Let's stop at the bar in our hotel for a nightcap. I'll tell you all about Mr. Phillip Palmer, the short version that is. The long version would take all night.'

HONG KONG, OCTOBER 22, TUESDAY, 6:10 A.M. LIN

It was early morning and the rising sun had not yet banished the shadows of night from the deserted streets of Hong Kong. Patchy fog drifted through the dark corridors of the city's high rise buildings; creating pockets of filmy gray mystery. Lost dreams mingled among the lingering shadows and drowsy stirrings of a few droopy-eyed pedestrians strolling under florescent signs dulled to soft shades of color in the dewy half-light of morning.

Lin Hung-Chao arrived at the entrance to his building early, as was his custom. The security guard for his Hong Kong Distribution House tipped his hat appropriately and held a door open for his boss. After crossing a spotless marble floor in the lobby at a steady pace, Lin pushed a button for an elevator. With many problems on his mind this morning, he had come in early to accomplish some unfinished paperwork so he would have an uncluttered day to accomplish his normal duties.

Once upstairs, he passed down a hall of open doors to empty offices. Soon, these offices would be filled with his fellow workers. They were important to him; his employees were his family, his responsibility, just as he had a responsibility to John in America and, more importantly, to his homeland. He frowned, thinking once again about how to solve his complex puzzle while keeping everyone satisfied. He would simply have to find a way. He was not the only person burdened with multiple life responsibilities. Others had found solutions to their problems. He would also.

His first obligation was to allow nothing to interfere with his good fortune. The Hong Kong Distribution House he managed was very profitable. It provided him the lavish lifestyle he now enjoyed. His second obligation was to his employees. His third was to John, who had made his good fortune possible. His final and perhaps most important obligation was to his country. His world was a very complicated puzzle.

Deliberately shelving his problems for another time, he had work to do today. After entering his office, he unlocked his desk drawer and was immediately startled by the sight of some very valuable gemstones he should have returned to the vault before he left work yesterday. He remembered examining the stones when his phone rang. He had hurriedly shoved the gems in his drawer and apparently forgotten them.

Holding one of the gems up to the sunlight filtering through the high windows of his top-floor office, he looked at the specimen- a pink sapphire sparkling in a myriad of cut facets. Returning the gem to its parcel paper, office protocol dictated he immediately take the stones to the vault. Instead, he returned the stones in his drawer where he could view them later when he had more time.

LONDON, 10:25 P.M. JOHN

The bar at the Ambassador Hotel had none of the traditional grandeur of Arthur's club.

Yet its simple elegance made for a pleasant atmosphere. It was a good place to have drink and conversation. M and I found a table in a quiet corner where we could have some privacy. The whiskey I ordered quickly worked its magic on my tired mind and I began to relax. M had asked about Phillip and I thought perhaps it wouldn't be so bad talking about him. It might even help get him out of my head.

'He's a gemologist, very bright.' I began. 'But his brilliant mind contains some flaws... serious flaws.'

I paused. 'Sorry, I'm getting ahead of myself. Let's begin at the beginning... I was introduced to him when working for a company in Chicago which marketed colored gemstones. The company was called Gems Unlimited or GU for short. I was an account executive at Anderson and Jones Advertising at the time. GU was my client and Phillip was an independent consultant to GU.'

Monica listened in silence.

'GU was not my only client. I had several others, but they were smaller companies, none as successful and ambitious as GU. As a result, my work for GU took most of my time and effort. And I think this was true for Phillip as well. Coincidentally, we learned we both came from the same small town in Michigan and went to the same high school. Although, he was ten years older than me and I never really knew him at school. Still, it was something we had in common, making it easy to form a casual friendship. Plus, we were both single and had time to kill after work, so we would go for drinks. He liked to talk, and I liked to listen, which was good because he could talk for hours about whatever was on his mind. It didn't matter what the subject was. He just liked to talk. And most of the time, he talked about his specialty, colored gemstones, which was great for me because I learned a lot from him.'

Monica didn't look too bored, so I continued. 'To do my job well, learning everything I could about my client and its business was important. And for this, Phillip was a great source of information. He made the world of gemstones sound fascinating.'

'Is GU still around?' Monica asked.

'No. Let me explain. They were ambitious. Investors were recruited. A chain of retail jewelry stores was purchased. Everything was good initially. Demand was strong. Sales were increasing. It seemed a no-brainer. My advertising budget expanded in concert with their desire for success and this made the agency I worked for happy. Talk about a raise at my next review was in the wind.'

I paused and took a deep breath, unsure I wanted to continue because the next chapter in this story was not pleasant. Dread passed quickly through my mind as I relived the events in my mind. I could still see it all clearly, just as if it occurred yesterday.

M looked at me, perplexed. 'What happened?'

'What happened was what usually happens when a company goes broke. It expands too fast, spends money recklessly; big salaries, huge bonuses, expensive offices, the normal reasons for failure.'

The bar was quiet now. The band was done for the evening. Patrons were slipping away, one by one. I sipped my drink slowly, remembering those days.

'Watching a company self-destruct is no fun,' I continued. 'And to make matters worse, my advertising firm started to have financial problems about the same time. It was all purely coincidental, but it happened. They were forced to downsize and

I became a casualty. Without income from GU, they couldn't afford to keep paying me. I was fired.'

I hadn't told many people this story. I kept it mostly to myself, but for some reason I didn't understand, I wanted to tell her.

'Your company, the one you run now?' she asked. 'How did it start?'

'Glad you asked,' I replied, happy to move on to a more pleasurable subject. 'I'm a quick study. I learned the gemstone business during the time I worked for GU. When I lost my job at my ad agency, I put together a strategic business plan for a new company. I put everything I had learned in my work with GU into it. It was a good plan, at least one I thought could be successful. All I needed was someone who believed in me and had the cash to finance a new company. Fortunately, I had been introduced to some wealthy investors as part of my previous job. When GU started to go bad, a few of these investors came to me for my assessment of what was going on. Obviously, they were not very happy.'

'Why did they ask you?' Monica interrupted.

'Good question. I don't really know why. Maybe because I have an honest face. Or maybe because when you are in advertising, you need to know everything there is to know about your clients. It's part of the job. Or perhaps they asked because sometime during my time with the client, I had demonstrated to these investors I was a good guy. And I was. I had been perfectly honest with them whenever they had a question and didn't try to sugarcoat facts. I think they appreciated that.'

'Did you go to them for money when you wanted to start a new company?'

'You're a quick study,' I complimented her.

She smiled, took a sip of her wine.

'Yes, and they agreed. I think because it was an opportunity for them to recoup the money they lost with GU. I didn't present my plan as such, but I believe this was how they took it.'

'Has your company delivered?' she asked.

'Yes, we have been very fortunate. We have made money for them, more than they expected; more than they lost at GU.'

'So, they are happy.'

'Very happy.'

'How did you become so successful?'

'By gaining control of a high percentage of one gemstone, sapphires. That put us in a position to dictate prices. Sapphires today are expensive, making them a very profitable item.'

'Isn't that bad for business?'

'What?'

'Higher prices.'

'Why?'

'Because don't high prices normally decrease sales.'

'Normally, but not for our product. Sapphires are a scarce natural commodity and incredibly beautiful. Price is only one factor that dictates demand.'

'What are your gross annual sales?' she asked.

I paused before answering. 'That information is not for public consumption.'

'I'm sorry. I didn't mean to pry.'

'No need to be sorry,' I replied.

'I see,' she backtracked. 'Phillip, what happened to him? You don't act like he's your friend anymore.'

'He's not.'

'Why?'

'Phillip didn't like the fact I started a new company without him. He thought I would fail. To him, I was just some dumb marketing guy who really didn't know anything about gemstones. Not like him, a brilliant gemologist. I think he had planned to do what I did: start a company to replace GU. But I beat him to it. And when it became obvious, even to him, that my company was a success, he demanded I make him a partner. He acted as if that was the most obvious move and that it was what I should have done from the very beginning. I turned him down. I didn't ever really trust him. I don't know why, but I always wondered if he may have been one reason for GU's failure.'

'How did he take it?'

'What, my refusing him a job?'

'Yes.'

'He wanted to know why the famous Phillip Palmer, a legend in his own mind and the master of all he surveyed, could possibly be refused. How could I, a nothing in the world of gemstones, do this to him? He was furious. He proceeded to form his own company, convinced he would put me out of business. But his company failed quickly. Because he only knew one side of the business, the product side. He didn't have other skills required to run a business.'

'Did he blame you for his misfortune?' M asked.

'Yes, of course. It's a lot easier to blame someone else than it is to take responsibility for failure on your shoulders.' With this pronouncement, conversation lagged. It was time to call it a night. I had hit a wall.

I walked her to her room, smiled and said goodnight at her door.

11:15 P.M. JOHN

Through a corner of my vision, I saw a fleeting shadow appeared out of nowhere in an empty hotel hallway.

I turned in adrenalin alarm, raising an arm in self-defense, but not fast enough to avoid a steel fist from hammering my forehead. Falling to the carpet in a semi-conscious state of fright, I rolled away from my attacker while kicking his knee. He winced, but the look on his face remained eerily calm. He came after me methodically as I vainly tried to crawl away. A glancing blow hit the side of my head. Anger took control of my brain; I got up to charge him, fists landing only a few good shots, but enough to deter him from continuing. Whiskey and jet lag combined slowed my reflexes and softened my defenses. He easily deflected my weak attempts to fight back, seemingly able to hit me at will, driving me against a wall. I fell slowly to the floor while holding my arms over my head.

Hotel guests arrived in the hall from an opposite direction, two men and two women dressed in suits and fine clothes. They started yelling.

My attacker, momentarily distracted by their demonstration, sighed as the men approached and calmly stood his ground. Dressed in a black suit with a gray shirt, head low, he stood very still for a moment before turning to escape down an exit stair.

One of the gentlemen helped me stand. I was hurt, but not too badly. Bruised and battered, but nothing broken.

I thanked him.

He asked if I was okay, if I needed assistance, a doctor, or an ambulance.

'No, I'm fine. Thanks, but no,' I heard myself say.

I limped to my hotel room door, inserted my key card, and locked the door behind me, leaning against a wall for support until I could stand steady as my breathing slowly returned to normal.

My face looked okay in the bathroom mirror, bruised some, but okay. I felt sick to my stomach, but mostly, I was disgusted, my personal space violated, my freedom to roam aborted. I needed to be more careful, watch, wait, be better prepared next time. Sickened from my experience, I washed my face, knowing I had dodged a bullet. If those people had not appeared, it could have been worse. I was lucky. But somehow, I didn't feel so lucky. I felt abused.

I was suddenly very tired. I got ready for bed while deciding not to report the incident to the police. Muggings are common in big cities. I didn't think the cops would do anything. Plus, I didn't need the hassle. I just wanted to forget the whole affair and get some sleep.

It hurt to slide my bruised body under the covers, afraid to sleep but badly needing oblivion, a retreat from reality in dreams.

HONG KONG, OCTOBER 23, WEDNESDAY, 11:40 A.M.

Two businessmen arrived at the Hong Kong Distribution House dressed neatly in dark blue suits, white shirts, and ties.

The receptionist took casual note of them as they entered the lobby and approached her desk. As was her habit, she put away her college textbook and smiled.

'Good morning, gentlemen. May I help you?' she asked politely.

'We are here to see Mr. Hung-Chao,' the first gentleman said in correct Mandarin Chinese.

Morning had been slow for the receptionist. But then, she was never very busy. The Distribution House where she worked was conducted mostly with assistance from instruments of long-distance communication, not close personal contact. She liked her job. It allowed her time to read or study. She was a student at a local university in the evening. Her job was a perfect fit. The only duties were to dress well and greet a few visitors with utmost respect.

'Yes. I will ring him,' she replied in their dialect while searching for his extension number.

The lobby began to quickly fill with new visitors, arriving in pairs, all well-dressed in white shirts and business suits. Concerned now, the receptionist had never experienced a large influx of guests into her lobby at one time. Working alone, except for a couple of security guards who usually sat or stood next to entrance doors to elevators, she suddenly felt vulnerable while noticing some of the visitors talking to the guards.

'Please do not call Mr. Hung-Chao,' her first visitor interrupted her before she could press an emergency button under her desk. 'Do exactly as my friend instructs.'

The man had walked behind her desk and taken hold of her arm. She tried to jerk away. Pain was instant, her shoulder burning where he touched her. She stood, trying desperately to escape her pain.

'Come with me,' the man said quietly.

She nodded. Her pain eased.

He directed her to follow the other intruders who were confidently passing disabled guards as they made their way through open security doors and down a hall.

11:58 A.M.

Sparkling blue sapphires lay in a pile on the top of a back-lit glass-top table.

The gemstones had been cut to an exact specification- the same size, shape, and carat weight.

An employee working at the table began meticulously separating the gems into groups of five for easy counting, five groups of five, twenty-five in a pile. A buy order called for seventy-two gemstones of the same size in matching blue. The work was monotonous, but the pay was good. He needed to concentrate. Exact quantities were required. However, his concentration was broken when his peripheral vision caught sight of men dressed in suits entering his room. Losing count, he swore under his breath, knowing he would have to start over. But then curiosity took over, and he stood to look over the heads of his fellow workers, wondering what was going on.

One of the visitors dressed in a blue suit approached his workstation.

'Please follow me,' the man said.

'What?'

'Follow me, please,' the man repeated, looking the employee directly in the eye.

The employee instantly disliked the man. Who was this guy anyway? And why was he giving orders? He was not the boss. The employee's gut instinct was to resist. He knew self-defense. Almost everyone in Hong Kong practiced some form of martial arts. He measured the guy's physical strength, trying to decide what to do.

Noticing two of the men near the doors holding automatic weapons, he watched his fellow workers moving towards a door as directed.

He decided it would be unwise to resist.

12:12 P.M.

A lone security guard sat on a folding chair in a corner of a back hallway.

The location was well chosen, far from activity. It was very unlikely anyone important would find him here. A couple of minutes off his feet was heaven. As was his custom, it was time for desert after lunch while conducting his rounds. A candy bar from an inside pocket of his uniform was carefully unwrapped and he began attempting not to spill telltale crumbs on the polished marble floor.

After taking a bite of chocolate-covered caramel, yelling and screaming interrupted his reprieve, echoing down the hall from somewhere around a corner. Unable to see what caused the noise, he got to his feet quickly, preparing to do his job. The business where he worked held a fortune in gemstones. His job was to protect the stones. Instinctively, he reached for the cold metal of his gun.

Then hesitating.

Suddenly uncertain.

He decided there was no need to rush to conclusions. It could be a false alarm. Slowly walking through a hall, his heart pounding, sounds of trouble and running footsteps echoed off the marble walls as he proceeded. The guard unfastened his holster strap. Didn't sound like a false alarm.

Fear took control, accompanied by a strong desire to run. Gun in his hand, he paused... Then took off running in the opposite direction.

They were waiting for him at the end of a hall.

Two men dressed in dark blue suits standing quietly in front of a door, blocking his exit.

He stopped when he saw them.

They didn't move.

'What do you want?' he asked, holding his gun in a trembling hand.

They didn't respond. He raised his gun cautiously, 'What is your purpose here?'

They stood their ground, not moving, not answering him.

Footsteps from behind. Distracting. He turned. A strong hand grabbed his arm. His gun fired high, carelessly, the bullet ricocheting harmlessly off marble walls.

Blinding pain followed, falling, reaching to protect his face. A blow cracked ribs deep inside his chest. He doubled over, gasping for air, falling onto the floor as acrid gas assaulted his nostrils.

Crying in revulsion, he vomited.

LONDON, ENGLAND, 2:00 A.M. JOHN

The phone beside my bed rang around two a.m., Greenwich Mean Time.

I felt like I'd been sleeping for only about five minutes when its incessant ringing reached through a long tunnel of deep, unconscious sleep to wake me. When I could no longer ignore the bloody thing, I rolled over to my nightstand, rubbed my bruised head, and picked up the phone to stop the intrusive thing from making any more noise.

'John,' said Lin quietly, knowing I was probably sleeping when he called.

'I'm awake, Lin,' instantly recognizing his voice.

'Sorry to disturb you in the middle of the night.'

'What's wrong, Lin?' I asked with growing impatience. 'You wouldn't be calling at this time in the night if it wasn't something really important. Skip the formality. Just tell me.'

'We've been robbed, John. Our inventory is gone.'

'Say again,' I bolted upright in bed, now fully awake. The inventory of gemstones at our Hong Kong Distribution House was not as large as in New York or London. Still, it was valued at anywhere from retail thirty-five to fifty million US dollars.

'It's gone, John. They took almost everything.'

'Impossible. Your security system is state of the art.'

'Of course,' Lin said. 'But that didn't stop them.'

'Stop who?'

'Don't know,' Lin continued without emotion.

'Who does know?' I asked stupidly, still hoping this was a nightmare.

'The thieves.'

'What thieves?'

'The thieves who robbed us.'

'Anyone hurt?'

'Not many, a few minor injuries; nothing serious.'

Lin gave me details of the robbery, the sparse details he knew. He said police were investigating. Slowly, I wrapped my mind around the fact I was not dreaming, even though I badly wanted to believe it couldn't be true. Because, if it was, my company was in trouble, serious trouble.

'Look, it's the middle of the night here. Can you book me a flight leaving London for Hong Kong...today? Make it today, this afternoon.' I stammered, still uncertain what to do or say, just knowing I needed to see what happened in person.

Monica came into my head at that moment; what to do about Monica, thinking about her while wondering at the same time why I was thinking about her. I was in the middle of a crisis. She should have been the last person I should be considering. But instead, I quickly rationalized taking her with me, thinking it would be good for her continuing education. I probably shouldn't have thought this, but I was in a state of shock, obviously not completely rational, my mind racing with possibilities.

'Lin, book the flight for two and get me two rooms at the usual hotel in Hong Kong.'

'As you wish,' Lin replied without comment.

'We'll talk later. Okay? Right now, I need to call Arthur and Bob, warn them. You haven't talked to them, have you?' I asked, words coming fast, one random thought after another in no order or coherence.

'No.'

'Okay, I'll tell them to increase security immediately. I can't let this happen to them.'

As soon as Lin hung up, I called Arthur and Bob. If this could happen in Hong Kong, it could happen in London and New York. I didn't even want to even think about such a possibility. It would mean the end of my company.

The next hour was spent on the phone. Waking Arthur at two-thirty a.m. was a treat, but he said he understood after I explained. Bob was still awake at home in New York when I called. We talked for a while. I couldn't tell him a great deal about what happened in Hong Kong, only what I knew. We agreed he should call his security company immediately, tell them to send additional guards, be on alert. We couldn't afford to lose any more gems. The loss of gems in Hong Kong put my company in serious jeopardy of not fulfilling contractual orders.

More than anything, our success was built on the premise of safe, secure, and on-time delivery of products. And nothing erodes confidence faster than late or non-delivery. And if confidence was completely broken, my company would disappear in a heartbeat.

After talking with Arthur and Bob, I phoned the hotel desk clerk and asked him to call Monica's room in the morning and instruct her to pack.

'Please tell her we will be leaving London in the afternoon ahead of schedule.'

3:10 A.M. JOHN

Sleep was an elusive animal prowling through the canyons of my mind.

A million questions raced through my head as I lay in bed. First, who was the man who had attacked me in the hall? Then, the robbery in Hong Kong, and finally, the lost shipments in

London. All directly related to me or my company. How was it possible? So many problems in so short a time span. Plus, the massacre in Cambodia still laid heavy on my troubled psyche; round and round like a never-ending roller coaster, nothing made sense, nothing but problems. I finally gave up, got out of bed, and called Lin because I couldn't think of anything else to do.

First, I apologized for asking him to arrange my travel.

'Sorry, I wasn't thinking straight.' I said, 'I'm sure you have enough to do.'

His world had to be vastly complicated by the robbery, yet he responded in his usual, unassuming fashion, saying I need not be concerned. Everything had been arranged. I would receive the travel details by e-mail in the morning.

I thanked him, apologizing again.

We discussed the robbery in more detail now that I was fully awake. Lin said some of his employees thought the robbers were Chinese, spoke Mandarin. One thing became perfectly clear as we talked. The thieves had done their homework. They were in and out in less than twenty minutes. After first disabling the computerized security system, rendering it useless, they incapacitated the guards. It was as if they had intimate knowledge of how everything worked and had a layout of the building. Plus, they seemed to understand the business: where the gems were kept, when they wouldn't be secure- out in the open for sorting and mailing. They wasted no time going directly to the vault and the sorting rooms. Gemstones were collected in briefcases and carried out of the building in a matter of minutes.

'How many men were involved?' I asked.

'That's the amazing part,' Lin replied. 'The number is not exact, but from what we can deduce, between twenty-five to fifty individuals. Each one had a function and performed it flawlessly. They covered every possible variable. After leaving the building, they simply disappeared into the passing crowds in multiple directions.'

'You mean they just walked away?' I asked, not believing what I was hearing.

'Yes, it appears so. Our employees were being held in conference rooms. No one witnessed the thieves leaving. They simply left as they arrived. Men in suits, ordinary-looking businessmen, nothing to distinguish them from the crowded sidewalks. Nothing unusual.'

'Any good news?'

'The only good news is because you held shipments from Sri Lanka, our inventory was unusually low. Had shipments come in from Vidu as expected, it would have been worse.'

'How low?'

'About ten percent below normal levels.'

'So, you can begin operating again as soon as the next shipment arrives?'

'Yes.' Lin replied.

'Okay, I'll talk to Vidu. I'll have him send the shipments today.'

'Good, we will start sorting as soon as the gems arrive. That is, if you approve, John.'

'Of course, Lin. I'm glad no one was badly hurt.'

'We are all fine John. Thank you for your concern.'

'Okay, we'll talk more when I arrive in Hong Kong. In the meantime, e-mail your client's needs to New York and London. Let the other Houses help you as much as they are able from their inventory. I know it's not efficient to ship from their locations, but your clients must be our first priority.'

'I'm sorry for this trouble,' Lin lamented.

'It's not your fault, Lin. You could not have anticipated something like this happening. There's no need to apologize.'

'I wish there was something I ...'

'Lin, it's okay.'

HONG KONG, OCTOBER 24, THURSDAY, 11:38 A.M. JOHN

Slicing through the clouds, over the highly congested city of Hong Kong; our 747 descended towards the main airport runway at the airport. After etching a haughty exclamation point of smoky, black rubber across the concrete runway, its powerful engines were thrown into full reverse to slow its momentum before it turned towards the terminal.

Thankfully, I was able to get some sleep during the flight. Although not entirely refreshed, I was at least awake and alert but not exactly looking forward to visiting this city. Hong Kong is my least favorite destination of our three Distribution Houses. The city is simply too busy for me. Something in my midwestern upbringing never allows me to fully acclimate to the anxious activity of a large metropolitan city, and Hong Kong is one of the worst. The best I can do is to tolerate these sprawling examples of man's inhumanity to nature. Still, if anything about this city captivated me, it was the vast, rich multicultural stew of its teeming masses that gave it an irresistible energy.

Before leaving London, I spent a few hours with Vidu on Wednesday morning. The bumps and bruises from my mugging were still in evidence, swelling, but I didn't think I looked too bad. I figured I could wing it. If asked, I would say I bumped into something in the night and fell down. Unfamiliar hotel rooms can be a nuisance, you know.

The robbery in Hong Kong was number one on my list of subjects I wanted to discuss with Vidu. As expected, he was shocked when he heard the news. He mentioned how Hong Kong was reported to be relatively free of major crime. I found his comment interesting but not pertinent.

We hastily reviewed his plans for two new factories. I had hoped to spend more time with him going over the plans in detail, but he said he understood my desire to get to Hong Kong quickly.

Before leaving, I told him I would phone Jason in Charlottesville and authorize a loan.

Vidu said he was grateful.

'No need,' I countered, 'It's a good investment.

After a casual lunch with Vidu, we briefly met with Arthur in his office to review new shipping routes. I reminded Arthur again how he had been warned about using Heathrow Airport in the past. Vidu nodded, adding that Indian baggage handlers often look for gem shipments from Sri Lanka. Arthur grudgingly agreed to stop sending shipments through that airport. Vidu stayed behind to work with Arthur on the new schedules, promising to email their recommendations to me.

I called Monica after my meetings to explain our travel plans. The hotel desk clerk had notified her she was leaving London this afternoon for a red-eye flight to Hong Kong. She said she was surprised, but after I told her the reason, she seemed to take it in stride even though I thought I heard some understandable stress in her voice.

Needless to say, my day was hectic, with no time to rest, meetings, packing, and rushing to Heathrow. Our flight was uneventful. I didn't talk much with Monica. I was dead tired and needed to sleep. In no time, we were landing. Lin's driver met us at the airport and drove us directly to his office.

The Hong Kong Distribution House is located in a new glass building in central Hong Kong. The building had been financed by my company. Lin and I consulted on its design, finally choosing a concept presented by a well-known local architect. As in London, his building leases space to other businesses. The Distribution House occupies only the top two floors.

The normally impeccably maintained interior of its top-floor lobby, marble walls, and expansive windows was a mess of broken glass and yellow police ribbons when we arrived. Lin met us at the elevator door and bowed in a traditional Chinese greeting before extending his hand to Monica.

Although I never asked him, I assumed Lin's ancestry was Chinese. He is a good-looking man with straight black hair neatly cut and average height for his island. Always impeccably dressed, he wore a light gray suit, white shirt, and dark red tie. His expressions are usually reserved, typical of his heritage and his approach to life. He welcomed Monica with a polite smile.

The Chief Inspector's name was Chang Furui. Forensic evaluations were still in process. Access to the main crime scene was therefore restricted to police personnel only. Avoiding areas sealed with yellow tape, we toured the building together. Gemstones could be seen lying unattended on the floor where the thieves had inadvertently dropped them in their haste to escape. Our inspector explained the elaborate sequence of events of the crime. Dried blood was evident in places. Although no one was seriously hurt, apparently, this was a minor miracle. Force had been used when an employee resisted.

My reasons for wanting to visit in person were twofold. First, I couldn't believe the robbery occurred in broad daylight. Second, I was curious to see if there was any evidence that it was an inside job. Although I implicitly trusted Lin, I didn't want to rely on second-hand observations.

The inspector's description of the events was intriguing. Occasionally, I glanced at Monica during our tour of the crime scene. She had come with me because we drove directly to Lin's office from the airport without stopping at a hotel. I wanted to arrive at the scene of the crime as quickly as possible before anything was altered. I expected M to be bored, instead she seemed to be very interested. I made a mental note to compare my observations with hers later.

My musings were abruptly interrupted by the police inspector when he noticed I had stopped paying attention to him.

He asked if I had any other questions. If not, could he please return to his urgent work?

'One question before you go, inspector.' I asked. 'How could the security system have failed? It is my understanding it has a backup, making it virtually failsafe.'

'Nothing in this world is completely foolproof,' he replied. 'In this case, the thieves rigged the system so all distress signals were sent to an undisclosed location while at the same time sending false signals indicating no problem to your off-site monitors. Simply speaking, no alarm was received during the entire time of the robbery.'

'I don't understand.'

A frown crossed his brow indicating some frustration with my questions, but he took the time to answer. 'Two telephone repairmen were reported to have visited an office next to yours the day before the robbery. I suspect they found a way into your system. The tap was probably in place before the robbery occurred.'

'Is it still there?'

'No, it's gone. We checked.'

'And the vault, how did they get into the vault?'

'I can answer your question,' Lin said. 'The robbery took place during the day when orders are being prepared for shipment. The vault was open. They didn't need to break in. No one ever considered a robbery occurring in the middle of the day.'

'What about your guards?' I looked at Lin. 'Why didn't they do their job?'

The inspector answered for Lin. 'Overpowered,' he said. 'The perpetrators had their people inside very quickly; they were very efficient. Debilitating gas was used and force when necessary.

It only took perhaps five to ten minutes to gain complete control of your facility.'

'Our employees didn't have time to react,' Lin apologized. 'Those who did were quickly and violently subdued.' Lin said he was in his office at the time of the robbery. Phone lines were cut. Before he could react, he was staring at the wrong end of a gun. He, along with other employees, were ordered into a large conference room where they were shut off from outside communication. They waited there, perhaps thirty minutes before leaving the room only after one of them braved opening a door. By this time, the thieves were gone.

The Inspector smiled tightly before asking if we had any other questions.

I thanked him. Then asked if we could use Lin's office.

He nodded his approval.

12:35 P.M. JOHN

The sun reflecting off the tall buildings of Hong Kong was an incredible sight when viewed from a top-floor window of Lin's office.

No frills in his workspace, and his office was utilitarian to a fault; efficiently organized, nothing ornate. Inexpensive metal furniture, filing cabinets, and bookshelves passed for interior decorating. A Formica-topped table covered with computers and electronic gadgets served as his desk.

To my knowledge, Monica was the first person of the female gender to have ever graced the interior of his office. His secretary was male, as were all his assistants. I had never seen a female anywhere near the inside of his office before. And I'm quite sure if it hadn't been for the robbery, she would not have been allowed inside his inner sanctum. Fact was, he seldom let me in. Business was always conducted in a catered conference room. Lin's office was for work, not show. He never relaxed during the day. In his world, after-hour clubs were where executives went to relax. At his invitation, I had, on occasion, accompanied him to one of his clubs. This was when the other side of Lin was exposed- when young girls danced and wine flowed.

I caught Lin stealing a quick look at M, accompanied by a slight, almost inconspicuous frown crossing his face. However, I was not unhappy she had come. Rather than openly questioning Lin's cultural preferences, I liked pushing his comfort level to the edge occasionally, just to see how he would react. From experience, I knew his mind was like a tightly woven rope; no deviation from historical cultural preferences was considered prudent. In some ways Lin was no different than my Dutch ancestors. They, like him, lived in a narrow-minded world defined by a set of rules handed down from their ancestors.

'Can I offer you and Miss Monica something to eat or drink?' he asked politely.

'Coffee would be excellent,' I replied. I wasn't hungry, caused by slightly upset stomach from long hours of travel.

M said she would appreciate something to eat if it wasn't too much trouble.

Lin nodded. Using his phone, he instructed a male secretary to bring food for M and coffee for me while absentmindedly opening his desk drawer and taking out several parcel papers containing gems, handing them to me as he talked.

Using parcel papers to store gemstones is an ancient custom. The paper is folded in such a way that a gem placed inside cannot escape. The outside of the paper is marked with the description and size of the stone contained inside. All this is done because gemstones are small and can be easily misplaced. Parcel papers are not so easily lost and can be stored upright in trays.

I unfolded one of the papers. A nice ruby of three and a half carats was inside. I showed it to M to view while I unfolded another.

'I had these gems in my office for examination.' Lin explained with a grin. 'The thieves didn't get them.'

'Good thing,' I replied while examining a deep pink sapphire. 'This one is a beauty.'

'Yes.' Lin answered simply. 'I should have sent them to the vault, but got busy and forgot.'

'Probably have to wait until the police are finished before you can send them now,' I suggested.

'Yes,' he glanced toward his door as if the robbery had slipped his mind.

It was possible to access the inventories of the London and New York Distribution Houses. We discussed sending a schedule of gemstones Lin needed to fulfill existing orders by e-mail to them. Hopefully they would be able to cover his emergency needs.

Before continuing, Lin called his chauffeur to have M driven to her hotel. I told her she was free for the rest of the afternoon. I would be with Lin. As I walked her to the door of his office, I asked if she would meet me for dinner. She agreed.

He was noticeably more comfortable once M was gone. Although he accepted my personal secretaries more readily than anyone else in my company, he was never comfortable when discussing business in their presence. He didn't like mixing business with pleasure. I had tried on more than one occasion to justify their need, said their primary function was to aid me while traveling. I spent more time on the road than I did in my office. Not having a secretary with me was inconvenient, a business necessity, no more. He would smile and say he understood, but I was pretty certain he did not agree. He saw them in a completely different light, more like geisha girls than executive assistants. Eventually, I gave up trying to convince him.

'She is very pretty,' he said unapologetically.

'You didn't like having her here,' I probed.

'Oh no, you misunderstand. It is just...we have much business to do.'

8:15 P.M. JOHN

The restaurant's décor was minimal, nothing fancy.

It's said a good Chinese restaurant is known for its food, not its furnishings. This was certainly true for this restaurant; the interior decorating was very casual. I slowly sipped a glass of wine while halfheartedly glancing at the entrees on the menu. Nothing looked interesting. I was tired and having a stunning woman sitting across the table from me wasn't helping me concentrate. Monica was overdressed for the occasion in a sculpted black suit with a revealing open collar, nylons, and high-heeled shoes. After her experience at Arthur's club, she probably assumed I only ate at fancy restaurants, but this was not true.

'I hope you don't mind I asked you to dinner,' I said.

She looked up from her menu, 'Not at all, but I am curious... Why did you invite me?'

'No reason really.' I paused before adding, 'I'm leaving for Australia in a few days. There's no need for you to tag along. You will be going home.'

'I see,' she replied. 'When do I leave?'

'Whenever you like. Just let me know and I'll have Helen arrange your flight. Stay a couple of days if you wish. See the city. It doesn't matter to me.'

'Your life, it's all so very interesting.'

'Sometimes. But most of the time, it's pretty dull: airports, hotels, and long hours of work,' I responded, assuming she didn't believe me. And I could understand why. After all, wasn't this evening just another example of my opulent lifestyle, traveling to Hong Kong, having dinner with a beautiful woman.

'Can I explain something to you?' I added, thinking it might help her understand.

'Sure,' she sipped her wine.

'Lin normally invites me to one of his clubs when I'm visiting his city. But I wasn't in the mood for geisha girls tonight. That's why I made a point of asking you to dinner when we were in his office. I didn't want him to feel obligated to entertain me.'

'I see,' she smiled.

'Sorry, dinner with the boss to avoid an excursion to a geisha club is not a typical paragraph in an employee manual.' I smiled.

'That's true,' she agreed.

I paused to sip some wine. 'As long as we're discussing duties not found in your manual, let me explain something else. It's something I seldom explain this to my secretaries.' I rattled on. 'But you seem like an intelligent person.'

'Is it necessary?'

'No.'

She smiled faintly; I suppose wondering where this conversation was headed.

I doggedly continued. I didn't know why. I had no reason to tell her. But for some reason, I wanted her to know, even when common sense dictated it would be better to say nothing.

'You remember we discussed social functions.'

'Yes,' she smiled.

'Well, I told you I don't like going alone, and that's true, but not completely. I'm antisocial, and having a woman with me at a social gathering is like having a human shield. A woman in a room naturally draws attention away from me and takes the pressure off; especially the company of a beautiful woman. Everything changes, the tone and the subject of conversations. She becomes the focal point and this allows me to retreat and observe, which is what I would prefer to do.'

'Does this mean I need to be able to carry a conversation?' she asked with a hint of sarcasm. 'Not just look pretty and keep my mouth shut?'

'Right,' I replied, now slightly embarrassed.

Fortunately, our hors d'oeuvres arrived at this moment.

The wine was good. Not too sweet, but with a full flavor. I'm not much of a wine connoisseur, never had the time to learn, but I have my preferences, not much more. Same for food, I try different foods when I travel, but again, I'm not knowledgeable and don't have the inclination or time to become an expert.

'How do you like this wine?' I asked

'Very good.'

I was beginning to relax, content for a moment.

'You were saying you would prefer I carry the conversation at social engagements?'

'Yes, hopefully you'll sense when it's important.'

'Okay.'

'Did I tell you I got mugged in London?' I mentioned after consuming an appetizer. Again, I had no idea why I brought up this subject. I had previously decided not to tell anyone. But with her, well...

She gave me a blank look.

I told her what happened, about being mugged in the hotel hall and the people who rescued me.

'Did you report it to the police?'

'No.'

'Why not?'

'It's London, people get mugged all the time.'

That is what I told her, but the truth was, something about the appearance of the mugger had been roaming around in my head ever since it happened. It didn't come to me right away, but after having time to think about him, the guy who mugged me looked a lot like the person who had been sitting with Phillip at Arthur's club. I couldn't be sure. It could have just been the product of my overactive imagination. So, I didn't mention it to Monica because I had no real basis for a conclusion.

Conversation lagged. She became quiet, and I took the opportunity to enjoy my meal, happy for some peace after a hectic day in Lin's office.

After a few minutes of pleasant solitude, M spoke up hesitantly. 'Mind if ask you a question on a different subject?'

'Sure.'

'Have you ever been investigated by the Anti-Trust Department of the US government?'

Somewhat perplexed, I put down my fork. 'Interesting question. Not that I haven't been asked before. I have, but never by one of my secretaries.'

She smiled.

'It's a good question, though, and I'll try to answer it for you,' I replied, thinking it would help pass our time. 'That is if you really want to know.'

When she didn't answer, I explained. 'The Anti-Trust Division of the federal government has looked at us very carefully. And although initially they made some noise, they backed off.'

'Why? Your case is so obvious,' she noted. 'You control a monopoly in one natural resource.'

I was startled at her audacity, her accusing me of something which was considered wrong in some circles. But I didn't say anything, just tried to explain. 'Yes, but we have not been prosecuted for good reasons. First, because we have been a positive influence in some third-world countries. Emerging economies is, I think, the current term to describe these countries. Let me explain. Gems are often used as the currency of choice by terrorists and drug lords. Taking this currency out of their hands has made it difficult for the other two sides of their triangle of fear to operate. It hasn't totally stopped them, of course. But in some cases, it has slowed them down.'

'The Feds saw this as a positive thing?'

'Yes, we were performing a service.'

When she didn't comment, I continued, 'I wouldn't say my company is completely out of the woods. But even if they wanted to go after us, we're not defenseless.'

'Why is that?' she asked before putting a single olive into her mouth.

'You really want to know?' I asked again, this time looking into her eyes, trying to fathom what was going on behind those beautiful dark brown orbs.

'I would.'

'Okay. I'll tell you. The truth is my company doesn't have a monopoly on anything. Therefore, we can't be prosecuted.'

'But you've told me you do.'

'I told you a monopoly exists. I didn't tell you my company controls a monopoly. The monopoly, if it exists, only exists because several independent businesses freely cooperate. Service contracts are the only concrete evidence of a relationship. And these are negotiated annually and can be dissolved anytime by either party without notice.'

'Oh,' she seemed surprised.

'So, do you get it?' I asked, convinced she had no idea what I was talking about.

'Sure, no permanent, traceable, legal connections exist between your company and these other companies. Therefore, you can't be tried in court as a monopoly.'

'Yes.'

'But just because these connections aren't visible and can't be traced doesn't mean they don't exist,' she stated as if it was a fact. 'They are just buried deep inside international banks or held in untraceable trusts?'

'No...'

'Of course,' she said with a wink. 'Mr. Van Laan. I'm not dumb. I know how this works. But it's okay. You don't have to defend yourself to me. I'm not here to judge you.'

'And I'm not asking for your judgment. I only want you to know the truth. And the truth is we have no buried or unburied legal ties.'

She looked at me. I could tell she wasn't buying it. I cursed myself for trying to explain. It was becoming apparent she was smart enough to understand the situation but not trusting enough to believe me. I decided it was time to change the subject. It had been a long day and it wasn't ending as I had hoped.

'Perhaps we should...' I began, looking for an out.

But she ignored me and asked another pointed question. 'Do you buy gems from strip miners?'

Now this question resonated with all the fervor of a righteous accusation from a born-again ecologist.

'Another question I often get asked.' I replied, now completely annoyed. 'Strip mining, sounds like a bad idea, right?'

'Well yes, I guess so.'

'And it's important to you, right?'

She immediately tried to backtrack. 'Well, no... I'm just curious... Look, we can talk about something...'

'No, I'll answer your question. It's obvious you assume your boss is a bad actor. So, please allow me an opportunity to defend myself.' I was beginning to sound irritated, but I didn't care. Our discussion had gone too far. Retreating was no longer possible. I launched into a defense.

'Some of our miners are strip miners,' I explained. 'And some are deep bore miners. But my company is not in the business of mining. We never have been. We simply buy rough stones; cut, polish and market them.'

'So, just because you don't actually do the mining, it's not your responsibility? You can wash your hands and blame others?'

'That's true and it's probably the answer you expected. But it's not the whole answer. The real answer is my company encourages land reclamation and environmental stewardship. We don't wash our hands of the issue. Here's what we do. We pay engineers to teach miners how to reclaim their land. And we pay miners to do reclamation. And we don't stop there. We also monitor their progress. And finally, we pay more for gemstones from miners who practice environmental reclamation than from those who don't.'

She raised an eyebrow. 'You actually pay higher priced for gemstones from reclaimed mines than you do for stones from other mines?'

Seeing the incredulity on her face offered some satisfaction, 'Yes, we make sure miners who follow our guidelines make a profit on their reclamation work. This way they cannot afford to ignore us.'

'I see.'

'Yes, but please understand. We don't control every mine in the world. Mining continues in parts of the globe where we have no influence. In these areas, mining is done as it has been for centuries.' I took a sip from my glass, feeling satisfied.

'Strip mining of sapphires continues?'

'Yes, despite the fact I wish it didn't.'

'Do you buy gems from these mines?' She was obviously on a roll.

'Yes. Our stated goal is to control as much of the world's supply of sapphire as possible.'

'Doesn't this make you responsible for what happens at these mines?' She countered. 'Higher prices mean more money for the miners. And this encourages more mining, which causes more damage to our environment.'

'You're right of course. But I have my limitations. I can only do so much.'

'Sounds like a cop-out?'

'Cop-out? No, not really, we're doing everything we can.'

'But strip mining continues.' She wasn't budging.

'Regrettably, it does. Look, sapphires are mined in many unstable regions around the world, some politically unstable, some economically unstable. It's not something we can control. Our buyers are sent to these regions, directly to these mines where possible. We offer to help miners reclaim their land; we encourage them. But most often, they continue as they have for hundreds of years. Old practices die hard.'

Monica didn't immediately respond. Her momentary silence was a welcome reprieve; no more probing questions. 'Well, do you want to resign now you think my company contributes to pollution?' I asked.

'No.'

'Okay,' I sighed.

It was time to call it a night. But then another bright idea took over my tired, beleaguered brain and unfortunately, I went with it.

'Look,' I suggested, sighing and looking around the room. 'Since you are so interested, perhaps you would like to come with me to see a mine where reclamation is practiced. Maybe this will make you think better of your boss.

'I sorry, I didn't mean to imply anything by my questions. I'm just a naturally curious person. It's always getting me into trouble.' She turned to me. 'I hope I haven't upset you.'

'No,' I lied. 'Your questions are good questions and I have tried to answer them. But sometimes; seeing is believing. You asked a question. Now would you like to see the answer to your question? Or would you prefer to assume I'm a bad guy?'

'I didn't....'

'You can go home if you wish,' I interrupted her. 'Or you to come with me to Australia instead.'

'I'm at your disposal according to my contract,' she countered.

'No, not in this case; I simply promised a mine manager I would visit him the next time I was in his part of the world. No business or social obligations are scheduled and I won't need your professional services. So, what do you want to do? I can put you on a plane for the States. Or you can come with me and get an in person answer to your question. It's totally your choice.'

'I would very much like to go to Australia,' she answered without hesitation.

I smiled. 'You sure? You've already flown around the world. You must be tired.'

'I want to go.' She began eating as if our conversation was now done.

'Alright, it's settled then. We leave for Australia Monday. In the meantime, I will require some typing from you. The rest of the time, you are free to enjoy Hong Kong. Just be prepared to leave our hotel early Monday morning.'

'I'll be ready.'

HONG KONG, OCTOBER 28, MONDAY, 11:25 A.M. JOHN

Leveling off at cruising altitude, I glanced out the plane's cabin window to be greeted by an infinite blue sky filled with a few wispy clouds freely riding high winds.

The peaceful scene visibly contrasted wildly with the mental confusion and hectic pace of Hong Kong we had just left behind as the concrete runway at the airport below us swiftly evolved into little more than a gray line marking an island of tall buildings occupied by too many anxious souls. I couldn't resist an involuntary sigh of relief. We were headed to a calmer place, which was more to my liking. The isolated hills of Eastern Australia were nothing like the frantic pace of Hong Kong.

M rested comfortably in a seat next to me. I had not talked to her since our dinner of many questions. Although we spent our weekend on the same island, we did not do it together. A courier was sent to her for work. Mostly, typing was required. My time was occupied with a telephone glued to my ear in Lin's office. The robbery created major logistical problems for our cherished delivery schedules. My business depended on reliability. Any glitch in delivery schedules worried the very core of the company. My job was to try to make sure that didn't happen as much as was humanly possible.

By Sunday, Lin and I had written new schedules designed to shore up holes in our supply chain. Sapphires and rubies were being shipped from New York and London to fill the gaps caused by the Hong Kong robbery. Cutters in Sri Lanka were working overtime to replenish our supply. In addition, clients were informed of delays, their computers updated. We hoped they wouldn't be too upset with the short-term problems caused by the robbery. We also knew the flow of product was pitifully thin. Any additional interruptions would create major problems. However, we didn't anticipate any more complications; hopefully confident our troubles were behind us.

I had promised Clarence Albridge a visit to his Nullamana Mining Company in Australia the next time I was in the area, meaning Southeast Asia. This seemed as good a time as any. In addition, M might learn something from visiting his operation; get her off my case about strip-mining. Australian mines operated under strict environmental controls monitored by their government's equivalent of the EPA.

Opening my computer, I began writing a letter, but concentration was lacking and the letter wasn't coming together. A side glance at M proved far more rewarding. Isn't it true that beautiful women get plenty of attention and I was sure she got more than her share? After attempting to return once more to my work, I stopped mid-sentence.

'Did you enjoy your free time in Hong Kong?' I gave in to distraction.

'Yes,' she sighed, putting down the magazine she was readings. 'It was interesting but so hectic; the lights, the buildings, so many people.'

'The next few days shouldn't be as difficult,' I suggested. 'We're flying to a small town called Inverell in Eastern Australia to visit a sapphire mining company. I'll introduce you to Marsha when we arrive. She's the mining company's secretary. She'll take you to an outfitter's store in town and help you pick out some clothes you'll need for visiting a mine. Buy whatever you wish. We have an account. It wouldn't cost you anything. A helicopter will take us to the mine site in the afternoon. First, we'll tour the company's laboratory at its headquarters.'

'Okay.'

I briefly considered returning to my letter, but it was pitifully obvious I was far more interested in talking to her. I wondered if I was being transparent. Did she know? Could she see right through me? She certainly had beautiful eyes, big browns. They say great models are blessed with great eyes. What was it about their eyes? What shines through those lovely orbs? I didn't know, but I did know M's eyes had it, and I liked looking into them.

She interrupted my contemplation. 'I've been thinking about what you told me at dinner the other night.'

'More questions?'

'I'm sorry.'

'It's okay, but I have to tell you, I can't recall receiving such intense grilling from anyone except perhaps the IRS,' I answered with a smile.

'Please forgive me. I don't mean to...'

I smiled again. 'Ask away. Anything you want to know.'

'You sure?' She moved so that her legs were towards me. 'I don't mean to be a pest.'

I paused to look at her, wondering what was going on inside the brain behind those big, beautiful eyes. 'Please ask your questions. Let's say I find them entertaining.'

'Really?'

I looked at her again. 'Please continue.'

'Okay,' she began, 'I know a little about international tax law.'

'Interesting subject, have at it.'

'Is any subsidiary or any part of your company offshore?'

'Hold on, I thought we covered this at dinner,' I replied, knowing offshore companies are usually established to avoid taxes and other government scrutiny. I began to wonder what was prompting her question. Had I missed something all along? Did her resume mention any experience in international tax law? Not that I could remember.

She continued. 'You explained that you have no legal connection except service contracts with your subsidiary companies. My question doesn't concern these other companies, it concerns your company.'

I have what I like to call a bullshit detector which goes off inside my head whenever something doesn't add up. At this moment, it was going off big time like a five-alarm fire. If I have a fault as a manager, it's that I always assume new employees are good people. I want them to succeed. I expect them to succeed. They have to go out of their way to prove me wrong. Only then do I acknowledge their shortcomings. This approach to hiring has cost me in the past, but I don't really want to change. I want to begin by trusting people, believing I may miss a rewarding relationship if I don't. And a beautiful woman like M. Wasn't she a classic case? I certainly wanted her to succeed. Plus, I assumed my staff had done a thorough background check on all the applicants, including Miss Monica Sorenson. No mental cases. No felons. But was there something they missed?

She paused, seeing the confused look in my eye. 'I guess I shouldn't have asked. The information is confidential... right? I understand.'

I didn't answer immediately.

'Can we talk about something else?' she continued to backtrack.

I wasn't quite sure where to go at this point in our conversation. I wasn't prepared for the possibility that she was not who I thought she was. But obviously, something needed to be said. Plus, now, I was curious. 'No. Your question is an interesting one. And I will answer it, but first, I have a few questions for you.'

'Look, I'm sorry... It's just, well... I'm naturally curious. I told you it gets me into trouble.' She avoided eye contact and moved away from me once again.

'No, it's a perfectly reasonable question. But it's not the kind of question I expect from a secretary, especially not one with your background. It is more like a question I might get from lawyers or accountants, not waitresses.'

'Oh,' she paled.

'So, will you answer my questions... truthfully?'

'Yes,' she hesitantly agreed.

'Truthfully.'

'I promise.'

'Okay. First question: Are you an undercover agent from the IRS...or any other government agency for that matter?'

'No, absolutely not,' she said emphatically.

'You sure? Because...'

'Mr. Van Laan, I would never agree to do something like that.'

I looked into her eyes, attempting to see if she was lying. All I saw honest conviction. It was how she answered my question, like it would be distasteful to cooperate with the government.

'So, if you're being truthful, then where did all these questions ...'

'Where did I acquire an interest in international law?' she finished my sentence.

'Well, yes... Let's begin there.'

'Okay,' she paused. 'I didn't exactly put everything on my resume,' she finally confessed. 'The job description I read in your ad didn't... well... I didn't think brains were what you were looking for. In fact, I thought being too smart might be a deterrent to getting the job.'

'Humm, interesting perspective. Not that I'm going to admit you're right, but I guess I get it. So, tell me. What did you leave off your resume?'

'Am I going to get fired over this?' she asked defensively.

'Not necessarily, but I place a high value on being truthful.'

She sighed inwardly.

She knew I was not happy. Probably already starting to shut her out. Like so many others before her who didn't make the grade for one reason or another. Like them, she would be history soon. My company and all its inherent problems were enough trouble. I didn't need more complications. But... I was curious.

'I'm a lawyer,' she began. 'I graduated from the University of Virginia Law School. It's my connection to Charlottesville I specialized in studying international and environmental law. I worked for the Environmental Protection Agency in Washington DC for seven years on their legal staff.'

She paused, wondering, I suppose, if this was enough to get her fired.

'Go on.'

'I became frustrated with the system like many other idealists. I quit and returned to Charlottesville and took a waitressing job. Got bored after a while. When I read your ad, I decided to apply. So, here we are... I'm sorry,' she continued without giving me an opportunity to speak, 'I didn't mean to get nosey. I'll do my job to the best of my ability from now on. And I will mind my own business. I promise... So, can we start over?'

I took a moment before answering. 'No, we can't start over... let's continue. Is there anything else you conveniently left off your resume? Like maybe being married.'

It was now her turn to go after me. And she did with a vengeance. 'That's personal, none of your business. You're my employer. By law, you are not allowed to ask me this question. You can be sued for sexual discrimination for asking,' she stated defiantly.

Okay, she had me. I knew it, but I wasn't ready to back down, not just yet. 'Fine, I have been sued before,' I countered. 'I have good lawyers.'

'Ever have to settle?'

'That's confidential.'

'You're right. There I go again being too nosey again,' she sighed.

'I withdraw my question, your honor. I don't want to be sued.'

'Duly noted... I won't sue you and I will answer your question. I wouldn't want you to think I'm hiding anything. My answer is I have been too busy to get involved with men.'

'Busy at what?'

'One question at a time. And, by the way, you still haven't answered my question. Not that I want an answer anymore.'

'No part of my company is offshore, in blind trusts, or any other kind of an invisible corporation. As I told you before, my partners run companies that are totally independent. I rely on their trust. That's it, nothing more.'

'That's not very American of you. Americans usually like everything tied together in volumes of legal paperwork.'

'That's true,' I said. 'But it's not my MO. I value trust more than legal constrictions.'

'Okay, I guess. Now, I'll finish answering your question.'

'Please don't,' I countered. 'On the advice of legal counsel, I withdraw my question.'

'I'm answering anyway,' she stated emphatically.

'Under protest for the record, your honor.'

She ignored me. 'I had a mission. I was either studying or working. Men, marriage; they were not what I wanted. I had other dreams. Men were simply a hindrance.'

'No interest at all.'

Now it was her turn to go on the offensive again. She laughed. 'Yes, I had an interest and sexual preference is not my problem. You can put that issue to rest,' she looked me squarely in my eye. 'I dated and I guess you could say I used some men. But they didn't seem to mind... most of them anyway.'

'Very pretty. All those broken hearts trailing off behind you.'

'Not my fault.' Her smile was charming. 'I never promised them anything.'

INVERELL, AUSTRALIA, 4:10 P.M. JOHN

Cousins Motor Inn was the best accommodations available in the small town of Inverell, Australia.

The Inn specialized in practicality, not elegance like the hotels in Hong Kong and London. Clarence, the company's CEO, sent Marsha, his do-everything secretary, to meet us at the airstrip. No limos this time, just a late model Land Rover. After depositing me at the Inn, Marsha drove M to a local outfitters store. We would be venturing into the dry dust and disorder of the Australian hills. M would need something to wear other than fancy suits and dresses.

I retreated to my room. It was late afternoon in Australia by the time we arrived. My visit with Clarence would have to wait until tomorrow morning. Meanwhile, a demanding mountain of faxes, e-mails, and telephone calls waited for me, all forwarded courtesy of Helen in Charlottesville and thoughtfully delivered by Marsha.

Already irritable from constant travel, the claustrophobic atmosphere of a small, gaudy motel room did nothing to help me concentrate on my work. A minuscule wooden desk served as a temporary office. Sometime in the late hours of the night, I finally gave up, concluding I didn't have enough time to get everything done.

Besides, I couldn't keep my eyes open anymore.

OCTOBER 29, TUESDAY, 8:05 A.M. JOHN

After only a couple of hours of fitful sleep, the sun came up completely out of sequence with the biological clock inside my overtaxed brain.

Jet lagged, overworked, overtired; it didn't matter; I had to get out of bed. Ignoring a deep desire to find a dark hole and crawl in it for a few more hours of rest, I half-slept through breakfast. And then, as if in a dream, M and I were herded by Marsha into a waiting Land Rover headed for the offices of the Nullamana Mining Company. A meeting with Clarence was scheduled before driving to his mine.

'Why here?' M asked as we rode through town. 'Why is the headquarters of the mining company located in this small town out here in the middle of nowhere? Why not in Melbourne or Sydney?'

'Because security is a big issue in the gemstone business. And security can be more easily monitored here. Understand, this is a small town, and a good share of the town's prosperity depends on mining. No one wants anything to go wrong. Everyone knows everyone here, and they help keep it secure. When someone new comes to town, everyone watches. You can't buy this kind of scrutiny in a large city.'

Our Land Rover drove past the local airport before turning down a road towards the mining office complex. The town of Inverell was too small to require a jet runway. We needed one, so I had it built.

'See that plane?' I said, pointing to an unmarked private jet parked next to a hangar. 'That is the mining company's jet. Several times a week it flies gemstones directly to Sri Lanka for cutting.'

The Nullamana Mine's office and laboratory were housed in two white, non-descript metal buildings on the edge of town. No windows could be seen in either structure except at the entrance to the lobby of the office building. Separating the two buildings was a tall, curving concrete wall with substantial metal supports painted red.

Clarence Albridge, a tall, slightly crumpled, balding figure with a beaming smile, greeted us in his lobby. He was your basic workaholic, just like me. But then he had to be. The busy activities of mines scattered throughout the region took his constant attention.

'Good to see you, John,' Clarence said, his handshake firm as always.

'You too, Clarence. May I introduce Monica Sorenson? Monica, Clarence.'

Clarence's world was far more orderly and conservative than mine. Married with two grown children and three grandchildren, he was a big man, slightly overweight, in his early sixties, with a great smile and wonderful sense of humor.

He extended his hand to M. 'Welcome to our part of the world.'

'Thank you,' M replied.

'So, what brings you here, John?' Clarence turned to me.

'I was in the neighborhood, Hong Kong, to visit Lin after the robbery. I told you I would stop in the next time I happened to be in your area. Here I am.'

'May I ask you a quick question before we get on to other business?' he interjected.

'Sure.'

'I got a fax asking for increased quotas for the month. Is it correct?'

'Yes, it's one of the reasons I came. We need to talk.'

'Sure. Say, I'll bet Miss Sorensen would like to see our operation. Why don't you let me show her around?' he was insistent. 'I'm sure you have some work you can do while I give her a tour.'

Somehow, I didn't have the heart to deny him. It was easy to see he was completely taken by M and what man wouldn't be. She looked great in her new mining outfit. The color suited her skin tone. 'Okay, I'll make a few calls from your office?'

He grinned and offered an elbow to M, swiftly escorting her towards a long white hallway before I had a chance to change my mind.

I headed for Clarence's office, making a mental list of the tasks I needed to accomplish during this brief intermission.

8:55 A.M. MONICA

Opening big double doors to a brightly lit room, Clarence escorted M inside.

Fifty-plus workers could be observed, laboring over lines of back-lit glass tables.

'Gemstones come here directly from our mines,' Clarence explained. 'But not all stones which arrive are sapphires. Ordinary stones need to be separated from sapphires and this is done by eye. It's demanding work.'

Clarence and M stopped to observe. The sorting tables had translucent glass tops. Underneath the glass were rows of florescent bulbs. Illuminated by light from below the glass, it was possible see that some of the stones were a dull, slightly transparent blue, different from other stones which simply appeared to be black.

'First, we separate stones which show color from ones which don't,' he explained. 'The colored stones are assumed to be sapphires. The discarded stones are deposited into a hole in the far-right corner of the table, where they are collected in a bag,' he pointed. 'The colored stones are placed in separate bags on the other side of the table. Occasionally, a gemstone with either extraordinary natural color or size is noticed. These exceptional stones are specially marked for careful inspection later.'

M reached over a sorter and selected a stone which looked dark blue with a hint of green. It was very dull and rough, but its color seemed to be easier to see than most of the other stones

She handed it to Clarence. 'This looks different.'

'It is,' he replied. 'You have a good eye.' He looked the stone over carefully and handed it to the female sorter who was working at the table. 'What do you think?' he asked.

She examined the stone.

'Some stones are blessed with clear natural color,' Clarence explained to M. 'Mother Nature has already done everything necessary for these stones. Let me show you.'

He led M to a flat round circulating wheel. Placing the stone in a tool which resembled pliers, he gently eased the stone against the wheel. The abrasive surface of the wheel polished a portion of the rough exterior of the stone revealing a beautiful clear blue color inside. After Clarence released the stone from the pliers, he showed it to M. The polished area gleamed under bright overhead lights.

'See,' he said, 'a naturally colored gemstone.'

'Beautiful,' M breathed, obviously impressed that a seemingly dull stone held such great beauty inside.

'These naturals are rare and deserve special attention,' Clarence held the stone in his hand as he talked. 'Properly certified, at market, they can bring two to three times more value than a treated stone.'

'What is a treated stone?' M asked.

'I'll show you in a minute.'

After the stone was returned to the sorter, M's tour continued. Exiting a back door in the office building, Clarence directed her outside, down a sidewalk through a grassy area towards a tall concrete wall. The wall was close to three feet wide and, in places, as much as fifteen feet tall. Supported on both sides by bright red steel girders, it could have passed for a modern art sculpture as it gently curved.

'The reason for the wall is to divert a possible explosion in the building we are going to visit from affecting the main office building,' Clarence explained as they continued. 'But don't worry; the chances of an explosion actually occurring are extremely remote.'

After entering the building on the other side of the wall, M viewed a room filled with rows of gleaming six-foot-high cylinders about four feet in diameter was next on her tour. Electric cables connected each cylinder to separate control panels covered with numerous dials. Long overhanging hoses and wires were attached to the top of each cylinder.

A white-coated lab technician was carrying a long white ceramic tube when M and Clarence approached.

'Harry,' Clarence said, 'show this young lady what you have in your tube.'

Harry smiled meekly at the beautiful girl standing next to his boss, turning the open end of the tube toward her so she could look inside. Rough stones like the ones M had seen in the building next door were inside the tube.

'Okay, put the tube into the furnace.' Clarence instructed the lab technician.

Harry loaded the ceramic tube into a cylinder-shaped furnace. He then proceeded to cover the top with a metal lid and securely fastened it with four hand-turned screws. Next, he set dials on a control panel.

Clarence explained the function of the furnace as Harry worked. 'We call this heat-treating or color-enhancement. What we really do here is to give Mother Nature a boost. You see, deep inside the earth where the clear sapphire crystals are formed, heat, pressure and outside elements come together to create color in gemstones. With some crystals, a perfect gemstone with good color and clarity is formed. Unfortunately, this is not true for a high percentage of sapphires. They either don't have very good color or they contain many small flaws which detract from their clarity. What we do here is to give Mother Nature some help. We effectively return these stones to conditions similar to where they were formed. Then we allow the process to continue to perfection. And of course, we accelerate the process. We don't want to wait thousands of years.'

After the technician set a timer and turned a switch, a temperature gauge on the furnace began to rise slowly as heat and pressure were applied inside the cylinder. Harry explained the process would take between forty-eight to sixty hours to complete. Temperatures inside the cylinder will reach as high as eighteen hundred degrees Celsius.

Clarence pointed toward some metal pipes running the length of the building, explaining, 'At monitored temperatures, the contents inside these furnaces are stable. But if it gets too hot, the furnace could explode like a bomb. To make sure this doesn't happen, heat inside the furnaces is constantly adjusted using cool water flowing through pipes you see above the furnaces.'

9:10 A.M. JOHN

The desk chair in Clarence's sparsely furnished office leaned way back.

Relaxing with a phone in my ear, my eyes naturally fell under the spell of Clarence's dysfunctional decorating tastes, which vacillated between English Victorian and Australian Bushman. Floral patterns better suited to an English country house covered a sofa in one corner of the office, but the walls of his office were decorated with Aboriginal artwork. I enjoyed teasing Clarence about his schizophrenic sense of style.

Vidu was on the phone. He knew where I was. Clarence told him. They were friends.

'I apologize for throwing rush orders at you,' I replied to him.

'It is no bother,' Vidu explained. 'I have directed one of my factories to begin cutting sapphires instead of diamonds. We were ahead of schedule on a diamond contract, so I was able to cut your sapphires instead. I think we will be able to get your inventories back to good levels in two to three weeks.'

'Thanks.'

'You do not need to ever thank me, John. I am a stock owner in your company. I have a duty to your company.'

'That's why I included you,' I said with a grin.

High-pitched sirens interrupted our conversation, wailing in loud screams, suspending all rational thought.

'Vidu, something is happening here,' I yelled into the phone, barely able to hear myself think above the noise of the sirens. 'I'll have to get back to you.'

I didn't know if he could hear me above the din of the sirens, but I had no choice except to hang up. The sirens were too loud.

Designed to get everyone out of the buildings if there was a fire or worse, they were very effective.

Calm down, I told myself; it's probably just a drill.

Confirming my suspicions, the staff looked completely unconcerned. Through the open office door, I could see them calmly passing down a hall towards exits in an orderly manner, laughing and joking. I decided to wait out the drill in Clarence's office even though I knew my reluctance to leave was a violation of company rules. Technically, I wasn't an employee. But I figured I could bend the rules. Besides, this would allow me time to finish my call to Vidu as soon as an all-clear sounded. And now that I had time to think about it, I suspected the drill was probably retaliation for my always getting on Clarence's case about safety. I chuckled to myself, thinking it was just the sort of thing he might do. I leaned back in his chair and rested for a few minutes, finding that difficult. The sirens were simply too bloody loud for comfort.

Dull booming vibrations suddenly began to shake the office building, forcing me to quickly reconsider my previous conclusion.

This was no drill.

This was a real problem.

Falling awkwardly to my knees on the floor, I ducked behind Clarence's desk for protection when another loud explosion resonated through the building, knocking pictures off the wall. I stayed down, mentally suspended in a nervous, deafening daze; wondering if the next explosion would end my life.

A brief silence followed instead, but it lasted only a few seconds. Employees began to scream and run for exits.

Trying to calculate how much time had passed from when I first heard the sirens until the explosions hit, I thought it might have been enough time for everyone to get out of the lab. I assumed this was where the explosions were coming from.

Nothing in the office building was explosive. The lab was where volatile chemicals were housed. However, my sense of time was deeply flawed. The explosions echoing through my brain made it difficult to think clearly, accompanied by fears rapidly processing through the dark corridors of my mind, beginning with Clarence and M... where were they?

Not inside the lab, I hoped.

This new, potentially dreadful complication ignited an incoherent need that could not be ignored. Getting up off the floor, I was determined to find them, desperate to know they were okay. Running down the hall toward the back exit doors leading to the lab was impossible. Employees were streaming in the opposite direction outside Clarence's office, headed towards a front exit. Like a panicked herd of cattle, they stampeded for the front doors in the lobby. It would be futile to try to go against the tide of bodies. Instead, I joined the frantic crowd, pushing and shoving, trying to avoid falling and being trampled.

Eventually, our mass of terrified flesh approached the exit doors in the lobby as one hopelessly condensed body, jammed together, pushed towards a narrow opening of two doors. A woman screamed. Another began to cry. An elbow jabbed my back. I began to fall, my shoe trapped under a foot. I pushed back, grabbing the shirt of a man in front of me to keep from falling. My foot released at the last moment, and I edged toward the door amid the crushing bodies, mingled with a stench of fearful sweat.

A violent explosion hit the building while we were trapped inside, shattering the lobby windows. Flying glass cut into the employees. Shrill screams blended with high-pitched sirens, like the pitiless crying of wounded animals. A gap in the now open windows made for an alternate escape route. Employees began stepping through the broken windows, releasing pressure off the rest of us who were nearer the front door, enough so we were able to lurch forward. Scraping against a door frame, I finally made it outside the building, only to be shoved from behind, tripping over a fallen employee face down on the lawn. The frantic herd behind me ran, screaming from the building, stepping on those of us who had fallen. Rolling and crawling on my hands and knees, I extricated myself from this hurting scene, finally reaching an open space on the grass where I could rest for a few minutes, breathing deeply.

Getting to my feet, I looked over the office building in the direction of the lab. Flames were shooting high into the air trailing clouds of black smoke. To my relief, the concrete wall standing between the two buildings was still visible, shielding us from the fire. The wall had done its job. The main office building, although visibly rattled, was not badly damaged. Employees on the front lawn stood around in absolute awe as the devastating flames rose high into the sky from the lab behind the wall. Some hurried away. Others looked dazed and shocked as I searched their faces for Monica and Clarence.

An employee approached who must have known my name from previous visits. 'Mr. Van Laan.'

I asked him if he had seen Clarence.

'No, sorry. What a tragedy.'

'Yes.'

'You might ask one of the lab guys over there if they know where Clarence is?' he pointed.

'Thanks.' I wandered in the direction he indicated. A crowd of white-coated lab technicians was a good sign. Hopefully, it meant the lab had been completely evacuated in time. I approached them and asked. 'Have you seen Clarence Albridge?' my voice sounding hollow in my ears.

'Who?' the man's gaze was vacant.

'Clarence Albridge. You know. Clarence, your boss.'

'Oh yeah. Sorry. No, haven't seen him. Sorry.'

'Thanks.'

'Ask Terry,' The guy pointed to another group of white coats. 'He might know.'

'Terry?'

'Yeah, the tall guy over there.'

I hurried towards the man. 'Sorry, excuse me. I'm looking for Clarence. Have you seen him?'

'He was right behind me,' Terry replied.

'Was there a young lady with him?'

He thought for a moment. 'Yes, yes, I saw her too.'

'Did everyone get out?'

'Think so.'

'Thanks.'

'Yes sir.'

'I'm John Van Laan, friend of Clarence.'

'You run the company in the US.'

'Yes. Can you tell me what happened?'

'Don't know. Everything failed. It happened fast.'

'Thanks, Terry. If you see Clarence, tell him I'm looking for him.'

A siren car marked with the Inverell fire chief's insignia interrupted our conversation, speeding through the parking lot, lights flashing, scattering workers in its way. I took a deep breath. Now was a time to be calm. I needed to stop running around mindlessly. Still, I badly wanted to know they were okay.

More fire trucks arrived, roaring through the crowded parking lot, stopping behind the south edge of the wall. Men jumped off, grabbing hoses. Some formed lines, pushing stupidly curious workers away from the wall. I decided to return to the empty office building, thinking, hoping maybe Clarence and M might be inside, but only empty rooms greeted me in my search, rooms with papers lying on the floor.

Hooper, an Aboriginal employee, Clarence's security chief was working in one of the sorting rooms with two other uniformed men, scooping loose stones into bags. Gemstones lay scattered everywhere, on the floor, on tables. It was a mess. They were carrying bags of stones to the vault, which was located in the rear of the building.

'G'day, Mr. Van Laan,' Hooper said.

'Hi Hooper,' I knew him well. He had been with Clarence for many years.

'Bad situation, sir.'

'Yes. I appreciate you taking care of the stones.'

'My job, sir. Can't leave these gemstones lying about for just anyone to pick up.'

'Might be dangerous working here.'

'The wall's still up. We'll be okay, Mr. Van Laan.'

'Ok, Hooper. Thanks again. Say, have you seen Clarence since the explosions?'

'No.'

'Tell him I'm looking for him if you see him.'

'Right,' Hooper replied. 'I'm sure he'll turn up.'

'Look, Hooper. Don't stay here any longer than necessary.'

'We won't. I promise. As soon as we get the stones into the vault, we'll lock up and get out.'

'Good.'

'Right,' Hopper replied. 'My men and I know what to do.'

9:25 A.M. JOHN

Remembering an emergency exit door somewhere in the back corner of the building, I headed in that direction in a hurry.

After some searching, I found the door and eased it open. Smoke immediately greeted my senses, eyes burning, lungs coughing foul smoke-filled air. The door led to a concrete sidewalk that cut through an open area at the rear of the office building on the opposite side of the safety wall from the burning lab. Although the area was filled with visually dense, suffocating smoke, I discovered if I got down low on my hands and knees, the air nearer to the ground was breathable. To my relief, the concrete wall looked solid, not near to collapsing, at least from what I could see through the smoke. It was still shielding the office building, protecting it from the heat of the fire on the other side but not from lung-choking smoke curling around and over it. The red steel girders supporting the wall showed no sign of bending. On the other side of the wall, I could hear the fire burning out of control.

I was alone.

Firefighters were working at the other end of the wall, closer to the parking lot and their fire trucks. Since I wasn't in anyone's way, I decided to take a look around the end of the wall, curious to see how much damage the explosions and fire had caused. A minor shock wave shook the air as I neared the end of the wall. I went down low on one knee, afraid the wall might collapse. It stood firm, so I continued.

Heat from the burning fire immediately scorched my face when I leaned around the edge of the wall. Complete destruction of the lab was the answer to my curiosity. Red hot plumes of fire rose from inside the building through what once was a roof. Another explosion sent sound waves reverberating through the canyons of my mind; I quickly retreated behind the wall, horrified by what I had seen. One image captured my attention. For one brief horrifying moment in time, a breeze had cleared the smoke and I thought I saw what appeared to be two objects lying inert under the smoke-filled gloom, two shadows which looked a lot like bodies.

I had to know; I couldn't ignore what I saw. Crawling on hands and knees to get a better look, I again eased around the edge of the wall. A large red water tank momentarily appeared out of the smoke. I knew from past experience that the tank was an essential part of a cooling system. It stood behind the main laboratory building, connected by pipes that fed water by gravity to furnaces inside for cooling in an emergency. Apparently, it had survived the blasts. From where I lay by the edge of the wall, perhaps thirty-five yards of grass separated me from the base of the tank. Beneath the tank was a pad of concrete supporting the steel girders which held the elevated tank in the air.

Smoke burned into my eyes while attempting to get a better picture of what was under the tank. I buried my head in cool grass for a moment, breathing air near the ground while wiping tears from my stinging eyes. The dark shadows could be bodies or merely debris from the explosions? I didn't know. Trying to see through the smoke was like looking through a moving gray fog against a backdrop of intense glaring heat. It was almost impossible to distinguish reality from illusion.

My knowledge of the lab offered a few clues in understanding what happened. The first big blasts were probably caused by exploding furnaces. Hopefully the furnaces had been disabled by now. No more big explosions. The secondary explosions were smaller, most likely from tanks of compressed gases normally used to supply ingredients to the furnaces' cylinders during heat treatment.

Wiping my eyes, I again attempted to look around the wall, hoping the smoke would clear. And for one brief moment, this is exactly what happened. My burning eyes clearly could see two distinct shadows lying under the tank. The steel girders which supported the water tank looked intact, but the tank was damaged. Water was leaking steadily onto the ground where the shadows were laying. After wiping tears out of my eyes, I looked again. Clouds of smoke again covered the scene and I could see nothing. Quickly retreating behind the wall, I buried my face in the cool grass and coughed to clear smoke from my lungs.

Were the shadows bodies? I had no way of knowing, not without getting closer. Cowering behind the wall for protection was no solution. My options were limited. I had no choice. I had to know.

Crawling on my belly close to the ground, I covered about a third of the distance to the tank before glancing up, greeted by a shimmering oasis like reflection which could only be a puddle of water surrounding two dull shadows. I wondered if the water from the tank was protecting whatever was under it from the fire. And if the shadows were bodies, could they still be alive? Maybe, but once the water from the tank was fully drained, the heat would... Some movement. Couldn't be sure. Could be a mirage caused by heat waves. And even if the bodies were real, what was the odd that they alive? Was I risking my life for nothing trying to rescue them? But on the chance that they were still alive, didn't I have to try, even if the odds were long, even if I died trying.

Too many questions. Too much confusion. No answers. Crawling seemed the only solution. Just keep going without thinking, periodically wiping my eyes, attempting to see, trying not to think about what I was doing because thinking offered no help. When I was finally able to clearly distinguish the bodies through the smoke; no movement, probably dead. It was time to turn back. Heat too intense, debilitating. Self-preservation took over.

One of the shadows moved.

Grabbing a fist full of grass in frustration, one of them was alive, eliminating my best option which was to get the hell out of there before I died. For a long moment I lay on the ground with my face buried in grass, feeling waves of heat pass over my back, trying to breathe the air near the ground. Coughing, choking, wondering how much water remained in the tanks. Briefly squinting into the smoke before burying my face again in the grass, water was dripping in a steady stream. Good because it was probably sheltering the bodies beneath it from the heat. But it also meant there couldn't be much water left in the tanks. If someone was going to rescue the poor souls lying under the tank, it had to be now.

And it had to be me.

Time stands still in moments like this. Decisions are not made in the conscious mind. Actions occur more by instinct than rationale. I am no hero. Only God knows why I continued to crawl on my belly away from the protection of the wall. It was what I knew I had to do; nothing more. Intense heat covered me like a suffocating pillow the nearer I crawled towards to bodies. I didn't want to continue, but as long as I stayed close to the ground, crawling slowly on my belly, the heat was tolerable, barely.

Another explosion set a plume of fire and smoke high into the air. I buried my head in my hands as a shock wave rolled over me. Holding my breath, I briefly thought I was a dead man.

The skin on my back felt hot, unbearably hot. How hot, how damaging I did not know. As I crawled closer, two bodies, one large, one smaller became more defined. I kept inching my way on the ground, increasingly conscious of growing heat and smoke filling my lungs. A sudden, desperate urge to turn and run; yet, I scraped along the ground, almost as fearful of turning back as moving forward. At some point I became aware I was crawling through water from the tank. It cooled my belly. Splashing water on the back of my head, I rolled over to immerse my clothes in the shallow wet coolness of the water before continuing to crawl over the grass in what seemed an endless journey. Closing my eyes to shield them from smoke, only occasionally looking up, I hoped I was moving in the right direction.

My elbows became painful from scrapping over rough concrete which told me I was under the tank in a shallow pool of cool water. Finally able to touch one of the faces, she turned towards me and my worst fear was realized. One of the bodies under the tank was Monica. She was alive, but only barely conscious.

'You okay?' I asked.

She didn't answer immediately as if she was hearing me at the end of a long tunnel.

'I think so,' she answered.

'Are you injured?' Can you move?'

'I don't know.'

'We need to go,' I tried to not alarm her, only give her simple instructions. Wiping my eyes to examine the bottom of the water tank, it was difficult to gauge, but it was possible the flow of water from the damaged tank was beginning to slow.

'Can you crawl?' I asked.

Another explosion ripped through the air. We both ducked our heads into the shallow puddle of water. It felt cool and good.

I looked at her again. Her eyes were open, but she seemed confused.

'Crawl.'

'What?'

I pointed in the direction of the wall and realized I could only faintly see it now through the thick smoke.

'Crawl,' I said, this time forcefully, pointing again in the direction I wanted her to go.

She started to stand.

'No!' I screamed and pulled her down into the cool water. 'Stay on your belly. Stay down, as low as you can.'

I pushed her gently in the right direction until slowly she began to crawl through the water.

The other body was Clarence. He lay motionless on his back, nose in the air, blood trickling down his face from a cut in his hair. He was out cold, but I saw movement in his chest. I splashed water over his body, grabbed an outstretched arm, closed my eyes against the smoke, and began to pull him behind me, holding on to his shirt sleeve. M crawled in front of me as I pushed her again in the proper direction, scraping on my belly, concrete cutting into my knees and elbows, heat penetrating the back of my head, sometimes stopping to splash water on my back and on Clarence and Monica with my free hand.

The distance to the wall appeared miles away as we inched along, crawling, pulling, sliding, scraping. My arm began to ache. Clarence is a big man. It was not easy pulling him. Stopping periodically to breathe and splash water, eventually we reached grass. Crawling was easier now, the grass smoother than concrete, not as painful, but no more water. Heat and smoke engulfed us in its suffocating glove.

M coughed.

I choked, trying to cover my mouth with my wet shirt, my eyes closed, smoke and heat blowing over us in endless waves.

'Stay low,' I yelled at M while pulling Clarence, fighting an urge to stand and dash for the wall and safety. She coughed and somehow kept sliding along the ground.

There are moments in life when you are convinced time has stopped, and you will forever be held in a hard, granite-like existence evidenced only by your current dire conditions, conditions of pain, and sacrifice, which will never end. I crawled, everything in mind and body dedicated to one simple discipline, one demand: breathe the smoke-filled air and crawl, try not to cough, breathe, crawl, nothing else, think about nothing, don't think about the heat. Don't think about what the heat is doing to your body. It hovered over us like a hot shower, seemingly penetrating the pores of our bodies. I crawled through the smoke, pulled Clarence, and pushed M, grass making my sliding progress only slightly less torturous, crawling through unyielding intervals of pain and heat. I crawled. I crawled. I tried not to think. I crawled, I coughed, I dragged Clarence. Nothing else existed.

And then, as if by a miracle, our ordeal was over.

It was over as though it had never happened. We were behind the wall. A fresh breeze blew away the smoke for a moment. I lay on my back in the cool grass and coughed and coughed to clear my lungs until I could finally speak.

'Can you walk?' I asked her.

She slowly sat up into a sitting position and looked at me with blank eyes.

'I think so,' she said.

10:20 A.M. JOHN

Clarence was lifted into an ambulance, not fully conscious, showing signs of movement.

According to the medic who was attending to him. A splint had been placed on one of his arms, which appeared to be broken. An IV was running into the other arm.

'Clarence protected me from the blast,' M huddled next to me in the corner of the ambulance with a blanket wrapped around her shoulders, shivering.

'What happened?' I asked, slipping an oxygen mask off my mouth so I could talk.

'I don't really know. An alarm sounded. Employees quickly began moving to exits. Clarence grabbed my arm while shouting instructions to technicians. Something wasn't working right, not sure what.' M spoke slowly, as if recalling a dream.

'The backup cooling system?' I asked.

'Yes. They couldn't understand why it wasn't working. Finally, Clarence gave up and yelled at everyone to get out.'

'You were the last ones out?' I asked hopefully.

'Yes, he wouldn't go until they were all out.   I thought we were okay. He seemed to know what he was doing. We were outside the building when a blast hit us from behind. The shock wave must have thrown us under the tank.'

INVERELL HOSPITAL, WEDNESDAY, OCTOBER 30, 10:35 A.M. JOHN

A local hospital admitted Monica and Clarence overnight for observation.

Me, they released; no real burns, no concussion, some smoke inhalation, nothing serious; just go away, they said.

I would rather have stayed.

No, doc said I had to go, get some rest. You will be fine.

Rest was not what I got.

After returning to my motel room, the unhappy task of calling my partners and telling them the bad news concerning our latest catastrophe was my required duty. Destruction of the lab-created major problems. Everyone listened quietly without comment. I didn't have to explain anything, only the facts. The problems were all too obvious. Besides, I didn't have the luxury of spending much time with any one person. Too many calls to make. When I finally couldn't talk anymore, my voice hoarse from smoke and exhaustion, I went to bed and slept, dreaming of fires.

By morning, Clarence was awake and making good progress towards recovery. In fact, he looked better than I felt after a mostly sleepless night. Better than I thought possible after the ordeal he had experienced the previous day.

'How you doing, mate?' I asked.

'Just dandy,' Clarence answered with as much resolve as he could muster, 'I'm ready to get out of here.'

'Best do what the doctor tells you.'

'I know, but I want to see the lab.'

'Not much to see.'

'That bad?'

'Yes, a blast from an exploding furnace knocked you unconscious under the water tank. After a second furnace blew, the lab began to burn, followed by secondary explosions.'

'Compressed gas cylinders going off?'

'Like small bombs,' I said.

'I hear you saved my life.'

'Not me, water from the emergency tank kept you alive.'

'But you got us out.'

'I was rescuing M. You just happened to be in the way.'

He smiled, then cringed as the abrasions on his face cracked.

'Thanks anyway, mate.'

'Act of pure stupidity on my part,' I joked. 'I should have let the firemen do their duty.'

'I was told it was a good thing you got to us before it was too late,' he replied un earnest.

'Don't know, just seemed like the thing to do at the time.' I paused, then asked him, 'So what do you think caused the furnaces to blow?'

'Hard to say,' Clarence replied. 'It all happened so fast. All systems went down at once.'

'All the back-up systems?' I asked in disbelief.

'We tried to get the water tank to work, but even it failed. Finally, we gave up and ran out of the building.' Clarence said with hollow resignation.

'Probably waited too long.'

'I couldn't believe every system failed. It seemed impossible.'

'Good thing we built a wall.'

'Yes, good thing,' he replied without enthusiasm. 'It saved our employees.'

He had not wanted to build the concrete safety wall when I first suggested it. He had argued the backup cooling systems were designed to avert explosions. They were bulletproof. The wall was a waste of money. Nothing short of a complete breakdown of the Inverell Town's electric grid would cause an interruption to the power supply. And we had backup generators to compensate for power outages. Besides, if all else failed, we had the water tank, which only needed gravity to keep water flowing to the furnaces. In theory, the system was foolproof.

But I knew how much projected force one of the furnaces would generate if it blew up. And that's why I had insisted on the building the wall for the safety of the employees. It was a paragraph in the loan contract, a requirement for receiving money from my company so they could build the lab. Now, I was glad. It probably saved a few hundred lives, mine included.

'How's Monica?' he asked.

'She's fine. The doctors are releasing her today.'

'Having the lab down is going to throw a monkey wrench in your supply chain.'

'Yes.' I acknowledged. The lab in Australia processed rough sapphires purchased from all over the globe. It operated under formulas that were proprietary, meaning I held the rights to the processes. These formulas, developed in our R&D lab in Charlottesville, were loaned to Clarence. We allowed no one else to use them. We simply could not risk having the secret formulas get into the hands of our competitors. The formulas were a large part of why we held a monopoly on the sapphire market. No one else was capable of doing what we were doing. The color-enhancement process wasn't something we could move to another lab. The work had to be done by people we trusted. The lab in Australia was the only lab that fit this description.

Problem was, we had no backup. With the lab down, all production would eventually come to a grinding halt. As soon as Vidu finished cutting the stones he had in Sri Lanka, we were out of product.

'Do you think someone sabotaged the lab?' I finally asked the question I didn't want to consider. Because if true, we were in a world of trouble. Considerable inside knowledge and the cooperation of some employees was required.

'I don't know,' said Clarence. 'It seems impossible all backup systems shut down at once. Foul play is an obvious answer, but currently, it's pure speculation. We really won't know until we have a chance to investigate, and that will take time.'

'And only if enough of the lab remains to be examined.'

'Exactly,' said Clarence. 'We may never know.'

'Look, Clarence. Too many problems are occurring, all at the same time, defying the laws of probability. Determining if this was an accident or sabotage could be a clue to what is going on.'

Clarence seemed to be lost in thought.

'I'll do my best,' he said while looking at the cast on his broken arm.

'Are you up to do the job? Because...'

'Don't even suggest it.' he interrupted.

11:45 A.M. JOHN

Our little side trip to Australia was ruined.

M and I drove directly from the hospital to the airport. Clarence arranged for his company plane to fly us to Sydney in time for a late afternoon Qantas flight to New York City. A long sixteen-hour journey home waited for us.

Marsha, his secretary, drove us on the first leg of the journey to the airport in the company Land Rover. M sat quietly in the back seat, staring out the window. I didn't disturb her, assuming peace was what she needed after the ordeal she had recently suffered. Doctors said she was okay, physically okay, that is. The water from the tank kept her from being burned. An overnight stay at the hospital for observation was recommended. Fortunately, no complications developed from her concussion. Scrapes, bruises, and minor burns were the worst of it. She was released in the morning.

Hooper met us on the runway before boarding the company plane. A small leather bag was in his hand. 'It's a stone from our mines,' he explained while handing it to her. 'The natural you found on a sorting table yesterday. Clarence wants you to have it. He deeply apologizes for any pain the fire caused you.'

'He wasn't responsible for what happened. No apologies are necessary.' she smiled and tried to give the stone back to Hooper, but he won't take it.

'Thanks, Hooper,' I smiled.

He nodded and walked away.

After she settled into a leather armchair inside the jet, I asked how she was doing.

'I'm okay,' she replied softly, sounding like a hurt animal wanting to curl up in its hole.

I had a passing desire to take her in my arms; protect her from the big bad world. If I had not foolishly rescued her, she would have died. And in no small way, I would have felt responsible, her death totally unacceptable; not something I wanted to even think about.

Captain revved the jet engines of the plane at the end of the runway. After releasing the brakes, the plane accelerated, gaining speed. Climbing into the air, rising quickly, it rode on the wings of flowing clouds into a bright morning sky. Once we reached cruising altitude, our flight settled into an uneasy and restless waiting.

I turned to M.

'Look,' I began, knowing this conversation would be difficult, but necessary. 'What happened yesterday is not found anywhere in your job description. And it is becoming increasingly obvious that my company is either extremely unlucky or someone is out to destroy us. Either way, I don't think you should be involved anymore.'

I paused before adding, 'I hope you understand. I don't want to be responsible for you getting hurt... or worse, killed.'

I waited. No response and when she didn't say anything, I continued, 'I'd like to make you an offer. But before I do... please know that I'm not trying to compensate you for what happened. I don't think I ever can.'

She sat, silently listening, staring at the leather satchel in her hand containing the gemstone Clarence gave her. It was difficult to gauge what was going on in her head,

I continued, 'I'd like to offer you one year's salary as severance pay, including full benefits. You can resign as soon as we arrive home, take the money and do what you want for a year: travel, take another job... Or just use the time to heal. You've been through a terrible experience.'

No response from her again, nothing; just sitting silently looking down at her bag. I began to become concerned. Damage caused by a concussion can be difficult to diagnose. Add the psychological trauma of almost being killed, and it was very possible she was hurting far worse than anyone knew.

'I hope you think that's fair?' I added.

'Was anyone else hurt in the fire?' she finally responded.

'No, it seems you and Clarence were the last ones out.'

'What caused the fire?' she asked.

'What?'

'The fire, what caused it?'

'We don't know.' I paused. 'The lab was built with safety in mind, but all the backup systems failed. We don't know why.'

'Do you think the fire is related to the robberies?'

'That's a good question. Fact is I don't know. But look, you don't need to be concerned. My offer is serious. I never intended to get you into something like what happened yesterday. And until we know what's going on, I don't think I'll be attending many social events. Point is, I don't really need a ...'

'But I'm part of this now,' M interrupted. 'I have the bruises to prove it.' She looked defiant.

'That's my point. I don't want to risk you getting hurt again.'

Silence momentarily reigned, except for a low rumble of anxious vibrations passing through the interior of a plane. Brochures for these luxury rides show pictures of smiling passengers relaxing in deluxe cabins surrounded by extravagance. But reality is different. The noise inside a jet plane can be unrelenting. Passengers are constantly aware of the fact they are flying in a small metal tube surrounded by volatile jet fuel, propelled by engines driven by continuous, controlled explosions.

'Are you firing me?' she asked.

'No.'

'Are you trying to get me to resign voluntarily to avoid a potential lawsuit?'

Her questions were unanticipated. I assumed she would take my offer, and why not? It was very generous. I was proposing to pay her eight thousand a month plus benefits for a year to do what? Absolutely nothing. Seemed like a no-brainer to me. My mind was already drifting to other problems; like finding solutions to a growing list of problems my company now faced.

'No,' I replied honestly. 'I just think it is the right thing to do under the circumstances. Look, I am trying to be fair with you, M. But if you think you deserve more money, just ask.'

'Money is not my concern. I'm trying to understand why you want to get rid of me.'

'Simple, one reason only, I don't want to see you get hurt.'

'Really, that's it?'

'Yes, it has nothing to do with money.'

'Okay, if that's true, then I want you to consider a few things first.' She paused before adding with emphasis, 'Perhaps you haven't noticed, but I'm not like your other social-event secretaries, personal secretaries, personal assistants, or whatever you call them. I'm different.'

I was speechless, but this hardly mattered because she wasn't about to give me an opportunity to react.

'Second, I'm no quitter, Mr. Van Laan. I think something is happening to your company, and I know I haven't been with you very long, but I feel like I'm a part of it now. Plus, you saved my life. We haven't talked about that, but you did. And I owe you.'

I tried to reply, but the lady was now on a roll. No way to shut her up.

She continued, 'Look, I'll do the stuff you hired me for, the social secretary stuff, but I want to do more. That is if you'll let me. I told you I'm a lawyer and I am, and a darn good one too. Plus, I'm smart. I graduated at the top of my class. Forget for a moment that I have long legs and look good. I'm more than just a pretty woman. And I have friends in Washington, friends who can help... Truth is, I want to help you, John Van Laan.'

I didn't know what to say.

'You're offering to pay me anyway. So, why not let me earn my money?' She paused, I guess, to give me a chance to respond, but then she started in again without really giving me an opportunity to say one word. 'And, just so you know. You're going to have to fire me to get rid of me. Because I'm in no mood to quit voluntarily.'

'Are you serious?' I interjected, totally stunned by the direction this conversation had taken.

'I am,' she said with great finality.

I was shocked and a little stupefied. I finally replied the only way I could think, in jest. 'Okay, if you're really serious, and from the tone of your voice, I have to assume you are, then you should be asking for a raise.'

'Right, and a new job description.'

'So, how much do I pay you?'

'Two hundred thousand a year.'

'Whoa, where is all this leading?' I was trying desperately to catch up, which wasn't easy with this lady.

'To an office near yours because I have a lot of questions.'

'I have to tell you, it never occurred to me you wouldn't take my offer.'

'That's because you don't know me,' she smiled.

I chuckled. 'I'm learning.'

'You still haven't answered my question,' she demanded. 'Do I get a raise and a new job description, or not?'

'Okay, okay, give me a minute to think about it,' I insisted. 'I don't usually make decisions on demand.'

She was momentarily silent. Obviously, this was something she had taken time to consider, but she had given me no time, and I needed a minute. When I finally replied, I tried to choose my words carefully. 'First, let me answer your question... No, I don't want to fire you.'

She looked at me, and I suddenly knew the last thing I wanted was to lose her. I liked what I saw in her: fierce determination and drive. 'I accept,' I responded. I don't know how we'll make it work, but we can try.'

'But I thought you said you wanted time to think it over.'

'No. Let's just do it. But one thing first.'

'What?'

'I still want you available for social events, assuming I have any. I don't want to hire anyone else right now. Okay?'

'I thought we had agreed to that.'

'I wasn't sure,' I shrugged.

'That's the deal,' she replied with a smile on her face.

Sometimes, it is not what is said that creates an understanding.   It is the accumulated clutter of shared experiences that makes it happen. I sensed we had just agreed to much more than a new job description. Plus, I couldn't help but wonder... do opportunities to be happy come to all of us? Are we all given a chance to be happy, to find the one person who is... if not perfect... the one who is right for us? And if we choose wisely, if we go down the right road... will it lead to a good life? Or...if we are afraid..., if we hesitate... if the pressures that surround us cause us to stumble and we choose wrong for the wrong reasons... Does our life change forever, immeasurably in ways we can never imagine, ways we will never understand... because we will never know the life we threw away?

I didn't know, but I sensed at that moment she was the road I was meant to travel. She was the one to accompany me on my journey.

If only I could keep her close.

2:15 P.M. JOHN

As soon as we landed in Sydney, a waiting car escorted us to the Qantas terminal, arriving shortly before our flight's departure time.

M, now apparently renewed in spirit by her new verbal employment contract, spent the first part of the flight across the Pacific quizzing me about different aspects of the company and my thoughts on possible explanations for recent events.

I finally pleaded with her for time to get some rest before touching down in New York. She reluctantly gave in and gave me some peace, although she didn't seem too happy about it. Lawyers, it seems, all of them, even the beautiful ones, have one thing in common- the ability to frustrate us with their endless questions. And the worst aspect of their breed is that you are never really sure why they are asking their interminable questions.

Our stewardess lowered my first-class seat, and I closed my eyes. Sleep was elusive. A myriad of unnerving questions raced through my mind like endless whirlwinds of sand rushing over a desert devoid of life. I wondered how one catastrophe could immediately be followed another. Was it all just coincidental or bad luck? Or was it possible that someone was actually intent on carving up the essential elements of my company until nothing of value remained? Too much was happening. Too much which pointed to someone who knew us from the inside, someone who was familiar with our weaknesses.

Our jumbo-sized Qantas 747 slowly dipped and rose when encountering turbulence over the Pacific at thirty-five thousand feet, rocking me like a baby in my mother's womb.

Mercifully... finally... I got some sleep.

BANGKOK, THAILAND, 3:15 P.M. LUANG

Deep lines of worry tightened between the eyes of the old patriarch, unable to relax as he read the report.

Some days are better than others. Some days are not. This was one of those bad days. He felt old and tired today. He had seen much trouble in his life. Nothing he read in his nephew's report gave him any relief: innocent miners killed, a factory destroyed, burned to the ground.

But, was this his fight? Hadn't he earned his retirement? He could ignore it all and enjoy the fruits of his labor, rest from his toil, and stop worrying about events that were no longer under his control. Life could go on without him now, just as it had before he was born and just as it would after he was dead and gone.

But as much as he wished he could do it, he simply couldn't. He wasn't dead. Not yet, anyway. He still had options. And he had a moral obligation to exert what influence he still had for as long as he was able.

Luang could not just stand by seeing disaster on the horizon and do nothing about it.

CHARLOTTESVILLE, VIRGINIA, NOVEMBER 1, FRIDAY, 9:20 A.M. JOHN

The steep hills of Charlottesville Virginia force the urban road system to twist and turn inexplicably, making it easy to get lost.

Roads named long ago for immigrant farmers have been unceremoniously replaced with the names of stuffy politicians, sometimes in the middle of random intersections. These needless changes are no help for already confused drivers. Fortunately, most travelers are eventually saved from wandering the streets of this city forever after arriving at the entrance to a ramp of the surrounding beltline. The only remaining challenge is to determine which direction to turn. Because by the time the hopelessly confused drivers approach the beltway, they are often so lost they have no idea which direction they are headed.

I know all this because I have been lost in Charlottesville too many times to mention. That doesn't mean I don't like this town. The natural beauty of its ancient trees and rolling hills is wonderful. It is a city enhanced by the presence of its historical heritage, evidenced primarily by the University of Virginia campus founded by Thomas Jefferson. This was the school where Monica got her law degree. Or so she said. I made a mental note to have personnel check into her past. Although I hoped she wasn't lying, it wouldn't hurt to double-check her story, given she had already admitted to not being totally truthful on her resume.

I was fortunate to get a few hours of sleep on the long plane ride from Australia, but not nearly enough. Landing in New York, we rushed to board a commuter plane to Charlottesville. Tired and worried, I headed for my office by taxi from the airport. It felt good to finally be home, and having a beautiful girl like M sitting beside me in the backseat of the taxi was wonderful.

Out of nowhere, a brief, undisciplined urge to slide over and cuddle with her like a teenager in heat passed over me.

Fortunately, enough residual sanity inhabited my weary brain to prevent calamity. Somehow, I was able to gain control of my weakening willpower and remain seated on my side of the taxi.

At my office, I instructed the taxi driver to take M home.

'Take a break,' I said to her as I got out of the car. 'See you in the morning.'

She countered; said she would be in the office that afternoon. Something about research was mentioned. New job description, she reminded me.

I was too fatigued to argue.

My office building is comparatively small for a corporation with earnings in the millions. This is fine with me. I'm in the business of making money, not providing a showpiece for its CEO, meaning me. The outside of the building is brick and glass. It is attractive but hardly distinguished in a way which would cause it to stand out from other buildings in our area. This is the way I like it. I don't want to draw any special attention. No one needs to know what goes on inside our walls or, more importantly, no one needs to know the value of the gemstones that reside in our vault.

Furnishings, although not elaborate, are expensive and tasteful. The atrium is two stories of glass and dark gray marble floors and walls. Its size dwarfs a modern wood reception desk situated at the rear of the voluminous space. Shelves displaying a collection of extraordinary cut and rough gemstones line one wall behind locked and bullet-proof glass. A large 'John Visser' abstract work of art covers another wall. Chrome and leather lounge chairs are reserved for visitors and guests.

A receptionist seated behind the desk smiled as I entered. I nodded to her and placed my hand on a palm reader next to the executive suite door. Once the reader registered my information, the system automatically opened the door to the office complex.

The building's interior is divided into four separate sections: lab, accounting, marketing, and executive. Each section has its own security code and is separated by thick interior cement walls for security.

A fifth section is not mentioned anywhere in the company's literature. It's where Arny and I live in our individual apartments.

The center of the building holds a vault built to the specifications of a bank. Although we never have large quantities of gems at the office, the vault holds some very special sapphire stones for both display and sale. These gems come from mines around the world. They are some of the most beautiful and expensive found anywhere. A small sales room illuminated by full spectrum lights and painted in neutral colors creates the necessary visual atmosphere for viewing these gems. Two large armchairs sit on opposite sides of the tables. One chair is for a sales representative. The other is reserved for a buyer. Although we discourage active bargaining, most buyers are not happy unless they are permitted to haggle over price. It is a time-honored method of purchasing gemstones. To some buyers, the process is more important than the price.

I tried to enter my office without Helen noticing but was unsuccessful. My eagle-eyed home secretary dutifully followed me with what I assumed was nothing but work on her mind.

'Here are the calls you received this morning,' she said. 'I won't even try to give you the calls from the last few days. I filtered some of the important ones and e-mailed those to your computer, but if you wish, I can give you a complete printed list.'

'Thank you, Helen,' I said, slumping into my desk chair. 'One thing I'll need you to do this morning is prepare an empty office in the executive section for Monica Sorensen. She will be in this afternoon, and she needs a place to work.'

Helen raised her eyebrows skeptically. 'The assistant you took with you?'

Helen's opinion of my personal assistants was colored with distaste. She dismissed them whenever she had an opportunity. In her defense, she worked far harder than they did and with much less glamour. I tolerated her attitude.

'She has a new job description,' I admitted. 'And just so you know, she's qualified for the job. But she will initially require some help, and I expect you to cooperate,' I added for emphasis.

I knew Helen wouldn't be too happy with her new assignment, but she would do it if I demanded her cooperation. I waited to see if she had anything more to say. She didn't.

'Hold my calls,' I added. 'I want some time to think. I'll let you know when I'm ready.'

'Jason wants to see you.'

'I'll see him when I'm ready,' I repeated with more emphasis than I intended.

'You okay?' she asked, now concerned.

'I'm tired. But I'll be okay. Just give me a few minutes to get my shit together.'

I was tempted to take a nap. The couch in my office looked good. Covered in soft gray leather, it faced a large expanse of windows that framed the rear of the office. The windows are curved, following the line of the hillside which supports the building. They view a valley and mountains in the distance. One corner of the office, next to the windows, was a door that opened to a small deck with stairs to the ground. The door was built to building code, an exit in case of a fire. Occasionally, I use the deck to take a break. It's a good place to escape my phone.

Opening the door to let in some fresh air, I stepped outside.

The State of Virginia in late fall is normally stark and leafless. The weather this day was no exception, gray and dreary. But the vista over the valley stretching to an ever-changing sky offered a sense of peace. I sat down on a chair to rest.

I like to travel.

I have never failed to enjoy the varied and beautiful landscapes which exist on our planet, but I'm always happy to return home to my valley. It is a great place to live and work. I have been fortunate. I was in the right place at the right time. And good people listened to me and understood my vision. Without their help, I would have nothing. Mostly it is a matter of luck. That's how I see it.

However, it would seem my luck was recently souring. If my intuition was right, someone was trying to destroy my company. And they were executing a well-designed plan to accomplish their goal. Major problems were mounting exponentially.

The winter sun broke through a crack in a gray overcast sky as I rested, sending a small spear of light shining down to the valley floor.

'Everything you need is at your home.' The words filtered through my exhausted consciousness, something I remembered reading in a book titled, Tao Te Ching.

I consider myself a spiritual man, perhaps not in the conventional sense of the word. But I do not dismiss the idea of God. In fact, it seems to me God has gone out of his way to communicate with us. We only need to take time to listen and learn. Our world is his microphone.

The Tao also stated: 'Success is as dangerous as failure.' And this was unfortunately becoming absurdly true in my life. I wondered if it was easier to build something than to keep it.

A ringing telephone brought me out of my reverie. I had left the door open, didn't think Helen would disobey my desire for a few minutes of solitude. I should have known better. Frustrated but suddenly concerned, pessimism took control of my brain. I feared more bad news and went inside to answer the inanimate instrument of communication that was causing a problem, hoping I was wrong.

'This had better be good,' I said to Helen. 'I asked not to be disturbed.'

'It's Arthur,' Helen replied without remorse. 'He insisted.'

'I'll take the call.' I resigned myself to my fate. 'But we'll talk about this later.'

'I'm sorry,' she said, but she didn't sound too sorry. Helen often thinks she knows better than I do what is good for me. Problem is, most of the time she's right.

I clicked an insistently blinking light for an outside line.

'Arthur.'

'John, I had to call,' he replied. 'Sorry, but people are concerned. I need something to tell them.'

'Calm down, old boy, we'll get through this.'

'Right, but what can I say.'

'Damage control.'

'Precisely.'

'So, what do you think we should be telling them?' I asked.

'Well, how about saying simply we're experiencing a run of bad luck, but not to worry. The company will sail on pretty much as expected. Just need to even the keel.'

'Really, is it wise to phrase our problems in sailing terms, given the severity of the situation?' I questioned, thinking this was just the sort of thing a Brit would do, bring up some silly sailing metaphor.

'Of course, we need to muster on like the good sailors we are,' Arthur stated unflappably.

'I know Arthur, but perhaps it would be better to tell them the truth rather than try to sugarcoat it.'

'And the truth is?' asked Arthur.

'Several unrelated incidents have severely damaged our company. If you're talking to clients, tell them this is going to slow delivery of product. If you are talking to our investors, tell them this is going to hurt our profits. It is unfortunate, but we will put the full resources of our company behind returning to normal delivery and profitability as quickly as possible.'

'Is it wise to be quite so blunt?' Arthur emphasized the word 'blunt' in his clipped English accent. 'They aren't going to like it.'

'True, but when something is seriously wrong, the best option is to tell the truth; the sooner, the better. Get it behind you fast. Because you know as well as I do, the truth will come out soon enough. If we try to bluff our way through this, we'll end up looking like fools.'

'I see your point, John. But perhaps we should wait before giving them the awful news. Admitting everything in one sitting might be a bit startling.'

'Sure, perhaps we could wait,' I said to placate him. 'But with the lab down in Australia, new production is currently on hold. In about three to four weeks' time, the full effect of our problems will be felt by everyone. Hong Kong first because they are already without inventory. Need I say more? We need to allocate remaining product in earnest, immediately. It's the only fair way to proceed.'

I wondered briefly why Arthur was advocating for a delay. One ugly reason came to mind. From computer read-outs, I knew Arthur's London House had a higher inventory level than New York. Maybe old Arthur wanted a delay so he could sell as much of his inventory as possible before I instituted a company-wide allocation, which meant he would have to send stones to the other houses for them to sell.

'Okay, but how about we hold off for a few days?' Arthur proclaimed with a tone of resignation in his voice. 'Then, out with the bad news.'

'No. I don't think so,' I sighed. 'Bad news out now and allocations put in place immediately.'

'Not sure I agree.'

'And Arthur,' I said, ignoring him for a moment.

'Yes?'

'Hold all deliveries until you get the allocations from me.'

When he didn't respond, I continued. 'And one more thing. No increase in prices. Hold the line. We're going to see shortages. Everyone is going to be unhappy. The worst thing we can do now is to be seen taking advantage of this situation by raising prices in a time of shortage.'

'Right,' he replied.

I couldn't see him, but his comment sounded almost snooty like he was mocking me. His words were right, but his attitude felt less than cooperative.

'When this is all over,' I continued, 'I want our clients to remember we treated them fairly.'

'That's the plan, then?' Arthur asked.

'That's it. Any questions?'

'No.'

'Good, Sorry old buddy, I know this isn't pleasant. But Arthur, you know it needs to be done.'

'Consider it done.'

'I'll start work on the allocations immediately. As soon as they are ready, I'll send them to you. And Arthur, remember, I asked you to put a freeze on all shipments.'

'Now?'

'Immediately, call your shipping department when we hang up and put everything on hold.'

'Okay,' Arthur replied with an obvious lack of enthusiasm.

1:20 P.M. ARNY

Arny looked out of place entering the company lobby.

Not because he was African American. It was more how he dressed. Wearing a Washington Redskins windbreaker and worn jeans seemed oddly out of place in the highly polished, marble floored lobby of the ultra-modern office building. In contrast, the other office staff were neatly attired in formal office business wear; white shirts, ties for the men and appropriate dresses for the ladies. They worked in the tradition-hardened Northeastern part of the country. Dressing up was in their blood. Arny seemed immune to their inbred habits. He dressed as he pleased.

The company employees knew him well, mostly because he was a difficult man to ignore. Greeting each of them with a casual remark and a smile as he passed was his trademark. He was a social animal, and no one minded. They enjoyed his spontaneous banter.

Behind Arny strolled James, a white man and company driver. One of his duties was to assist Arny when he went shopping for apartment supplies. James was lugging three or four bags of groceries, whereas Arny carried only one small plastic bag, thus implementing his right of superiority.

After a small red wagon was retrieved from a closet near the receptionist's desk by Arny; James dutifully placed his grocery bags in the cart and turned to leave. He was not allowed to follow Arny down the hall to the apartments. Only Arny had security clearance for this area of the building. From this point forward, Arny pulled the cart, looking slightly comical, but he didn't care. As he passed Helen's desk, he made some off-hand remarks about her necklace and how beautiful she looked today. Maybe, he briefly suggested, she might like to go dancing at the Blue Note Lounge this evening, one of his hangouts.

Helen was not unattractive, but she had passed her prime a few years back. She knew Arny was kidding. It was the game they played.

'You should be so lucky,' Helen replied.

'But, my lovely, I've been waiting so long,' Arny continued. 'Tonight could be our big night.'

'In your dreams,' Helen smiled.

Arny always hated going through security. He had been with the company long before the latest security system was installed. He figured the system was for other employees, not him. But I insisted he use the main entrance leading to the security checkpoint in the executive office as his designed route, and he reluctantly agreed, although he made it clear he didn't like it.

He was semi-retired, and he never ceased reminding me of this fact. He came and went pretty much as he pleased, which was fine with me because most of the time, I was either busy or gone. And when I needed him, he was always there, somehow intuitively knowing when his services were required. I never asked him how he accomplished this seemingly impossible task; just accepted it as standard practice.

He claimed to be sixty-eight years old, but I never knew if this was his real age or just the age he wanted to be. He was a handsome man regardless, very trim and strong.

'I can kill a tree that's already dead,' was a favorite expression.

4:20 P.M. JOHN

I hung up my phone after discussing with Lin how many gemstones would be allocated to Hong Kong from our London and New York distribution houses.

Lin was grateful. Said the newly allocated gemstones would be used immediately to fulfill existing orders to his clients.

By the time I finished talking to Lin, it was late in the afternoon and I needed a break. I had been cooped up in my office too long. My phone was beginning to feel like an extension of my ear. Besides, I was curious to see if M had come into the office as promised.

'She's here,' Helen announced pertly after I passed her desk.

'Who's here?' I stopped to ask.

'You know who,' Helen reiterated with a hint of sarcasm in her voice.

'Where is she?'

'Next office down the hall.'

'What's she doing?'

'Asking questions, wants to know everything,' Helen added indignantly. 'Company history, corporation documents. Am I to assume you'd want me to give her everything she wants?'

'Yes,' I nodded.

'Okay,' she sighed, hesitated... then asked again, 'You sure?'

'I'm sure.'

But I wasn't really sure at all. I had not yet ordered an in-depth security check on Monica. Probably should have. It was common sense to thoroughly check any employee's history before turning over confidential company information. I didn't really know her that well, and she was a lawyer. That wasn't a good combination, but I also knew we were in a crisis, and I wasn't sure I had time to be prudent. I wanted answers, and I wanted them fast. Hopefully, she could help.

Sometimes, someone new examining a problem with no preconceived notions. Sometimes, this person can see flaws that others have missed. Being too close to a situation can often make you blind to what is obvious. I hoped M might bring a different perspective to our problems. I figured it was worth the risk. However, I still was determined to call our security firm and have them do a detailed background check on Ms. Sorenson.

When I went to find her, she was sitting at a desk in a workstation not far from Helen. This was not the executive office; I had suggested Helen give her, but apparently, my loyal secretary, Helen, was not yet ready to give Monica any special priority. I let it go.

Papers were scattered everywhere inside her small cubicle. M was hunched over her desk reading and didn't even look up when I entered. 'Why didn't you go public?' she asked without so much as acknowledging my presence.

'Didn't have to,' I replied. 'We had adequate private funding. And I didn't need the SEC constantly looking over my shoulder.'

'That's understandable,' she stated with a touch of sarcasm in her voice.

'Besides, I thought it would be unwise to solicit investors who didn't completely understand our business.

'A company with a conscience?' she mused.

'Let's say it made sense in more ways than one.'

'You don't really own anything.' she added, immediately changing the subject.

'Not for very long.'

'Yet people are willing to pay you a lot of money. Why?'

'I offer valuable services,' I said with a grin.

'Services for what?'

I started to answer her question, but before I could get one word out of my mouth, another question passed her sweet lips.

'Hasn't anyone ever asked you where all this money comes from?' she wanted to know.

'Yes, lots of times.'

'I don't understand.'

'Okay, I'll explain it to you. But let's do it at dinner.'

'Sorry, I have too much work to do,' she finally lifted her head from the paperwork to look at me.

Bruises from the fire were still clearly visible on her face. Some swelling around her eyes had turned dark, shades of black and blue. But her eyes were still beautiful even though it was obvious she had spent almost no time on makeup before coming into work. Looked like she had simply changed her clothes, driven to work, and dived into research.

'May I remind you,' I countered in jest. 'About the social functions clause in your contract,'

'The what?' she asked, distracted.

'Social functions clause,' I said. 'You remember, I asked you on the plane if I could still use you for social functions. You said yes.'

'You have a social function tonight, and you want me to go with you?' she asked skeptically.

'Yes.'

'Where are we going?'

'Out for dinner.'

'Who's going to be there?'

'You and me.'

'That's not company business. Therefore, I'm not required...'

'I'm still your boss, and your presence is requested,' I interjected with as much authority as I could muster without smiling.

She hesitated, and I knew if she said no, I would have reluctantly backed down. I wasn't going to demand she go to dinner with me. But nothing in her contract stated I couldn't ask. Besides, a man has to do what a man has to do.

'Okay,' she finally agreed. 'Where are we going?'

'I'll have Arny prepare something.'

'Who is Arny?'

'He's my chef and housekeeper.'

'You're taking me to your house?' she asked like she couldn't believe what she was hearing. Her already huge eyes were opened wide.

By this point in our conversation, it was pretty obvious even to me that I had made a serious error in judgment. I guess I wasn't thinking clearly. Jet lag had obviously taken control of my pea-sized brain. 'We can go to a restaurant if you would prefer. Or we could just skip it,' I backtracked.

She smiles softly. 'No. Your place is fine. I don't really want to go out looking like this. Where do you live?'

'I live here,' I admitted, regretting more than ever I had started down this road. 'It's convenient and...'

'You live here?' she looked me straight in my eye.

'Yes, I live in a small apartment attached to this building. And Arny is a good cook.'

'Does he make a good chaperone too?' she asked with a smile.

By this time, it was painfully obvious she had me in deep water way over my head. I nodded, 'I'll come and get you around seven.'

'You know where to find me,' she immediately returned to her work.

I retreated to my office like a dog with my tail between my legs. Helen must have heard every word of my pathetic example of male incompetence. I didn't dare look at her as I passed her desk.

I was afraid I would see her trying not to laugh.

7:20 P.M. JOHN

Couldn't get off my phone.

It was late by the time I went to find M for dinner, but that didn't seem to matter to her. She was deep into reading some documents working in her small office with papers strewn across her desk. She was so completely engrossed in her reading material that I wasn't sure she even knew of my presence.

'Dinner,' I finally said to break her concentration

She looked up, genuinely surprised to see me, 'Oh, sorry... Is it that time already?'

'Aren't you hungry?'

'Yes, I guess.... But can I ask you a few questions before...'

'That's why we're doing dinner, remember?'

'Dinner... Right... Okay. I'd like clean up first?'

'You can do it in my apartment.'

'Apartment?' she questioned blankly... then remembering. 'Yes, you live here.'

I ushered her down deserted halls. Staff had gone home long ago. The building was only partially lit. A few security guards were the only employees still inside. She must have been wondering what she had gotten herself into, but she didn't back down. I'm not sure I would have done the same if I was her.

Placing my hand on a palm reader next to the door to my apartment, I waited. As expected, the polished steel door clicked and slowly opened electronically. Arny and I were the only two people whose palm prints activated this door. An emergency procedure was available, but it required going through our security firm. Otherwise, no one entered my apartment without me because this was as I wanted it; private.

The automated door led to a small entrance hall. At the end of the hall was another secure metal door, opened by a key.

A room with a high ceiling greeted us when we entered the apartment. Windows covering the far end of the room overlooked the same valley scene as my office. In the middle of the windows stood a fieldstone fireplace, which rose to the ceiling. Decorated in warm natural tones, the room felt less austere than my office. Couches covered in brown leather faced the fireplace. A high-tech audio-video system had been built into one wall. A display case made of stone and wood shelves covered the opposite wall of the room, filled with pictures and artifacts I had collected from my travels.

M stood very still for a moment, simply taking it all in. It was difficult to determine what she was thinking. I hoped she was impressed, but it was possible her tastes in interior design were different from mine and she didn't especially like what she was seeing; too modern, too austere.

Wandering, slowing to look at the display case, she examined several objects located on the shelves.

I don't collect very much, but occasionally, I find a piece of artwork or a historical artifact that is beautiful or symbolic of the people and culture I am visiting. M picked up a small wooden porpoise craving from one of the shelves. It was probably the least expensive piece on display. Made by hand from dark mahogany, it was beautiful in its simplicity.

'I'm sorry,' she apologized. 'Should I have touched this?'

'Please feel free to handle the pieces. I placed them there to enjoy.'

'Where's this one from?' she asked.

'Belize.'

'Business trip?'

'No, that trip was for pleasure. Belize has some of the best scuba diving in the world. I stopped there once on a return trip from South America.'

She gently turned the porpoise over in her hand, caressing its polished wood surface with her long fingers, exploring its soft design with her eyes.

I sometimes think a simple act, like how a person responds to a piece of artwork can express more about their inner soul than anything else. I suddenly felt drawn to her. But at the same time,

I felt slightly guilty, as if I were invading her private space. It was as if she was allowing me a rare glimpse into her heart. It was a moment I have never forgotten.

After placing the porpoise carving back on a shelf, she wandered over to the windows to take in the view. The valley was dark that evening filled with homes, their windows emanating a warm glow filtering through tree shadows in the night.

'I wanted to look out the windows in your office when you first interviewed me,' she said, 'but I thought it would be unprofessional to ask.'

'Maybe you should have. It would have told me something about you,' I replied as I came up behind her.

I wanted to touch her in the worst way, but I knew it would be wrong; a violation of our assumed professional relationship. Timing wasn't right. And yet, she was had come into my apartment voluntarily. This in itself was a departure from professional standards. I personally had only allowed a few of my secretaries into my apartment. And truth was, I had invited them here for less than altruistic reasons which I regretted later. Because apparently the act of allowing them into my inner sanctum suggested more to them than I intended. Eventually, I decided it wasn't worth it and instituted a self-imposed rule about keeping my apartment strictly private. But with Monica, well.... I immediately broke another of my cherished rules, reverting back to behavior more like a child, breaking rules and testing authority.

'Maybe I didn't want to tell you anything about me,' she replied.

'Well, you're telling me now.'

'Yes, that's true, I guess,' she turned to look at me as if she was trying to ascertain what was happening inside my head. Then, perhaps assuming I was more or less harmless, she gently moved away. I sighed inwardly, knowing the moment had passed. A moment that could have gone differently.

'I want you to meet someone,' I suggested in an attempt to move on from my juvenile obsessions.

Arny could be heard humming to himself in my kitchen at the time. He was a man who didn't like being ignored. I had called him earlier in the afternoon and told him I was bringing someone to dinner before quickly hanging up before he could start asking questions, knowing he would give me no end of grief if I gave him the opportunity.

Ushering M past the formal dining room which paralleled the living room. A large oak table and chairs capable of accommodating as many as eight people occupied the room. The size of the room and the table were ridiculous because I almost never entertained anyone in my apartment. I don't enjoy eating in groups any larger than four or five. It is my experience that large group conversations often deteriorate quickly to nothing more than grandstanding.

Arny was preparing our meal in the kitchen when we entered. He didn't look up; just continued his dinner preparations, ignoring us like we didn't exist. M stood across the counter from him, expecting an introduction. I waited, knowing Arny's act couldn't last long. His natural curiosity would take over long before he could play out his little charade. Because when he finally realized a beautiful woman was in the room, well... then everything would immediately change. I only had to wait.

Monica turned to me with a confused look on her face. She didn't understand our game. I smiled and held a finger to my mouth indicating a request to wait quietly.

'Well?' Arny finally asked, his head still down, working at the stove.

'Well, what?'

'Well,' he said when he couldn't stand it any longer. 'Aren't you going to introduce me?' And then without hesitation, he added after looking up, 'to this beautiful lady?' He smiled. 'Or are you afraid I'll sweep her off her feet and take her away from you like all your other women?' He grinned mischievously. 'Well, well,' he said to Monica without missing a beat. 'Where have you been all my life? And I thought I knew all the beautiful women in Charlottesville.'

And so began the inevitable flirtation, which Arny enjoyed with all women he met, especially the pretty ones.

M smiled demurely, charmed.

'Let me look at you, gal,' he began.

Immediately dropping a fork he had been using to fix our supper, he went around the counter as if he was a French aristocrat, bowed, and kissed her hand. 'Say, I know a great place, good music and yummy food. Let's leave this lonely bachelor boy and have some fun tonight.'

'Arny, this is Monica,' I interrupted. 'She likes to be called M.'

'You mean M for magnificent.'

I assumed someone had warned him she was coming, given him her name, probably Helen. It was obvious he was prepared. I should have known.

'How's dinner?' I asked in a ploy to get him back on track.

'Ah, dinner,' he seemed temporarily unaware of the pans which were still sizzling on the stove. 'Some other time then, baby?' he winked at M.

She looked a little unsure; his behavior slightly unnerving.

Even though Arny was an old man, he still had the hard body of an athlete. His hair had begun to show some gray, but he was a very attractive man. I was sure he did very well with the ladies. Or this was what he bragged to me, and I believed him. Most of the secretaries I introduced to Arny didn't quite know what to make of him.   Some became uneasy. I was interested in seeing how Monica would handle him. So far, she was doing fine and didn't seem too flustered by his advances.

Arny returned to his cooking, every burner hissing as he deftly moved from one to the next. The kitchen was furnished with commercial-grade appliances. He insisted I buy the best if he was going to cook for me. He had worked in restaurants for most of his life. He knew appliances.

'You're late, by the way,' he chastised. 'Everything's overcooked. I expected you here an hour ago.'

'Sorry, you know...' I started to explain.

'Sure, sure, business, business, I know. Well, don't blame me if your dinner is overdone.'

'It smells delicious,' M tried to pacify him.

She didn't know we always indulged in this kind of banter. We were friends but verbal combatants all the same.

'Well, it would be nice if you and your lady showed up on time,' he looked at M with a smile.

'Sorry,' I chuckled, knowing he didn't mean it.

'Why don't you go sit down?' he said. 'Dinner will be served shortly.'

'Want to join us?'

'Nah, got things to do in town tonight,' he replied with a wave.

I started for a small table by a window in a dinette off my kitchen. He and I usually ate there for dinner when I was in town.

'Formal dining room,' he directed instead.

'Why not here?'

'All set up in there,' he shrugged.

'Okay.'

Arny had readied two place settings at a far end of the dining room table near the windows. A bottle of wine was open. I poured a couple of glasses.

'He doesn't seem too happy,' M queried.

That was possible, but I didn't want to explain to M what could really be bothering him. Truth was, he liked his life as it was. Bringing a woman into my apartment was; well... a break in his routine and maybe even a threat to his lifestyle.

'Just his way,' I said. 'Don't mind him.'

'Okay,' she replied with a quizzical look on her face.

Arny brought plates filled with Cornish hen, scalloped potatoes, and a spinach salad; dinner for two.

'Okay, eat while it's hot,' he demanded. 'I've worked my fingers to the bone, so you better enjoy... Got things to do tonight, I can't stay. Dessert is in the fridge, key lime pie. Don't forget about it.

'Thanks. You sure you don't want to join us?'

'No, no, got things to do.'

'This looks wonderful, Arny,' M smiled. 'Thank you so very much.'

Arny was a happy man. 'I'm glad someone around here appreciates me,' he jested. 'You're so pretty. How come you're hanging out with this deadbeat?'

'Just business,' she replied with a grin as he headed for the door.

We sat down to an uneasy silence. Food was delicious, but the atmosphere was uncomfortable.

'Want to get started on your questions?' I asked to break the mood.

'Okay. Let's begin with the question I asked you before.'

'Fire away.'

'Why do people pay your company so much money?'

'Services, I told you.' I replied.

'But Gemstone International doesn't appear on paper to offer services deserving the kind of money you charge,' she countered.

I started to say something, but she interrupted before I could answer.

'In addition, your company doesn't own large assets. Most companies which make as much money as you do own factories, machinery, physical property.' She paused, frowning. 'Your company, on the other hand, doesn't own anything besides this office building. You don't own mines. Your stones come from like your buddy in Australia. And you don't own a lab... except a small R&D lab in this building. From what I've seen so far, there isn't any real substance to your company. It appears to be nothing more than smoke and mirrors. The only thing you seem to do well is to make money.'

'Isn't that the reason for business?'

'Yes, but most companies make money by building assets, hiring employees; you know, the usual way of growing a business.'

'So, what's your conclusion?' I asked when she finally took a breath. I was beginning to learn that once she was on a roll, there was no stopping her.

'I'm not ready to express an opinion.' she answered like a lawyer. 'Except maybe... you're hiding something.'

I laughed. 'But I have given you access to everything. So, what am I hiding?'

She didn't answer, probably because she was still processing data. A slight frownline deepened between her eyebrows, and it appeared to indicate she wasn't happy with her preliminary conclusions.

Her frown line, I thought it was cute. It was the one aspect of her face that wasn't perfect. It was slightly off-center between her eyes. When something was bothering her, I noticed her frowny line became more noticeable. It was a dead giveaway.

I sipped some wine as she silently continued to process data. Soft red curls of hair fell unkempt over her forehead as I waited. She wore almost no makeup that evening, but still, she was very attractive. Her big browns were bright and alert. Something about her was undeniably enticing. I wondered obliquely if I would be able to keep up with her once she got going. It was obvious a world of smarts circulated behind those big browns. I knew I couldn't be complacent when around her or she would quickly find my weaknesses and run me over.

'Let me give you a brief history of Gemstone International,' I finally suggested. 'Maybe this will help answer your question.'

9:20 P.M.

Only two security guards were on duty when they approached.

The guard in the operations center never heard or saw them. Truth was, he was half asleep at the time, watching monitors with his eyes closed.

Before entering the building, the intruders disarmed the alarms. He had no warning before they hit him on the back of his neck, immediately falling to the floor unconscious.

The other guard did not go as easy. He was making rounds. The intruders found him without too much difficulty by tracking his movements on the monitors surveying various areas in the building. They ambushed him at a corner of a hall. Although he gave them a fight, he was quickly rendered unconscious for his efforts, bruised and bloodied. Tying his hands and legs together with duct tape, they covered his mouth so he could not scream when he woke up. After dragging him into the operations center, they placed him on the floor next to his companion.

Then they waited.

9:55 P.M. JOHN

Flashes of blue reflected off the highly polished facets of the sapphire she held in her hand.

The gemstone, I had given M, sparkled under a recessed light as she viewed it. I said nothing; simply let the stone speak to her as she held it up to the light, turning it slowly.

Dinner was great. Arny had worked his magic, but I wasn't sure she noticed. She didn't eat much, simply picked at her food while spending most of her time mentally exhausting me with her interminable questions. When I was finally too tired to answer, I gave her a sapphire to examine. Her question, or should I more accurately say, her accusation, the one she made at dinner about how much money my company made; it bothered me. It deserved an answer.

'So, do you think this stone is worth the money we charge for it?' I asked.

'It is very appealing,' she admitted.

When words fail to win arguments, sometimes it is better to let the gemstones speak for themself. Normally I have a few sapphires in my apartment, some of very best stones which I store in a small vault hidden in my library. I like to look at them occasionally. The one I gave her was an especially bright and vibrant blue stone, several carats in size.

'Yes, but is the price justified by the beauty of the stone?' I asked again.

'Maybe, but it still doesn't explain why your company makes so much money,' she interjected, not yet ready to concede.

I didn't answer immediately. Not many people saw the gross sales numbers of my company. I wondered if I should have been open with her, but I couldn't take back the information now.

'Look,' I began. 'The fees we charge are not exorbitant on a percentage basis. What you need to understand is this is a worldwide business, and the fees add up rather quickly. Plus, relative to the value we add to the stones, I don't believe our fees are exorbitant. For instance, the value added from our marketing and advertising programs alone contributes far more than what we are compensated.'

'You say,' she countered.

'If you knew how much our ad program has contributed to increased sales over the last few years, then yes, I think you would agree.'

'But surely some buyers are circumventing your cherished distribution system, buying gemstones from other dealers.'

'Of course, I can't control every gem in the marketplace. At any given moment, at least thirty to forty percent of the market escapes our control.'

'Is this okay with you?'

'I never expected to control the market completely. That's not possible.'

She didn't immediately respond.

'Want some dessert?' I interjected to change the subject. 'Key lime pie, Arny's specialty.'

'No, thank you.'

'It's great. You should at least try a small piece.'

'Okay,' she finally relented.

'Why don't you go to the living room?' I suggested. 'I'll get the pie.'

When I returned, she had settled into one of the large armchairs near the fireplace, looking relaxed and comfortable. A half-moon high in the sky cast faint shadows through the trees in the valley below. Despite the black and blue swelling under her eyes, she looked beautiful.

'Your business is so tenuous, nothing substantial,' she observed.

'But it works.'

No reply, she was looking down at her food with her hair hanging around her face, making it difficult to see her reaction.

We ate our pie in silence, both temporarily lost in thought. Our discussion had been long and tiring. The tension from lingering questions still hung in the air, it was late, and we both were tired.

Time to call it a night

10:05 P.M. ARNY

Arny pulled his late model Lincoln into a reserved parking spot next to the office building.

He would always inform me he would be staying out late, visiting his buddies, enjoying his ladies, but he seldom did. Tonight was no exception. He had fun. Cards had gone his way;

he made some pocket change. But mostly, he enjoyed the conversation and companionship of his friends. Long before he became too tired, he decided to head home.

They came out of shadows in a dark hallway in the office. They were on him before he knew what hit him. He resisted, but unseen blows came hard and often. His strength only prolonged a beating. Finally, bloodied and subdued, he could do no more to resist. Bound and gagged, they dragged him past the operations office where he saw two security guards tied up on the floor. A pool of dried blood lay next to the head of one of the guards, still unconscious. The other guard was sitting, propped up at an awkward angle with an anxious look in his eyes.

Arny wondered if he would see the morning. He was scared. Duct tape on his mouth hurt. He struggled; breathing difficult. One side of his nose had swelled shut from a blow and the other side wasn't working very well. Blood dripped from his forehead, covering his eyes, making it difficult to see. A massive pain convulsed through his side with each breath, probably from a cracked rib. His bad knee throbbed; the knee damaged in a baseball injury. It had never healed properly. But at this moment, his knee was the least of his concerns.

His attackers dragged him down a hall and placed his palm on a security pad. He heard the door click open to his and the boss's apartments.

Overwhelming dread washed over him in panic.

He now knew what they wanted.

10:10 P.M. JOHN

'Can I drive you home.' I suggested.

'My car is here,' she countered.

'I would feel better if I knew you made it home safely,' I argued.

At that moment she was probably wondering if I was hoping for more than simply a discussion of business. And if I didn't get it, sex that is, here in my apartment; then maybe I would ask to come in when I arrived at her place. She decided to put an end to my charade.

'No,' she answered emphatically.

I understood her reluctance, but it wasn't true. I didn't really expect anything more from her. Not that I wouldn't have accepted it if it had been offered. I am a guy after all.

'Okay,' I said, trying not to show too much disappointment.

She stood and started for the door.

'Will you at least allow me to walk you to your car?'

She nodded after taking a moment to consider my offer; probably thought this too was a sexist thing. She could obviously make it from the building to her car in the parking lot without my help. But she relented, I suppose to be nice and allow me some semblance of chivalry.

That's when it occurred to me; it might not be prudent to walk past my security guards. The sight of the boss and the new girl leaving his apartment at night might not look too good. Rumors would fly. Tongues would waggle the next day in the office. I suggested we exit the back way to avoid the guards.

She smiled knowingly.

The back way was through a lower-level garage where I parked my cars; down a flight of stairs from my apartment. It was the only entrance and exit in the building which didn't go through the main lobby and a security checkpoint. And I was the only one allowed to use it. This did not meet with my security firm's approval, but I had insisted. I did not want to have to go through the office and around the outside of the building every time I wanted to take a drive. From the garage it was possible to walk around the outside of the building up to the main parking lot in front where her car was parked. I directed her towards the back door of the apartment which opened to stairs.

When I closed the door, I heard a noise.

Now this was odd. Couldn't be anyone in my apartment, Arny was the only person who had a key and he never came into my apartment at this late hour.

'Just a minute,' I said to M after we had gone down the stairs and into the garage. She looked confused but stayed in place. I couldn't get the noise out of my head. I made up an excuse so she wouldn't worry. 'I forgot something.'

Leaving M stranded inside the big garage must have seemed strange to her, but I needed to know what made that sound. As quietly as possible, I climbed the stairs toward the apartment. Standing very still with the door ajar, I listened. Nothing, then something like a brushing noise, very faint, and then quiet again. Another slight scratching sound was followed by quiet again. I waited, nothing, no new noises. Could be an animal or could be my overactive brain imagining things. M had to be wondering what I was doing. I decided to deal with the noises later. Locking the door to the apartment, I headed down the stairs. After reentering the garage, I locked the door to the garage. And just to be certain, I found a board and jammed it against the knob.

'What's wrong?' she asked.

'Oh, nothing,' I attempted to sound unconcerned, but it didn't pass muster with her. She looked at me carefully, like maybe she had miscalculated. Was her boss crazy after all? Was he locking her inside his garage? Was he in the process of kidnapping her?

'You don't always do that, do you? Put a board against the door?' she asked, moving her eyes from the door and back to me.

'You're very observant.'

'What's going on?' She looked scared which was not unexpected given the kinds of experiences she had recently been through.

'I'm not sure,' I answered truthfully. 'I thought I heard something in my apartment. It's probably nothing.'

M stared at me. 'I would like to leave. Now, if you don't mind.'

'Sorry, but I would really feel better if you would allow me to drive you home. Too much has happened lately.'

She didn't respond immediately. 'Okay,' she finally agreed. 'If we can go now.'

'We'll take my Mercedes,' I said, pointing to a two-door silver SLC Mercedes in the center of the garage.

'You have a few cars,' she responded, understating my obvious love affair with automobiles.

The spotless garage currently contained no less than five automobiles: a vintage Ferrari Daytona, a new Ferrari Maranello, a Porsche Cabriolet, an M5 BMW, and the silver Mercedes. I chose the Mercedes-Benz because it and the BMW had been fitted with bulletproof glass after I watched a TV program on carjacking. Occasionally, I drive into DC or New York for business. Usually, I fly, but sometimes I drive for a change of pace. I have never had any problems, but I thought the glass was a good idea for big-city driving. It never hurts to be prepared.

M slipped into the passenger seat. I put the key in the ignition and locked the car doors as a precaution.

'I'm going to call security on my cell before we go, have them check on my apartment while I'm driving you home. This will just take a minute.'

'Can't you do that while you are driving?' she clicked her seat belt into place.

Ignoring her request, I listened to my cell phone ring. When no one picked up immediately, an increasing sense of foreboding began to take control of my tired brain. I was becoming more and more concerned. Usually, it takes only one ring for a guard to pick up. Someone is assigned to the security desk at all times. I listened to the phone ring several more times before... finally.

'Hello,' a voice said.

I hesitated. Something was wrong. The voice did not immediately ask my name which was the normal procedure.

'This is the south station operator,' I said. 'Everything okay?'

'Yes, sir.'

'Okay then.' I hung up.

'Well,' M asked, seeing the puzzled look on my face.

'No problem,' I didn't want to alarm her.

'But it's not okay, is it?'

'No, it's not. Security didn't follow protocol,' my jaw tightened. 'And we don't have a south station.'

The interior garage lights were on a timer. I waited for the lights to turn off before starting the car. After the engine came to life with a mild purr. I put the car into drive without turning on its headlights; I didn't want anyone to see us leaving. It was difficult to see the driveway as I drove, but I knew it by heart. Shades of gray moonlight helped.

Nothing seemed out of place as we slowly drove up the back driveway to the front parking lot. A spec of light on my right flashed, saw it out of the corner of my eye, looked like a firefly, bursting out of the black night sky, followed by dull thuds jarring the car.

M screamed.

'Get down!' I yelled and hit the accelerator.

Staccato thuds in rapid succession hit the right-side window, transforming it into a spider web of distorted glass. Engine came to life. M shielded her head with her arms. Fear-induced adrenaline pulsed through my veins. Thud, the back window blossomed into hurt glass. I turned on the headlights once we were in the parking lot, hitting the brakes hard approaching the exit to the main road.

A pair of car lights lit the road on my right. I quickly gauged the automobile's speed, hitting the gas, thinking I would easily turn on the road before the car arrived. Not a problem until the lights increased in speed; the approaching car was not acting logically, not slowing when he saw me as I expected, accelerating to collision speed.

I have a knack for calculating the odds of things, especially in tight situations. I thought as I watched the lights approach, I thought I still had a sixty/forty chance of accelerating onto the road before he hit me. I kept going, accelerator on the floor, tires screaming.

'What's he doing?' she screamed in panic as the approaching car lights glared through the broken door window glass, eerily lighting her face.

I was wrong, odds off. The car easily arrived at the intersection first, blocking my path. I hit the brakes, four wheels in full lock, lifting, swerving furiously to the right, trying to avoid a collision. Lights spit out of a side window of the blocking car. Door of my car absorbed the full force of several shots. My Mercedes careened off his rear bumper before heading towards a ditch at the edge of the road. Accelerating, turning hard now, gravel ricocheting off the rocker panels. Momentarily leaning into the ditch for a split second on the edge of disaster, the rear tires dug into the hard pavement, driving past the stopped car up onto the road, hoping there were no other cars up ahead blocking my path. It didn't matter, we couldn't wait, couldn't avoid a crash if another car was in our path, nothing I could do, had to get away, accelerating in a panic, open road ahead.

Normally, this road is sparsely driven at night. Not many people live up here. Just a few commercial buildings exit onto the road along with some older houses, not much. Most residential traffic is farther down the road closer to the city and civilization. M turned to look behind through the rear window.

'You okay?' I shouted, hoping she had not been hit, my eyes never leaving the road. Heartbeat quickening, hands shaking I had to remain steady, waiting for her to reply.

'I'm okay,' she gasped.

'Anyone following? See any lights?'

'Maybe, I'm not sure.'

Trees beside the road slowly blurred together in a patchy white wall illuminated in my headlights as I accelerated. I drove as fast as I dared, desperate to escape the nightmare in the parking lot. Had to get to town somehow, get some help. This section of road was isolated, vulnerable. I knew the road, but I had never driven this fast at night. Even with high beams, I was out-driving my lights at speed, desperately trying to see through the dark.

'Car lights behind us,' M said in a quivering voice. 'They are still coming.'

'Stay low.' I commanded.

The road was a series of switchbacks meandering down hills towards town. If we crashed, we were dead. If they caught us, we were dead. I had no choice, had to move. Each corner in the road felt like it lasted a lifetime, one mini-crisis after another, with death looming around every bend. My Mercedes fought for adhesion, braking, leaning as it slid into the corners, speeding through straight sections, braking hard for the next corner. I strained to see into the dark, out driving my headlights, trying to remember what I could not see ahead, fighting for the right combination of brakes and acceleration, needing to guess because at these speeds, my car was through a corner before I could make an adjustment, the present passing quickly to the past, an eternity evaporating into each stark, fearful second.

M stared silently ahead; her hands balled in fists in her lap.

A car followed. I could see it in my mirrors. But we had a lead, not much of lead, not enough. Flashes of light told me they were firing, but no thuds. The road curved dramatically. They couldn't get off a good shot. I drove as if in a trance, faster than I imagined possible as the lights behind us slowly faded behind.

Suddenly remembering my Mercedes had an emergency button, I searched urgently with my left hand and finally found the button while steering through curves.

'Yes, Mr. Van Laan,' a female voice spoke out of the dashboard. 'Can I be of assistance?'

'Can you tell me where I am?' I asked, hoping my car had a locator.

The operator paused for a moment. 'You are on a two-lane road near I-64 just southwest of Charlottesville, Virginia. You don't seem to be stationary,' she noted. 'Are you experiencing a problem with your car?'

'No,' I said, 'Please listen carefully. This is an emergency. I need you to contact the Charlottesville Police Department. Have them meet me at the nearest intersection.'

'Where would you like to meet them?' she asked politely.

'I don't care!' I yelled in frustration. 'I'm being chased by another car. People are shooting at me. The situation is very dangerous. Do you understand?'

'Yes, sir.' Her voice was bright and pleasant.

The road suddenly veered right in my lights. I hit the brakes hard, remembering this corner was tight. I hadn't been concentrating on driving while talking to the operator. Slowing fast, but not fast enough, fighting for grip, rear end broke loose, tires skidding across the road towards a gravel shoulder, sliding sideways, out of control. A tree on the side of the road was in my path. The car lurched when its tires hit loose gravel, fell into a rut on the shoulder, and leaned over on two wheels. I straightened the wheel, regained traction in the dirt, sliding past the tree, missing by fractions. Easing back onto the blacktop, exhaling slowly.

'See anything behind?' I asked M.

'Not sure. Your rear window is badly cracked.'

Unless the gunman had a very good car or was a professional driver, I didn't think he could catch us. Still, I didn't want to test my theory. I stayed hard on the accelerator.

Operator. 'Police will meet you at the southbound exit of 29 and I-64. Is that okay?'

'I'll get there.'

'Are you hurt, Mr. Van Laan?' the operator asked. 'Do you need medical assistance?'

'Not yet.'

'You okay?' I asked M.

'I think so.

After slowing for the entrance ramp to I-64 off Highway 20, I accelerated onto the expressway. Traffic on the freeway was sparse this late in the evening. It was an opportunity for my Mercedes to lay down some speed, put more distance between us and the boogeymen behind us, run from the demons in the night.

My body, every nerve ending vibrated with a rush of adrenaline, my foot hard against the accelerator as if this act alone would save us, we passed a few slower cars so fast, it was like they were parked.

'Maybe you should slow down,' M said.

I knew she was right, but I had been running scared, not acting rational, still hell-bent determined to lose the idiots behind us.

'Okay,' I finally acknowledged her advice, noticing my speedometer was buried above one hundred twenty miles per hour. The next exit approached fast. I hit the brakes and slid onto the off-ramp, merging quickly onto 29. Flashing lights ahead, two police cars waited on the side of the brightly lit road. I pulled off the road in front of the cruisers.

Deep breath.

'That was fun.' M whispered.

NOVEMBER 2, SATURDAY, 9:35 A.M. JOHN

My eyelids began to droop.

I hit a wall. Needed sleep.

Cops were relentless. Questions and questions. Most of the time, the same questions... just different cops. They didn't understand why someone wanted to kill me. I didn't understand either. I wasn't much help.

When they were finally done harassing me, I asked them a few questions for a change. Cops nodded. They told me their initial findings indicated the intruders hadn't touched anything except the guards. They didn't steal anything; they didn't destroy anything. It all seemed strange. The vault in my building held millions of dollars in gemstones, but they needed the combination for access and according to the police, they hadn't asked Arny or the guards for the combination before leaving the building. So, stealing gemstones apparently was not their motive.

Cops said Arny and the security guards were okay, stable except for being badly bruised. Next, I asked about Monica. They said they had taken her home hours ago. Police protection had been established. They promised to keep an eye on her apartment for a few days. I hoped she wouldn't need it. I told them I thought the gunmen were after me, not her.

Finally, I asked if I could go home.

A detective insisted on driving me. While walking to his car, I surveyed the damage to my Mercedes. Without bulletproof glass we would not have survived. Every window except the windshield was broken or cracked. Sheet metal was pockmarked. We were saved only because the gunmen didn't know about the glass. According to the detective, they vanished into the night. He guessed they hadn't followed us past the two-lane road down the hill.

The road to my company looked very different. Circumstances change the way we view ordinary objects. I had driven this road many times, but I never saw the trees and hills as I did that morning. At each bend in the road, I imagined a bullet-marred Mercedes wrapped around a tree. Truth was, my world had changed overnight. It was a harsher, crueler place, now. A world filled with nightmares and dangers I could not control.

Unbuckling my seatbelt after arriving at my office, fatigue washed over me like a man drugged. I needed sleep, but I had nowhere to go except my office. The detective apologized, but insisted, apartment was off limits, still being checked for finger prints and trace evidence.

I collapsed on my favorite reading couch after entering my office, shutting down completely, both mentally and physically, wanting nothing more than to escape into a few hours of sleep. Yet, all out of proportion with my desire, the windows in my office windows were filled with bright sunlight. The sun had risen, casting long shadows through the barren leafless forest valley below my building. Winter still dominated the land. Spring was a long way off. I tried to visualize how the lush green valley would look in the warm sunshine of spring; dogwoods and redbud trees spreading irresistible color through what was now a drab brown landscape.

I wondered as I settled onto my couch. I wondered if I waited long enough... would my life emerge from this cold nightmare I now inhabited? Would it evolve into something good again, something which was more closely evidenced by the flowers of spring?

Spring was months in the future. Winter was my reality. And winter is a silent time of waiting, a time of endless gray days.

3:35 P.M. JOHN

Slipping silently around an outside corner of the building. casting tree shadows over the siding; the afternoon sun eventually drifted in through the windows of my office, spreading a warm glow across the room where I lay sleeping on a couch.

A busy computer screen on my desk was on, dutifully reporting sales numbers in dollars and pounds from distant Distribution Houses as far away as New York, Hong Kong, and London. It cared not that no one was paying any attention. It simply continued to steadfastly display figures representing rough stones purchased from mines around the world, along with quantities of cut stones ready for shipment from Sri Lanka and India. Showing no sympathy for absent numbers which should have represented the quantities of color-enhanced gemstones produced in our Australian laboratory, a chorus of statistics, a silent hum of activity continued to emanate from the unemotional technological marvel as if nothing was wrong; no apologies for displaying conclusive evidence of a failing company which was operating at a deficit in various time zones around the world.

Equally unacknowledged on the desktop was a telephone console whose blinking green lights were begging for attention. Not one sound escaped from the internal office phone system to the right of the computer. It was strangely silent in the middle of what should have been a busy afternoon.

When her motherly regard for my mental stability finally dissolved by midafternoon and Helen could wait no longer, she opened one of the two tall varnished oak doors which served as an official entrance to my office and peeked inside. Seeing me still sleeping on the couch, she stepped inside, slowly easing the door closed behind her, releasing the silver handle with a slight click. Tiptoeing softy across the Oriental carpets covering the wood floor, standing for a minute over my sleeping body, she couldn't decide what to do about my current state of errant absence.

'John,' she softly said.

No response. My eyes remained closed; breathing slow.

'John,' louder this time.

Still no response.

Unsure... she turned to go.

'I heard you,' I replied.

Opening my eyes was a relief. I had been dreaming, flying at great speed through a forest of tall trees... hard trees, unforgiving trees that lacked pity, trees ready to attack me on every side should I make one mistake, one wrong turn and I would crash into one of these trees with painful if not fatal consequences.

'You awake?' Helen asked.

'I am now,' I replied.

'Everyone is asking for you. I couldn't let you sleep any longer.' She cast an apologetic glance toward my desk, where multiple green lights continued to blink on the telephone console. 'I'm sorry.'

'What are you doing here on a Saturday?' I asked, ignoring her apology.

'I heard what happened,' she explained. 'I came in to see if you were okay. The phones were ringing when I entered the office, and I ...'

'Have you seen Arny?' I interrupted, sitting up.

'Yes.'

'Is he okay?'

'He's limping on one leg and holding his chest kind of funny. I think his side is taped up. He may have a broken rib. But his mouth is working just fine.'

She loved Arny in her own way. However, if you listened to the two of them when they were together, you would think you were listening to two spoiled kids begging for attention. They were always bickering. Lighthearted fun most of the time. Sometimes, it got serious. That's when I needed to referee.

'Hold my calls. I'll let you know when I'm ready.'

'Okay,' Helen nodded and headed for the door.

I sat up on the couch, still exhausted, trying to find the will to stand. Every bone in my body ached, every muscle rebelled. I reached for the portable phone on a table next to my couch and dialed an internal extension number.

'Yeah,' Arny answered.

'How you doing?'

'Okay for almost getting killed.'

'Come to my office. I want to see you. And bring some food, will you? I'm hungry.'

'Hey, I got beat up bad last night' he objected. 'Doesn't that entitle me to a day off?'

'Sure, take a day off. Just do it when I'm out of town.' I sighed heavily. 'And for the record, I do care.'

'I suppose that redhead is with you. Is she hungry too?'

'Monica? She's not here. She's home.'

'No, she ain't boss. She's in the office.'

'She is?'

'Would I lie to you?'

'No...I guess not... Okay, come to my office. I want to talk to you. And don't forget, bring some food... please.'

Hanging up my phone before he could give me any more flack, I stood up and paced around my office to get my blood moving. I couldn't believe M was here. I hadn't thought about how she would react to last night's disaster. But I knew how I would act. And it wouldn't be to come into work on a Saturday. I decided to see for myself.

Helen turned as I passed her desk.

And Jason came out of his office down a hall when he heard my footsteps. 'You okay, sir?' he asked.

'Why are you here?'

'I have some questions and ...'

'Later Jason, I'll call you when I'm ready.'   I continued walking.

Papers could be heard rustling in her workstation, evidence of a real person working inside. I poked my head inside to be sure.

'I can't believe you're here,' I began.

'You're here,' she replied calmly.

'I live here. I had nowhere else to go. What's your excuse?'

'Law school taught me how to work seven days a week with no sleep,' she shrugged. 'I'm fine.'

She looked good, hard at work. Better than me. I was barely functioning.

'I need to talk to you,' she said without missing a beat.

'Okay, but I have some work to do first. I'll call you when I have a minute.'

'I don't think this can wait.'

'Give me a couple of hours.'

She shot me a typical female look which is usually followed by the word 'fine.' I got away fast while I still could.

What remained of my afternoon flew by. Everyone wanted to know what happened. Jason came in with new allocation figures from accounting. I reviewed them quickly, then told him to e-mail the numbers to the three Distribution Houses. His calculations indicated our entire operation was walking a tightrope. With a chill, I realized my company's survival was no longer guaranteed. Its existence was tenuous at best, but only if I was optimistic. Truth was, it was failing.

Helen called. 'It's that girl,' she said without explanation.

'That girl?' I asked my head somewhere else.

'You know who,' Helen replied, apparently finding it either difficult or distasteful to pronounce Monica's name.

'What about her?' I replied when I realized who she was talking about.

'She keeps bothering me with questions.'

'Okay, I'll talk to her when I have a few minutes. Now leave me alone.'

At some point during the afternoon, my adrenaline, the little amount which still resided in my body after last night; the hormone which had been helping me to function; finally wore off. An ache began in my head, working its way down my neck and into the muscles of my shoulder. All I really wanted to do was to crawl into a warm bed somewhere and sleep. But apparently, I was required to deal with Monica before I could achieve any peace.

Now... I think I have more stamina than almost anyone alive. But in actuality, no matter how good you think you are at any particular skill, there is always someone who is better. And when it came to having stamina, it seemed one of those better persons than me was Miss Monica. She had me in the endurance department. If I were her, I would have gone home hours before, but when I dialed her number, she was still working. I asked her to come to my office so we could talk.

Then I called Arny.

Earlier he had brought lunch. I was on my phone at the time. Bandages covered one side of his head. I motioned for him to sit down, but he had just waved me off dismissively and limped out.

'How's my apartment?' I asked him after he answered his phone.

'Not bad. The cops are done. I cleaned it.'

'Good.'

'Aren't you going to ask how I am?' he demanded.

'How are you?'

'Fine. Thanks for asking.'

'Sorry. You didn't look too bad when I saw you this afternoon,' I lied.

'Can't get to me, boss. I'm a rock.'

'Yeah, and I am an island,' I retorted with a smile. 'By the way, police told me they're going to set up twenty-four-hour surveillance at my office for the next few days. I guess we're okay here for now, but please feel free to leave if you don't feel safe.'

'Look, boss. This is my home. No slitty-eyed bastards are going to make me leave.'

'What did you say?' My heart skipped a beat.

'Sorry, don't mean to offend anyone, but the guys who attacked me looked Chinese.'

'Did you see their faces?' I asked carefully.

'No. not really, but I saw their eyes through their masks.'

'Did you tell the police?'

'Yeah, but I was occupied at the time. You know, trying to stay alive. I told the cops it was no big deal because I wasn't sure.'

'Okay,' I sighed. 'And Arny, thanks.'

'For what?'

'For putting up a fight. I appreciate what you did.'

'Didn't do enough,' he said, fatigue and regret echoing through his words.

'Arny, you did everything you could.'

I hung up when M arrived in my office. She looked good in blue jeans and a cream-colored sweater, probably cashmere. I was dead tired, but seeing her revived me. In my opinion, blue jeans can be more glamorous than an evening dress and jewels. And the luscious curves of her sweater... well, I must have been staring because she stopped and gave me an inquisitive look.

A beautiful girl like M must have already heard every pick-up line in the book. I was embarrassed to hear myself say, 'Nice sweater.' I had no idea why I said something about her sweater, just tired, I guessed, lack of self-control. I silently chastised myself.

'Okay, thanks,' she shrugged off my remark as if it deserved about as much attention as she gave it. 'But I didn't come in here to talk about me. I want to talk about you.'

'Doesn't sound like an interesting subject.'

'Not really,' she replied. 'First, I think you had better seriously consider the possibility someone is trying to destroy your company. And second, you need to find out who and why quickly if you want to stay alive.'

'Have a seat,' I replied, as if we were discussing nothing important. 'Would you like a glass of wine?' I grabbed a couple of aspirin from a shelf in my office wall before she could reply. Then poured two glasses of wine.

'Sure, but we need to talk,' she said impatiently.

I stopped, wine in hand, curiously unsure what to do next.

'You okay?'

'Why?'

'Because you're not moving.'

'It's you,' I said, couldn't help it. Words kept slipping from my mouth like someone else was doing the talking.

'Me?' she seemed confused.

'Don't you ever have a bad day?'

'Oh, I have my bad days,' she smiled.

'I haven't seen one yet.' I laughed.

'Look,' an air of resignation sounded in her voice. 'Do you think you can sit down and concentrate on something more important than how I look... like how are we going to keep you from dying?'

I wasn't accustomed to being told what to do, especially not by a secretary. She got under my skin just a little with her remark, and I wasn't in the mood to be irritated. But she was right. My perennial optimism, embodied by a belief that the nightmarish events of my recent past was hopefully nothing more than coincidental bad luck; the theory had not been serving me very well lately.

I stealthily slipped the aspirin into my mouth and downed it with a sip of wine. Unfortunately, my temples were throbbing from a dull headache at the time, threatening to take over what little remained of my limited mental capacity. Placing a glass of wine on a coffee table for her, I sat down, attempting to act rational through a tired, twisting blur of conflicting impulses.

She must have read my confusion and immediately used my silence to introduce a subject she wanted to discuss and it quickly became obvious she was more prepared for our conversation than me.

'And please don't tell me this is none of my business,' she began.

'What's none of your business?'

'That I'm not involved in this as much as you.'

'You don't have to be.'

'That's where you're wrong. I almost burned to death in Australia. And last night someone shot at me. That's twice I've nearly been killed. Therefore, it is my business.'

'You can walk,' I countered. 'I'm the problem, not you. As soon as you get away from me, you'll be safe. And that's exactly what you should do.'

She glared at me. It was clear she was one woman who didn't like having other people dictating her life.

I smiled.

'I already told you I want to see this through,' she answered tersely.

'But I insist. I don't want to be responsible for getting you killed or injured... Monica. Don't you understand? This thing is turning very ugly, very fast. If something happens to you... well... I don't want to even think about that possibility.'

'Forget it,' she sounded determined. 'Because you can't force me to leave. Not now. I'm in too deep. And besides, I have a friend in Washington who works at the CIA. I can call him and ask for help. And you need help... the kind of help he can give you.'

'I'll take your help, but you don't need to continue to work for me. It's too dangerous.'

'I'll take the risk. It's my decision, not yours.' Her voice was rising.

'No, not as long as you work for me, you are my responsibility. Look, I appreciate your guts and your desire, but you have nothing more to prove.'

'I didn't think I had to prove anything.'

'I didn't mean it that way.'

'Okay, what way did you mean it?'

The look on her face, disdain, anger, told me I should back down and fortunately, aspirin had kicked in, just enough that I was beginning to think clearly. I knew I shouldn't be arguing with her. She was smart and she was a lawyer, a bad combination when arguing a point. I chose the only out available to me at the time.

'You're fired,' I said, assuming I was the boss and firing her would put an end to our conversation.

She was hurt. It was immediately apparent she was hurt. She sat silently on the couch without looking in my direction. Obviously, I had made a mistake.

'Damn it, John. We've been through this before,' she finally shot back. 'I don't want to quit. And for the record... you can't fire me,' she said with a tremor in her voice, appearing for a moment to be on the verge of crying.

'Why can't I fire you?' I asked stupidly.

'Because I will sue you for sexual discrimination if you do!' she hit back. 'You wouldn't fire a man in the same situation.'

'But you're not a man,' I replied, only digging myself into a deeper legal hole.

'That statement can and will be used against you in court,' she said emphatically.

'Look, I'm only trying to do what is right,' I replied, now exasperated.

The sky outside my office windows was turning dark. Clouds were gathering. I stood up to walk towards the windows to take a break. She was wearing me down.

'May I suggest you begin by shutting the drapes,' she interjected. 'You are a perfect target for a sniper standing there.' She paused. 'John, you need to start thinking differently.'

I turned to face her. Every time I thought I could control her, something new popped out of her sweet lips, some new issue I had not previously considered. I didn't want to close my drapes. I seldom, if ever, closed them. I liked the expansive view of the valley. But I closed the drapes anyway, mostly because I didn't want to argue with her and because she was probably right. Someone could be outside with a gun.

'And...' she continued after I finished my assignment.

'What now?'

'I didn't want to say this before, but you leave me no choice.' She paused before continuing, looking down at her hands which were folded tightly in her lap. Finally, she sighed, and it came out. 'I feel somehow connected to this... and to you.' She looked into my eyes, imploring, pleading her case.

I said nothing because I didn't know what to say. I was too stunned.

'Do you believe in God?' she continued.

Still trying to decide how to react to her last bombshell announcement, I had no idea what believing in God had to do with what we were discussing, but I answered her question anyway, as honestly as I could.

'I believe in a God,' I said. 'Although I'm not sure anyone or any religion really understands God. But, yes, I believe in God.'

'Do you believe God has a plan for us?'

'I believe his plans are complex and inconceivable. I also think it's impossible to believe in God without accepting some order in our universe.'

She rose and approached me. 'I belong here with you, John. That's the plan. I don't know why. And I'm not going to pretend I can explain it. Please don't push me out. Please let me stay and help.'

I knew I should send her home. I had no business exposing her to the danger which seemed to have taken over my world, but I couldn't do it. I couldn't send her away because, more than anything, I wanted her to stay. Even though logic dictated I send her packing, I couldn't do it.

'Are you sure?' I asked, thinking I should give her one more opportunity to get out alive while she still could.

'Yes, I'm sure,' she replied, although I sensed a slight tremor in her voice which belied the confidence she sought to display.

'Okay.'

'Good,' she replied confidently, sounding like a lawyer in a trial who had just been issued an opinion in her favor by a judge. She had won, and it was now time to move on to other issues. She gathered her papers from the floor as if nothing important had happened, nothing monumental anyway. Moving to my desk with her pile of goodies, she motioned for me to follow and immediately launched into a barrage of questions before I could even sit down. At some point in our conversation, I called Arny and begged him to please bring some food; pizza, whatever edibles he could find. I was hungry and still slightly in shock I had let her stay. I didn't quite know how to act except to do exactly what she wanted, answer her questions as best as I could. And in order to do this, I badly needed food. I simply couldn't continue without some nourishment because it appeared as if nothing was going to deter Miss Monica from her predetermined path. She didn't even slow down when Arny showed up; just continued to motor on like a lawyer in a deposition, munching pizza and firing questions at me... now her witless witness.

'Are you sure there's nothing illegal about your overseas operations?' she asked again. 'No tax-dodging offshore corporations, etc.? Because if I go to the CIA, they'll start asking questions. Now is the time to come clean.'

'Nothing,' I replied. 'We've discussed this before, and besides, I've been investigated by better organizations than the CIA.'

'What are you talking about?' she was momentarily speechless.

'The Internal Revenue Service.'

'Okay, but just for the record. Is there anything they couldn't find? I have to ask. No foreign tax havens? No blind trusts? I don't want to get you in trouble.'

'No and no,' I replied.

'Not anywhere?'

'No!'

Exasperated, I raised my hands in mock submission. I was beginning to wonder if every lawyer, even the beautiful ones like Monica take a class in law school which teaches them how to ask onerous, obnoxious questions devised to keep their witness on the defensive with no chance of a reprieve in sight.

'Look, I have enough money,' I continued. 'I don't need, nor do I want that kind of exposure or risk. Sure, I could have set up any number of tax havens if I wanted. In most countries they would be perfectly legal. But I didn't. Okay... so can we move on?'

She looked at me intently as if I were some kind of foreign spy. All her training must have pointed to a contrary conclusion. Could I really be different from the norm, from the portrayal of a dishonest businessman she had learned about in law school? I suspected she had been educated to distrust honesty. She probably thought most men lie. It was clearly evident she was a hard sell, but that was okay with me. I knew I would eventually win because I was telling the truth. I just hoped she would eventually believe me.

We continued and I was trying to concentrate, but finally, I began to fade, couldn't help it. At some point in our conversation, I suggested we move to a couch where we could be more comfortable.

She agreed.

Once there, I must have leaned back after answering a few more questions. Then I slouched down, allowing my head to rest on the couch's soft leather. I could still hear her voice as she continued her relentless, endless questions; questions, questions... and fell asleep.

Sometime later in the night I woke up mostly because I was uncomfortable in a half sitting, half lying position on the couch. I chuckled while attempting to stretch the kinks out of my aching back. I had never before fallen asleep in the middle of a conversation. I must have been very tired.

That's when I saw M stretched out on the couch with her head on a pillow. Finding a blanket in a closet, I laid it gently over her body before unlocking the door to my apartment and turning out the lights in my office. But not before taking one more look.

She looked very beautiful as she slept.

BANGKOK THAILAND, SUNDAY NOVEMBER 3, 4:00 P.M. LUANG

His nephew was late.

Luang had called him. Suggested a meeting, just the two of them for an informal discussion. He made it clear he would not take 'no' for an answer. But his determination didn't deter his nephew from politely declining, claiming he was too busy. However, the old patriarch had prepared for his response. He began by pointing out that he was the oldest living member of this family. His nephew should show some respect. Please meet me in the grand hall at four this afternoon, no excuses. He didn't wait for his nephew's reply.

His hands had trembled when he put down his phone. He hoped his voice had not given away his apprehension. Even if it did, he could do nothing about that. He needed to talk to his nephew.

Now that the time had come for the meeting, his nephew was absent. As Luang waited in the grand hall, his anger grew. He was not accustomed to waiting for others, especially not a young nephew. The nephew's absence demonstrated a lack of respect. It was intolerable.

But perhaps his anger was good. Perhaps his anger would assist him when it came time to say what was on his mind. Perhaps he would be so angry he wouldn't care how he sounded.

But that wasn't really true.

He didn't want to sound like a pathetic old man. He wanted to appear composed and in control. Still, he did nothing to quell the anger building deep in his gut.

Sitting in a chair at one end of the long conference table, the chair currently reserved for him at formal meetings of his family; he didn't know why he had chosen to sit in this chair. He could have sat in any one of the chairs which surrounded the table. They were all empty. It just seemed like this chair belonged to him, the only piece of furniture in this house which still belonged to him. Everything else was gone. He no longer lived in this house. When he retired from his job, he had been forced to leave.

Retiring had seemed right at the time. He was getting old. Now he regretted his decision. He longed to roam the halls of this house again. Revisit the memories which lingered here. Memories which were once his life. But his time in this house was over. He had to be content with other duties.

However, contentment had not come as easy as he expected. He wondered if he should not have stepped down. Ancestors before him had died in this house. He could have done as they did, lived in the house until he was dead. But he had thought himself wiser than his predecessors. He believed he should step down while he still had his health and the ability to enjoy the remaining years of his life.

He had been wrong. Nothing had prepared him for the useless feelings which accompanied his new life.

He looked around the grand hall to regain his focus. Gold-embossed framed pictures on the walls stared down at him as he waited in nervous anger: pictures of ancient battle scenes, warriors on their grand horses, their swords raised in a victory salute... As if they were saying to him; see... you should have stayed the course, seen the battle to the end, tasted victory as we did. Instead, you fled the field of combat. Now you have no one to blame except yourself.

He suddenly felt very alone and very afraid; more alone and afraid than he had ever felt in his life.

CHARLOTTESVILLE, VIRGINIA, NOVEMBER 7, THURSDAY, 2:30 P.M. JOHN

He walked into my office with a confident athletic stride.

It was late afternoon at the time and I was working at my desk, studying inventory numbers, trying to make sense of shrinking figures, trying to stretch them beyond their physical limits.

M was with me at the time, sitting at my conference table, buried in some legal documents. She had so many questions in the days following our attack that she became tired of walking back and forth from her small cubicle to my office. Eventually, without asking my permission, she simply settled into a chair at the conference table and spread out her work.

Outwardly I expressed only a mild tolerance for this new development. But the truth was I rather liked having her where I could see her.

Our afternoon visitor was expected, ushered into my office by Helen. He was a tall, handsome, and African American.

M rose when she saw him. They politely embraced.

He smiled and stepped back. 'Great to see you again, Monica,' he said warmly.

She smiled in return.

I came out from behind my desk to greet him.

'John, I would like you to meet Agent Charles Stewart,' she introduced him. 'Charlie, this is John Van Laan.'

He extended his hand and gave me his business card. I immediately liked the man. He had a great smile. His black hair was closely cropped, dressed in a typical Washingtonian bureaucratic dress code, a dark suit, white shirt, and tie. His card read:

Charles M. Stewart, Special Agent, Central Intelligence Agency.

'May I get you something to drink?' I asked, gesturing toward the informal seating area in my office,

'No, thank you,' he replied in a deep strong voice.

I suggested we sit in the casual seating area because my desk seemed too formal and the conference table was well... totally cluttered with M's work papers. He chose one of two leather chairs with M sitting opposite him on a couch beside me.

'How have you been?' Charles asked her.

'I'm fine.'

'Not at the EPA anymore?'

'Got burned out.'

'I understand.'

'And you, Charlie? How are you?'

'Oh, just trying to navigate the bureaucratic obstacle course at the agency. You know, career advancement.'

'Charlie, can I still call you Charlie? Or does everyone now call you Charles?' M asked with a slight smirk.

He gave her a sly smile. 'You can call me, Charlie.'

'We went to law school together at UVA,' she turned to me. 'After school, Charlie chose to take a job at the CIA for reasons I still don't understand.'

'I don't understand it either,' he smiled.

'We continued to stay in touch in Washington's 'young professionals' social scene, but only as friends. Mostly because our work was our life,' she added.

'Workaholics, one characteristic we have in common.'

'Law school to the CIA, an interesting career choice,' I questioned.

'Yeah, I guess.' He smiled affably.

'M told me you graduated at the top of your class. You could be making a lot more money in private practice,' I observed.

'Maybe, but nothing is easy for a black man in the business world. Besides, I always wanted to join the CIA. Had to give it a try.'

My first impression was good; I liked Charlie and I'm seldom wrong about people. He had a quiet confidence about him, something which often is coupled with intelligence.

'Monica calls me Charlie,' he said. 'So please, just call me Charlie.'

'Thank you and you can call me John.'

Formalities over, M was all business. 'Charlie, I asked you here because we have a situation at Gemstone International that I thought you may find interesting.'

'I know,' he replied. 'I looked into your boss's company before driving here, including a recent police report which was very interesting.'

'You did?' M asked.

'Yes, the report reads like a botched robbery, but you don't need the CIA for something like that. So, how can I help you?'

'Here's what you don't know.' Monica explained. 'First, nothing was taken at this alleged robbery. We think John was the target. They either wanted to kill or kidnap him.'

Charlie didn't comment.

'Second,' M continued. 'John and I were in Australia last week visiting a lab owned by a company which does business with John's company. The lab exploded and burned to the ground while we were there. I was nearly killed.'

She paused for effect before continuing. 'Third, only days before the fire, a business in Hong Kong was robbed. The business works closely with John's company. In addition, a series of robberies in London have affected another company which is associated with John's company. In total, these events have seriously jeopardized the ability of John's company.'

'You say these companies are associated with John's company. How so? Are they a conglomerate?' Charles asked.

'No,' M replied. 'They're loosely connected in a distribution and sales network.'

'Is this a case of competitors fighting with each other?'

'No. They work together. What happens to one affects the others.'

Charles looked at me. 'You do very well for being such young company.'

He then paused and turned to Monica. 'I checked the financials of Mr. Van Laan's company. Gemstone International's financial success is off the charts. For starters, the gross sales last year were one hundred and fifty-one million with operating costs under twenty-four million annually. That's a pre-tax profit of one hundred and twenty-seven million. Great numbers for a six-and-a-half-year-old company with very few assets. Now, I'm not trained in economics, but I talked to a few of my friends who are and they said this is virtually impossible to achieve.'

M glanced at me apprehensively.

I was starting to become annoyed. My company was a private business. Its financial records are not for public consumption, but apparently, that didn't stop the prying eyes of the CIA.

'Look,' Charlie said to Monica, 'I don't want to sound argumentative, but something doesn't add up here and I not sure you want me involved.'

'Hold on, Charlie,' M interrupted, 'I told you I checked everything before I called...'

I stood to interrupt her. 'Monica, this is not the kind of help we need. As far as I'm concerned, this meeting is over.'

M ignored me, challenging Charlie with a vengeance. 'If the company is illegal,' she argued, 'Why would it bother to report a profit of one hundred and twenty-seven million? Do you know how much corporate income tax they have to pay based on these numbers?'

'Because maybe they should be paying more,' Charlie looked her directly in the eye.

'Come on, Charlie,' M responded.

'You explain it then,' he said. 'Look, I came here as a favor to you, but I have some concerns. And I wouldn't be honest if I didn't express them.'

'And I wouldn't have asked you to come without first verifying the legitimacy of John's company,' she shot back.

He smiled. 'Working at the EPA doesn't exactly qualify you for investigating financial fraud.'

'Sure, and working at the CIA probably disqualifies you from understanding anything,' she responded.

I smiled and returned to my seat. She was easily his match.

They paused like two stunned prize fighters who had each taken a hard blow, waiting to see if the other guy would fall first. It suddenly occurred to me this wasn't the first time they had traded verbal blows. I decided it was time to intervene before their contest got too bloody.

'Okay, okay,' I interrupted. 'I think it's clear Mr. Stewart is not here to help. Apparently, he would rather bring down my evil empire.'

Their gazes had been locked in combat. They turned to me as if they were wondering who I was and how I became involved in their fight. Their difference of opinion had become real personal, real fast.

Charlie backed off. 'Alright, sorry... I didn't mean to sound so antagonistic,' he said, sitting on the edge of his chair.

M stared at him. 'That's bullshit, Charlie! You know exactly how you sound. Do you think becoming a CIA agent entitles you to say whatever flashes through your pea brain?'

'Look, can we call a truce?' I raised his hands in the air, signaling surrender.

'Just because you apologized, doesn't make it okay?' she continued without bothering to acknowledge my presence.

I was almost beginning to enjoy their contest, couldn't help noticing M was utterly gorgeous when she got angry.

'Okay, okay... I give,' Charlie conceded, hanging his head. 'If you say John's company is solid, I'll believe you.'

At this point, I personally wasn't in the mood to continue. 'May I suggest we shake hands and go our separate ways? This is getting us nowhere.'

'We need him, John,' she wasn't ready to give up. 'Don't worry. I know him. He loses his way from time to time, but I can keep him focused.'

'Thanks, M. I assume you meant that as a compliment?' Charlie responded.

'As close to one as you are going to get from me today.'

These two had gone at it before. That much was obvious. I didn't know if that was good or a hindrance. I sighed. Our discussion certainly had not gotten off to a good start. But M was right. We needed help.

'Charlie,' I cleared my throat. 'I'm going to defer to Monica on this even though I want you to know I'm uncomfortable with your attitude. But she's right. My company does need help. Before we continue, I want to state for the record I'm not too happy you looked at my financials. Gemstone International is a private company and I think this should still mean something in this country. The information you read is privileged and not for public consumption. But having said this, I'll open my books to you any time you want. You may scrutinize our financials to your heart's content. And if you find anything illegal, I expect you to act on it. In the meantime, please offer me the presumption of innocence which I believe the law affords.'

Charlie looked mystified by my statement. I don't think he anticipated I would be so open. He probably thought I would run for the hole in the ground I had crawled out of. I wasn't fitting the bad guy profile he anticipated.

'Charlie, you have to trust me on this,' M interjected. 'Initially, I thought the same thing, but I checked it all out. John's telling the truth.'

'Okay, Monica,' Charlie replied.

'Do you really think he can help?' I asked M.

'I know it doesn't look like it now,' she answered, putting her hand on my arm. 'But yes. He can help and it's the kind of help we need.'

'Okay,' I said with resignation. 'Then let's clarify some things for Agent Stewart before we go any farther.'

I spent the next hour explaining the colored stone business to Charlie.

'You still look confused,' I said after finishing.

'What you are saying may be true,' he replied, 'But if you don't mind, I would like to withhold judgment.'

'Of course, but please try to understand, Charles. Naturally produced gemstones like sapphires are not a renewable resource. They are scarce and becoming scarcer. We have raised the value of these stones by multiples of their price in a very short period. Even so, the current prices don't reflect the true value of the gemstones, not in my opinion.'

Charles didn't comment.

'Here's something which should interest you. We have removed gemstones in some countries from the age-old triangle of guns, terror, and drugs. As I am sure you know; gems have frequently been used by terrorists and criminals as their commodity of choice to launder money. Because of our efforts, these gemstones are now flowing directly through our company to manufacturers; eliminated from being a valuable tool of drug cartels and terrorists.'

'And,' added M, 'rural third-world miners and their communities are now benefiting from their natural resources in ways which were never true before. These people were badly exploited under the old system. In addition, John's company has set up a foundation to help the miners. A percentage of his profit every year goes to fund that foundation.'

'Okay, okay,' Charlie appeared to be finally giving in. 'Let's say I believe you. Why do you need me?'

'The events I described to you earlier are beginning to form a pattern,' Monica explained. 'We think the true purpose for all these crimes is to destroy John's company.'

'Could the crimes be purely coincidental, just bad luck having them all come at once?' Charles responded.

'Could be. but highly improbable.'

'Okay,' Charlie acknowledged. 'But I'm still having trouble understanding. If you're helping so many people, where's the motive? Who benefits if your company goes belly up?'

'Charlie, I hardly know where to begin to answer your question,' I intervened. 'You must understand GI has changed the economies of some small nations. We are not as big as big oil. But what we have accomplished has affected many people. And not everyone likes the change or welcomes its consequences. We have eliminated whole industries in some countries. But for every job lost, we have created new jobs, good ones; just not always in the same region. And many of the jobs we eliminated, they weren't good ones. Workers were severely misused. Some were child laborers. Greedy men were getting rich from exploitation. Charlie, we've made some enemies along the way.'

'Like who, where?' asked Charles.

'Hong Kong, Thailand, and India, for instance. These countries have a huge stake in the sale of gemstones. In places like Zaire and Sierra Leone; drugs, guns, and gems are intricately woven into their political struggles. Places like New York, London, and Brussels have whole segments of their economy connected to cheap gems and jewelry. We are in the process of eliminating some of these industries.'

'What do want from me?' asked Charlie.

'Find out who is doing this to us. The situation has gotten seriously out of control. I can deal with lab fires, robberies. But there is something amazingly real about the sound of bullets slamming into my car's windshield on my home turf. I should be dead now if not for my paranoia.'

'How so?'

'I had bulletproof glass installed in my car.'

'Why? Were you afraid something like this might happen?'

'No,' I shrugged sheepishly. 'I saw a program about a carjacking in New York and...'

He looked at me suspiciously, probably thinking that installing bulletproof glass in one's car was self-incriminating. Why do it unless you're involved in drugs and guns?

'Look, Charlie, I know what you're thinking. But you're wrong. I'm not a crook. You must believe me.'

'Convince me,' he stated firmly.

'How... I don't know how. But I do know I need help and M tells me you can help. Look, you seem to be an ethical person. I get it. All the self-righteous accusations you keep tossing at me, misguided as they are, point to one thing and that is you don't like crooks. And although I personally don't appreciate your attitude towards me, I do like your drive. So, help me if you really are who I think you are. Prove it by helping me.'

'You wouldn't be bullshitting me?'

I couldn't help but laugh.

'Charlie,' M said in exasperation. 'The man is not lying to you. Get off your high horse for a minute and listen to him.'

'Charlie, I'm not bullshitting you.'

'Are you going to help or not?' M asked with an air of finality. I could tell she was at the end of her patience. Either Charlie was in or he was out.

He thought for a minute and finally replied, 'Well, it certainly is interesting. I guess you can count me in.'

'Are you in a position to help?' M asked. 'I mean, you aren't going to get in trouble over this, are you? I mean at the agency.'

'Because we don't want that,' I finished her thought.

'No. I've moved up the ladder at the CIA since I last saw you, Monica. I have the freedom to look into something like this if I choose. I'll start by doing a preliminary investigation; maybe talk to some folks at Interpol and the police in Hong Kong.'

'Good,' said M. 'I have the name of cop in Hong Kong.'

After searching through her purse, she found the business card of the police captain in charge of the robbery. Handing him the card effectively sealed our working relationship.

6:25 P.M. JOHN

Charlie finally left the building after we discussed a few avenues to investigate.

M quietly returned to her pile of papers on the conference table and I to having my telephone firmly attached to my ear; which was not necessarily a bad idea. It meant M had no opportunity to question me about anything.

When I finally put down my phone, I was drained, worn out from talking. However, more than anything else, concerns about the meeting with Charlie were still circulating through my brain. The meeting didn't feel particularly productive. I had been on the defensive for most of the discussion. Regardless, I sensed a preemptive strike was required to avoid another session of attorney/client interrogation from the lady lawyer who was sitting at the conference table. She looked ready to strike, to start asking questions as soon as she sensed I was free. I wasn't in the mood.

'I'm really tired,' I said with a sigh. 'How about taking a break from work? Want to join me for dinner?'

'I have work to do,' she replied, giving my offer no serious consideration.

'Must I remind you again? Dinner with me is within the terms of your employment contract?' I mentioned in jest.

'Demand all you want. It won't do you any good this time.'

'Okay, how about this? I need a break, M. And I would really like it if you'd have dinner with me.' I pleaded in as conciliatory a tone as I could muster.

She studied me for a moment. 'Alright,' she finally conceded.

'Thanks. I have two more calls to make and then I'll be ready.'

Having made up her mind to stay for dinner, she immediately ceased work, stood for a moment as if she was unsure what to do next. 'I think I'll find Arny,' she concluded. 'Where's that hidden door which leads to your apartment?'

I sighed, 'You're not supposed to know about that.'

'You're the one who showed it to me.'

'Oh yah, forgot.

'You have no secrets from me, John. I know everything.'

'Really?'

'Yes, Helen and I have been talking.'

A mild look of surprise crossed my face. 'Is that so? Maybe I should have a talk with Helen.'

'Oh, come on, John. She hasn't told me anything important. Just girl talk, you know,' she winked.

7:10 P.M. JOHN

Two phone calls turned into a half-hour of agitated international dialog.

When I was finally able to escape to my apartment, M and Arny were deep into telling stories. A couple of beers sat on the kitchen counter. Obviously, they were having a good time.

Outwardly, Arny was making dinner, but I suspected he was working M more than he was working the stove. I wasn't worried. Despite his apparent lack of attention to dinner, I knew his knack for cooking would result in a meal which tasted as good as any prepared by a master chef.

M quickly informed me she had asked Arny to stay and enjoy the meal with us. According to her, it was her idea. But my guess was, the idea had been planted in her brain by the master of manipulation, Mr. Arny. I knew how his mind worked and I knew his talents. However, I was not unhappy with the suggestion. I knew it would be very relaxing to sit back and listen to my friend Arny mesmerize Monica with his silver tongue. Along with his other talents, Arny was a terrific storyteller; many delightful tales from his days in minor league baseball. To hear him tell it, he never pitched anything but no-hitters. And when not pitching, he was hitting game-winning home runs.

A few years ago, I had a chance conversation with a knowledgeable baseball historian. He confirmed the truth in many of Arny's stories. Said Arny's problem wasn't talent, it was his skin color. It kept him in the minors too long. A career-ending knee injury destroyed forever any chance he might have had for fame and glory. The injury happened shortly before he was scheduled to move to the majors.

I never heard a bitter word from Arny about his bad luck. Instead, he seemed to enjoy his memories of life in the minors with great fondness. Perhaps he felt lucky to have what he had. After baseball, life for Arny was difficult. He was a black man with no formal education. Along with his bum knee went any hope of making big money. That didn't stop him. He worked odd jobs, associated with a variety of women, and enjoyed life as only he could. He was a well-known character in some quarters of Charlottesville. An easy gift of gab was his entry key.

M had fallen quickly under his spell.

The steaks Arny prepared for dinner were exceptionally good along with some beans and corn. I sipped a glass of wine while Arny and M ate ice cream for dessert.

Personally, I'm not much into desserts. Instead, I indulged in one of life's sweeter pleasures. And that was to quietly enjoy the presence of a beautiful woman. The line of her brow, the curve of her mouth, the fullness of her breasts under her sweater. Small details, but when observed at leisure they can be extremely sensual and a source of great pleasure and wonder.

I have often wondered how something as insignificant as the line of a woman's jaw can become a pure art form. Or what makes a woman so desirable in the first place? Is it physical beauty alone or is it the way a beautiful woman expresses herself? Is it her smile or the way she moves in self-assurance? Can it be how she runs her hand through her hair? Or is it her intelligence and her wit? I didn't know. I simply watched in subdued pleasure as she laughed and traded jokes with Arny.

'You're not saying much, boss,' Arny said, breaking my reverie.

'Don't need to,' I grinned. 'You do enough talking for three people.'

'You're just jealous,' he replied. 'Your life is boring compared to mine.'

'You're right, Arny. Maybe we should take M to one of your nightclub haunts and show her the real Charlottesville.'

'What is this 'we' business? I'll take her.'

'Of course, what was I thinking? You take her.'

'Not tonight, boss. I'm pretty tuckered out. Mind if I clean up the mess of dishes tomorrow?'

Perhaps Arny sensed it was time to retreat and leave us alone, but there was no need. I had been comfortable having him control the conversation.

I read somewhere: there are two types of people. One type is energized by being with people and the other type is drained by the experience. I am the second type. I enjoy being with people, but it's exhausting. After Arny left, M was my responsibility. I wasn't sure I was up to the task.

I was preparing to offer to take her home when she asked, 'What do you do most evenings after Arny leaves?'

'I work. Or I read or listen to music.'

'What kind of music do you like?'

'Just like music. I find almost any style of music can be enjoyable.'

'And your favorites?'

'How about you?'

'No, you first.'

'Okay, but I don't think music should be discussed. It should be heard.'

I went into the living room to search through my CD collection. After selecting a Leonard Cohen album, the mellow notes of his bass vocals filled the vaulted ceiling in the room, permitting the music to reach full volume without becoming harsh.

M settled into a leather couch which faced the windows overlooking the valley. Arny always placed some fresh firewood in the fireplace hearth. I lit a match to the kindling. Soon the warmth of the fire cast flickering shadows over the sparsely lit room. M looked comfortable like she belonged. Her black turtleneck framed her face, reflecting the warm colors of the fire's glow dancing off her shiny, dark red hair.

Music is one of life's wonders. Its abstract nature seems to communicate with us in ways words can never reach. Perhaps this is because life is far more intangible than we think; filled with vague, uncertainty; shapes and concepts in constant tension and release. Regardless of race or culture, humans never stray far from making or listening to music in all its expressive and infinite variations.

As we quietly listened to the CD with the fire's flickering shapes playing in our eyes, light from the homes down the hill reflected off a few gray-white luminescent clouds hovering in an otherwise black, star-filled sky.

'What kind of music do you like?' I asked her after the last deep notes from Leonard Cohen's voice had faded.

'Bocelli is one my favorites,' she said after thinking for a moment. 'Do you have any of his albums?'

Fortunately, my music library contained a few of the Italian tenor's albums. Soon his rich voice filled the room. I stood for a moment by the fire, listening to his music, wanting to touch her, to cross the physical and emotional barrier which separated us. Without thinking, I went behind the couch where she was sitting and began to lightly massage her shoulders; drawing in a sense of her body through my hands.

There was comfort in the act but also fear. I had wanted to be with her for some time. But I had always hesitated, afraid she would pull away and reject me. To my relief, she did not. She took my hand and held it to her shoulder for a moment. Then, letting go, she asked me to sit down beside her.

'No talk,' she instructed. 'Just listen.'

Music spread over us like a blanket as the sky subtly shifted in shades of gray. Placing her small slender hand inside mine, she rested beside me, enjoying the warmth of my body and the fire. Eventually, the music died away, but she didn't move away, just continued to sit beside me in comfortable silence as the fire played in our eyes.

'I'd like you to stay,' I said softly.

She didn't respond, just held my hand. After a few minutes, she stood up without speaking, without asking, and simply led me to my bedroom as if it were the most natural act in the world.

Releasing my hand, she rolled back the covers on my bed.

Soft light from the fire peeked around the corner of the bedroom door like a voyeur wishing to revel in the long beautiful lines of her body slowly emerging from beneath her clothes as she undressed. That winter night we lay naked together for endless moments of pure unassailable delight. We touched in slow anticipation, forcing nothing. I felt her body through my body, resting together, my foot caressing her foot, my hand touching her face softly exploring her closed eyes. I combed through her long red hair, brushing it from her face; resting in silence before again stirring to her small movements, feeling the curve of her smooth thigh, her gently flowing waist. She took my hand to hold her firm round breasts and then we rested again in a time caught between anxious dreams of longing. Times of unimaginable ecstasy until we made love.

And then I slept in a quiet place which was closer to peace than anything I had known for a long time.

NOVEMBER 8, FRIDAY, 8:05 A.M. JOHN

The smell of coffee woke me in the morning.

Unconsciously rolling over in bed, hoping to touch a warm body, wishing last night was more than a dream; my bed was empty, cold on the other side. Only the scent of her perfume lingered in the sheets testifying to the possibility of her reality. Suddenly, without notice, the jubilant cords of a Miles Davis horn reverberated through the apartment, offering clear evidence the lady in question was not gone.

I was a happy man.

Mornings are normally pragmatic for me. Exercise, eggs, or cereal, and I'm off, out of my apartment and through the concealed door in the bookcase to my office to work. The concept of a leisurely morning is not part of my makeup. But last night had left me feeling lethargic. Coffee smelled good. I decided to put on jeans and a shirt to look for her.

I found her in the dinette in my kitchen.

Like most of the rooms in my apartment, the dinette faced southwest. The sun rises on the other side of the building. The dinette is normally not bright in the morning with soft light reflecting off a stand of sheltering trees in gentle shadows. M was wearing an old University of Michigan sweatshirt with a big yellow M in the middle, she must have found in my closet.

I smiled. M is for Monica, how perfect.

A cup of hot coffee was in her hand and a newspaper lay open on a table. She looked content and at home.

'Good morning,' I greeted her with a kiss on her cheek. 'Are you quite comfortable, need anything?'

'I'm fine,' she replied with a smile.

I poured a cup of coffee while noticing her beautiful bare legs had somehow escaped from under the oversized sweatshirt. Even in the morning, even in simple attire, she was stunning. The gentle flow of her auburn hair around her face got lost in my imagination.

Sitting down on a chair beside her, I asked, 'Do you talk in the morning or should I leave you to enjoy your coffee and newspaper in peaceful solitude?'

'No, I talk. I was just waiting for you. Would you like me to fix you some breakfast or does Arny do that too?' she smiled.

'I don't see Arny until noon most days.'

'Hmm, breakfast then?'

'Okay, but just so this doesn't feel too domestic, let me do my part.'

She looked at me quizzically and asked, 'Are you afraid of domesticity?'

'No, let's just say... I'm content without it.'

A small frown crossed her face. Apparently, my attempt at morning humor had not gone over well.

'I make good scrambled eggs,' I volunteered, hoping to change the subject.

Working together in a small kitchen became somewhat hazardous. We tripped over each other, knocked elbows a few times. It was obvious neither of us was accustomed to sharing space. I didn't mind. Casually touching her while cooking was rather enjoyable.

'We need to talk,' she pronounced as I placed some scrambled eggs on her plate.

'Okay...What about?' An alarm bell was going off in my head, thinking a discussion of last night's amorous activities might get serious.

'About what you need to do,' she replied as I held my breath. 'From everything I've learned, your company has been seriously hurt by the so-called unrelated incidents.'

With a sigh I gave the choice of the kitchen conversation to her, slumping on a bar stool on the other side of the countertop. Nothing wonderful lasts forever. The pleasant memories of our carefree evening faded quickly while I listened helplessly to her describe my dire economic situation as she understood it.

The difficulties my company was facing; the problems which had been consigned to irrelevance in the amorous shadows of last evening; once again reared their head in harsh reality.

NEW YORK, NEW YORK, DECEMBER 2, MONDAY, 4:15 P.M. JOHN

The cushy, black leather seats in our chauffeured, luxury ride were comfortable in a way that was totally out of sync with the anxiety occupying my mind and body.

I stared out the limo's rain-splattered windows at the skyline of Manhattan as we drove across the Queensbury Bridge from La Guardia Airport with M quietly sitting beside me, wearing a gray suit under her black raincoat. She was dressed for upscale New York. I understood. Even though personally I don't like suits and wear them infrequently; certain places and occasions demand formal business attire; places like New York City. She looked good. I assumed the Big Apple would not be a problem for her. She must have become accustomed to city life while living and working in Washington, D.C.

Once on the island, the towering skyscrapers of Manhattan quickly encapsulated our ride and our progress stalled in an inevitable traffic jam. Horns blared. Pedestrians scurried down the sidewalks, attempting to avoid becoming drenched in the rain. New York City is an unnecessarily harried place by nature. I'm a Midwestern boy at heart. My roots are in small villages. I tolerate the confusion of big cities like New York and enjoy their attractions for short periods, but I am never completely comfortable on this small island inhabited by millions of aggressive humans. Money helps. Places like New York demand money. It isn't a luxury. It's a necessity. When in New York, I'm happy to be rich.

The last few weeks at the office had been a nightmare, continuously patching holes in leaky shipment schedules, trying to keep our clients reasonably happy. Daily visions of the Dutch boy averting catastrophe with his finger in a dyke danced through my brain. I felt like this boy most of the time.

Thanksgiving had come and gone without notice. I didn't bother to fly to my family's home in Grand Haven, Michigan for a visit. I had too much work to do. Everyone associated with the company was becoming anxious. Major decisions had been put off pending the next scheduled board meeting. This was the reason for our trip. We were in New York for the meeting. On the surface, it was a normal quarterly meeting of the board of directors, but it felt like much more. First, because it should have been held a month earlier, but due to our multilayered problems, it had been postponed. Now it was upon us. Members had flown in from all over the world.

I am the Chairman of the Board and CEO of the company. I own more stock than anyone else, but not a majority. I am a minority holder. The other minority stockholders are heads of key resource companies such as Vidu who owns the cutting facilities in Sri Lanka and Clarence, the CEO of an Australian mining company. They, along with the men like Arthur and Lin who manage our three distribution houses are permanent members.

Permanent members of the board also include investors who made the company possible. Not all of them are still with us. Some disappeared after taking a healthy return on their investment when the company offered to purchase their stock. Investors who choose to stay have a permanent chair at the table through their stock ownership.

Non-permanent members are appointed on a rotated basis. They are members of the board for one-year appointments. These include the CEOs of mining companies who supply our business with gemstones. Not every company is represented at any given time. The board would become too big and cumbersome if we tried to include everyone.

Democratic rule governs all decisions of the board. Most decisions are unanimous, but if there is a dispute among the members; it is the permanent members who effectively take control of the board. And that's fine with me. Without their help and cooperation, there would be no company.

Slowly, painfully, we progressed towards our hotel; the chauffeured vehicle alternately stopping and starting, moving to the rhythm of an erratic New York traffic dance. A dull gray winter sky contributed to my growing sense of unease. Not since the early days of the company had I come to a board meeting with such a great sense of uncertainty. For the last six-plus years when the company was growing on a solid pattern of success, the board meetings were fun. Now, however, everything felt different. But then, I always knew the good times couldn't last forever. I just never anticipated that everything would change so abruptly and violently with such overwhelmingly negative consequences.

I reached over and touched M's hand. She intertwined her fingers in mine as she gazed intently at the bustling people on the sidewalks and the lofty buildings of the city. It was late afternoon. The meeting was not until tomorrow morning. I always arrived a day early, giving me time to mentally prepare without having to worry about travel delays.

Finally, the maze of moving vehicles which had entrapped us released its grip and we weaved our way across town to the entrance of the Plaza Hotel. Porters quickly ran down the steps. One opened a car door while holding an umbrella. M slid easily out of the backseat as if she came here every day. With poise, she stood straight and tall under the umbrella before walking up the steps toward the Hotel's brass-handled glass doors. A porter followed, holding an umbrella over her head. She seemed not to notice.

I lagged behind with a second porter, directing him to take our suitcases from the trunk, acting more like her butler than her boss.

'Good evening, Mr. Van Laan,' a desk clerk personally welcomed me once I was inside the lobby. 'Your suite is ready.'

'Thank you,' I acknowledged, signing in.

The expansive lobby inside the Plaza sparkled brightly in contrast to the dull gray day outside its gleaming windows. Each time I enter this hotel, I remember the first time I was here, the day I was asked to leave. I was a vagabond student in faded jeans with a dirty backpack draped over a worn jacket at the time. I had been exploring a city I had never seen before and needed a bathroom. I assumed they had one in the Plaza, but apparently, the uniformed staff of the Plaza Hotel didn't think I was the right sort. They politely asked me to leave. It was a humbling experience that made my subsequent visits to the Plaza bittersweet.

M waited patiently with our bags as I completed check-in. A porter stood by ready to help.

In retrospect, it was no wonder they threw me out back then. My dirty clothes hardly fit with the polished brass, gleaming marble floors, and cushioned furniture of the Plaza. The rich and famous lounge here in quiet, unhurried luxury. I have often wondered if their demeanor is an act. Or is it true, having money all your life makes you content? Or does one simply pretend to be relaxed when they are rich because it is expected?

I am new rich, so I didn't know. But I do know I can walk in now without worrying that the hotel staff will throw me out. However, the truth is... deep inside, I'm not really much different than that traveling Midwestern college student who had been curious. Some days I wish I could go back to being him again.

Our suite was spacious and elegantly decorated in what I call early American, overstuffed overkill. Too many patterns on the wallpaper, on the furniture, on everything. Just too much visual clutter for my taste.

Our relationship, M and me, had progressed since our first amorous evening together. Although... we didn't talk about it, didn't have time. We worked together during the day and she returned to her apartment in the evening. That is, most evenings she went home. Some nights she stayed with me.

So, it seemed to be no big deal on the surface to ask her if she would like to accompany me to New York for the board meeting. I told her it was her decision. I wasn't going to require her presence. I would not invoke the clause in her contract which obligated her to go.

Gratefully, she said yes.

Probably because she thought I needed her. And she was right. In a way I did. Or perhaps she was just curious. I didn't know. But for whatever reason, she agreed. And it was her idea to stay with me in my hotel room even though I initially suggested getting her a separate room. She had insisted, said a separate room was an unnecessary expense. I didn't argue the point.

'I'm meeting Lin, Bob, and Arthur for dinner at my Club,' I explained as I unpacked my suitcase. 'It's a working dinner, but why don't you come with me before dinner and have a drink at the bar?'

'Okay,' she answered, sounding subdued.

'You all right?'

'A bit overwhelmed,' she replied tersely as she brushed her hair. 'This is just too much. You know, New York, the Plaza, your Club.'

We had agreed to elevate her status to a legal advisor for the board meeting. This way she could attend the meetings. As a result, she had spent considerable time reading everything she could find on board protocol and fiduciary board responsibility. In addition, she researched the background of the members of the board. I attempted to help by filling in the gaps in her research when I had the time. But even for a quick study like her, this was a tall task. It had taken me years of working in the business to learn what she was trying to absorb in several days. I sensed she was exhausted. Perhaps we had pushed too hard.

I stopped unpacking for a moment and sat on the bed. 'You look tired. Maybe you should stay here and get some rest.'

'Oh, no. I want to see this famous club of yours.'

'You sure?'

'I'll be alright. It's just... you know I want to help, John. And I know I can. But well... coming here, this place, facing the reality of it all...well...it's a lot to take in.'

'Do you want to return to Charlottesville? You don't really need to be here.'

'No,' she said emphatically. 'I'm not a quitter.'

'Okay, then let's look at this realistically. You don't need to do anything at the meeting other than answer a few legal questions if asked.'

'I can do that.'

'Frankly, they're all going to be so stunned by your beauty. They'll be too awe-struck to ask you anything critical,' I teased, half-smiling.

'Stop. I hate that. That's not why I'm here.'

I tried not to laugh, knowing how sensitive she was about the brains versus beauty issue. 'Okay, look. Don't get uptight. Just observe, that's all I ask. Be my eyes at the meeting tomorrow. It's difficult for me to observe everything which is going on; especially when it's my responsibility to chair the meeting. I can use a second set of eyes in the room. Watch what other members are doing. Be aware of the small gestures, whispers, eye signals; little actions which can sometimes say more than words.'

She nodded, and I knew by the look of determination in her eyes, she was up to the task.

6:35 P.M. JOHN

We didn't need to take a cab to the Club.

Rain had stopped and it was only a few blocks. We could walk from the Plaza.

Before leaving our hotel room, I told M the Club had been originally built by a wealthy New York banker. In many ways, it resembled Arthur's hallowed club in London, just not as old. Loaded with luxury and tradition, the place was rumored to have originally been a haven for the rich banker and his buddies; drinking, playing cards; males only, no wives.

I'm not a member, but I'm allowed the use the Club because it is affiliated with a club in Hong Kong of which I am a member. Lin secured that membership for me as a great favor. I exercise my reciprocal privileges at the Club in New York more often than I use the one in Hong Kong.

A courtyard off the street in front of the Club's building was originally a circular drive designed for horse-drawn carriages. A black wrought iron fence now closes this area to traffic. It's only accessible through a walking path from the sidewalk leading to a small flight of stairs where very ordinary-looking doors open into a wood-paneled hallway manned by an employee who politely greets visitors. Only those entitled to be here are permitted entrance to its hallowed premises.

The main lobby is a special place, showcased by a marble staircase rising three stories. I said nothing to M after we entered, just let her take her time looking around. Ornate furnishings included gold-engraved picture frames holding paintings portrayed fox-hunting outings replete with red-coated horsemen and packs of barking hounds. By modern standards, the lighting was subdued which only seemed to enhance its ambiance. A few overstuffed chairs furnished the lobby. Although rich in luxury, the interior always looked slightly worn to me, in need of minor repair. However, redecorating was apparently not a priority at the

Club. Tradition was a far more important fixture. The Club's rich history as evidenced by its interior decor has passed from previous generations to the present and was not to be pushed aside for the sake of gaudy newness.

I pointed M towards a bar on the other side of the lobby. Garish, dark red, flocked wallpaper greeted us when we entered the hallowed grounds of this watering hole. The bar's ceiling was twelve to eighteen feet high in the shape of a concave semicircle, painted with a muted mural of little angel figures flying over a classical country scene. Although not exactly the Sistine Chapel, the bar had a distinctly Italian flare. Waiters in pressed white coats stood at its carved-wood oak bar, ready to serve drinks.

I like this place. It's a step back into history, a place to rest from the modern-day New York turmoil which exists only a few feet outside the club's hallowed, stone walls.

During winter months, a fire burns in its carved marble fireplace, casting a warm glow over the room. In years past, real wood was used, burning and crackling, providing heat to the spacious room. Now an antiseptic gas-fired, wrought iron sculpture has replaced natural elements.

Bob, Lin, and Arthur were sitting in overstuffed armchairs at a table near the fireplace.

'Excuse us,' I said as they rose in unison to greet M. All but Lin that is; who stood quietly to one side, looking amused. After introducing M to Bob who had not previously met her, I said I would be taking a few minutes to show her the Club.

Arthur suggested, perhaps she would like a drink first.

M smiled. 'No, no. I'll just be in your way.'

He looked just a little disappointed.

'Carry on gentlemen. I'll be back in a few minutes.'

After climbing the staircase in the lobby to the second floor, we entered a large conference room that had been reserved for our board meeting the next day. I explained the Club would handle all the arrangements, including serving us lunch. Extra security had been ordered. In addition, I had hired a personal bodyguard assigned to her while she was in New York. The man was now downstairs in the lobby, waiting to return her to our hotel. She was not too thrilled with this arrangement, but when I reminded her that the bodyguard was a precondition to her coming to New York; she reluctantly agreed.

Once our tour was complete, Monica headed toward the exit. I watched as her bodyguard picked up his pace in an effort to keep up with her as she crossed the stone floor lobby towards the exit door in a rush.

I chuckled. The woman could be stubborn.

7:05 P.M. JOHN

Returning to the bar, I ordered a drink after dropping into one of the cushy armchairs which surrounded the table occupied by my partners and allowed myself the luxury of enjoying the atmosphere, of being swept back to a time when problems were less complicated and the world outside these walls was not burdened by a highly condensed mass of exasperated humans.

My partners were deep into a brisk conversation about politics at the time. I listened in silence, not really interested in joining the discussion. They were all very intelligent and clever. When they had an occasion to be together; they liked to challenge each other to games of verbal gymnastics. Even though they all spoke the same language and used the same vocabulary; if you listened carefully, you could distinguish their diverse cultures in their words.

'Well John, you've had a few sips of your drink,' Bob Anderson interrupted my reverie. 'Are you sufficiently relaxed now? Can we talk business?'

'I think so,' I said. 'That's why we're here, isn't it?'

'We're a bit concerned about you, John,' Arthur quickly interjected without further pleasantries. 'You have been through a good deal of strain lately.'

'If you're referring to being shot at and nearly burned to death, then yes... I guess you could say that,' I replied.

'We don't question your ability, John, but traumatic experiences can take a toll,' Bob continued. 'Arthur suggested you might want to consider having someone else chair the meeting tomorrow, you know, take some pressure off you.'

The notion I needed to be relieved of my chairman's duty came as a complete surprise. In previous conversations, none of my partners had hinted at the possibility of my not chairing the meeting. However, trying not to overthink the matter or give it too much credence, I briefly considered giving in, thinking they were honestly concerned about me and meant no harm.

Or...

A wayward notion quickly passed through my brain in combination with my shit detector going off. I didn't really want to consider the possibility, but couldn't help it. Was this the beginning of a power play for control of my company. An involuntary shudder ran down my back as the possibility hit me like an ice-cold shower. I didn't think anyone saw it, but inwardly I cringed at the thought.

It was time to take a deep breath. Step back and think realistically. I had no real reason to think they wanted my job. When something like this normally happens in a corporation, it is generally for reasons of neglect of duty or outright misdeeds.

And surely, they knew none of GI's current problems were my fault.

'I'm fine,' I replied firmly. 'It's been difficult, but don't worry about me.'

'John, you know we have every confidence in you,' Arthur stated. 'But tomorrow's meeting is likely to be difficult. So perhaps...'

'I'll be ready, Arthur,' I abruptly cut him off, now becoming slightly annoyed. 'Can we move on to another subject?'

An awkward moment of silence followed.

'Any news?' Arthur finally asked.

'Nothing,' I replied. 'I had hoped the police would have discovered something by this time.'

'The board is not in an overly cheerful mood,' Arthur remarked, glancing at the others. 'They've been talking to us, John.'

Bob and Lin were oddly silent, allowing Arthur to take the lead in discussing whatever was really on their minds. I searched their faces for a clue, wondering who they had been talking to.

'Are you implying they are not talking to me?' I asked.

'No, no,' Lin protested. 'That's not what Arthur meant.'

'It's just... everything had been going so well. And now,' Bob interjected apologetically. 'Everyone is upset and ...'

'I'm upset too,' I cut him off. 'I want this to end as much as anyone.'

'That's the problem,' Arthur interjected. 'After the news of your attack last week, it suddenly occurred to everyone how dependent the company is on one man, on you.'

I took a long sip of whiskey. This conversation was like being drowned in warm water. The water was comfortable, but I felt like I was dying.

'Let's get something straight,' I said. 'I have no intentions of dying anytime soon.' When no one responded, I continued. 'I believe it is vitally important we present a unified front tomorrow, gentlemen. If the question of my succession is mentioned, we should say we will deal with it after this crisis has passed. And just for the record between us friends, I'm not opposed to accepting a smaller role in the company in the future. It has been a long, hard six years, and I wouldn't mind slowing down. But not now, not in the middle of a crisis. Right now, the company needs firm leadership.'

Silence.

'Very good,' Lin finally concluded, seemingly relieved this conversation had reached an end.

'I agree,' Bob concurred.

'Good, good,' Arthur flippantly remarked.

'One last item,' Bob interjected. 'This Monica, your new secretary. I see from the board packet she's taking on a larger role than expected.'

'Don't be sensitive about this old chap,' Arthur remarked. 'I personally have had the pleasure of getting to know her. And she is positively delightful, but...'

'But are we to understand she will be at the meeting tomorrow in some sort of official capacity?' Bob finished Arthur's statement with a question.

They had me and I knew it. My relationship with M looked irresponsible on the surface. I could easily be accused of thinking with my penis and not my brain.

Bob continued, 'John, we've always been tolerant of your lifestyle, mostly because it never interfered with the company before, but this is different.'

'We're asking if it's wise to bring your girlfriend to a board meeting in the middle of a crisis.' Arthur finished their presentation. 'We don't question your judgment, John. But the timing may not give the board the right impression.'

I took a deep breath. Lin had added nothing to this last exchange. I wondered what he was thinking. I looked at him and asked, 'Perception is reality. Right, Lin?'

'Yes,' Lin responded without further comment.

'Okay, guys. I will admit, on the surface you are right. And I'm not going to deny having a relationship with Monica. But ... and I'm asking you to take my word on this, she is far more than meets the eye. Let me give you some of her background.' I explained Monica's education, her previous job experience, and the fact she had contacts in Washington. Although, I didn't mention Charlie by name because he had asked me to keep his involvement confidential.

'So how did someone this smart get through your pre-employment screening?' Bob laughed.

'Every system has its flaws, Bob,' I smiled.

Bob laughed.

I looked at Arthur.

'Well, old chap,' he said reluctantly. 'If you're sure you want her there, John. It's up to you, but it might be a tough road at the board meeting tomorrow. And having someone new like her at the meeting may not send the right sort of signal.'

'That's why I invited her, Arthur. Don't you understand? She's new. She comes into the room with no prejudices. I want her opinion.'

'What do you mean?' Arthur asked, almost in alarm.

'Look at the situation gentlemen,' I explained. 'If it is true someone wants to take this company down, it's just possible the source of our problems could be inside? Too much has happened pointing to an inside source. Maybe, just maybe, someone on our board is part of a conspiracy.'

They looked stunned. I guessed they hadn't considered this possibility.

'Aren't you jumping to conclusions?' Bob said. 'Conspiracy, traitors, all sounds melodramatic to me.'

'Maybe, Bob, but in the absence of proof, we can't rule out the possibility.'

'Don't you think that's a trifle extreme, John?' Arthur retorted. 'I hope you don't plan to introduce your theory to the board.'

'No, Arthur,' I said dryly. 'But thanks for your advice.'

'Do you really think a conspiracy is possible?' asked Arthur.

'Don't you?'

'I suppose it's possible, but without proof, it is just a theory.'

'I think it's more than theory,' I responded angrily.

'Do you have proof?' Arthur forced me to be defensive.

'No, I don't.'

They sat in silence for a moment until Lin interjected. 'We should not dismiss the possibility.' Asian culture is filled with ancient conspiracies. I knew Lin would not discount the possibility. Bob, on the other hand, was an American. He was an individual. He would not accept anything until it was proven beyond a reasonable doubt. And Arthur, well, he was a Brit and

Brits always seemed to be hiding a wayward plot or two in their closet.

'Well, okay for now,' said Bob. 'But let's just keep this to ourselves until we have hard evidence. In the meantime, we were discussing Miss Sorenson when we started this discussion. My opinion, for what it's worth... if you think she has a role to play, then let her stay.'

'I agree,' Lin supported Bob much to my surprise.

Old Arthur wasn't quite so ready to give in. 'Personally, I'm not overjoyed about inviting your consort to the meeting. But it's still your board, John,' he added.

7:40 P.M. JOHN

The night air had turned bitter cold with a damp drizzle mirroring my mood.

Under stark streetlights, a chilled wind whipped across the shimmering black pavement as I waited impatiently for a stoplight at an intersection. The icy sting of cold rain hit the exposed skin of my face as I walked across the wide intersection when the light finally turned green, heading to the Plaza at a brisk pace.

I had begged off dinner with my partners. Our pre-dinner conversation put me in a bad mood, my appetite was gone. After Arthur's last comment, I told the guys I was tired. I wouldn't be dining with them tonight. They looked surprised, but I didn't give them an opportunity to change my mind. I simply got up from the table and walked away. My sudden exit probably wasn't the most intelligent move under the circumstances, but I didn't care. I'd had enough of their nonsense for one night.

Hitting the up button in the lobby of the Plaza Hotel, the elevator door slid open. Like all elevators, it operated a small, uncomfortable room filled with strangers forced into a confining space for a brief nervous time, hoping to avoid conversation. I don't like hotel elevators. The stifling interior traps me. I'm always anxious to get out of them. I also don't like the long halls in hotels any more than I like their elevators. The halls are narrow, empty traffic lanes devoid of life, lined with closed doors, which are uninviting examples of exclusion. Comfort and rest may reside behind all these silent portals, rife with emptiness but only if you have a key.

Ignoring my discomfort for a moment, I headed down the hall, daydreaming about what might be happening inside the rooms on the other side of all the shiny doors, all in an effort to take my mind off the conversation I had at the bar. The discussion with my partners had been disturbing. I was looking forward to greeting the lovely redhead who was behind one of these doors.

'Hi,' a surprised expression covered her face when I entered our suite.

She was sitting on an upholstered couch, wrapped in a soft white terrycloth robe furnished by the Plaza. A book was in her hand, and a half-finished room service dinner tray sat next to her on a table. M looked warm, happy, and well-fed. I, on the other hand, was dripping wet, cold, and miserable.

'You're back early,' she commented.

'I decided not to stay for dinner.' I peeled off my damp coat.

'Anything wrong?' her brow furrowed slightly.

'No,' I lied, turning around so that I did not face her. 'I'm going to change...'

I hurried into the bedroom before she could ask any more questions and quickly removed the Club's required dress code of a sports coat and tie. Changing into a pair of comfortable jeans and a sweater helped me relax. Poking my head into the sitting room of our suite, I asked M if she would please order a room service dinner for me. She opened her mouth to ask what I wanted, prompting a dismissive wave of the hand. Anything, I didn't care.

The bathroom was elegantly furnished with more wrapped soaps and plastic shampoo bottles than anyone could ever use in a day.   Fresh, white, fluffy towels were hung everywhere. I splashed my face with soap and water hoping to complete a transformation which would put the conversation at the bar behind me.

M was still sitting curled up on a couch when I reentered the sitting room. Beautiful bare legs peeked deliciously from under her flowing white robe. Her hair was damp and combed back like she had recently taken a bath. No makeup, and still, she looked magnificent. I was glad to have returned to our hotel. Dinner with her was a far more enticing choice than spending time with my brooding partners.

'You look comfortable?' I commented. 'Good book?'

'Jim Harrison,' she replied. 'I picked it out of your library before we left. Do you like his writing?'

'One of my favorite authors,' I nodded. 'Which book are you reading?'

'*Dalva.*'

'Good choice.'

'Want to talk about what happened?' she closed her book. 'You don't look too happy.'

'No questions, please.' I knelt down on my knees in front of her and slowly moved my hands up her bare thighs under her robe.

She took my hands and held them tightly, bending over to kiss the top of my head. 'Stop now. You'll spoil my surprise. I'm not quite ready for you.'

'I'm ready. What's your surprise?'

'Not now. I think we need to talk first. What happened at your Club?'

I sighed.

She was a very perceptive lady and could be incredibly persistent when she wanted something. That much I had learned. I retreated to an armchair and told her about my conversation at the bar. Room service arrived with my dinner as we talked. She had ordered salmon, asparagus green and crisp. The meal looked appetizing. I began to eat because I thought I was hungry, but somewhere in the middle of telling M about the conversation with my partners, I lost my appetite again. Placing a polished silver cover over the uneaten food, I pushed the tray away. Getting up, I went over to the room service bar, thinking a glass of whiskey might settle my nerves. After pouring some calming liquid into a clear glass, I took a sip while crossing the room to a window.

Across the sparsely lit void of Central Park, the lights of New York sparkled in the night, each light a room, each room a living space in a tall building. Few sights can compare to New York at night. A vista of towering buildings adorned with a myriad of indiscriminate lights. I wondered how many other lost souls were looking out their windows at this moment, marveling at the sight, just like me.

'Do you really think they're planning something?' M asked, pulling me mentally back inside.

'No, I don't think so.' I sat down beside her.

'But you don't feel good about what they said, do you?'

'No, I don't.'

We were both silent, my mind rushing like a wind through countless conflicting emotions.

'It may appear to you I never lost anything in my life,' I confessed. 'All you have seen of my life is success. And I have been blessed. That is true. But that's now. It hasn't always been true. I have lost more battles than I have won. And I know how it feels to lose. And I know how it begins.'

M looked at me inquisitively. 'But these men are your friends. You've said so yourself.'

'Yes, they are my friends. But money and power are very strong motivators. Understand, I control a company and with control comes privileges. Maybe they want what I have. Maybe they want control. Maybe they see an opening, a weakness, an opportunity to take my job.'

M just looked at me silently.

'They'll rationalize it somehow,' I rambled on. 'They'll say he did his best, but it's time for someone else to take over. Or... he's not tough enough. He's not smart enough. If we don't take over, all will be lost. We'll do him a favor. Save the company for him. That's what they'll say. But in the end, it will be nothing more than justification for taking something which doesn't belong to them.'

'Do you really believe they are plotting against you?'

'I don't know what to believe.' I shook my head.

M sat with her legs tucked under her in one corner of a couch, silent for the moment; her oversized terrycloth robe draped over her like a blanket. I reached over to touch her bare foot, absentmindedly stroking her toes.

'Let's talk about something else. You, for instance. You looked tired earlier at the Club,' I said.

'I'm fine. I just wish I could do something to help you.'

'By the way, they also objected to your sitting with the board tomorrow,' I added, changing the subject.

'Why?'

'They said the other directors might find you a distraction.'

'That's what they said?'

'No, that's my thought.' I laughed. 'And it's fine as far as I'm concerned. Your beauty will take their collective minds off the problems of the company.'

'Thanks a lot. You're telling me I'm nothing more than window dressing.'

I smiled. 'We both know you are so much more.'

'What did they really say?' she asked indignantly.

'They said bringing my girlfriend to an important board meeting might indicate a lack of judgment on my part.'

She considered this possibility for a moment. 'That's plausible. Perhaps I shouldn't go.'

'No! You're going,' I said with more vehemence than I thought I had in me. Realizing I was sounding angry, I reached over and took her hand. 'Sorry, M. I didn't mean to sound upset.'

'It's okay, John,' she said softly. 'I understand. But it might be better if I didn't go.'

'Please don't fight me on this,' I half begged her.

'I'm not fighting you, John. I'm only trying to be logical. I don't want to do anything to hurt you.'

'You won't. I won't let that happen. And let me be clear. I want you at the meeting. I want your eyes in the room. Now more than ever.'

'Okay,' she gave in after a minute. 'If you want me to go, I'll go.'

'Thanks.' I was feeling more frustrated than I intended. The last thing I wanted was an argument with her. It just happened. Standing, I went over to look out the windows again to calm down.

She came behind me, wrapped her arms around my waist, leaning her head on my back. The feel of her warm body against me was comforting, relaxing. A half-moon momentarily emerged from the edges of a racing storm cloud. The rain had passed and clouds in the sky were being swept clean by a strong wind. Moonlight spread a fleeting halo of soft light through one of the clouds, glowing in brilliance against a clear black sky.

Saying nothing before moving around to stand in front with her back to me. Taking my hand, she slid it inside the warmth of her robe to touch the smooth curve of her bare hip, then gently up her belly to cup a full round breast. Opening her robe, she let it slip off her shoulders to the floor. Turning around, she slowly began to undress me, her hands brushing over my body as she carefully removed each article of clothing. I marveled at the beauty of her shadowed body in the moonlight.

In a way I could not comprehend, her image entered my poor, disturbed soul and brought comfort as only she could.

11:40 P.M. JOHN

To me, nothing is more beautiful than the face of a sleeping woman, her eyes closed in the faint light of night, her flowing hair falling carelessly across a pillow.

After we made love, I lay awake for some time, sleep elusive. The joy she brought me for a short time had passed, replaced by a dread mood of failure polluting musty corners of my mind. The scene at the bar kept replaying in my head. I wanted to believe it was nothing more than the result of the frustration we all felt from the horrible events the company had recently endured. But as I lay between sleep and consciousness with my eyes closed, I couldn't stop mulling over our conversation. And I couldn't help but wonder if they really were trying to steal my job.

The memory of last time I had been fired returned like a bad dream. I groaned inside thinking about it, wondering if that memory would ever leave me alone. Or would it always appear at times like this from somewhere deep in my skull. In my sleepless nightmare, I again saw the CEO of Anderson and Jones Advertising Agency arrive solemnly in my office followed by the CFO.

'May we have a word with you?' the CFO spoke politely.

Apparently, he had been assigned the task of firing me. The CEO came with him only as an impartial observer.

'Sure,' I replied. 'Why don't you take a seat.'

I never liked the CFO. He talked too much, always assuming he knew everything. He was a tax expert, full of book knowledge, but totally lacking in common sense. Despite his flaws and for reasons I never completely understood, the CEO liked him. Probably because the CFO didn't mind doing his dirty work, such as firing employees, the ugly deeds which the CEO didn't have the guts to do himself.

'Sorry,' the CFO began. 'We really didn't want it to come to this, but it has been decided. We must ask for your resignation.'

His words hit me hard; I had not been expecting them. 'Why?'

Opening my eyes, the dark walls of the Plaza Hotel bedroom did nothing to stop the haunting memories of being fired from roaming freely through my weary brain. I tried concentrating on something far more enjoyable, such as M, her body, her smile, her eyes. And just to be sure she was real, I reached over to touch her thigh softly under the bedcovers. Everything was fine, I told myself. But that did stop the memories from that day, the day I was fired, that didn't stop them from reappearing in my troubled thoughts as I lay half-awake, badly wanting to sleep.

'Why?' I had asked.

The CFO responded dryly, 'Isn't it obvious?'

I knew the company had lost several big clients, mine included. Rumors had been circulating for days. I had talked to some of my fellow employees in accounting. I knew what was happening. I had made it my business because I assumed it might come to this.

'No, it's not obvious to me,' I replied, even though I knew it would be fruitless to attempt to change their minds. 'I know we have recently lost some clients,' I argued. 'But in my opinion, this company needs all of us working and pulling together. I can bring in new clients. I know I can. Give me a chance,' I responded because I had to try; I couldn't go down without a fight.

'That may be true. But in our opinion, we need people with more education,' the CFO countered. 'You understand? If the company is to grow, it needs credibility.'

I couldn't argue with him. I was a small-town guy from the Midwest with an undergraduate degree in marketing from a local liberal arts college. I was just a hardworking fellow trying to climb the ladder to success using determination and guts. What he said was true. I didn't have much in the way of academic credentials.

'Let me state for the record I think you're wrong,' I argued, 'I can do this job better than anyone.'

'We're very sorry. Our decision has been made.'

I was done.

The agony following my firing was the worst part. It was like slowly dying. If your life is your job, if you wake every morning thinking about your work, spending countless hours at your job, if your office is your home and money defines who you are, then being fired is like being executed. Your home, your activities, the clothes you wear, the people you associate with; everything changes after you lose your job. You are alive, but the life you knew, the life you dreamed of, everything is gone.

You die inside when this happens.

My mother had always chastised me when I wasn't doing well in school. She told me I was going to grow up to be a ditch digger if I didn't improve my grades. After being fired, I remembered her words and I had the feeling she might be right.

TUESDAY, DECEMBER 3, 8:25 A.M. MONICA

It was time to go.

She knew she should be excited, but the only emotion she felt was pure dread.

All her preparation, her hard work, her research into every nook and cranny of John's company was not enough, not nearly enough. And then came John's story about what happened, which made him skip dinner with his colleagues. After that news, her feelings of insecurity only got worse. A sense of being utterly overwhelmed swept up from somewhere deep inside her.

She was a small-town girl from Ohio. Sure, she was smart, she was pretty, but this was New York. This was the board meeting of a very important company. Men had come from all over the globe to attend this meeting. This was the big time. She had never attended a meeting like this before.

She looked at herself in the bathroom mirror, checked her makeup one more time. Truth was, she didn't want to go. More than anything, she did not want to go. She did not think she belonged across the street in that elegant boardroom, in that fabled club with all its luxurious fixtures. She was afraid she would do something that might hurt John. He had enough problems. He didn't need his inexperienced girlfriend doing something wrong.

Not at this meeting anyway. This one was important, too important.

When she came out of the bathroom, his briefcase was in his hand.

'John,' she began. 'Perhaps it would be better if I didn't go today.'

'No,' he responded firmly. 'I want you there. Now get your coat. I don't want to be late.'

8:45 A.M. JOHN

Neatly arranged trays of bagels had been placed next to muffins and rolls on a spotless white tablecloth covering a long table located against a wall in the boardroom. Tall silver coffee dispensers steamed next to the food. Pitchers filled with orange and grapefruit juice were available next to an assortment of the Club's heavy ornate silverware, small clear glasses, China white coffee cups, and folded cloth napkins.

Board members milled around the table dressed in suits and ties, sampling the food and drink. Unenthusiastic conversation typical of early mornings roamed throughout the room; nothing special spoken, no great concerns expressed, no crisis discussed. Just the usual, how are you? Good to see you again, a handshake, a smile. The difficult business of the company was slated for later.

A polished wood conference table sat in the center of the room. Dark brown upholstered leather armchairs were equally spaced around the table. A presentation folder containing an assortment of company literature, including current financial data, mine output reports, distribution schedules, and sales figures for the last quarter, was placed on the table for each participant. Reprints of the company's recent advertising campaign were also included, along with a DVD disk featuring a TV ad.

The room was the largest boardroom available at the Club. Its vaulted ceiling gave it a feeling of spacious grandeur. Beyond curtained windows, the towering trees of Central Park were visible across the street. Several chairs had been placed against an inside wall for those attendees who were not board members, visitors who were allowed at the meetings but only after having received an invitation cleared through my office. These normally included executives from our advertising, accounting, and law firms, jewelry manufacturers, retailers, people connected to our company in one way or another. Today's meeting included very few invitees because I didn't want to discuss the company's current problems in front of a large audience. As it turned out, this was a good decision.

Seeing Vidu as I entered the room with Monica made me recall a conversation I had with him several years ago. He, as much as anyone, had taught me to appreciate the gemstone business. On more than one occasion he had taken time to explain the history of colored stones. It was during one of these early conversations when it first occurred to me that certain changes were necessary if the industry was to grow. That was when I suggested to Vidu that the only way to effectively change the culture of the colored stone business was to gain control of a majority of the world's supply. This conversation, more than anything, was the reason why all these people were gathered together in this room.

'Vidu, how are you, my friend?' I shook his hand. 'Did you have a good trip?'

'It was a long and difficult flight, John,' Vidu responded with a tired smile.

'May I introduce Monica to you? You didn't get an opportunity to meet her in London.'

'Ah, it is surely a great pleasure to finally meet you. The rumors of your beauty were not exaggerated.'

'Thank you,' M responded demurely.

'I would like to talk with you privately before you leave town,' I said to him.

'Yes, it would be good for us to talk.'

'Thanks. I'll give you a call after the meeting.'

He nodded.

Board members and visitors filed in. I introduced M to most of them, clarifying her purpose at the meeting. She was my legal advisor, I explained, hoping this would ease her discomfort. A hum of quiet conversation grew in the room as board members slowly arrived, mingling with the others, drinking coffee and eating rolls from the continental breakfast table. I was in no hurry to begin the meeting. I took my time, poured a cup of coffee, and selected an oat bran muffin from the table. It was not my custom to adhere to a tightly wound schedule. I purposely waited to begin until after everyone had the opportunity to become reacquainted with their fellow board members through casual conversation. When I was satisfied the board was comfortable, I made my way to the head of the conference table.

Two visitors were at the meeting. Manuel Ortega was from Colombia and represented emerald mining in his country. Henry Mudantoo was the other invitee. He was the current supervisor of the Sandawana emerald mine in Zimbabwe. These two gentlemen had been invited because Gemstone International's future plans included buying and selling emeralds. It was our hope that inviting these gentlemen would help them become comfortable with our methods of operation. Perhaps, allowing us to one day market their stones. It seemed a good idea when their invitations were offered, but given our current situation, I wasn't so sure now. However, asking them to leave was not an option at this late date.

Non-permanent members of the board included Vidu's brother, along with a representative from a Russian sapphire mine and the CFO of the Nullamana Mining Company of Australia. Mining interests in countries such as India, Madagascar, and Zambia were also represented.

I sipped my coffee and patiently waited, standing at the head of the table for the board members to assume their seats. M was sitting in one of the chairs against the wall reserved for visitors. I had suggested she sit with the board, but she must have felt more comfortable away from the main table.

Eventually, everyone noticed I was waiting for their attention, and they slowly found their respective seats. The meeting was called to order with a few opening remarks. I welcomed our visitors and thanked everyone for coming. The agenda began with a recitation of normal business information supplied in their board packet, such as the financial condition of the company, which I briefly presented. Losses we had suffered in recent months due to our problems were indicated by negative numbers. I made no attempt to hide bad news from the board. Each loss was duly noted with a footnote at the bottom of the page detailing the cause of the problem. I finished by saying our profits were still reasonably healthy for the current fiscal year. Not as good as hoped, but we were in the black.

It was then time for representatives from various mines around the world to present cautious projections of future production. In his report, Robert Stevens, CFO at Nullamana, reported it would be several months before his lab was rebuilt and fully functional. I noted that the delay would not affect the company's purchase of rough stones from mines. We would continue as before without interruption. We did not wish the company's problems to cause economic hardship for the miners. Even though I knew this would adversely affect our own bottom line, it needed to be done. The long-term consequences of cutting off our loyal miners would surely sink our company. We had no choice in this matter. It was essential for our survival. If we lost the confidence of our miners, we lost everything.

Before long, lunch was served in a different room down the hall. I finished my food quickly, taking little notice of what I was eating. Standing to stretch my legs, I decided to return to the board room. Glancing out a window at the wooded expanses of Central Park across the street, a fleeting desire came over me. I briefly considered taking a walk in the park, forgetting my current problems, and never returning.

M approached from behind, touching my shoulder. Sensing my mood, she asked, 'You okay, John?'

'Yes,' I replied grimly, although clearly, I was not okay. A premonition of doom had continued to cloud my mood throughout the morning. I didn't know why. The meeting had gone well so far. Still, I was having trouble dodging the notion that something was wrong.

I turned to face her. 'What's your impression so far?'

'I think it's going well,' she replied quietly.

'It's almost time to begin the afternoon session. You doing okay?'

'I'm fine.'

The Club's staff brought in fresh coffee, placing the dispensers on the table against the wall along with clean cups and saucers, everything in an orderly fashion. The agenda for the afternoon session included a few more reports before moving to our major topic of discussion, the subject everyone had been anticipating: the cycle of unfortunate events that was gripping the company. I didn't push. Even though everyone knew this was the most important item on the agenda, it was business as usual first. Then, on to the mess we were in.

When the last formal report concluded, I paused for a moment; again, no need to be in a hurry.

I smiled at M and began. 'I wish to thank everyone for their contributions. It is a sincere pleasure to work with so many talented professionals. It certainly makes my job easier.' I paused and looked pointedly around the room. 'Of course, we are all aware of several unfortunate events which have recently occurred. Cumulatively, they have severely damaged our production and sales.'

I paused again, trying to make eye contact with each member before I continued. 'Unfortunately, I cannot tell you we have been able to apprehend the criminals who perpetrated these crimes. To date, no connection between these isolated events has been proven. Apart from the coincidence of all the crimes occurring within a relatively short period of time, we have nothing to demonstrate they are related, but this is not because we are not trying. In your folders, you will see a report that documents efforts being made to solve these crimes. These include ongoing investigations conducted by the FBI, Interpol, and the police in Hong Kong and Australia.'

I took a deep breath. I didn't want to bring up the next topic, but I knew it was necessary.

'Unfortunately, I have to add one more bit of bad news to the report. As you may have heard, a former member of our board, Loc Tran, was killed in the attack on his mine in Cambodia. His death was only recently confirmed. Many of you knew him well. I considered him a good friend. We will miss him.'

I paused before continuing. 'Again, let me emphasize we have no evidence suggesting the slaughter in Cambodia was anything more than another isolated event. Most likely, it is an example of the ongoing problems in this area of the world where pirating is not uncommon. However, we cannot rule out the possibility it is related to our other problems. As a result, I urge each of you to institute good security measures to protect your interests. Let me add the company stands ready to offer you advice and economic assistance if you require it.'

I paused to let the members think about what I had just said before continuing. I wanted to present the company in a proactive light, moving forward to deal with its problems, not regressing from the blows it had sustained. 'Although the company has been adversely affected,' I continued, 'I'm confident these problems will sort themselves out in the future. The biggest mistake we can make now is to panic and abandon strategies which have brought us phenomenal growth in the past. The progress we have made in the last few years is something we can all be proud of. We should not become discouraged.'

I waited for a response. When no one spoke, I continued. 'Okay, let's open the floor now for discussion with one possible exception, please. Several of you have expressed concerns for my safety. I want to thank you. But please note I am here and I am in good health. No discussion, please, concerning my personal well-being. Otherwise, the floor is open.'

Silence... finally Vidu spoke, expressing a conclusion I hoped would be reached by the board.

'The report is exceedingly well done,' he said. 'We are all very worried, but the company is doing everything possible to solve these crimes.'

Lin spoke next, agreeing with Vidu. 'Our clients have pushed us hard, but I am not worried. Because we have treated them well in the past, I believe they will stand by us during this crisis.'

I smiled, happy with their leadership. Everything was going well. A few other board members spoke in agreement, and for a moment, I thought we would finish shortly. It was time for cocktails. I took a deep breath and looked down the long table of men. The board seemed ready for adjournment.

Then Arthur spoke.

'Very good, John, all in good order,' his plucky English accent sounded through the room. 'However, it's important the board fully recognize that any further unpleasant complications could quickly put us into a serious deficit condition. Truth is, we are within weeks of being unable to supply even a portion of our client's needs. I'm not saying this to be an alarmist, but facts are facts... Remember,' continued Arthur, 'Our clients are paying us ridiculously high prices because we give them what they need when they need it. However, it is important to recognize that their factories and clients require constant attention. And they can not, nor will they, wait for us to solve our problems. If we are unable to supply them with gemstones in quantity soon... well... I think you know what will happen.'

'Back to the old ways,' interjected Mr. Piat from Madagascar.

'Right,' Arthur agreed. 'In fact, for all our optimism and wishing it weren't so, the truth is our company is in a very precarious position. I have prepared several charts which I believe illustrate my point.'

At this juncture, Arthur jumped out of his chair and, to my shock, retrieved a floor easel that had been innocuously placed against a wall. He set the easel at the end of the table where everyone could see it and placed a large white pad on it. Innocently, he lifted the plain white cover sheet over the pad to reveal a chart underneath, comprised of a series of broadly colored lines meant to illustrate our dwindling reserves in various sizes and colors of sapphires.

Astonished, I had difficulty containing my intense displeasure. Never had a board member introduced a presentation without my previous knowledge or permission. I was furious, immediately wanting to shut him up. It was within my rights to do so. I was the chairman of the board. I could say he was out of order. I could say the time for such a report was earlier in the meeting. But I was powerless. None of these options would do. My hands were tied, and Arthur knew it. Any action on my part to silence him now would be perceived by the board as an attempt to hide the truth. In fact, any effort to do anything which indicated a rift between us could be interpreted as a further weakness in the company. And this was not what I needed, not now. I had to let him continue.

Arthur turned over the second sheet, revealing another chart with two converging colored lines. In blue was a timeline illustrating current reserves. The other line in red showed the known requirements of our clients. The place where the lines converged was when our reserves and our client's requirements were equal. Where the lines separated on the chart illustrated when the company would be unable to fulfill the minimum requirements of our clients. According to Arthur's chart, this time was four to five weeks more or less from today. He then flipped over another sheet, exposing a chart concerning high-end gemstones, the very expensive stones. This illustration clearly demonstrated how any further deterioration of our reserves would cause severe shortages in sales of these stones. Everyone on the board knew why this was a matter of serious concern. These expensive stones were the greatest source of income and profit.

I watched the faces of the board members in both fascination and fear as Arthur chirped away, destroying everything I had attempted to accomplish during this meeting, throwing a dark pall of ruin over our proceedings, a train wreck ready to happen, no chance to avoid catastrophe. Occasionally, a member looked towards me as if pleading for answers to Arthur's accusations. I had none. Everything he said was true. And the board knew it. In countless phone conversations prior to this meeting; I had discussed the situation with everyone. Of course, I had not used the negative connotations that Arthur was carelessly throwing about in his explanation, words such as disaster, unemployment, and net loss. I had tried to be more positive, but the facts were facts.

'If anything else goes wrong,' Arthur concluded, 'our clients will go from having one of their best years to having one of their worst if they continue to rely on us. And this is not something they will tolerate.'

He paused before glancing at Bob for confirmation.

On cue, Bob stepped in, reading from a sheet of prepared notes. 'I have spoken with many of my clients. To date they have been very gracious, expressing a willingness to help us through our crisis. But they have also told me they cannot continue for more than a few more weeks on our limited delivery schedules. And what they did not say is what they will be forced to do when that happens. I didn't ask. I didn't have to. I know their answer. They will go to someone else for product.'

I needed to respond.

I knew I needed to say something. But what? Nothing seemed right. I had talked with many of the same clients as Arthur and Bob. Our clients knew we were doing everything possible to provide them product. And yes, they had indicated they would continue to work with us. But Bob had a point. When their inventories ran low and their clients were screaming for product, they would buy from whatever source they could find. I couldn't control them, and I didn't blame them. They had a business to run. Arthur was right. And any attempt on my part to refute Arthur's accusations might, I suppose, save the meeting today. But I knew I would have to eat my words later. It wasn't worth it.

I spotted M. She too was staring at me, urging me to say something...

I remained silent.

Arthur continued without waiting for a response. 'When we lose our clients to our competition, everything will change, regress. The cumulative effect will unravel our pricing and undo the work we have accomplished in the last six years.' He paused for effect. 'And this, as we know, would be the end of this company,' he finished with flair.

'Thank you, Arthur,' I finally found my voice. 'I think we all know the gravity of our situation. Your charts certainly illustrate this.'

'I don't think you fully understand, John,' Arthur stated emphatically.

Now... the truth was out. His last statement implied a clear split between us, a disagreement, and a difference of opinion between assumed friends and partners. He was openly questioning my ability to run the company. Last night's conversation at the bar with my three partners echoed in my mind, along with all my brooding thoughts of doom during the night, urging... *I told you so! Why weren't you listening?*

The only possible conclusion I could come to now was to assume my friend Arthur had not made his presentation simply out of the goodness of his heart. No, he had an ulterior motive in mind. He wanted something and I could only guess what that might be. And I didn't think I wasn't going to like it.

Plus, the fact that he hadn't informed me of his intentions clearly indicated he didn't want to give me time to prepare, time to lobby the board to stop his unpleasant power play. I briefly wondered if he had majority support for what I assumed he was about to propose. I had to conclude he did. If not, why challenge me? I wondered furiously how many board members were on his side. I guessed I would find out soon.

It was game on.

I decided it was time to be proactive. I had nothing to gain by letting him continue, no reason to give him an opportunity to do whatever dirty deed he was contemplating.

'Thank you, Arthur,' I said forcefully. 'I think we all understand how serious this is.'

'But…' Arthur tried to interject.

'Just a minute, Arthur,' I cut him off, looking him squarely in the eye with all the intensity I could muster. 'As I'm sure you are painfully aware, none of these problems are our doing. And you do understand everything possible is being done to deal with them. Now, I assure you, we will discover who is causing these problems. And we will put Gemstone International back on track. In the meantime, it is imperative we remain positive. It is my belief a stronger and more secure company will emerge in the future if we continue to work together.'

'But, John,' Bob stated, 'The consequences are…'

'Yes, Bob, they are indeed unfortunate. I know this as well as you do, perhaps better. But I'm also confident we will soon learn the truth. Either all this is the effort of someone or some group trying to destroy this company. Or it is an incredible coincidence which could not have been anticipated. My point is none of us knows the answer. I don't and you don't. But I am confident that either way, we will survive.'

'John,' Arthur tried to interject.

'That's enough, Arthur,' I insisted, thinking it was time to find out if Arthur had the votes to shut me up.

'Your presentation was very informative,' I persisted, staring at Arthur. 'Thank you, we all appreciate your work. Now, it's been a long day. I wish to thank everyone for their contributions. A nice dinner is presently being prepared for us across the street at the Plaza. I think it's time we adjourn. Do I have a second to the motion?'

To my intense relief, Vidu offered a second.

I didn't wait for a discussion, immediately asked for a voice vote. 'All in favor of adjourning?'

'Yes,' votes responded weakly across the table.

'All opposed?'

Nay votes were just as feeble or maybe not. Regardless, I announced without delay, 'Motion carries.'

The motion had passed as far as I was concerned. Although, to be honest, I wasn't sure it did. Didn't matter. This meeting needed to come to an immediate end, and I ended it.

Standing, I gathered my papers and placed them in my briefcase.

Thankfully, several other members joined me by also standing, signaling they too were done for the day.

I immediately exited the room.

7:10 P.M. JOHN

Tradition called for board members to have dinner together after our meeting.

Some members leave early due to pressing business or travel arrangements, but most usually stay. It is a time to relax; break bread together after a day of decisions and hard work. However, this time, I feared we would experience no such relief. And to confirm my apprehension, when Monica and I entered the dining room, we were greeted by noticeably hushed conversations which simultaneously fell silent. The only exception was Bob and Arthur who continued to converse without interruption.

I assumed the reason for this hushed behavior was that permanent members of the board had never seen me unprepared for an issue at a meeting. They knew what happened this afternoon was not business as usual. They were sensing the same discomfort I felt hanging over the room.

But then I wondered if I was overreacting. The circumstances surrounding this meeting were irregular from the beginning. And it was just possible Bob and Arthur were right to bring the company's dire situation into clear view. Perhaps I had been too passive in my approach.

The problem was I couldn't get the word 'conspiracy' out of my head. It seemed more appropriate to the circumstances. But was this a fair representation? Were my partners really involved in a conspiracy? I didn't know. But I did know Bob and Arthur had never done something like this before.

I badly wanted answers. I also knew that until I learned the truth I shouldn't jump to conclusions. The consequences could be disastrous if I was wrong. I had to be patient.

'Would you like a glass of wine?' I asked M.

'Sure.'

After retrieving two glasses of red wine from an open bar, I took a deep breath and surveyed the room for her, eventually finding her surrounded by several members of the board. After arriving at the place where she was holding court, I discreetly passed her a glass of wine and slipped away unnoticed with a smile.

Wandering the room, I began to feel like an uninvited party crasher. Whenever I approached a group, conversation waned so I never stayed long in one place. It was too awkward. Just said a word of greeting and I moved on.

Unlike me, M drew a crowd wherever she went.

I purposefully avoided her, drifting through the room, listening. However, I couldn't help overhearing several conversations she had with some of the board members. These men were not stupid and it wasn't just her beauty which was attracting their attention. It was her intelligence. Consistently she answered their questions, never hesitating; legal opinions given with precision, or politics diffused with common sense and wit. She was having no problem holding them at bay.

Bob eventually approached me; I assumed to be conciliatory, but he had something else on his mind. 'She really does know her stuff,' he said with a smile. 'I thought you were putting us on about her legal talents.'

'Would I do that?'

'With someone that pretty, yes. Where did you find her?'

'She found me, answered one of my ads. Seems she was burned out by Washington bureaucracy and wanted a change of pace.'

'Really?'

'Really.'

'So, you didn't hire her for her brains.'

'Do I look that smart?' I chuckled.

'No, you don't,' Bob stated sarcastically.

'Thanks, Bob.'

'It was just dumb luck then?'

'Just dumb luck,' I admitted.

'I thought so.'

His comment was disturbing on a number of levels. I made a snap decision.

'Bob,' I began calmly, holding his arm to stop him from walking away, 'I would like to talk to you privately.'

'Sure. Anytime.'

'No, I mean tonight.'

'Tonight? It's been a long...' his words drifted off.

'It has to be tonight, Bob. It's urgent. Please meet me in my hotel room after dinner.' I wrote my room number on a business card, handed it to him, and walked away before he could refuse.

Mercifully, the dinner didn't last long. Most directors immediately headed to their respective hotels as soon as they finished eating. Only a few stayed on, enjoying the free bar. I ate in silence, with M sitting next to me, carrying the conversation for both of us. I purposely chose to sit at a table occupied by board members from the Far East. I didn't want to sit with Arthur and Bob until I discovered why Arthur had acted as he did at our meeting.

Before leaving, I found Lin and asked him to also meet me in my room.

I wanted him present when I confronted Bob in private.

8:20 P.M. JOHN

The plastic key card slid easily into the polished brass insert on the hotel door. A small green light flickered, the door clicked open, and I went safely inside.

I had asked M to return early to our hotel room to greet Bob and Lin when they arrived. Normally, I stay long enough after dinner to say a few words of goodbye to the members as they exit, thanking them for coming as was my custom. I wondered if anyone would question me about the meeting. No one did, almost as if they didn't want to talk about it any more than I did. When most of the members were gone, I left to go to my room. Bob and Lin were already inside. Avoiding eye contact, they were seemingly more content to continue their conversation with M than to bother greeting me. She was sitting on a couch in one corner of the studio hotel room, her legs comfortably folded beneath her skirt, her jacket lying over a chair, and the top button of her blouse open. She looked beautiful and at ease, courteously talking to Bob. From what I could observe, he was intent on catching her in some sort of legal misinterpretation. Bob was very intelligent and had a wealth of experience in the legal side of business. He was badgering M with questions, which I assumed mostly for his entertainment because it didn't appear that he was attempting to learn anything; he just wanted to trip her up. However, from what I could hear, he didn't seem to be making much progress. M was politely answering all his questions. Lin, as was his manner, was passively listening, seemingly disinterested in their contest.

Ignoring Bob's genteel bantering for a moment, I headed for the room's liquor cabinet. The situation called for a whiskey. I already had a glass of wine with dinner, which was against my better instincts. Normally I do not make a habit of drinking at business functions, especially something as important as a dinner with the board. It is better to be alert and pay attention. Casual conversations can sometimes be revealing. Subtle references implied in relaxed discussions may contain warning signs. And I was fully aware that I shouldn't be having another drink, but the day had been long and stressful. I needed some liquid reinforcement.

Oddly, a strange impression passed over me as I took a sip of whiskey. It was as if no one knew I was in the room. It felt like I was already a ghost, a relic of the past, just a footnote in the history of the company. I wondered if this would soon be my fate. Shaking the illusion off, it was time to get back in the game, first by rescuing Monica from Bob.

Sitting down purposely on the couch between the two of them to break up their conversation, Bob gave me a look of annoyance.

I smiled at Bob. 'I think Monica has had enough grilling for one evening, don't you? Perhaps you can administer the rest of her legal examination the next time you two get together.'

He leaned back into his chair, obviously irritated.

Body language, it is said, is the only true international language, much more accurate than words. Words are merely symbols that, on occasion, create common images in our minds. When this occurs, communication is facilitated. But more often than not, the process breaks down. Conversations become tainted. Even people speaking the same language can become easily confused. Because words are understood through learned images based on individual experiences that relate to the words. And when our backgrounds are diverse, as is most often the case, the images in our minds may not be similar. As a result, our words do not communicate the same meaning.

Body language is different. It never lies. The way Bob leaned into his chair told me he was reluctant to speak with me, but I couldn't let this deter me. I needed to know what Bob was thinking.

Of my three partners, I felt Bob was the key. Mostly because I knew I could trust what Bob said. Arthur, on the other hand, was different. I was never quite sure what old Arthur was thinking any more than he did. I was never totally confident he would tell me what was really on his mind, even if he knew what it was. My third partner, Lin, was... well... I simply didn't believe he was involved in a conspiracy. I trusted Lin. I was certain I knew where he stood. Bob was another matter. I needed to know if my friend Bob was still my friend. Or was he working behind my back with Arthur to take my job?

'So how did you think the board meeting went today?' I casually asked no one in particular.

Silence.

M knew it was not her place to comment.

Bob attempted to look preoccupied, apparently unwilling to answer.

Finally, Lin answered, 'I thought it went well until Arthur made his presentation.'

'How about you, Bob? What do you think?' I asked him directly, refusing to accept his reluctance to talk.

'I thought it went as well as could be expected under the circumstances,' he replied evasively.

'Did you know Arthur intended to make a presentation?' I asked him, point blank.

'He had to. No one else was raising the pertinent facts,' he replied. 'The board was acting as if this was just another meeting.'

'So, you felt the presentation was necessary?'

'Yeah, I did,' he returned my gaze.

'Okay. Let me ask you if you knew before the meeting what Arthur planned to do?'

I don't think Bob expected me to be this direct. He looked down at his hands for a moment before answering. 'It was important someone make the case.'

'Yes, I know. You already said that, but I want to know if you knew about it in advance. And if you did, why didn't you tell me? Because isn't it common practice at our board meetings for members to inform me of their intentions before making a presentation?' I pressed him.

Bob didn't answer.

Lin answered for him, 'Yes, this is our custom, John.'

'So why did Arthur do it?' I asked Bob. 'Why did he make a presentation without informing me first?'

When Bob again refused to answer, I pressed him. 'Look, Bob, I want to know if Arthur's presentation was more than what it appeared to be on the surface.'

'Like what?'

'I don't know, you tell me.' I asked, feeling like the parent of an insolent child.

'I didn't read anything more into it,' Bob quickly replied.

Bob was a man who always made swift decisions. He was equally hasty to express them, expecting others to accept his logic and wisdom at face value.

Lin, on the other hand, was more thoughtful. I wanted Bob to hear what Lin would say. Bob could possibly discount what Lin or I said individually, but I knew he would have a hard time dismissing both of us if we stood together in solidarity.

Lin sensed intuitively I was waiting for him to speak because it didn't take long for him to reply. 'I believe Arthur's presentation was more than an innocent presentation of the facts.'

'That's preposterous!' Bob retorted defensively.

'Is it?' I replied, more forcefully than I intended. 'Then please explain to me why Arthur made the presentation without first informing me. Because I'm not sure it was in the best interest of the company. Remember, I had asked both of you before the meeting to stay calm, try not to sound discouraging. We have enough problems without blowing the situation out of proportion.'

When Bob said nothing, I continued. 'Everything leading up to Arthur's presentation was fine. The board meeting could have ended quite successfully without Arthur's comments. He knew this, but still, he chose to stir things up. So why did he do it, Bob? And more importantly, why did he choose to discredit the management of this company, namely me, in the process?' I paused before continuing, 'I'm not going to pretend to know his precise motivation, but I do know I didn't like it. And it sure begs a few questions.'

'I think you're both making something out of nothing,' Bob said stubbornly.

M sat very still, visibly uncomfortable.

I was angry. I wanted answers. I knew Bob. I knew he would tell Arthur what I said, but this was okay with me. I wanted our conversation to be related to Arthur. I wanted him to know I was unhappy with him. But more than this, I wanted to discern Arthur's real motive.

'John has a right to ask.' Lin said calmly after a pause. 'Did Arthur have more than one reason for making his presentation.'

'Well, Bob? What was Arthur really after?' I pushed him for an answer. 'Was he intending to make a motion after his presentation? Was he going to ask for my job?'

Bob sat quietly without saying a word. Now, this was not normal for Bob. He was seldom at a loss for words. I waited. When he still refused to answer, I decided it was time to let it drop. I could have pressed him harder. But if I was in for a fight, I knew I might need his help in the future. I didn't want to lose him... not just yet.

'Okay, Bob,' I said. 'Enough for one night. I'll talk to Arthur myself. Perhaps he can clear this up.'

'Look, John,' he replied. 'You've been under a lot of strain lately. Let me apologize for Arthur. I'm sure he intended no harm. If he made an error, it was to be unsympathetic to your situation.'

'Okay, let me talk to him.'

Bob nodded.

9:25 P.M. JOHN

Curiously, Lin seemed to be in no hurry to leave.

When I returned to the sitting room after seeing Bob to the door, Lin was calmly listening to M ask the question which had been worrying me.

'Do you think Bob and Arthur are working together to take over the company?' she probed.

'Let's let John answer your question,' Lin replied.

'It's possible. They have been buddies for a long time,' I began. 'They met about the same time I got to know them when I was in advertising, and GU was my client. Phillip was also a friend of theirs.'

'Phillip Palmer?' asked M. 'The gentleman we saw in London at Arthur's club? The man who made you look like you had seen a ghost?'

'I haven't told you about that, Lin,' I quickly added. 'When I was having dinner in London with Arthur, we saw Phillip sitting at a nearby table.'

'Interesting,' Lin remarked.

'Getting back to your question, M. Truth is I really don't know. That's why I invited Bob here tonight. I was hoping he would tell me the real reason for Arthur's presentation.' I paused, 'What's your opinion, Lin?'

'He said nothing to indicate he knew,' Lin responded in his normal impassionate manner.

I took a sip of whiskey.

'Has John told you about Phillip?' Lin asked Monica.

'John told me some things,' M replied.

'Do you know the connection Arthur has with Phillip Palmer?' Lin asked.

'No,' M replied.

'Maybe you would like to explain, John.'

'Phillip knew Arthur long before they worked together at GU.'

'So, Arthur also has a connection to that business?' M took a sip of a soft drink.

'Yes, at one time he was a small-time colored stone dealer. Rumor has it that he had been smuggling emeralds for years using diplomatic pouches. It was a common method of transporting gems out of Rhodesia at the time.'

'Rhodesia eventually became Zimbabwe?' Monica queried.

'Yes, when Mugabe became its ruler.'

'How did Arthur and Phillip meet?' she asked.

'Phillip said he became acquainted with Arthur in his travels. He asked Arthur to introduce him to the Minister of Mines in Zimbabwe. Arthur agreed, but the association proved to be a dead end for Phillip. The minister was found floating in a river a few days later.'

'How did Arthur get involved in GU?' M asked.

'Originally, he sold emeralds to the company. Eventually, he convinced them to hire him as a buyer. It was a great job for as long as it lasted.'

'And this is how you got to know him?' M asked me.

'Yes, I ran into him often at GU. We hit it off. He was fun to talk to, British accent coupled with a great sense of humor.'

'Tell her about Bob Anderson,' Lin suggested.

'Bob worked at GU after it acquired a string of jewelry stores. He was hired to run that business for them.'

'So, Bob was introduced to Arthur at GU?' Monica settled on the couch, a soft drink in her hand.

'Yes,' I replied.

'As was I,' Lin said. 'GU also lured me in. I represented a firm in Hong Kong which invested money in start-up companies.'

Both Lin and I fell silent for a moment, remembering those days. Dreams had turned to dust. The impossible had happened. A business which was full of promise, destroyed; so much effort down the drain.

'When did you first get involved with GU?' M asked Lin.

'Not long before the company shut down,' Lin answered simply. 'During the time when it was operating on other people's money.'

'So, all of you are connected through your previous association with GU?'

'Yes,' Lin answered simply.

'Why did you decide to work with John? Wasn't GU's collapse enough to convince you to stay out of the business?' M asked Lin while glancing at me.

'Because I convinced Lin that money could be made in the business,' I replied for Lin. 'But only if it was done the right way.'

'Did you help John find money to finance his company?' she asked Lin directly.

'Yes,' he responded.

'And now you run one of his three Distribution Houses?'

'He offered me the job.'

'And you also own stock in John's company?' she asked.

'Yes, I'm responsible for voting stock,' Lin replied simply without further explanation.

'Is there anything which legally ties your Distribution House to John's company?' M asked Lin. Seemed she was still not fully convinced I was telling the truth. Or perhaps she simply wanted absolute confirmation. Either way, I was happy to hear Lin's answer.

'No.'

'Remember, M,' I intervened. 'We had just worked for a company which had been papered to death by lawyers. All very proper, but in reality, it was just a house of cards.'

'Paper doesn't make things right, doesn't make a company work,' Lin explained.

'And sometimes it can actually be a deterrent.' I added.

'And Arthur, did he ask to join John's new company?' she questioned.

'Begged,' Lin replied for me.

'The present goes back to the past,' M mused, having finally put the pieces together.

'Yes,' I answered.

'What happened to Phillip?' asked M.

'After his company failed?'

'Yes.'

'I'm not sure what's happened to Phillip,' I responded. 'Truth is I've been purposely avoiding him. But now I wonder.'

'Wonder what?' M asked.

'If he could be involved in all this?' I looked at Lin.

'We have no reason to suspect him,' Lin responded.

'But still, it's possible.'

'Doesn't seem possible to me,' Lin stated unemotionally.

DECEMBER 4, WEDNESDAY, 9:15 A.M. JOHN

The high-pitched scream of its twin jet engines filled the interior of the helicopter's cabin as the mechanical bird broke free from gravity and lifted off the roof of a tall building, rising high into a blue sky above towering buildings and miniaturized humans below.

I have often wondered what draws the hordes of lonely souls to this island encapsulated by water. I have heard it said that many New Yorkers never leave this city, never climb a mountain, never sail to another country, never ever hear the quiet sounds of nature on a summer evening. Their universe consists of nothing more than a densely populated piece of expensive real estate compressed into a state of constant human turmoil.

'You seem lost in thought,' M reached over to take my hand.

'Just wondering why some New Yorkers never leave this city. They're born here and die here without ever stepping off this island.'

'Is that good or bad?'

'I'm not sure. I'm just happy when I can escape.'

Wind currents jolted our helicopter as we flew over the eastern seaboard before turning west to head inland toward Charlottesville. After my board meeting, I felt I needed to return to my office quickly, get back to work. That's why I hired a helicopter. My world was under attack from every angle. I needed to be in position to respond quickly.

Truth is, I love to fly. I take to the air every time I can justify the expense. I enjoy viewing the shifting landscapes passing below. I was reminded of a time flying over the Rocky Mountains. It was a cloudless winter day. Smoke rose gently from isolated cabins perched high on snow-covered mountains far below. Curving single-lane roads wound through the tranquil terrain connecting inhabitants, often with great distances between houses. I wondered what makes people choose to live on a mountainside far removed from civilization. Do they have something to hide, or are they simply tired of dealing with other people? The only life they know is a lonely existence.

How different from the life of the inhabitants of New York City.

The insistent ringing of my cell phone broke my reprieve.

M answered for me, 'John Van Laan's phone. May I help you?'

'I'm fine,' she said after a pause. 'Yes, we're flying to Charlottesville. Would you like to talk to John?'

7:40 P.M. JOHN

The night air had turned bitter cold, with a damp drizzle mirroring my mood.

Under stark streetlights, a chilled wind whipped across the shimmering black pavement as I waited impatiently for a stoplight at an intersection. An icy sting of cold rain hit the exposed skin of my face as I walked across the wide intersection when the light finally turned green, heading to the Plaza at a brisk pace.

I had begged off dinner with my partners. Our pre-dinner conversation put me in a bad mood, appetite was gone. After Arthur's last comment, I told the guys I was tired. I wouldn't be dining with them tonight. They looked surprised, but I didn't give them an opportunity to change my mind. I simply got up from the table and walked away. My sudden exit probably wasn't the most intelligent move under the circumstances, but I didn't care. I'd had enough of their nonsense for one night.

Hitting the up button in the lobby of the Plaza Hotel, the elevator door slid open. Like all elevators, it opened to a small, uncomfortable room filled with strangers forced into a confining space for a brief nervous time, hoping to avoid conversation. I don't like hotel elevators. I'm always anxious to get out of them. I also don't like the long halls in hotels any more than I like their elevators. The halls are narrow, empty traffic lanes devoid of life, lined with closed doors, which are uninviting examples of exclusion. Comfort and rest may reside behind all these silent portals, but only if you have a key.

Ignoring my discomfort momentarily, I headed down the hall, daydreaming about what might be happening inside the rooms on the other side of all the shiny doors, all in an effort to take my mind off the conversation I had at the bar. The discussion with my partners had been disturbing. I was looking forward to greeting the lovely redhead behind one of these doors.

'Hi,' a surprised expression covered her face when I entered our suite. Sitting on an upholstered couch, wrapped in a soft white terrycloth robe furnished by the Plaza; a book was in her hand, and a half-finished room service dinner tray sat next to her on a table. M looked warm, happy, and well-fed. I, on the other hand, was dripping wet, cold, and miserable.

'You're back early,' she commented.

'I decided not to stay for dinner.' I peeled off my damp coat.

'Anything wrong?' her brow furrowed slightly.

'No,' I lied. 'I'm going to change...'

Before she could ask any more questions, I hurried into the bedroom and quickly removed the Club's required dress code of a sports coat and tie. Changing into a pair of comfortable jeans and a sweater helped me relax. Poking my head into the sitting room of our suite, I asked M if she would please order a room service dinner for me. Anything, I didn't care.

The bathroom was elegantly furnished with more wrapped soaps and plastic shampoo bottles than anyone could ever use in a day.   Fresh, white, fluffy towels were hung everywhere. I splashed my face with soap and water, hoping to complete a transformation that would put the conversation at the bar behind me.

When I reentered the sitting room, M was still curled up on a couch. Beautiful bare legs peeked deliciously from under her flowing white robe. Her hair was damp and combed back like she had recently taken a bath. She had no makeup, and still, she looked magnificent. I was glad to have returned to our hotel. Dinner with her was a far more enticing choice than spending time with my brooding partners.

'You look comfortable?' I commented. 'Good book?'

'Jim Harrison,' she replied. 'I picked it out of your library before we left. Do you like his writing?'

'One of my favorite authors,' I nodded. 'Which book are you reading?'

'*Dalva.*'

'Good choice.'

'Want to talk about what happened?' she closed her book. 'You don't look too happy.'

'No questions, please.' I knelt down on my knees in front of her and slowly moved my hands up her bare thighs under her robe.

She took my hands and held them tightly, bending over to kiss the top of my head. 'Stop now. You'll spoil my surprise. I'm not quite ready for you.'

'I'm ready. What's your surprise?'

'Not now. I think we need to talk first. What happened at your Club?'

I sighed.

She was a very perceptive lady and could be incredibly persistent when she wanted something. That much I had learned. I retreated to an armchair and told her about my conversation at the bar. Room service arrived with my dinner as we talked. She had ordered salmon, asparagus green and crisp. The meal looked appetizing. I began to eat because I thought I was hungry, but somewhere in the middle of telling M about the conversation with my partners, I lost my appetite again. Placing a polished silver cover over the uneaten food, I pushed the tray away. Getting up, I went over to the room service bar, thinking a glass of whiskey might settle my nerves. After pouring some calming liquid into a clear glass, I took a sip while crossing the room to a window.

Across the sparsely lit void of Central Park, the lights of New York sparkled in the night, each light a room, each room a living space in a tall building. Few sights can compare to New York at night. A vista of towering buildings adorned with a myriad of indiscriminate lights. I wondered how many other lost souls were looking out their windows at this moment, marveling at the sight, just like me.

'Do you really think they're planning something?' M asked, pulling me mentally back inside.

'No, I don't think so.' I sat down beside her.

'But you don't feel good about what they said, do you?'

'No, I don't.'

We were both silent, my mind rushing through countless conflicting emotions like a wind.

'It may appear to you I never lost anything in my life,' I confessed. 'All you have seen of my life is success. And I have been blessed. That is true. But that's now. It hasn't always been true. I have lost more battles than I have won. And I know how it feels to lose. And I know how it begins.'

M looked at me inquisitively. 'But these men are your friends. You've said so yourself.'

'Yes, they are my friends. But money and power are very strong motivators. Understand, I control a company and with control comes privileges. Maybe they want what I have. Maybe they want control. Maybe they see an opening, a weakness, an opportunity to take my job.'

M just looked at me silently.

'They'll rationalize it somehow,' I rambled on. 'They'll say he did his best, but it's time for someone else to take over. Or... he's not tough enough. He's not smart enough. If we don't take over, all will be lost. We'll do him a favor. Save the company for him. That's what they'll say. But in the end, it will be nothing more than justification for taking something which doesn't belong to them.'

'Do you really believe they are plotting against you?'

'I don't know what to believe.' I shook my head.

M sat with her legs tucked under her in one corner of a couch, silent for the moment; her oversized terrycloth robe draped over her like a blanket. I reached over to touch her bare foot, absentmindedly stroking her toes.

'Let's talk about something else. You, for instance. You looked tired earlier at the Club,' I said.

'I'm fine. I just wish I could do something to help you.'

'By the way, they also objected to your sitting with the board tomorrow,' I added, changing the subject.

'Why?'

'They said the other directors might find you a distraction.'

'That's what they said?'

'No, that's my thought.' I laughed. 'And it's fine as far as I'm concerned. Your beauty will take their collective minds off the company's problems.'

'Thanks a lot. You're telling me I'm nothing more than window dressing.'

I smiled. 'We both know you are so much more.'

'What did they really say?' she asked indignantly.

'They said bringing my girlfriend to an important board meeting might indicate a lack of judgment on my part.'

She considered this possibility for a moment. 'That's plausible. Perhaps I shouldn't go.'

'No! You're going,' I said with more vehemence than I thought I had in me. Realizing I was sounding angry, I reached over and took her hand. 'Sorry, M. I didn't mean to sound upset.'

'It's okay, John,' she said softly. 'I understand. But it might be better if I didn't go.'

'Please don't fight me on this,' I half begged her.

'I'm not fighting you, John. I'm only trying to be logical. I don't want to do anything to hurt you.'

'You won't. I won't let that happen. And let me be clear. I want you at the meeting. I want your eyes in the room. Now more than ever.'

'Okay,' she gave in after a minute. 'If you want me to go, I'll go.'

'Thanks.' I was feeling more frustrated than I intended. The last thing I wanted was an argument with her. It just happened. Standing, I went over to look out the windows again to calm down.

She came behind me, wrapped her arms around my waist, leaning her head on my back. The feel of her warm body against me was comforting and relaxing. A half-moon momentarily emerged from the edges of a racing storm cloud. The rain had passed, and clouds in the sky were being swept clean by a strong wind. Moonlight spread a fleeting halo of soft light through one of the clouds, glowing in brilliance against a clear black sky.

Saying nothing before moving around to stand in front with her back to me. Taking my hand, she slid it inside the warmth of her robe to touch the smooth curve of her bare hip, then gently up her belly to cup a full round breast. Opening her robe, she let it slip off her shoulders to the floor. Turning around, she slowly began to undress me, her hands brushing over my body as she carefully removed each article of clothing. I marveled at the beauty of her shadowed body in the moonlight.

In a way which I could not comprehend, her image entered my poor disturbed soul and brought comfort as only she could.

11:40 P.M. JOHN

To me, nothing is more beautiful than the face of a sleeping woman, her eyes closed in the faint light of night, her flowing hair falling carelessly across a pillow.

After we made love, I lay awake for some time, sleep elusive. The joy she brought me for a short time had passed, replaced by a dread mood of failure polluting musty corners of my mind. The scene at the bar kept replaying in my head. I wanted to believe it was nothing more than the result of the frustration we all felt from the horrible events the company had recently endured. But as I lay between sleep and consciousness with my eyes closed, I couldn't stop mulling over our conversation. And I couldn't help but wonder if they really were trying to steal my job.

The memory of the last time I had been fired returned like a bad dream. I groaned inside, thinking about it, wondering if that memory would ever leave me alone. Or would it always appear at times like this from somewhere deep in my skull? In my sleepless nightmare, I again saw the CEO of Anderson and Jones Advertising Agency arrive solemnly in my office, followed by the CFO.

'May we have a word with you?' the CFO spoke politely.

Apparently, he had been assigned the task of firing me. The CEO came with him only as an impartial observer.

'Sure,' I replied. 'Why don't you take a seat.'

I never liked the CFO. He talked too much, always assuming he knew everything. He was a tax expert, full of book knowledge, but totally lacking in common sense. Despite his flaws and for reasons I never completely understood, the CEO liked him. Probably because the CFO didn't mind doing his dirty work, such as firing employees, the ugly deeds that the CEO didn't have the guts to do himself.

'Sorry,' the CFO began. 'We really didn't want it to come to this, but it has been decided. We must ask for your resignation.'

'Why?'

Opening my eyes, the dark walls of the Plaza Hotel bedroom did nothing to stop the haunting memories of being fired from roaming freely through my weary brain. I tried concentrating on something far more enjoyable- M, her body, her smile, and her eyes. And just to be sure she was real, I reached over to touch her thigh softly under the bedcovers. Everything was fine, I told myself. But that did stop the memories from that day, the day I was fired, that didn't stop them from reappearing in my troubled thoughts as I lay half-awake, badly wanting to sleep.

'Why?' I had asked.

The CFO responded dryly, 'Isn't it obvious?'

I knew the company had lost several big clients, mine included. Rumors had been circulating for days. I had talked to some of my fellow employees in accounting. I knew what was happening. I had made it my business because I assumed it might come to this.

'No, it's not obvious to me,' I replied, even though I knew it would be fruitless to attempt to change their minds. 'I know we have recently lost some clients,' I argued. 'But in my opinion, this company needs all of us working and pulling together. I can bring in new clients. I know I can. Give me a chance,' I responded because I had to try; I couldn't go down without a fight.

'That may be true. But in our opinion, we need people with more education,' the CFO countered. 'You understand? If the company is to grow, it needs credibility.'

I couldn't argue with him. I was a small-town guy from the Midwest with an undergraduate degree in marketing from a local liberal arts college. I was just a hardworking fellow trying to climb the ladder to success using determination and guts. What he said was true. I didn't have much in the way of academic credentials.

'Let me state for the record I think you're wrong,' I argued, 'I can do this job better than anyone.'

'We're very sorry. Our decision has been made.'

I was done.

The agony following my firing was the worst part. It was like slowly dying. If your life is your job, if you wake every morning thinking about your work, spending countless hours at your job, if your office is your home and money defines who you are, then being fired is like being executed. Your home, your activities, the clothes you wear, the people you associate with; everything changes after you lose your job. You are alive, but the life you knew, the life you dreamed of, everything is gone.

You die inside when this happens.

My mother had always chastised me when I wasn't doing well in school. She told me I would grow up to be a ditch digger if I didn't improve my grades. After being fired, I remembered her words and I had the feeling she might be right.

TUESDAY, DECEMBER 3, 8:25 A.M. MONICA

It was time to go.

She knew she should be excited, but her only emotion was pure dread.

All her preparation, her hard work, and her research into every nook and cranny of John's company was not enough, not nearly enough. And then came John's story about what happened last night, what made him skip dinner with his colleagues. After that news, her feelings of insecurity only got worse. A sense of being utterly overwhelmed swept up from somewhere deep inside her.

She was a small-town girl from Ohio. Sure, she was smart and pretty, but this was New York. This was the board meeting of a very important company. Men had come from all over the globe to attend this meeting. This was the big time. She had never attended a meeting like this before.

She looked at herself in the bathroom mirror, checked her makeup one more time. Truth was, she didn't want to go. More than anything, she did not want to go. She did not think she belonged across the street in that elegant boardroom, in that fabled club with all its luxurious fixtures. She was afraid she would do something that might hurt John. He had enough problems. He didn't need his inexperienced girlfriend doing something wrong. Not at this meeting, anyway. This one was important, too important.

When she exited the bathroom, his briefcase was in his hand.

'John,' she began. 'Perhaps it would be better if I didn't go today.'

'No,' he responded firmly. 'I want you there. Now get your coat. I don't want to be late.'

8:45 A.M. JOHN

Neatly arranged trays of bagels had been placed next to muffins and rolls on a spotless white tablecloth covering a long table located against a wall in the boardroom. Tall silver coffee dispensers steamed next to the food. Pitchers filled with orange and grapefruit juice were available next to an assortment of the Club's heavy ornate silverware, small clear glasses, China white coffee cups, and folded cloth napkins.

Board members milled around the table dressed in suits and ties, sampling the food and drink. Unenthusiastic conversation typical of early mornings roamed throughout the room; nothing special spoken, no great concerns expressed, no crisis discussed. Just the usual, how are you? Good to see you again, a handshake, a smile. The difficult business of the company was slated for later.

A polished wood conference table sat in the center of the room. Surrounding the table were dark brown upholstered leather armchairs equally spaced.   A presentation folder containing an assortment of company literature, including current financial data, mine output reports, distribution schedules, and sales figures for the last quarter, was placed on the table for each participant.   Reprints of the company's recent advertising campaign were also included, along with a DVD featuring a TV ad.

The room was the largest boardroom available at the Club. Its vaulted ceiling gave it a feeling of spacious grandeur. Beyond curtained windows, the towering trees of Central Park were visible across the street. Several chairs had been placed against an inside wall for those attendees who were not board members, visitors who were allowed at the meetings but only after having received an invitation cleared through my office. These normally included executives from our advertising, accounting, and law firms, jewelry manufacturers, retailers, people connected to our company in one way or another. Today's meeting included very few invitees because I didn't want to discuss the company's current problems in front of a large audience. As it turned out, this was a good decision.

Seeing Vidu as I entered the room with Monica made me recall a conversation I had with him several years ago. He, as much as anyone, had taught me to appreciate the gemstone business. On more than one occasion he had taken time to explain the history of colored stones. It was during one of these early conversations when it first occurred to me that certain changes were necessary if the industry was to grow. That was when I suggested to Vidu that the only way to effectively change the culture of the colored stone business was to gain control of a majority of the world's supply. This conversation, more than anything, was the reason why all these people were gathered together in this room.

'Vidu, how are you, my friend?' I shook his hand. 'Did you have a good trip?'

'It was a long and difficult flight, John,' Vidu responded with a tired smile.

'May I introduce Monica to you? You didn't get an opportunity to meet her in London.'

'Ah, it is surely a great pleasure to finally meet you. The rumors of your beauty were not exaggerated.'

'Thank you,' M responded demurely.

'I would like to talk with you privately before you leave town,' I told him.

'Yes, it would be good for us to talk.'

'Thanks. I'll give you a call after the meeting.'

He nodded.

Board members and visitors filed in. I introduced M to most of them, clarifying her purpose at the meeting. I explained that she was my legal advisor, hoping this would ease her discomfort. A hum of quiet conversation grew in the room as board members slowly arrived, mingling with the others, drinking coffee and eating rolls from the continental breakfast table. I was in no hurry to begin the meeting. I took my time, poured a cup of coffee, and selected an oat bran muffin from the table. It was not my custom to adhere to a tightly wound schedule. I purposely waited to begin until after everyone had the opportunity to become reacquainted with their fellow board members through casual conversation. When I was satisfied the board was comfortable, I made my way to the head of the conference table.

Two visitors were at the meeting. Manuel Ortega was from Colombia represented emerald mining in his country. Henry Mudantoo was the other invitee. He was the current supervisor of the Sandawana emerald mine in Zimbabwe. These two gentlemen had been invited because Gemstone International's future plans included buying and selling emeralds. It was our hope that inviting these gentlemen would help them become comfortable with our methods of operation. Perhaps, allowing us to one day market their stones. It seemed a good idea when their invitations were offered, but I wasn't so sure now given our current situation. However, asking them to leave was not an option at this late date.

Non-permanent members of the board included Vidu's brother, a representative from a Russian sapphire mine, and the CFO of the Nullamana Mining Company of Australia. Mining interests in countries such as India, Madagascar, and Zambia were also represented.

I sipped my coffee and patiently waited, standing at the head of the table for the board members to assume their seats. M was sitting in one of the chairs against the wall reserved for visitors. I had suggested she sit with the board, but she must have felt more comfortable away from the main table.

Eventually, everyone noticed I was waiting for their attention, and they slowly found their respective seats. The meeting was called to order with a few opening remarks. I welcomed our visitors and thanked everyone for coming. The agenda began with a recitation of normal business information supplied in their board packet, such as the company's financial condition, which I briefly presented. Negative numbers indicated losses we had suffered in recent months due to our problems. I made no attempt to hide bad news from the board. Each loss was duly noted with a footnote at the bottom of the page detailing the cause of the problem. I finished by saying our profits were still reasonably healthy for the current fiscal year. Not as good as hoped, but we were in the black.

It was then time for representatives from various mines around the world to present cautious projections of future production. In his report, Robert Stevens, CFO at Nullamana, reported it would be several months before his lab was rebuilt and fully functional. I noted that the delay would not affect the company's purchase of rough stones from mines. We would continue as before without interruption. We did not wish the company's problems to cause the miners economic hardship. Even though I knew this would adversely affect our own bottom line, it needed to be done. The long-term consequences of cutting off our loyal miners would surely sink our company. We had no choice in this matter. It was essential for our survival. If we lost the confidence of our miners, we lost everything.

Before long, it was time for lunch, served in a different room down the hall. I finished my food quickly, taking little notice of what I was eating. Standing to stretch my legs, I decided to return to the board room. Glancing out a window at the wooded expanses of Central Park across the street, a fleeting desire came over me. I briefly considered taking a walk in the park, forgetting my current problems, and never returning.

M approached from behind, touching my shoulder. Sensing my mood, she asked, 'You okay, John?'

'Yes,' I replied grimly, although clearly, I was not okay. A premonition of doom had continued to cloud my mood throughout the morning. I didn't know why. The meeting had gone well so far. Still, I was having trouble dodging the notion that something was wrong.

I turned to face her. 'What's your impression so far?'

'I think it's going well,' she replied quietly.

'It's almost time to begin the afternoon session. You doing okay?'

'I'm fine.'

The Club's staff brought in fresh coffee, placing the dispensers on the table against the wall along with clean cups and saucers, everything in an orderly fashion. The agenda for the afternoon session included a few more reports before moving to our major topic of discussion; the subject everyone had been anticipating: the cycle of unfortunate events that was gripping the company. I didn't push. Even though everyone knew this was the most important item on the agenda, it was business as usual first. Then, on to the mess we were in.

When the last formal report concluded, I paused for a moment; again, no need to be in a hurry.

I smiled at M and began. 'I wish to thank everyone for their contributions. It is a sincere pleasure to work with so many talented professionals. It certainly makes my job easier.' I paused and looked pointedly around the room. 'Of course, we are all aware of several unfortunate events which have recently occurred.

Cumulatively, they have severely damaged our production and sales.'

I paused again, trying to make eye contact with each member before I continued. 'Unfortunately, I cannot tell you we have been able to apprehend the criminals who perpetrated these crimes. To date, no connection between these isolated events has been proven. Apart from the coincidence of all the crimes occurring within a relatively short period of time, we have nothing to demonstrate they are related, but this is not because we are not trying. In your folders, you will see a report that documents efforts being made to solve these crimes. These include ongoing investigations conducted by the FBI, Interpol, and the police in Hong Kong and Australia.'

I took a deep breath. I didn't want to bring up the next topic, but I knew it was necessary.

'Unfortunately, I have to add one more bit of bad news to the report. As you may have heard, a former member of our board, Loc Tran, was killed in the attack on his mine in Cambodia. His death was only recently confirmed. Many of you knew him well. I considered him a good friend. We will miss him.'

I paused before continuing. 'Again, let me emphasize we have no evidence suggesting the slaughter in Cambodia was anything more than another isolated event. Most likely, it is an example of the ongoing problems in this area of the world where pirating is not uncommon. However, we cannot rule out the possibility it is related to our other problems. As a result, I urge each of you to institute good security measures to protect your interests. Let me add the company stands ready to offer you advice and economic assistance if you require it.'

Before continuing, I paused to let the members think about what I had just said. I wanted to present the company in a proactive light, moving forward to deal with its problems, not regressing from the blows it had sustained. 'Although the company has been adversely affected,' I continued, 'I'm confident these problems will sort themselves out in the future. The biggest mistake we can make now is to panic and abandon strategies that have brought us phenomenal growth in the past. The progress we have made in the last few years is something we can all be proud of. We should not become discouraged.'

I waited for a response. When no one spoke, I continued. 'Okay, let's open the floor now for discussion with one possible exception, please. Several of you have expressed concerns for my safety. I want to thank you. But please note I am here and I am in good health. No discussion, please, concerning my personal well-being. Otherwise, the floor is open.'

Silence... finally, Vidu spoke, expressing a conclusion I hoped would be reached by the board.

'The report is exceedingly well done,' he said. 'We are all very worried, but the company is doing everything possible to solve these crimes.'

Lin spoke next, agreeing with Vidu. 'Our clients have pushed us hard, but I am not worried. Because we have treated them well in the past, I believe they will stand by us during this crisis.'

I smiled, happy with their leadership. Everything was going well. A few other board members spoke in agreement, and for a moment, I thought we would finish shortly. It was time for cocktails. I took a deep breath and looked down the long table of men. The board seemed ready for adjournment.

Then Arthur spoke.

'Very good, John, all in good order,' his plucky English accent sounded through the room. 'However, it's important the board fully recognize that any further unpleasant complications could quickly put us into a serious deficit condition. Truth is, we are within weeks of being unable to supply even a portion of our client's needs. I'm not saying this to be an alarmist, but facts are facts... Remember,' continued Arthur, 'Our clients are paying us ridiculously high prices because we give them what they need when they need it. However, it is important to recognize that their factories and clients require constant attention. And they cannot, nor will they, wait for us to solve our problems. If we are unable to supply them with gemstones in quantity soon... well... I think you know what will happen.'

'Back to the old ways,' interjected Mr. Piat from Madagascar.

'Right,' Arthur agreed. 'In fact, for all our optimism and wishing it weren't so, the truth is our company is in a very precarious position. I have prepared several charts which I believe illustrate my point.'

At this juncture, Arthur jumped out of his chair and, to my shock, retrieved a floor easel that had been innocuously placed against a wall. He set the easel at the end of the table where everyone could see it and placed a large white pad on it. Innocently, he lifted the plain white cover sheet over the pad to reveal a chart underneath, comprised of a series of broadly colored lines meant to illustrate our dwindling reserves in various sizes and colors of sapphires.

Astonished, I had difficulty containing my intense displeasure. Never had a board member introduced a presentation without my previous knowledge or permission. I was furious, immediately wanting to shut him up. It was within my rights to do so. I was the chairman of the board. I could say he was out of order. I could say the time for such a report was earlier in the meeting. But I was powerless. None of these options would do. My hands were tied, and Arthur knew it. The board would perceive any action on my part to silence him now as an attempt to hide the truth. In fact, any effort to do anything that indicated a rift between us could be interpreted as a further weakness in the company. And this was not what I needed, not now. I had to let him continue.

Arthur turned over the second sheet, revealing another chart with two converging colored lines. In blue was a timeline illustrating current reserves. The other line in red shows the known requirements of our clients. The place where the lines converged was when our reserves and our client's requirements were equal. Where the lines separated on the chart illustrated when the company would be unable to fulfill the minimum requirements of our clients. According to Arthur's chart, this time was four to five weeks more or less from today. He then flipped over another sheet, exposing a chart concerning high-end gemstones, the very expensive stones. This illustration clearly demonstrated how any further deterioration of our reserves would cause severe shortages in sales of these stones. Everyone on the board knew why this was a matter of serious concern. These expensive stones were the greatest source of income and profit.

I watched the faces of the board members in both fascination and fear as Arthur chirped away, destroying everything I had attempted to accomplish during this meeting, throwing a dark pall of ruin over our proceedings, a train wreck ready to happen, no chance to avoid catastrophe. Occasionally, a member looked towards me as if pleading for answers to Arthur's accusations. I had none. Everything he said was true. And the board knew it. In countless phone conversations prior to this meeting; I had discussed the situation with everyone. Of course, I had not used the negative connotations that Arthur was carelessly throwing about in his explanation, words such as disaster, unemployment, and net loss. I had tried to be more positive, but the facts were facts.

'If anything, else goes wrong,' Arthur concluded, 'our clients will go from having one of their best years to having one of their worst if they continue to rely on us. And this is not something they will tolerate.'

He paused before glancing at Bob for confirmation.

On cue, Bob stepped in, reading from a sheet of prepared notes. 'I have spoken with many of my clients. To date they have been very gracious, expressing a willingness to help us through our crisis. But they have also told me they cannot continue for more than a few more weeks on our limited delivery schedules. And what they did not say is what they will be forced to do when that happens. I didn't ask. I didn't have to. I know their answer. They will go to someone else for product.'

I needed to respond.

I knew I needed to say something. But what? Nothing seemed right. I had talked with many of the same clients as Arthur and Bob. Our clients knew we were doing everything possible to provide them product. And yes, they had indicated they would continue to work with us. But Bob had a point. When their inventories ran low and their clients were screaming for product, they would buy from whatever source they could find. I couldn't control them, and I didn't blame them. They had a business to run. Arthur was right. And any attempt on my part to refute Arthur's accusations might, I suppose, save the meeting today. But I knew I would have to eat my words later. It wasn't worth it.

I spotted M. She too was staring at me, urging me to say something...

I remained silent.

Arthur continued without waiting for a response. 'When we lose our clients to our competition, everything will change, regress. The cumulative effect will unravel our pricing and undo the work we have accomplished in the last six years.' He paused for effect. 'And this, as we know, would be the end of this company,' he finished with flair.

'Thank you, Arthur,' I finally found my voice. 'I think we all know the gravity of our situation. Your charts certainly illustrate this.'

'I don't think you fully understand, John,' Arthur stated emphatically.

Now... the truth was out. His last statement implied a clear split between us, a disagreement, and a difference of opinion between assumed friends and partners. He was openly questioning my ability to run the company. Last night's conversation at the bar with my three partners echoed in my mind, along with all my brooding thoughts of doom during the night, urging... *I told you so! Why weren't you listening?*

The only possible conclusion I could come to now was to assume my friend Arthur had not made his presentation simply out of the goodness of his heart. No, he had an ulterior motive in mind. He wanted something, and I could only guess what that might be. And I didn't think I wasn't going to like it.

Plus, the fact that he hadn't informed me of his intentions clearly indicated he didn't want to give me time to prepare, time to lobby the board to stop his unpleasant power play. I briefly wondered if he had majority support for what I assumed he was about to propose. I had to conclude he did. If not, why challenge me? I wondered furiously how many board members were on his side. I guessed I would find out soon.

It was game on.

I decided it was time to be proactive. I had nothing to gain by letting him continue, no reason to give him an opportunity to do whatever dirty deed he was contemplating.

'Thank you, Arthur,' I said forcefully. 'I think we all understand how serious this is.'

'But...' Arthur tried to interject.

'Just a minute, Arthur,' I cut him off, looking him squarely in the eye with all the intensity I could muster. 'As I'm sure you are painfully aware, none of these problems are our doing. And you do understand everything possible is being done to deal with them. Now, I assure you, we will discover who is causing these problems. And we will put Gemstone International back on track. In the meantime, it is imperative we remain positive. It is my belief a stronger and more secure company will emerge in the future if we continue to work together.'

'But, John,' Bob stated, 'The consequences are...'

'Yes, Bob, they are indeed unfortunate. I know this as well as you do, perhaps better. But I'm also confident we will soon learn the truth. Either all this is the effort of someone or some group trying to destroy this company. Or it is an incredible coincidence which could not have been anticipated. My point is none of us knows the answer. I don't, and you don't. But I am confident that either way, we will survive.'

'John,' Arthur tried to interject.

'That's enough, Arthur,' I insisted, thinking it was time to find out if Arthur had the votes to shut me up.

'Your presentation was very informative,' I persisted, staring at Arthur. 'Thank you, we all appreciate your work. Now, it's been a long day. I wish to thank everyone for their contributions. A nice dinner is presently being prepared for us across the street at the Plaza. I think it's time we adjourn. Do I have a second to the motion?'

To my intense relief, Vidu offered a second.

I didn't wait for a discussion and immediately asked for a voice vote. 'All in favor of adjourning?'

'Yes,' votes responded weakly across the table.

'All opposed?'

Nay votes were just as feeble or maybe not. Regardless, I announced without delay, 'Motion carries.'

The motion had passed as far as I was concerned. Although to be honest, I wasn't sure it did. Didn't matter. This meeting needed to come to an immediate end and I ended it.

Standing, I gathered my papers and placed them in my briefcase.

Thankfully, several other members joined me by also standing, signaling they, too, were done for the day.

I immediately exited the room.

7:10 P.M. JOHN

Tradition called for board members to have dinner together after our meeting.

Some members leave early due to pressing business or travel arrangements, but most usually stay. It is a time to relax; break bread together after a day of decisions and hard work. However, this time, I feared we would experience no such relief. And to confirm my apprehension, when Monica and I entered the dining room, we were greeted by noticeably hushed conversations that simultaneously fell silent. The only exception was Bob and Arthur who continued to converse without interruption.

I assumed the reason for this hushed behavior was that permanent members of the board had never seen me unprepared for an issue at a meeting. They knew what happened this afternoon was not business as usual. They were sensing the same discomfort I felt hanging over the room.

But then I wondered if I was overreacting. The circumstances surrounding this meeting were irregular from the beginning. And it was just possible Bob and Arthur were right to bring the company's dire situation into clear view. Perhaps I had been too passive in my approach.

Problem was I couldn't get the word 'conspiracy' out of my head. It seemed more appropriate to the circumstances. But was this a fair representation? Were my partners really involved a conspiracy? I didn't know. But I did know Bob and Arthur had never done something like this before.

I badly wanted answers, but I also knew that I shouldn't jump to conclusions until I learned the truth. If I was wrong, the consequences could be disastrous. I had to be patient.

'Would you like a glass of wine?' I asked M.

'Sure.'

After retrieving two glasses of red wine from an open bar, I took a deep breath and surveyed the room for her, eventually finding her surrounded by several members of the board. After arriving at the place where she was holding court, I discreetly passed her a glass of wine and slipped away unnoticed with a smile.

Wandering the room, I began to feel like an uninvited party crasher. Whenever I approached a group, conversation waned so I never stayed long in one place. It was too awkward. Just said a word of greeting and I moved on.

Unlike me, M drew a crowd wherever she went.

I purposefully avoided her, drifting through the room, listening. However, I couldn't help overhearing several conversations she had with some of the board members. These men were not stupid, and it wasn't just her beauty that was attracting their attention. It was her intelligence. Consistently she answered their questions, never hesitating; legal opinions given with precision, or politics diffused with common sense and wit. She was having no problem holding them at bay.

Bob eventually approached me; I assumed to be conciliatory, but he had something else on his mind. 'She really does know her stuff,' he said with a smile. 'I thought you were putting us on about her legal talents.'

'Would I do that?'

'With someone that pretty, yes. Where did you find her?'

'She found me, answered one of my ads. Seems she was burned out by Washington bureaucracy and wanted a change of pace.'

'Really?'

'Really.'

'So, you didn't hire her for her brains.'

'Do I look that smart?' I chuckled.

'No, you don't,' Bob stated sarcastically.

'Thanks, Bob.'

'It was just dumb luck then?'

'Just dumb luck,' I admitted.

'I thought so.'

His comment was disturbing on a number of levels. I made a snap decision.

'Bob,' I began calmly, holding his arm to stop him from walking away, 'I would like to talk to you privately.'

'Sure. Anytime.'

'No, I mean tonight.'

'Tonight? It's been a long...' his words drifted off.

'It has to be tonight, Bob. It's urgent. Please meet me in my hotel room after dinner.' I wrote my room number on a business card, handed it to him, and walked away before he could refuse.

Mercifully, the dinner didn't last long. Most directors immediately headed to their respective hotels as soon as they finished eating. Only a few stayed on, enjoying the free bar. I ate in silence, with M sitting next to me, carrying the conversation for both of us. I purposely chose to sit at a table occupied by board members from the Far East. I didn't want to sit with Arthur and Bob until I discovered why Arthur had acted as he did at our meeting.

Before leaving, I found Lin and asked him to also meet me in my room.

I wanted him present when I confronted Bob in private.

8:20 P.M. JOHN

The plastic key card slid easily into the polished brass insert on the hotel door. A small green light flickered, the door clicked open, and I went safely inside.

I had asked M to return early to our hotel room to greet Bob and Lin when they arrived. Normally, I stay long enough after dinner to say a few words of goodbye to the members as they exit, thanking them for coming as was my custom. I wondered if anyone would question me about the meeting. No one did, almost as if they didn't want to talk about it anymore than I did. When most of the members were gone, I left to go to my room. Bob and Lin were already inside. Avoiding eye contact, they were seemingly more content to continue their conversation with M than to bother greeting me. She was sitting on a couch in one corner of the studio hotel room, her legs comfortably folded beneath her skirt, her jacket lying over a chair, and the top button of her blouse open. She looked beautiful and at ease, courteously talking to Bob. From what I could observe, he was intent on catching her in some sort of legal misinterpretation. Bob was very intelligent and had a wealth of experience in the legal side of business. He was badgering M with questions, which I assumed mostly for his entertainment because it didn't appear that he was attempting to learn anything; he just wanted to trip her up. However, from what I could hear, he didn't seem to be making much progress. M was politely answering all his questions. Lin, as was his manner, was passively listening, seemingly disinterested in their contest.

Ignoring Bob's genteel bantering for a moment, I headed for the room's liquor cabinet. The situation called for a whiskey. I already had a glass of wine with dinner, which was against my better instincts. Normally I do not make a habit of drinking at business functions, especially something as important as a dinner with the board. It is better to be alert and pay attention. Casual conversations can sometimes be revealing. Subtle references implied in relaxed discussions may contain warning signs. And I was fully aware that I shouldn't be having another drink, but the day had been long and stressful. I needed some liquid reinforcement.

Oddly, a strange impression passed over me as I took a sip of whiskey. It was as if no one knew I was in the room. It felt like I was already a ghost, a relic of the past, just a footnote in the company's history. I wondered if this would soon be my fate. Shaking the illusion off, it was time to get back in the game, first by rescuing Monica from Bob.

Sitting down purposely on the couch between the two of them to break up their conversation, Bob gave me a look of annoyance.

I smiled at Bob. 'I think Monica has had enough grilling for one evening, don't you? Perhaps you can administer the rest of her legal examination the next time you two get together.'

He leaned back into his chair, obviously irritated.

Body language, it is said, is the only true international language, much more accurate than words. Words are merely symbols that, on occasion, create common images in our minds. When this occurs, communication is facilitated. But more often than not, the process breaks down. Conversations become tainted. Even people speaking the same language can become easily confused because words are understood through learned images based on individual experiences that relate to the words. And when our backgrounds are diverse, as is most often the case, the images in our minds may not be similar. As a result, our words may not communicate the same meaning.

Body language is different. It never lies. The way Bob leaned into his chair told me he was reluctant to speak with me, but I couldn't let this deter me. I needed to know what Bob was thinking.

Of my three partners, I felt Bob was the key. Mostly because I knew I could trust what Bob said. Arthur, on the other hand, was different. I was never quite sure what old Arthur was thinking any more than he did. I was never totally confident he would tell me what was really on his mind, even if he knew what it was. My third partner, Lin, was... well... I simply didn't believe he was involved in a conspiracy. I trusted Lin. I was certain I knew where he stood. Bob was another matter. I needed to know if my friend Bob was still my friend. Or was he working behind my back with Arthur to take my job?

'So how did you think the board meeting went today?' I casually asked no one in particular.

Silence.

M knew it was not her place to comment.

Bob attempted to look preoccupied, apparently unwilling to answer.

Finally, Lin answered, 'I thought it went well until Arthur made his presentation.'

'How about you, Bob? What do you think?' I asked him directly, refusing to accept his reluctance to talk.

'I thought it went as well as could be expected under the circumstances,' he replied evasively.

'Did you know Arthur intended to make a presentation?' I asked him, point blank.

'He had to. No one else was raising the pertinent facts,' he replied. 'The board was acting as if this was just another meeting.'

'So, you felt the presentation was necessary?'

'Yeah, I did,' he returned my gaze.

'Okay. Let me ask if you knew what Arthur planned to do before the meeting?'

I don't think Bob expected me to be this direct. He looked down at his hands for a moment before answering. 'It was important someone make the case.'

'Yes, I know. You already said that, but I want to know if you knew about it in advance. And if you did, why didn't you tell me? Because isn't it common practice at our board meetings for members to inform me of their intentions before making a presentation?' I pressed him.

Bob didn't answer.

Lin answered for him, 'Yes, this is our custom, John.'

'So why did Arthur do it?' I asked Bob. 'Why did he make a presentation without informing me first?'

When Bob again refused to answer, I pressed him. 'Look, Bob, I want to know if Arthur's presentation was more than what it appeared to be on the surface.'

'Like what?'

'I don't know, you tell me.' I asked, feeling like the parent of an insolent child.

'I didn't read anything more into it,' Bob quickly replied.

Bob was a man who always made swift decisions. He was equally hasty to express them, expecting others to accept his logic and wisdom at face value.

Lin, on the other hand, was more thoughtful. I wanted Bob to hear what Lin would say. Bob could possibly discount what Lin or I said individually, but I knew he would have a hard time dismissing both of us if we stood together in solidarity.

Lin sensed intuitively I was waiting for him to speak because it didn't take long for him to reply. 'I believe Arthur's presentation was more than an innocent presentation of the facts.'

'That's preposterous!' Bob retorted defensively.

'Is it?' I replied more forcefully than I intended. 'Then please explain to me why Arthur made the presentation without first informing me. Because I'm not sure, it was in the company's best interest. Remember, I had asked both of you before the meeting to stay calm and try not to sound discouraging. We have enough problems without blowing the situation out of proportion.'

When Bob said nothing, I continued. 'Everything leading up to Arthur's presentation was fine. The board meeting could have ended quite successfully without Arthur's comments. He knew this, but still, he chose to stir things up. So why did he do it, Bob? And more importantly, why did he choose to discredit the management of this company, namely me, in the process?' I paused before continuing, 'I'm not going to pretend to know his precise motivation, but I do know I didn't like it. And it sure begs a few questions.'

'I think you're both making something out of nothing,' Bob said stubbornly.

M sat very still, visibly uncomfortable.

I was angry. I wanted answers. I knew Bob. I knew he would tell Arthur what I said, but this was okay with me. I wanted our conversation to be related to Arthur. I wanted him to know I was unhappy with him. But more than this, I wanted to discern Arthur's real motive.

'John has a right to ask.' Lin said calmly after a pause. 'Did Arthur have more than one reason for making his presentation.'

'Well, Bob? What was Arthur really after?' I pushed him for an answer. 'Was he intending to make a motion after his presentation? Was he going to ask for my job?'

Bob sat quietly without saying a word. Now, this was not normal for Bob. He was seldom at a loss for words. I waited. When he still refused to answer, I decided it was time to let it drop. I could have pressed him harder. But if I was in for a fight, I knew I might need his help in the future. I didn't want to lose him... not just yet.

'Okay, Bob,' I said. 'Enough for one night. I'll talk to Arthur myself. Perhaps he can clear this up.'

'Look, John,' he replied. 'You've been under a lot of strain lately. Let me apologize to Arthur. I'm sure he intended no harm. If he made an error, it was to be unsympathetic to your situation.'

'Okay, let me talk to him.'

Bob nodded.

9:25 P.M. JOHN

Curiously, Lin seemed to be in no hurry to leave.

When I returned to the sitting room after seeing Bob at the door, Lin was calmly listening to M ask the question that had been worrying me.

'Do you think Bob and Arthur are working together to take over the company?' she probed.

'Let's let John answer your question,' Lin replied.

'It's possible. They have been buddies for a long time,' I began. 'They met about the same time I got to know them when I was in advertising, and GU was my client. Phillip was also a friend of theirs.'

'Phillip Palmer?' asked M. 'The gentleman we saw in London at Arthur's club? The man who made you look like you had seen a ghost?'

'I haven't told you about that, Lin,' I quickly added. 'When I was having dinner in London with Arthur, we saw Phillip sitting at a nearby table.'

'Interesting,' Lin remarked.

'Getting back to your question, M. Truth is I really don't know. That's why I invited Bob here tonight. I was hoping he would tell me the real reason for Arthur's presentation.' I paused, 'What's your opinion, Lin?'

'He said nothing to indicate he knew,' Lin responded in his normal impassionate manner.

I took a sip of whiskey.

'Has John told you about Phillip?' Lin asked Monica.

'John told me some things,' M replied.

'Do you know the connection Arthur has with Phillip Palmer?' Lin asked.

'No,' M replied.

'Maybe you would like to explain, John.'

'Phillip knew Arthur long before they worked together at GU.'

'So, Arthur also has a connection to that business?' M took a sip of a soft drink.

'Yes, at one time, he was a small-time colored stone dealer. Rumor has it that he had been smuggling emeralds for years using diplomatic pouches. It was a common method of transporting gems out of Rhodesia at the time.'

'Rhodesia eventually became Zimbabwe?' Monica queried.

'Yes, when Mugabe became its ruler.'

'How did Arthur and Phillip meet?' she asked.

'Phillip said he became acquainted with Arthur in his travels. He asked Arthur to introduce him to the Minister of Mines in Zimbabwe. Arthur agreed, but the association proved to be a dead end for Phillip. The minister was found floating in a river a few days later.'

'How did Arthur get involved in GU?' M asked.

'Originally, he sold emeralds to the company. Eventually, he convinced them to hire him as a buyer. It was a great job for as long as it lasted.'

'And this is how you got to know him?' M asked me.

'Yes, I ran into him often at GU. We hit it off. He was fun to talk to, British accent coupled with a great sense of humor.'

'Tell her about Bob Anderson,' Lin suggested.

'Bob worked at GU after it acquired a string of jewelry stores. He was hired to run that business for them.'

'So, Bob was introduced to Arthur at GU?' Monica settled on the couch, a soft drink in her hand.

'Yes,' I replied.

'As was I,' Lin said. 'GU also lured me in. I represented a firm in Hong Kong which invested money in start-up companies.'

Both Lin and I fell silent for a moment, remembering those days. Dreams had turned to dust. The impossible had happened.

A business which was full of promise, destroyed; so much effort down the drain.

'When did you first get involved with GU?' M asked Lin.

'Not long before the company shut down,' Lin answered simply. 'During the time when it operated on other people's money.'

'So, all of you are connected through your previous association with GU?'

'Yes,' Lin answered simply.

'Why did you decide to work with John? Wasn't GU's collapse enough to convince you to stay out of the business?' M asked Lin while glancing at me.

'Because I convinced Lin that money could be made in the business,' I replied for Lin. 'But only if it was done the right way.'

'Did you help John find money to finance his company?' she asked Lin directly.

'Yes,' he responded.

'And now you run one of his three Distribution Houses?'

'He offered me the job.'

'And you also own stock in John's company?' she asked.

'Yes, I'm responsible for voting stock,' Lin replied simply without further explanation.

'Is there anything which legally ties your Distribution House to John's company?' M asked Lin. Seemed she was still not fully convinced I was telling the truth. Or perhaps she simply wanted absolute confirmation. Either way, I was happy to hear Lin's answer.

'No.'

'Remember, M,' I intervened. 'We had just worked for a company which had been papered to death by lawyers. All very proper, but in reality, it was just a house of cards.'

'Paper doesn't make things right, doesn't make a company work,' Lin explained.

'And sometimes it can actually be a deterrent.' I added.

'And Arthur, did he ask to join John's new company?' she questioned.

'Begged,' Lin replied for me.

'The present goes back to the past,' M mused, finally putting the pieces together.

'Yes,' I answered.

'What happened to Phillip?' asked M.

'After his company failed?'

'Yes.'

'I'm not sure what's happened to Phillip,' I responded. 'Truth is I've been purposely avoiding him. But now I wonder.'

'Wonder what?' M asked.

'If he could be involved in all this?' I looked at Lin.

'We have no reason to suspect him,' Lin responded.

'But still, it's possible.'

'Doesn't seem possible to me,' Lin stated unemotionally.

DECEMBER 4, WEDNESDAY, 9:15 A.M. JOHN

The high-pitched scream of its twin jet engines filled the interior of the helicopter's cabin as the mechanical bird broke free from gravity and lifted off the roof of a tall building, rising high into a blue sky above towering buildings and miniaturized humans below.

I have often wondered what draws the hordes of lonely souls to this island encapsulated by water. I have heard it said that many New Yorkers never leave this city, never climb a mountain, never sail to another country, never ever hear the quiet sounds of nature on a summer evening. Their universe consists of nothing more than a densely populated piece of expensive real estate compressed into a state of constant human turmoil.

'You seem lost in thought,' M reached over to take my hand.

'Just wondering why some New Yorkers never leave this city. They're born here and die here without ever stepping off this island.'

'Is that good or bad?'

'I'm not sure. I'm just happy when I can escape.'

Wind currents jolted our helicopter as we flew over the eastern seaboard before turning west to head inland toward Charlottesville. After my board meeting, I felt I needed to return to my office quickly, get back to work. That's why I hired a helicopter. My world was under attack from every angle. I needed to be in position to respond quickly.

Truth is, I love to fly. I take to the air every time I can justify the expense. I enjoy viewing the shifting landscapes passing below. I was reminded of a time flying over the Rocky Mountains. It was a cloudless winter day. Smoke rose gently from isolated cabins perched high on snow-covered mountains far below. Curving single-lane roads wound through the tranquil terrain connecting inhabitants, often with great distances between houses. I wondered what makes people choose to live on a mountainside far removed from civilization. Do they have something to hide, or are they simply tired of dealing with other people? The only life they know is a lonely existence.

How different from the life of the inhabitants of New York City?

The insistent ringing of my cell phone broke my reprieve.

M answered for me, 'John Van Laan's phone. May I help you?'

'I'm fine,' she said after a pause. 'Yes, we're flying to Charlottesville. Would you like to talk to John?'

9:25 A.M. VIDU

A bellhop stood next to Vidu while he was waiting for a cab on the sidewalk outside the Plaza Hotel.

A gust of wind swept through his curly black hair as he turned away from the glaring morning sun with his cell phone firmly pressed against his ear. It was difficult to understand John's words due to the constant clutter of irritating background noise inhabiting the cabin of John's helicopter.

'John?' Vidu spoke as clearly as he could. 'John, yes John, I have been doing some checking, and I have the most important information... I am very sorry. The news is not good.'

'Yes,' he replied after pausing when the noise of a departing taxi gunning its motor, made it impossible to hear.

Another yellow cab immediately arrived at the curb.

'Your cab is ready, sir,' the bellhop announced.

'Just a moment, please, John,' Vidu spoke into his phone.

Giving the bellhop a tip, he opened the door of the waiting cab as the bellhop threw his luggage in the trunk and slammed the lid.

'Where to, sir?' the cabby asked.

'LaGuardia,' Vidu replied as he settled into the back seat.

The cab jerked forward, abruptly blending into a maze of New York morning traffic.

'John, can you hear me, John?' Vidu asked, placing his free hand on the back seat of the cab to maintain his balance as the automobile swerved in and out of traffic.

'Yes, I have been waiting for a friend to report to me. My friend has just now called and the information I received from him is most troubling.'

His cab abruptly stopped for a traffic light, throwing Vidu forward, frustrating the normally calm, deliberate man. He was never comfortable in a cab, but he had no choice. This was just one of many American inconveniences he was forced to endure for his work. He could do it. He had done it before. With his phone held tightly to his ear, he listened intently to John's question before replying.

'It is the Thai. I think they are the source of our problems.' he answered simply. 'Yes, I know, John. I have been suspicious of them ever since our problems began, but I didn't want to say anything until I had evidence to support my fears.'

Vidu concentrated on listening to John as his cab bounced over uneven streets.

'No, John, do not send a plane for me,' he replied. 'I have a meeting in Chicago tomorrow morning. Bob made this meeting possible. I am driving to an airport to fly there now.'

'No, John, I don't want to say any more on my phone.'

'No,' he said again.

'Okay, John, you can send a plane to Chicago for me, Midway Airport. Yes, that would be very fine. I will call you when I have finished my meeting. Yes, John, we will talk tomorrow. I will explain everything then.'

Squinting through the bright sunlight shining into his cab's window, he answered John's question. 'No, Bob doesn't know any of this... Yes, I wanted to discuss it with you first.' He paused to listen before continuing. 'It is a client meeting, John, nothing for you to be concerned about. Bob asked me to go with him. It could mean some cutting business for my company.'

A brief pause. 'Okay, John, I promise. I will be careful.'

Vidu pressed a button on his cell phone to end his conversation, squinting nervously out the windshield as his cab drove towards the airport.

CHARLOTTESVILLE, VIRGINIA, DECEMBER 5, THURSDAY, 10:55 A.M. JOHN

It was an unusually warm day for early December.

I'm an avid golfer, even though it's a difficult game and not always a pleasure. However, as a balance against the pressures of work, it is often a welcome relief. Fresh air and lush green landscapes are a pleasant contrast to the sterile white walls of my office. Only rarely is it possible to play golf in December where I live. Normally, the weather is too cold and rainy in Charlottesville. However, occasionally a mild day comes along; an opportunity to get outside for a few hours. When I have the time, I take the opportunity to hit some balls at a practice range while dreaming of warm summer days.

I badly needed to get away from work for a few hours. The acrid atmosphere from the previous day's board meeting was still churning in my gut, gnawing at my innards like a devouring animal. And Vidu's phone call did nothing to ease my mind. I was anxious to talk to him. He was not due to arrive until late in the afternoon. I would have to wait.

My phone had been unusually quiet, no pressing business. Going to the golf club seemed an excellent opportunity to get fresh air, sunshine, and exercise to revive my lagging spirits. M came with me. Not voluntarily, I should add. When I first suggested going to my club, she smiled and refused as I knew she would, complaining about all the work she had to accomplish. It wasn't until after I bribed and threatened her that she finally agreed. I bribed her by promising to buy her a wonderful lunch. The threat was refusing to answer any more of her incessant questions if she didn't agree.

I was glad she came. She looked terrific in a new baby-blue windbreaker, matching hat, and white golf shoes. The pro shop at my club had supplied everything she needed including golf clubs. Of course, she had vigorously fought the notion she needed anything, but I had patiently explained to her how difficult it would be to play golf without the proper attire and equipment.

Exactly, she had countered. She didn't want to play golf. She didn't need anything. That's when I had to remind her about the clause in her employment contract which required playing social golf. She asked where in her contract did it say anything about social golf. I told her it was under the 'other useless duties' paragraph. She didn't find my comment amusing. I promised to show her the wording when we returned to my office.

Of course, there is no such provision in her contract.

I smiled as we drove to the practice range in a golf cart. She, however, was not smiling, staring straight ahead, holding on tightly, looking oddly out of her element, something which was very rare for her. I'm sure she had never imagined her retreat from the oppressive Washington scene would someday take her to a snooty Charlottesville country club.

I told her I was a member because this was the best golf course in the city.

She asked why that was important.

I smiled without answering, enjoying her indignant discomfort.

The grass was a rich shade of green under the warm sun after days of rain. Most of the trees were devoid of leaves by this time in late fall. Only a few oaks still held some brown, dried-up remnants from summer. Winter would soon have its way with the land. Spring was months from now.

Spreading some golf balls on the grass in front of her at the practice range, I selected a nine iron. Now some people are naturals at this game. They don't need much instruction. I thought I should let M take a few swings first before offering suggestions. After showing her an appropriate grip on a club, I demonstrated an easy swing.

'Go ahead, just let it happen. Enjoy hitting the ball,' I said as I gave her the club.

Stepping aside, I left her alone and waited to see what would happen. Either she had a gift for the game, or she would need expensive instruction.

Walking a few paces away, I was looking forward to a few minutes of contented solitude.

CHICAGO, ILLINOIS, 10:10 A.M. VIDU

Vidu hurried across the upper floor of the building's lobby, heading towards a waiting escalator to carry him down to the ground floor.

An expansive, two-story glass atrium spread out below him. Insidious Christmas music spoiled its otherwise comfortable, warm atmosphere. Outside the lobby's windows, Christmas shoppers trudged the cold sidewalks, leaning into a brisk, damp wind off Lake Michigan. Reaching to take hold of the shiny black rubber handgrip, Vidu steadied himself as the moving stairs traveled at a persistent speed down to the building's main floor exit doors.

Vidu had finished his meeting in Chicago. It had gone well. A topaz-cutting contract had been secured for his factories in Sri Lanka. Bob had helped smooth the way. His trip to Chicago had proved to be profitable as promised. Vidu was pleased, but already his active mind was moving to new challenges. His meeting with John in the evening was at the top of his list. Excusing himself early from his meeting had been awkward. Bob had suggested he stay, visit one of the client's showrooms and have lunch. Ordinarily, Vidu would have accepted, but today, he had politely declined, explaining urgent business demanding his attention. He left the meeting abruptly, hoping he had not offended his new clients.

John sent a plane as promised. It was waiting for him at Midway.

He did not often take advantage of his close relationship with John, but he was always appreciative when a favor was offered. In his world, it was better to be offered a favor than to ask for one. Today, he was happy to have a private plane available. It meant he would not have to wait at the airport.

Walking at a steady pace towards the lobby door, Vidu was intent on arriving at the airport as quickly as possible. Once he was outside, a stiff, bitter Chicago wind greeted him, swirling around and over the tall buildings as he waited at a street corner, hoping to hail a cab as crowds of shoppers seeking Christmas bargains strolled past him.

Vidu never saw the man in the gray overcoat approach him from behind. He was too busy waiting at the curb, looking expectantly up the street for an available cab. The initial prick of a needle pressed into his back was so very slight, he did not immediately react. A few seconds passed before the injected fluid caused the first spasm of pain to shoot up his spine. Turning quickly, Vidu caught a brief glimpse of a man getting into the backseat of a waiting car, which quickly disappeared up the avenue.

As the poison seeped steadily into his cells, great pain began to rack his body. Like a knife had been jabbed into his back, Vidu jerked forward, leaning involuntarily towards the street as streams of passing cars raced by. Holding his balance, he closed his eyes against the pain. He had been bitten by a poisonous snake when he was a young boy in Sri Lanka. He knew how it felt. This was worse, far worse. Looking around helplessly, convulsing in pain, badly needing attention, people hurried past him, ignoring a man who was obviously in distress. Paralysis swiftly overtook his body. He tried to remain upright but finally gave in, slumping over uncontrollably, falling in epileptic seizures on a cold, hard sidewalk.

Chicago traffic honked and drove past as Vidu lay convulsing on the sidewalk. Christmas shoppers turned away to avoid the revolting spectacle, wanting nothing to do with a man writhing in pain. He did not fit their Christmas spirit. One man reached into his coat pocket for his cell phone and dialed 911.

Through the pain, a vision of his lovely wife and the green hills of Sri Lanka passed over Vidu before he lost consciousness.

CHARLOTTESVILLE, 11:25 A.M. JOHN

Taking a moment to check on M, I just happened to be privileged to observe a particularly awkward swing of her golf club.

The small white orb she was attempting to launch airborne accidentally shot off the face of her club, fully encased in a mess of muddy grass. Skidding across the surface of the turf, the ball came to rest about twenty yards from its original position.

So much for being a natural. It was painfully obvious this woman was going to require expensive lessons should she ever hope to play golf with any competence. But in one respect, she was a natural. She looked great in her new outfit: dark blue golf pants nicely complimented by a powder blue jacket. Even though she didn't appear to be especially skillful in hitting a golf ball, she was still breathtakingly beautiful in my eyes.

Preparing to take another mighty swing, she hesitated... perhaps sensing my voyeurism. 'See something you like?'

'Just you, kid.' I smiled meekly, trying to stifle of laugh before returning to where I was practicing. Swinging a golf club after days of being cooped up inside my office felt like something oppressive had been lifted off my body. I didn't know why exactly. Perhaps it was nothing more than the opportunity to feel like I was a young boy again, indulging in one of the simple pleasures of youth.

My first few shots were weak; the ball rising feebly into the air before quickly diving for the ground like a wounded duck. But after a while, rhythm and timing returned. The balls flew higher into the blue sky as my muscles loosened and my mind relaxed. After swinging a few more clubs from my bag, I turned again to observe M, hoping to see some progress.

She was still struggling. Great messes of slimy mud and wet grass sailing through the air were occasionally accompanied by a golf ball looking as if it was an incidental compliment to the orbit of muddy chunks of flying earth. On more than one occasion, the grass-filled mud propelled by her club actually flew farther than the small white ball she was attempting to hit.

'How are you doing?' I sheepishly approached the area M had been furiously relandscaping.

She looked up at me in disgust. 'This is a stupid game.'

'Of course, it is. How about allowing me to give you a few tips?'

I think she would have told me where to shove it if she had been given the opportunity, but mercifully, my cell phone rang before she could respond. I briefly debated not answering the call. I was having too much fun. Relenting at the last second, I walked away from the practice tee to take the call in private.

'Hello?'

'John, it's Bob,' he sounded out of breath.

'What's up, Bob?'

'Vidu, he collapsed. It doesn't look good. Ambulance is on the way.'

'What?' I asked, confused.

'Heart attack, don't know. I found him outside, lying on the sidewalk. Just wanted to give you a heads up.'

'Call me as soon as you know something,' I responded as the dire scream of an ambulance siren was heard in the background of his call.

'I will.' he answered before clicking off.

Seeing a look of panic on my face, M approached. 'What is it, John?'

'It's Vidu. He collapsed in Chicago. Bob is with him.'

'Is there anything we can do?'

'No.'

The wonder and escape of the small boy who lived inside me vanished. I was once again forced to return to the world's harsh schoolroom to be educated by a teacher named Reality, who required me to endure another class of undisciplined chaos.

Placing my golf club back in its bag, I abandoned the golf balls lying on the green grass, begging to be hit.

11:30 A.M. JOHN

The clubhouse sits on top of a hill overlooking a gently sloping vista of green grassy fairways and tall trees.

Not nearly as formal as the city club in New York, the dining room was still a special place in a rural fashion, evidenced by wood-beamed ceilings, large windows, and comfortable furniture. Silverware had been neatly wrapped in dark blue cloth napkins and placed on the table next to the plates and water glasses. After we sat down, a waitress dressed in a black-and-white uniform unfolded the napkin and placed the silverware next to the plates. Our water glasses were filled while we read the menus.

'Would you like some coffee?' the waitress asked.

I nodded.

We were early for lunch. The room was almost completely empty.

'Do you mind if I ask a question?' M said.

I had not spoken a word to her since leaving the driving range, silenced by a growing sense of alarm that was sitting in my gut like a stone. I'm an optimistic man by nature. I'm optimistic that solutions to problems can be found by sheer force of will. But the current situation was different. Things were spiraling out of control in increasing speed and magnitude. People were dying. And death has no solution.

I nodded, even though I wasn't in the mood to talk.

'Tell me about the Thai. You said earlier Vidu mentioned them in his last call to you.'

'Yes.'

'Do you think they could be the source of your problems?'

'Vidu does.'

'Yes, but do you?'

'It's possible.'

'Why?'

'Let me give you some history.' I began. 'For years, the Thais bought the sapphires, which were mined in Sri Lankan, based on an old international treaty that gave them exclusive rights, meaning no other country was allowed to purchase the stones. Gemstones from Sri Lanka were sent to Thailand for cutting and sale on the international market. The treaty clearly served the economic interests of Thailand but did very little to help the people of Sri Lanka. The local miners received only a token amount for their work. The real money made from the gemstones went to merchants in Thailand. Thousands are employed in the industry. The whole affair was corrupt. For years, Bangkok was a leading international center for gemstone sales.'

I paused, remembering Vidu explaining all this to me. It was an important part of my education at his hands. He was a very patient man. He knew Americans thought in time spans of no more than five years. He told me if I wanted to be involved in the gem business, I needed to start thinking in terms of decades and centuries.

I continued, 'Citizens of Sri Lanka considered the treaty unfair. They thought gemstones mined in Sri Lanka should primarily benefit Sri Lanka, not Thailand. They wanted to cut and market the gems themselves. Their goal was to end the Thai's influence over a natural resource that belonged to their country. I first met Vidu when he was in the US looking for help to accomplish this goal.'

'Did you help him?'

'Not in the beginning. In the beginning, I asked him for help. I wanted his advice.'

'Did he help you?'

'Yes.'

'So, you helped him?'

'Exactly, it was a partnership. We helped each other. I trusted him.'

'Did you help him put an end to the Thai's dominance of Sri Lanka?'

'Yes,' I replied, my sense of unease deepening. 'I helped him find the money he needed to build his factories so he could cut the sapphires mined on his island.'

'And you marketed these gemstones through your company.' M said, understanding quickly.

'Yes.'

'How did the Thai react?' M asked.

'They had to know the sapphire business would change. It was inevitable. The old treaty was an artificial windfall for them that couldn't last forever. '

'But they were not happy?'

'They were not.'

M thought for a moment. 'Vidu's comment about the Thai could be important?'

'Yes.'

I sipped my coffee. Vidu's condition weighed heavily on my mind. He was my friend, but more than that, he was my mentor. He had taught me about the world of gemstones. When I had a question, I always called Vidu and he would answer my questions with unfailing patience. Few people understood how dependent I was on him.

My cell phone rang. I went outside to answer it. Cell phones were prohibited inside the clubhouse.

'John?'

'Yes, Bob.'

'He's dead.'

'Please, no. Don't tell me that.'

'Sorry, John. He died before reaching the hospital.'

My shoulders slumped in defeat.

'I can't tell you how sorry I am.' Bob continued.

I squeezed my cell phone tightly to suppress my anger.

'I will make arrangements to fly his body to Sri Lanka for burial,' Bob said into a temporarily silent phone.

'Okay,' I muttered softly when I could speak again.

'I'm going to ask for an autopsy first?'

'Why, don't you know what killed him?'

'No, I don't know, and that's why I think we need an autopsy.'

'Do it, Bob. Too much has happened lately. I hope he died of natural causes, but we need to know the truth.'

'I'll take care of it,'

'Bob, one question.'

'Sure.'

'Did Vidu say anything to you before he died?'

'No, he was unconscious when I found him lying on a sidewalk... I'm sorry, John.'

12:40 P.M. JOHN

Vidu's death lay heavy on my mind.

The clubhouse was the last place I wanted to be at that moment. I needed to get away, drive away, escape the demons who were chasing me. M and I walked out immediately after my conversation with Bob.

On the drive back to the office, a roadside café in the country came into view. I was familiar with the place. The décor was a log cabin. The food was home-cooked, and the atmosphere was cozy and warm. I suggested we stop.

It was a good choice. I began to relax as we ate, trying not to think about Vidu. M's smiles helped. We fantasized about heading out on the road for destinations unknown. The idea had a certain appeal. Maybe it was time to let someone else deal with the company's problems. But we both knew that wasn't going to happen. After lunch, we headed back to the office.

The electric garage door under my office building slowly opened as we approached. After driving inside, I turned off the engine but didn't immediately get out of the car. Serenity existed inside. Just being alone with her brought a level of contentment. Upstairs in my office, another world existed. Chaos reigned there.

Phone calls demanding attention... questions asked which had no answers. Vidu's death would need to be addressed.

I didn't want to think about him. I didn't want to deal with the problems. I only wanted to get back on the road and run away... run away with her, with the lovely redhead who sat beside me.

The signs were eminently clear by now to anyone who was paying attention... even me. I was aware of the danger. I knew I was falling for her. Not that I was too worried yet. I was still confident I could sound a retreat any time I chose and run like hell for the hills if required. I wasn't in that deep, not yet, anyway. Because wasn't she just a secretary, I rationalized, hired under an employment contract. An at-will employee; I could let her go anytime... It was just business as usual, wasn't it... or so I reasoned.

But the truth was she was no ordinary secretary, and I knew it. She was a lawyer, for one thing. She could probably beat me over the head with her employment contract in court if she chose. And she had me in the other department, the falling in love department. If I had taken even a millisecond to seriously think about her, about us, about what was happening... I would have known I was in way over my head.

But why think about that now? I could do that later, couldn't I? In the meantime, the only thing that mattered to me was her. How she looked, so wonderfully beautiful, her long red hair falling casually over her shoulders as she turned to me, wondering, I suppose, why I was sitting motionless in the car, acting like an idiot without a clue about what to do next. The answer was simple. Because she was in the car, that's why. The lure of her flashing eyes, the long line of her neck, so much to see, so much to enjoy. I wanted to forget about everything else. I was only interested in her...

'What are you doing?' she finally asked with her car door open, ready to step out.

'I'm desiring you. Isn't it obvious?'

'Stop that. If you only want me for my body, I'm leaving.'

'No, no, you don't understand. I want you for your mind,' I argued. 'So quick and nimble, so subtle, soft and tender...'

'Stop that, John.' She reached over to punch me in the shoulder. 'You're acting like some sex-starved teenager.'

'What's your point, counselor?'

'I don't know. Just grow up.' She started to get out of the car.

'And I thought I was all grown up.' I countered, 'What a disappointment. You mean I still have two things to learn?'

'Yes.' She leaned over and winked seductively.

'Please teach me,' I begged. 'As long as I can gaze into your eyes while you instruct me in the fine art of being an adult. I promise I'll behave...'

'Enough... I'm going home.'

'Okay, Okay.' I raised both hands in surrender. 'I'll be good. If you promise to stay with me tonight, I'll be good. Well... maybe a little bad. But you know, mostly good.'

'I'll think about it,' she turned to walk away.

Something like a hundred messages were on my phone when I sat down at my office desk. Bob had called to say the autopsy was scheduled for the morning. Arthur called, expressing deep regret. I sensed he meant it. But even in this, there seemed to be something odd about the way Arthur said it; more like he was apologizing than expressing sympathy. But I didn't have the time to think about him. Too many other phone calls occupied what remained of my day. When I finished talking to everyone, it was late. The relaxed mood of our afternoon drive had long ago dissipated into thin air, replaced by anger growing in the dark, fertile soil of my frustration. Problem was; I had no one to blame.

I didn't even know if anyone was to blame. It was just possible, against all odds, Vidu had died of natural causes. Death occurs every day. Perhaps God was talking to me, reminding me that life is fleeting.

One fact was undeniable. Vidu was dead, and I would miss his sly smile. I would miss my friend. Sadness seeped into my bones as I thought about him.

He had never stopped thanking me for his success. Even when I patiently explained how we did it together, he wanted to give me the credit. Whenever I visited Sri Lanka, he would take me to see his factories. We would go inside, and he would say, 'Look, John. Look at what you have done.' He would point to rows and rows of cutters working in his factories, bent over their spinning wheels, polishing gemstones. 'Look, John, you have made this happen. Each worker makes a good living. Their families have food and good homes. You did this, John.'

'No, Vidu, we did it together.'

'No, John, your money built these factories. You did this.'

'No, Vidu...'

'John, John,' he refused to listen, walking away with a dismissive wave.

He never knew how much I depended on him. He deserved more, much more credit than he ever received. I was going to miss his counsel, his advice. When my business was new, when it was critical that we stay on course, whenever an unexpected delay or difficult timetable looked as though it might sink us, I would call him.

Just to hear him say, 'It will happen, John. It is meant to be. You only need to be patient.'

7:40 P.M. JOHN

By the time I finished the long list of tasks Helen had marked urgent, it was dark outside.

Night is different from day. Night seems to inhabit your mind with a different sense of reality. Issues seem more depressing at night. Tasks that appear to be easy during the day... or at least manageable, can often feel impossible at night.

After putting down the phone, I silently headed for the door in my office bookcase to my apartment. M followed and poured me a drink. She knew I needed one. Arny had prepared dinner. It was in the fridge. He left a message on the kitchen counter which said all I had to do was to warm it in the oven.

'John, I think it is time for you to make some decisions,' she suggested.

'What?'

I was exhausted, hoping for relief from an intensely busy day. But apparently, my leggy legal advisor had other matters on her beautiful mind—important matters that demanded my attention. I took a sip of my drink.

'You have options.'

'I'm listening.'

'You can wait and hope for no more problems. Pray that this nightmare will end as quickly as it started,' she paused. 'Or you could run away like we talked about at lunch. You have more money than you can spend. You've won the game of life. To stay now may be a losing strategy.'

'Why?'

'Because whether you want to admit it or not. The truth is that you may be next on the list to die... John. Think about it.'

'I have.'

'Have you really?'

After a prolonged pause, I asked, 'Is there a third choice?' I wasn't in the mood to think about dying. And I wasn't sure I was ready to run.

'You can fight... find out who's doing this and make them stop.'

'Okay, given the alternatives... I say we run away. What island shall we inhabit?'

She didn't reply. Just sat, sipping her drink, gazing at me deliberately.

'Okay, you know I'll fight,' I finally relented.

'You didn't get what you have without fighting. I doubt you will stop now.'

'You don't really know me, M. I could quit. I've spent a lifetime fighting. I'm getting tired of this... I could walk away, but not now... Maybe later.'

'Vidu?' she questioned

'Yes, I owe Vidu's family an answer for why this happened, if nothing else.'

'But what if Vidu died of natural causes?'

'I don't believe he did.'

THURSDAY, DECEMBER 12, 7:35 P.M. JOHN

A Leonard Cohen album played in the background as I sipped a beer on my kitchen counter.

Holidays were closing in. Family obligations were beckoning. But Vidu's death was still pressing on my mind like a heavy iron bar, dispelling any pretense of interest in coming festivities. An unending tension like a cold winter rain penetrated the very pores of my inner being. I couldn't stop thinking about him. I feared this Christmas season would be even more difficult to tolerate than normal.

Arny was busy preparing dinner that evening. M had gone to Washington DC early in the morning to talk with Charlie. She had not returned, but called from the airport to say she landed and would be here shortly. Don't eat without me, she demanded. I want to have dinner with you guys.

Now, this made Arny happy. Seems he was no longer content hanging out with only lonely me. He preferred the company of a certain redhead.

After a couple of beers, Arny covered the pans and held off on dinner, obviously intent on waiting for M even though I had suggested we get started. My body wanted food, but apparently, from Arny's point of view, my needs were secondary to Miss Monica's.

When the lady in question finally called from the lobby, I hit the button on my apartment security door and listened for her shoes clicking down the hall. She had dressed up for her trip to Washington, wearing high heels and a power business suit. Ritual nonsense, as far as I was concerned, and I told her so. But she ignored me, claiming to know more about how to play the game in the city of desperate politicians than I did.

'I'm back,' she called before heading for the bedroom. 'Smells good, Arny.'

Arny smiled like a Cheshire cat, making no pretense of denying the fact he preferred her company. They had clearly bonded and it was for life.

Not that I didn't enjoy having her around as well. The sounds of her laughter and humming in the bathroom in the morning, the scent of her perfume in the air; signs of her presence had become familiar. And although I wasn't totally committed to abandoning my bachelor lifestyle, I had to admit, like Arny, my mood improved the nights when she stayed. It didn't happen often. But more and more it was becoming routine. I poured a beer for her and waited for her to change into something comfortable.

Arny gave me one of his knowing looks. 'Getting pretty domestic around here, boss,' he smiled.

I ignored him even though I knew he wouldn't let up.

'Have you decided where to put the nursery?' he asked, now on a mission.

'Just pay attention to your cooking, please.'

M came into the kitchen.

'What are you boys talking about?' she asked.

'Oh, nothing,' I handed her a beer.

'Nurseries, I think we were talking about nurseries, weren't we, boss?' Arny replied under his breath.

'What's that?' asked M.

'Nothing, nothing at all,' I interjected. 'Just ignore him.' I took her by the arm and led her out of the kitchen.

Arny grinned.

'How did it go with Charlie?' I asked, listening to a cold rain pelt the windows.

'He had no news,' M began. 'And he wasn't very impressed with your Thai theory. However, he did agree to check it out anyway and call in a couple of days. I also outlined your case against Phillip Palmer. He was even less impressed with that.'

'He's right, of course. We have no concrete evidence to implicate either of them.'

'Doesn't matter, Charlie will check on Phillip and the Thai. I know him. He's too thorough to let anything go without checking it out first. You'll see.'

'Did he have anything to say about Vidu?' I asked, feeling the dull agony of regret in my gut every time Vidu was mentioned.

'I told him about the autopsy?'

The report clearly indicated Vidu was murdered by a lethal injection. A poison the doctors were still trying to identify, possibly from an exotic snake not common to the US. Charlie found that interesting, but he noted a man like Vidu could have many enemies. His death might have nothing to do with my company's problems.'

I took a sip of beer, thinking she had accomplished nothing and this begged the question of why it was so important for her to go to Washington in the first place. She could have simply called Charlie. Did she really need to see him in person?

'Thanks for going,' I temporarily put aside my paranoia because it accomplished nothing.

'You're welcome.'

'I've been thinking about Phillip.' I changed the subject. 'Can't get him out of my head.'

'Why? Nothing in any of this implicates him,' she insisted, echoing Lin's argument when we last discussed Phillip.

I didn't respond.

'What's his motive?' M probed.

'He wants my company. He thinks I took it from him.'

'You didn't take his company. You said so yourself. You said his company failed because of what he did, not you.'

'Yes, I know, but that's not how Phillip thinks. He always blames someone else for his failures, never himself.'

'That's why you think Phillip might be the source of your problems.'

'Yes.'

'Okay, let's assume for a minute you are right. That would make Phillip responsible for arranging the robbery of the inventory in Hong Kong. And he would also be responsible for starting a fire in your ruined lab in Australia? And it was him who hired men to kill you here in Charlottesville.'

She paused for a moment. 'Do you really think it is possible he could be behind all these incidents?' she argued like a lawyer in front of a jury.

I didn't respond.

'One man did it all?' she pressed her case. 'A man who lives in a small town in Michigan, in the middle of the country, works out of a two-person office. He's the guy responsible for an international crime spree?'

'You don't know Phillip.'

'Come on, John. You're not being rational.'

'All right, all right, one man couldn't do it all. But before you completely dismiss Phillip, consider this. Every one of our recent problems has hurt us in an area where we are very vulnerable. And that points to someone who knows my company from the inside.'

'So how does that implicate Phillip?'

'He knows how my company works. And more importantly, he knows where it is vulnerable.'

'Okay,' M conceded. 'You keep bringing up this inside conspiracy theory of yours. And you think it points to Phillip. Well, maybe it does, but it also points to any number of other people. He's not the only person who knows your company from the inside. In fact, how could he know everything? He never worked for you.'

'Yes, but he worked at the company that preceded GI. And the two corporations are not that dissimilar.'

'So what? That doesn't mean he's responsible.'

'Yes, but it doesn't mean he isn't either.'

M gave me one of her looks like she was questioning my mental aptitude.

'Look, M, you're right in one regard,' I argued. 'No one person could have done it alone. But every gang needs an instigator, someone who brings them together. Phillip fits this profile, and he has all the right contacts.'

'Okay, but you're forgetting one thing. Motive, what does Phillip gain if your company fails?'

I hesitated.

'That's where your argument fails,' she concluded.

'Revenge is his motive.'

'Because you ruined his company. So now he wants to ruin yours?' she questioned.

'Yes, he believes if I had not started my company, he would have succeeded.'

'Could he really have done what you did?'

'No.'

'He just thinks he could?'

'Yes.'

'Why?'

'Because he can't face reality. '

'So instead, he blames you?'

'Yes.'

'Dinner,' Arny called from the kitchen.

M was silent for a moment, which was not normal for her. Another question always lingered on her sweet lips, just waiting for the right time to be presented. I personally hoped she was done. I was hungry. The steaks Arny was cooking on the grill smelled good.

My home phone rang. Arny answered it from the kitchen.

I don't normally answer this phone when I'm in my apartment; just let it go to voicemail. If it's important, I call back. If not, later or never. And I don't remember how many times I told Arny to let it ring. But he had a habit of answering it anyway, an old habit he had trouble breaking. So, I was not pleased to hear him answer it, and I was even more annoyed when he kept talking. I could see him through the kitchen door, sounding like he was having an argument with someone, with a frown covering his face. Not a good sign.

'Sorry, boss.' He came into the dining room. 'But I think you need to take this call.' He shrugged, handing me the portable phone.

'Who?' I asked, getting out of my chair.

'Arthur.'

'Hello,' I tried to sound calm while answering.

'John, so sorry to disturb you at this hour.' Arthur replied.

I immediately knew something was wrong. His usual nasal tone was elevated a few notes above normal; his words loud and fast.

'You know I was expecting a large shipment from Vidu's factory,' he said in a hurry. 'It was supposed to cover my needs for the next few weeks. Well, it didn't arrive. I tracked it to Liverpool, where we had it shipped for security reasons. A courier service was scheduled to pick it up there and deliver it to our London office, but they couldn't because it never arrived in Liverpool.'

'Could it be temporarily displaced?'

'Could be.'

'You okay, Arthur?'

'No, I'm in real trouble with my clients. Losing that shipment is a big problem!' his voice rose in volume as he spoke. 'It's a disaster, John. I don't know what to do.'

'Arthur, calm down. We'll get through this. Now tell me what you know.'

'Sure, sure, what do I know?' he blurted. 'Nothing really; the courier said the manifest showed the package on the plane, but it wasn't there when he arrived in Liverpool at the airport.'

'That's impossible.'

'It's what happened.'

'Could it have been misplaced at the airport?'

'Could be, I just don't know,' Arthur sounded extremely exasperated... 'John, what am I supposed to tell my clients? I have nothing for them. Can't say, 'Sorry, just another unfortunate problem. Please be kind and bear with us',' he continued, now sounding sarcastic.

I didn't know what to say.

'This is a disaster. I'm ruined,' he continued. 'After all, we have accomplished... now this,' he muttered repetitiously.

'Have you called the police?'

'Of course, I called the police. Do you know how much that shipment is worth?'

CHARLOTTESVILLE, VIRGINIA, JANUARY 8, WEDNESDAY, 1:45 P.M. JOHN

Somehow, my company survived the holidays.

This was mostly because our clients were more occupied with getting product into stores for Christmas than they were with making new jewelry. However, when the holidays were over, and they returned to producing produce, our inability to supply their needs became a big problem. The loss of the London shipment put a large hole in our carefully devised plans to shore up their minimum requirements.

To make matters worse, the lab's reconstruction in Australia was badly behind schedule when we needed it to be ahead. The cause of the delay was new furnaces. They had not been delivered on schedule due to unforeseeable problems, according to their manufacturer. As a result, the bloody machines were still not on the continent of koalas and kangaroos where they should have been.

I had been on the phone with the factory daily, saying I would pay for overtime, anything, just get the furnaces on transport planes to Australia in a hurry. But for all my frustration with the furnaces, I knew the furnaces were not the real problem. Even with the lab working at peak production, it would be weeks before our inventory returned to normal. What I needed was product and I needed it now. Without product to sell, I was helpless. Nothing I could do.

Complaints from our clients became a daily problem, resulting in multiple tiresome phone calls. To the best of my ability; I answered every call, explained we were doing everything we could to supply them product. I apologized for the delays, but eventually my words began to sound hollow, tiresome... even to me. Then, almost as if the storm had passed, my phone stopped ringing. No one called because no one had a reason to call. They knew I had no inventory. No inventory, no business. No business, no phone calls.

A major consequence of change is; it never feels right. After years of incessant phone calls and constantly flickering computer screens, I felt lost and depressed. Even though I knew I had done everything possible, the silence was unnerving.

I placed a call to Lin, just to talk to someone.

'How are things in Hong Kong?' I began.

'Damage control is the phrase I think you Americans use.'

'I see'

'More important, how are you, John?'

'What do you think?'

'Not good. You are a builder, not a watcher.'

'Very perceptive.'

'You must be patient now, John. All will be known in time.'

'What do you mean?'

'We have had it easy, John. Everything went our way for the last six years. And when you consider we changed the course of the gemstone business as it had operated for hundreds of years, you must realize how far we have come and how much we have accomplished. It was good, but for some time now, I have been expecting a backlash.'

'Explain.' I thought I knew what he was going to say, but I wanted to hear the words from his perspective.

'Did you think the people whose businesses we destroyed; did you think they would simply disappear without a fight?'

'No, I guess not.'

'John, you have changed the lives of thousands of people. For some of them, it has been a disaster.'

'Yes, but we also made it better for many other folks.'

'I agree, but the people who have not benefited, the people who have lost their source of income and power, what about them?'

'What we did was a natural evolution in the world of business. It just took someone to orchestrate it.' I argued.

'Maybe so, John, but that didn't guarantee everyone would simply give in. No, eventually someone would decide to fight.'

I was silent.

'Maybe the only mistake we made, John,' Lin continued, 'is not anticipating and preparing for the eventuality of a backlash.'

As usual, Lin was logical to a fault. 'Okay, Lin. Let's say I agree with you, what now?'

'Now we are in a fight. And this fight will determine who will win, our way or the old way. It has always been like this in history.'

'Will our way win?'

'Yes,' he replied quickly. 'Because the world is always changing and our way will be included in the future. Even if we lose this fight, the industry cannot return to operating like before us. Too much has changed for that to happen. Control is another question. This fight will determine who will control the industry in the future.'

'You mean our company may not emerge a winner when this is over.'

'I fear this is exactly what may happen.'

'Okay, so what do we do?'

'For now, we have done all we can. Until we discover who our enemies are. Only then can we determine how to fight them.'

'Are you on my side?' I asked without thinking.

Lin was silent for a moment. 'I am disappointed you asked me this question,' he answered quietly.

'I take it back, Lin. I'm sorry.'

'No need to apologize. You have been under tremendous strain. I understand.'

SWISS ALPS, JANUARY 13, SUNDAY, 1:35 P.M.
JOHN

Eyelids heavy, my head rested against the cushioned seat in the train's compartment, content for the moment to let the gently swaying synchronized click, click, clicking of the train's heavy metal wheels on the rails lull me into a false sense of peace.

Picture postcards passed my window in dreamscapes as I rested. Alpine villages painted in bright colors, yellow and pink stucco, forests of evergreens filling snow covered valleys, distant mountain peaks rising into a blue sky.

However, I had not been dwelling on the passing landscapes. I had been otherwise occupied with the small details of the woman who sat across from me on the train. The soft flow of her red hair fell off her shoulders how she sat up so straight, so strong and sure; her posture neither arrogant nor pushy; gentle in expression, calm and secure. She was a mystery I was intent on solving.

Leaning back into my seat for a moment, I closed my eyes to get some rest.

That's when he came to me in a dream, Vidu. He smiled and I reached out to shake his hand, wanting to keep him near. But he turned away quickly, swept into a vast sparkling sea of gemstones shining in brilliant color; my dream quickly evaporating into a disappointing reality which no longer contained my friend.

I sat up and took a deep breath.

M was sitting comfortably across from me, looking outside. Snow dust flew past the frosted glass windows of our train, not enough to obscure the scenery of natural rock sculptures rising like ghosts out of the smooth contours of snow-white landscapes, sweeping breathtakingly across steep mountainsides and down into valleys.

I had decided to get out of Charlottesville. With nothing to do there but wait and worry, work had become an exercise in futility and frustration. I was helpless to make the situation better. I could do nothing and nothing was something I could do anywhere in the world.

Hoping a change of scenery might lift my otherwise worsening moods; I convinced M to take a trip with me. We packed at the last minute and caught a red eye flight to Zurich from New York. From there, a train to St Moritz was booked. The annual meeting of my foundation board was to be held in Switzerland. I decided to attend.

When my company was nothing more than an idea on a piece of paper, I envisioned a percentage of the company's profits given annually to a foundation dedicated to helping miners. The foundation was written into our original articles of incorporation. Before we ever made a dime, my company was obligated to fund the foundation. Only an amendment approved by the board and a majority of the stockholders could eliminate the obligation. And that was not going to happen, not as long as I was the chairman. I wouldn't allow it.

In fact, over the first few years, I lobbied my board to give the foundation more money than our charter required. I wanted the foundation to have enough money so it could continue its work regardless of what happened to the company. Arthur had been the most vocal objector, saying the foundation was something better left for the future. It was all a bit premature, he complained. The company was young and needed money to grow.

I disagreed, saying we were making money, enough to give some away, enough for the foundation to be firmly established.

The foundation always holds its annual meetings in a resort. This is to entice good people to serve on its board and make the meetings fun and enjoyable. This year's annual meeting was scheduled in St Moritz during the prime ski season.

Originally, I had decided not to go; too busy with the problems of the company. Besides, the foundation board was working well without any interference on my part. It did not need me. It was set up to be completely independent. Even though my company funded it, it was not under my control. Decisions on how to spend its money were made by its board. As a result, my attendance was not required, but at the last minute, I decided to attend.

'I never realized the Alps were this beautiful,' M commented after I woke from my nap. 'I've been to Colorado, and I love the scenery. But these mountains are different and so grand.'

'Are you happy you decided to go?' I reached to touch her hand.

She had originally declined my invitation but changed her mind at the last minute, perhaps intuitively understanding how badly I needed this trip.

'This is one of my favorite places on earth,' I explained. 'I came here when I was in college, took a semester off to ski. Probably the best time of my life.'

She didn't respond, simply looking out the window, mesmerized by bright sunlight reflecting off snow covered mountains as our train climbed high and the view fell off steep cliffs into vast empty valleys stretching to mountains in the distance. Villages of brightly colored chalets occupied the valleys. Ice covered streams occasionally paralleled the train tracks.

Remnants of lunch; bread crumbs and cheese slices, empty soup bowls and soiled silverware sat on a small table between our facing seats, waiting for a porter to take away. I sipped a glass of wine as high mountain peaks passed outside our window in all their natural beauty. Wine with lunch was not my habit, but when in Europe; well... live as the Europeans lived. At least, that was my excuse.

M looked particularly gorgeous, dressed in a tight green turtleneck which nicely contoured her fine figure. Suede walking boots adorned her pretty feet. I had insisted she buy boots for our trip, told her to expect snow when we arrived in St Moritz. Warned her she would fall on her sweet derrière if she tried to walk around the town on the smooth soled shoes she wore in Charlottesville.

Helen was the only person in the office who knew where we were going. I didn't even tell Paul Edwards, the executive director of the foundation. I decided to wait until we arrived in Switzerland. I knew he wouldn't mind my coming unannounced. He was a friend and the foundation board meetings were casual affairs with limited pomp and circumstance.

I was a permanent member by virtue of my position as CEO of my company. Serving on the foundation board was one of the most enjoyable aspects of my job. Not that I didn't take it seriously. The humanitarian work facilitated by the foundation was good work. Walking through villages of the miners and seeing their happy faces, children in their new schools and medical offices was a joy.

I smiled at M. 'Having a good time?'

'This is beautiful, John.'

'My pleasure.'

I closed my eyes again, remembering another time and another beautiful girl on a train.

I was traveling Europe as a young college student. At the end of my trip, after a two-week visit to London, I took a train to South Hampton. A passage on the SS France to New York had been booked. I was returning home. With a few dollars still in my pocket, I decided to buy a first-class ticket for a train from London to South Hampton. After boarding, I found an enclosed empty compartment and waited for the train to begin its journey. My ticket indicated I would be served lunch. Good because it was morning, and my next meal was not until evening on the boat.

A beautiful blond girl about my age opened the compartment door as I waited for the train to begin its journey. She looked in and to my amazement, asked in an English accent if she could join me. We had laughed and talked, sharing the compartment as the train clicked over the tracks. I told her about my adventures on the continent. She said she was traveling to South Hampton to visit her family. I think she said she went to a boarding school and was on holiday. Towards the end of our journey, she asked me if I would like to come with her and spend some time at her home. She said she lived in a big house on the coast.

She was very kind, and we both knew in those few hours on the train that we had found something special. Would I please come, she asked. It would be fun. Come stay with me and meet my family. They wouldn't mind.

I was astounded and flattered. She smiled. I thanked her but told her no. My boat was leaving that night. I had a ticket in my pocket. My journey had been long. It was time to go home. She smiled and said she understood.

To this day, I still don't understand why I didn't go with her. What difference did a few more days make? My life might have changed if I had gone with this girl from South Hampton.

A door closed when I said no.

I never saw her again.

ST. MORITZ, SWITZERLAND, MONDAY, JANUARY 14, 9:55 A.M. JOHN

Rubber-soled walking boots squeaked self-consciously as I crossed the polished gold and white stone tiles covering the floor of the lobby at the Palace Hotel in St Moritz.

Tall marble arches supported a vast ceiling of stained, intricate mosaics. The most notable item in this exquisite room of our five-star hotel was a carved Madonna statue looking demurely down from a platform, casting her melancholy aura over the upholstered furniture covered in haughty reds and yellows. Extravagant silver and gold patterned wallpaper adorned the walls. Brass lamps with frosted glass cast shadows over luxurious satin furniture.

I couldn't help but wonder what the real Madonna, the mother of Jesus, would have thought if she could have seen this place. She was a simple woman living in a poor time. Wouldn't she have felt completely out of place in this grand hotel? And yet, someone thought it proper to have her statue in this bastion of luxury to the extreme.

Arriving in St Moritz after a day of travel, we were slightly jet-lagged the next morning. Had a late breakfast in the hotel restaurant. Coffee helped. Eggs and a jellied croissant were M's nourishment, an omelet for me. When we were done eating, a taxi waited outside the lobby to take us to the ski resort of Corvatsch, a short distance from town.

Paul Edwards, the foundation's chairman, had been called before breakfast. I informed him I would be attending the board meeting. However, it was not scheduled until tomorrow morning. We had a free day to ourselves.

Ski touring, I explained to M at breakfast... why don't we go ski touring?

It had been years since I skied, but we were in the mountains and I decided I wanted to ski again to revisit my youth. I said we would take it easy, be smart, just go slow, and enjoy the scenery. This was okay with her, no problem. She admitted to having skied on occasion in high school and college. Good, I commented, hoping this meant I wouldn't have to help her down the mountain.

While driving to the lifts at the advice of our cabby, we stopped at a local store he recommended to purchase ski outfits along with rented skis and boots. Once inside, the store clerk suggested the name of a guide. I agreed, told him to make arrangements.

It was a beautiful winter day, temperatures in the upper thirties; blue sky and sunshine with a light breeze. Our mountain guide's name was Hans Becker. He greeted us warmly when we arrived at the entrance to the ski resort. The store clerk had given him our description over his phone including M's new dark red ski jacket and matching pants. He easily identified us when we arrived.

Hans told us he was a local policeman when he was not working as a mountain guide.

'Where would you like to ski today?' he smiled broadly, displaying a perfect set of sparkling white teeth set in a deeply tanned, handsome face. Wearing a light blue nylon ski jacket over a black and white alpine sweater, his long, curly blond hair had been bleached white by the sun.

Speaking with a heavy German brogue in simple English phrases, 'This is a fine day,' Hans noted. 'New snow fell last night. We will have only sunshine today.'

He was right. It looked like this was going to be a great day in the mountains.

11:10 A.M. JOHN

It is easy to get lost while skiing in the Alps.

The mountains are immense. The trails are narrow and steep in places. It is possible to fall off a cliff and never be found until the sun thaws the winter snow in the spring, and trekkers find your picked-over bones. Apprehension began to gather in my gut as I looked down at the steep slopes falling far beneath our enclosed glass gondola as it rose high into the mountains. It had been years since I last skied. The snow-covered ski trails below us were filled with miniature skiers flanked by tall stands of pine trees. A second gondola ride took us even higher up the mountain, above the tree line. Outcroppings of rocks interrupted the otherwise smooth, snow-covered mountain slopes, which seemed to rise forever into a clear blue sky. The sun felt warm and good on my back when we finally got out of the gondola, but it didn't take long for my lungs to crave oxygen in the rarified mountain air. And this was before we began our arduous descent down the steep mountain trails.

The last time I was in the mountains, I had spent several days at lower altitudes to allow my body time to adapt, get acclimatized to the thin air before tackling higher trails. Lack of oxygen can cause dizziness; or worse, vomiting and black outs. I was reminded that we needed to take it easy.

After stepping into my skis, I joined M, who was waiting at the beginning of the ski run, looking down a near vertical drop-off. According to our guide, Hans, the only trail down this mountain was this one that began with a rather steep fall before leveling out. I told Hans I was in no shape to fly down the mountain. Not that I didn't want to. I did. I just knew disaster would be my reward for such stupidity.

'It is no problem.' Hans assured me, seeing the slightly terrified look in my eyes. 'We go slow at the top, ski simple traverses. Then, the trail gets easier after this. You will see.'

I hoped Hans was right.

Two men exited a gondola behind us. Quickly retrieving their skis, they stepped into their bindings. It was obvious they were experienced skiers. Without hesitation, they effortlessly skied to the edge of the drop-off where we lingered in anxious awe. I envied their natural grace as they dropped down the steep slope, making quick, snow spraying turns, gliding down the mountain and disappearing around a bend in the trail.

It was time.

The moment of truth had arrived. I wondered if I should have stayed at the hotel. Was I out of my element? Flexing my knees to get loose, I leaned on my poles to the left and right, trying to remember what it was like to feel skis under my feet again. Taking a deep breath of cool air, I pushed off my poles toward the beginning of the trail, following M and Hans, sliding easily over the snow, leaning into the slope, the edges of my skis clinging to a gentle incline before hesitating at the top of the drop-off.

'Come,' said Hans with a magnificent, white tooth smile. He pushed off over the edge and slipped down the steep incline, making slow progress, his skis drifting, traversing against the side of the slope before making simple, gentle turns, always in complete control.

M looked at me and forced a smile. Hesitating only briefly, she turned her skies downhill to follow Hans. I watched her for a moment, hoping she would be alright. No problem, it was immediately obvious she was not an expert, but she had no reason to fear the mountain. She could ski. I was relieved. I had been afraid I was getting her into something she was not properly equipped to handle. I should have known better.

I pushed off, down, and across the slope, allowing gravity to take me, edging my skis into the slope for control, letting the skis slide, then checking my speed, slowing by leaning into the slope with my edges.

An overnight snowfall had left a foot or two of powder snow, which felt soft yet firm for control under my skies. I lifted, transferring weight, using some forgotten muscle memory to turn down the slope. Slide, flow, edge back into the slope for control, slide, check, turn, white powder, blue skies; the rhythm of skiing returning from somewhere in my memory banks, gaining confidence, enjoying a sense of floating effortlessly over the snow-covered mountain.

M and Hans schussed quietly and confidently in front of me, making a trail of precision turns to follow in the new soft snow. Lift: transfer your weight, turn, slide, check, speed, freedom, and sunshine. Lift again; confidence building; it was easy to temporarily forget the air was rare, and my legs were not as strong as they once were.

Real freedom is to be a spirit. Spirits don't have limitations. Spirits glide over snow-covered mountains without stress and strain. But I was not a spirit. A small bump in the slope, partially disguised by new snow, suddenly came out of nowhere when I wasn't paying close attention. I caught an edge, leaned too far inside to compensate, skies lifting into the rarified air, white powder flying, falling hard on my butt, sliding down the slope on my side, rolling, grasping for anything, trying to slow my slide on a steep grade. Finally, mercifully, stopping, loose skis trailing behind me attached by safety bindings. Snow covered my chagrined face like the victim of a custard-pie-throwing contest. I could barely see through my snow-encased sunglasses.

The two of them, Hans and M had stopped a short distance down the slope and were looking up at me.

'You all right, sir?' Hans asked, starting to climb skis horizontally to the slope, working up the slope to assist me.

'Let me check,' I answered, testing limbs, one after the other, hoping no extreme pain indicated an injury or maybe a broken bone. I was fine. A sore butt and a bruised ego seemed to be the extent of my injuries. I brushed snow from my face, cleaned my glasses with my sweater, and smiled. 'No problem. Just give me a minute to reattach my skis.'

Fortunately, after my rather spectacular crash, Hans decided to go slow and stop numerous times to allow us to catch our breath. He said we should enjoy the grandeur of the high mountain scenery. Visions of soft white snow, interrupted by large boulders, cliffs and steep drop offs greeted us wherever we rested. He was right, the views were breathtaking.

Thunder interrupted us on one such reprieve, growing loud in the distance, echoing between mountains. I briefly wondered how it could thunder in a clear blue sky with no clouds, no lightening. Then I remembered.

'Avalanche?' I asked Hans.

'Ya, lots of snow already this winter. The warm temperatures are breaking the heavy snow off the high mountain peaks.'

'Any danger for us?'

'No, no. We will not ski in avalanche areas today. You do not need to worry

2:10 P.M. JOHN

We stopped for lunch, sunning on a warm restaurant deck high in the mountains.

I stripped off my sweater and rested in the rarified mountain air. M sat next to me in a patio chair, sunglasses forming tan lines around her eyes. Hans was somewhere nearby, busy tantalizing the waitresses, flashing his brilliant smile to their delight. He knew all the ladies by name.

For brief moments, I actually forgot about my company and its attendant problems. The mountains provided a reprieve, an escape I badly needed. I rested under a clear blue sky, momentarily content. Worry would return tomorrow, but today, I was determined to enjoy this place God made far from fear.

'Time to go,' I heard Hans say somewhere in a dream.

I took a deep breath to wake up, must have drifted off. It was time to move. After retrieving my skis which were standing upright in the snow, I followed M and Hans, heading toward a gondola.

'This afternoon, we ski the south trail.' Hans announced with a smile as we traveled up the mountain. 'It is not hard, only a few steep sections. The scenery is spectacular. You will like it.'

He was right; most of the trail was not too difficult, and we did not ski fast; we simply made slow progress down the mountain, stopping frequently for breathers. The views were awesome. Mountain peaks that appeared close enough to touch in the clear blue sky were far away across valleys stretching below us into the distance. No one spoke as we rested, each of us content to let the magnificent scenery whisper to us before again heading down the trail.

A loud noise, like a cannon shot, rolled down the mountain.

Hans slid to a stop. I skied up behind him. We had just finished skiing a smooth section of open slope that rose high above us. M had continued to ski below us. Hans turned to look up the sloop, sensing something in the air. A low rumble followed a second loud crack, which immediately began to sound like waves of rolling thunder coming out of the sky from somewhere high above us.

'Avalanche,' Hans saw it first, shouting over the increasing din. 'Go, go.'

Panicked, I pushed off immediately pointing my skis straight down the slope, skating to gain speed. Hans followed close behind as the constant rumble grew louder. The open section of the trail where we were skiing led into a steep and bumpy area of moguls. Gaining speed, headed straight down the slope, quickly exceeding my skill level. Moguls came at me fast, faster than I could absorb them with my knees, lifting me into the air, landings which jolted my bone marrow. Somehow, I managed to stay upright, headed towards where M was waiting far down the slope.

The cloud of white snow began to rise high above us, rushing down the mountain.

'Avalanche,' I yelled at her.

She quickly turned and skied towards some boulders, creating a natural shelter.

The rumbling thunder above us closed in quickly, sending shock waves penetrating my body and filling my mind with terror. I dared not look back, continuing as fast as gravity and the mountain slope allowed. To my right was a vertical drop-off. Briefly, I considered diving over the side of the mountain and disappearing down the slope, falling away from the threatening thunder. I did not, too scared I would crash. The slope looked too steep for my skill level. Ahead lay the rocky boulders where M was waiting in safety, hoping to get to her before the avalanche got me.

Bending my knees in a tuck, the ledge came up fast, only a few more yards. I could hear her yelling and for one brief instant, I thought I was going to make it.

And I almost did before the crashing jaws of icy snow caught me, grabbed me; turning, twisting me like some forlorn animal, sucking the breath out of my lungs. Held in the death grip of this white monster, I rolled over and over, reaching for the surface of the pounding, hazy white frenzy, caught uncontrollably in a blast of bitter white cold snow, falling, falling, until it all... stopped...

Dark...

Blank...

Nothing.

11:50 A.M. MONICA

M thought she saw him fall; thought she could easily find the place where John had disappeared under the snow.

But she had been forced to look away when the giant snow blizzard passed over the boulders that were protecting her. She briefly lost sight of his location. She had no choice at the time. She had to close her eyes as the massive thundering whiteout overpowered her senses, blinding her eyes, roaring through her head until she covered her ears with her gloved hands to prevent the pounding noise from piercing her brain.

And then it was gone. As quickly as it arrived, the horrible snow monster was gone, rumbling down slopes far below her. She waited for the wind to clean the air of snow dust before beginning to look for him in earnest.

A fresh blanket of hard snow left her few clues to his location. No ski tracks, no evidence which could help her identify the area where she last saw him. Only layers of hard packed snow spread across a mountainside.

Slowly, she skied from beneath her safe shelter, afraid the ground would begin to move again. The surface was hard and crusty, making it difficult to maneuver her skies in the chunky snow. Releasing her bindings, she discarded her skis and began to walk in her boots, searching for any sign of him. Hard white snow was all she found; no clothing, no skis or poles sticking up in the air, only a vast sea of white remnants of a deadly avalanche.

Exasperated, she began to dig into the snow. Her hands quickly became numb.

Despite the cold, she continued to dig furiously while screaming for help.

12:10 P.M. JOHN

I woke to gray ambiguity.

A pocket of loose snow lay above my head, close to the surface. I could see some light, not much, just enough to know what way was up. I thought I might be able to dig myself out... up...

I soon discovered that wasn't possible. My body was encased, held tight in hard-packed snow. I was in a vice. I tried to move. I could not. Except for my head, which lay in a pocket of open air, my tomb of white death held me firmly.

I was dead.

I knew I was dead if I could not get out. And I could not get out.

The open pocket of air above my head held only a limited supply of oxygen. How much, I did not know.

I was getting cold, and hypothermia was closing in.

I yelled for help. Yelled and yelled for rescue.

The cold became my worst enemy, seeping into my limbs; painful aching cold. I yelled until I became exhausted and then I stopped, stopped yelling, unable to move, entombed.

I was afraid to close my eyes, afraid the white ice was my death tomb if I blanked out. Wave after wave of panic racked my body, heart racing, lungs breathing deeply, encased in an icy grip of snow... cold snow... getting colder.

And then something completely unexpected happened.

I gave up, gave in, no longer afraid.

I felt relief, only relief.

The fighting, the pain, the panic... all of it lifted.

I accepted the fact that my life was over. It was time to die. I had no choice. My day had been glorious, and I had spent it with the one person I truly loved, surrounded by the beauty of the mountains.

I was content.

As I lay encased in my tomb, I had only one regret. I wanted to say the words I had been afraid to say. I wanted to tell her, 'I love you' before I died.

Cold crept slowly into my core, stealthily spreading through every tissue of my body. I had skied the last section of the trail dressed only in a turtleneck, perspiring under a hot sun in thin air. My sweater and jacket were in Hans' backpack. I had no protection from the cold. I wondered how it was going to feel to die in this cold white ice tomb, strangely devoid of definition. I waited, saying a silent prayer, asking God for grace to die in peace.

Cold was like a drug. I shivered, shivered uncontrollably. And then I stopped shivering, just stopped and waited, relieved, feeling tired and strangely content.

Finally, I closed my eyes.

My heart relaxed...

My breathing slowed...

9:10 P.M. MONICA

Her meal at the Palace Hotel restaurant had been delicious.

While sipping a glass of wine in quiet contemplation, her attention was momentarily captured by lights shining from a building across Lake Moritz, reflecting off the snow and ice against a black night sky.

Seeing but not really seeing, the lights were merely a distraction as Monica gazed out the window next to her table. She wasn't really paying attention because her mind was in another place, another time. Tears formed in her eyes as she remembered how John had almost made it to safety. She had witnessed it all from beneath the safety of a rocky outcrop, which saved her life from the avalanche but did not stop her from witnessing the raw force of the swirling snow gather him up like a rag doll before she was forced to look away and he disappeared into a windy white haze.

Hans had continued to ski down the mountain. Apparently, fearing he would not reach the shelter of the boulders before the avalanche caught him, he had dropped down a vertical slope off one side of the trail and shot straight down the mountain in a brave attempt to outrun the avalanche. It eventually caught him before he reached safety, burying him deep in its cold, hard grip. His body was found too late. He was dead.

Rescuers had arrived quickly to help M look for John. They asked where she thought her friend had fallen.

She said she wasn't sure.

Perhaps over there.

But she quickly began to doubt her first suggestion because they could not find him.

Okay, maybe over there, she suggested.

No, nothing they found nothing, only hard-packed snow in the holes they dug. It took time, too much time. One of the men yelled for help while digging in the snow. John's body was found. He was not breathing. They worked over him feverishly.

She waited, and she watched, screaming silently inside, looking for any signs of life. After long minutes of CPR, they revived him. He slowly came out of his cold-induced coma and began to exhibit some signs of life: breathing restored, heart pumping again. After being carted down the mountain, he was airlifted to a local hospital. X-rays indicated nothing broken, only a few bruises and scrapes. He was lucky, the docs said; no major injuries, just a bad case of hypothermia, which probably saved his life, cooled his body and slowed his heart rate while he was buried in an oxygen-deprived atmosphere until he could be found.

'Have you ever thought you were going to die?' he asked, sitting across the table from her at the restaurant.

'Only when I'm around you,' she smiled.

'No, I mean, have you ever really thought you were going to die, and you had no choice but to accept death? Did you feel like that in Australia in the fire?'

She tried to remember. 'No, she finally answered. 'I was in shock. I'm not sure I knew what was happening until it was over, and I had no reason to be afraid anymore.'

He took a sip of wine.

'I thought I was going to die in the snow,' he admitted. 'At first, I panicked. But after a while, I wasn't afraid anymore. I said a prayer to God. Then I waited to die.'

She was silent.

'But look,' he tried to lighten their mood, 'Thanks for saving me. I guess we're even now. You saved me, and I saved you.'

'Not exactly; I didn't risk my life to do it,' she smiled.

'Well, a save is a save. It doesn't matter how.'

'It does, but we don't need to talk about that right now. I'm just glad you're okay.'

Seeing the faraway look in his eyes, she crinkled her eyebrows as she always did when she was trying to understand what was going on in his snow-packed brain.

9:15 P.M. JOHN

I didn't really understand it completely myself.

I didn't know how I could have felt what I did while lying in my cold white tomb. And I didn't try to explain it to her because it only would have hurt her. Because how could I tell her I had almost regretted being saved by the paramedics? I couldn't tell her that, but it was the truth. So, I let it go.

And I also didn't tell her about the other matter I had admitted to myself as I lay entombed in the snow, about being in love with her and wanting to tell her. Like a fool, I also let that go.

'There's something I need to tell you,' She interrupted my train of thought.

'What?' I asked.

'The rescuers told me they thought they heard a sound like an explosion before the avalanche began as if someone purposely set off some dynamite to break the snow free.'

After allowing this new information to process in my brain for a minute, I asked, 'Besides Hans and me, was anyone else hurt?'

'No, you were the only ones.'

ZURICH, SWITZERLAND, WEDNESDAY, JANUARY 16, 6:05 A.M. JOHN

My body ached... ached everywhere.

I wanted nothing more than to go to bed Monday night and sleep.

But apparently, M wanted something more.

Personally, I would have been fine without it... the sex, that is. However, this didn't mean I didn't like it. The fact was, it was great. Her body, strong and graceful, more than made up for my weakened, injury plagued, pitiful attempt to participate. She made the experience good for both of us. And then, thankfully, she allowed me to sleep. But as much as I needed to rest, I got very little sleep that night. I lay awake most of the night, drifting between fitful dreams of snow-cold tombs and images of Hans' white-tooth grin. Getting out of bed early before dawn to escape my nightmares, I found a chair near a window in our hotel bedroom and sipped some hot coffee while watching a new dawn appear from behind distant mountain peaks.

M continued to sleep peacefully while I alternated between being transfixed by the sight of her lovely silhouette beneath the blankets in our dimly lit bedroom... and a mesmerizing view of the Alps outside my window. Slowly, over time, the dark night sky faded into gray as the sun rose behind the mountains to bathe the valley in a bright, sunny blue day.

The foundation board meeting was held on Tuesday. It was uneventful. I contributed almost nothing to the discussion. I don't think the other board members expected much from me. They had been told about my accident prior to the meeting.

After the meeting, M and I had planned to stay for a few more days to enjoy the mountains, but I no longer felt safe after she mentioned it was possible an explosion had caused the avalanche. I feared we could be in danger. Although no real evidence was discovered to justify my suspicion, that didn't stop me from assuming the worst possible explanation, meaning someone may have tried to kill me.

I booked an early flight out of Zurich. A car and driver were hired to drive us to a hotel near the airport, where we stayed overnight. Pre-dawn, Wednesday morning, we boarded our plane. After being cleared for takeoff, the big mechanical bird gained altitude quickly, and the lights of the Swiss city below us slowly disappeared behind mountains. I tried to relax, sitting beside M in the first-class section of the plane. Her hand felt warm when I wrapped my usually cold, bloodless fingers with hers. She smiled but said nothing, thankfully not complaining about my normally cold hands.

The Alps slowly receded into the distance as I stared out the window. I love the mountains. The sheer power of the rising slopes, driven upward from beneath the dark earth by unstoppable natural forces, rising to fill the land with coarse rocks and jagged peaks, growing immensely to heights which dominate vast expanses of previously void sky. Experiencing the views, the rare mountain air and the warm unfiltered sunshine is a wonder unparalleled in any other environment.

But the mountains were not on my mind as our plane made steady progress toward our destination. I was fixated on the devastating event which had almost taken my life... An avalanche, an agent of death and destruction that hides unseen in the high snow peaks of these glorious mountains. Hans had died surrounded by a place he loved, a horrible, lonely death. I knew because I had almost died like him, entombed in an embrace of cold, hard snow. I wondered briefly if he had given up as I had. Did he accept his death? Did he feel a sense of relief when he knew he was going to die?

Personally, I didn't think I would ever give in to death...

But I had. And it had felt good.

And that made me wonder...

Is it better to have never lived, to never have been born? Is it better to never have to deal with the catastrophes in life or the agony of an eventual death? Is death better than birth?

I didn't know.

But I did know by some miracle I had been reborn out of my tomb of icy snow, saved from a still-cold death. My tomb, my comfortable place to die, to cease to exist, to never again have to face the complications that seem to invade life at every turn. My icy tomb had become, instead, for me, a womb, a place to start over... to be reborn.

But I had not chosen life. I had chosen death. Choose to fade into a peaceful oblivion that knows no evil.

I chose death.

But... I didn't die. Because life chose me instead. I lived despite my desire to die. And the life I had not chosen; my life, had not changed. All the problems I faced before my brief encounter with death were as real as they had been before my near-death experience. And the minute I walk through that hidden door into my office in Charlottesville, I know I will once again be forced to face all my problems.

And my biggest problem was that I was having difficulty processing what was happening to me. It seemed so completely unfathomable. I had no idea how to understand what was going on in my life. By most standards, I was successful beyond my wildest expectations. I had money, more money than a boy raised in middle class America could ever think of spending. And I had a beautiful woman sitting beside me, holding my hand. That, in itself, was a minor miracle; just having a relationship with someone as lovely and wonderful as M was a miracle. Fact was I was living the American dream. Success, money, power, and a beautiful woman; I had it all. I should have been ridiculously happy.

Instead, I was living in fear, in constantly shifting sad shades of anxious agony. The success which had given me riches and power had also brought with it fear and death. And these two evil demons now lived with me as companions. They were my problem buddies and I needed to quickly find a way to deal with them.

And what about the woman who was holding my hand? She was a mystery of another sort, a mystery which also needed to be solved. Love does not come easy. I know this. But I was also beginning to understand that love holds uncertainties I may never completely understand.

She turned and smiled at me.

I had no idea why she chose that moment to smile at me.

Was it because she intuitively knew how much I needed her, needed her now more than ever, needed to see the light in her eyes, needed to feel the lingering comfort found only in her smiles?

THE END

See excerpts below from BOOK 2, LIVING WITH DEATH.

JANUARY 24, FRIDAY, 11:06 A.M. JOHN

At approximately five minutes after eleven, the large wooden doors to my office opened, and Helen, my office secretary, showed two gentlemen inside who looked strangely as if this was their first visit.

It was not.

They had been to my office many times in the past. Bob Anderson and Arthur Wilson were business partners, heads of two of our three Distribution Houses and members of my board.

My mood all morning had been particularly dour. I didn't know why. But for whatever reason I had the distinct feeling my buddies were not coming to town for my personal health and well-being. I feared they might have something else in mind. However, I was determined to begin our meeting assuming they came to discuss business, nothing more.

I walked around my desk to greet them with a handshake as Helen politely closed the doors behind her.

To facilitate my hoped-for air of casual civility, I had dressed in long sleeved polo shirt, sweater and khaki pants. They on the other hand, arrived dressed in big city power suits, white shirts and ties. I didn't really mind. They always dressed this way. I sometimes wondered where I found these two guys. In many ways they were very different from me.

'Good morning, Arthur.' I extended my hand while noticing something seemed slightly untidy about his appearance this morning like he hadn't slept well. His curly red hair was more than simply fashionably out of place. An air of dishevelment seemed to have permeated his normally tidy attitude, and his usual sardonic smile was oddly missing.

Bob, on the other hand, was his normal, unaffected self. A big, broad-shouldered man, and his hair was cut short like an ex-Army officer who is exactly what he was. In contrast to Arthur, it was almost impossible for Bob to look untidy, given his strict dress code. A stern, tight-lipped expression always covered his face, highlighted by a permanent frown, which was the product of years of disciplined behavior.

'Please sit down, gentlemen.' I motioned towards the leather couches in my office, normally used for informal conversations. 'Can I get you some coffee, a roll perhaps? This is Charlottesville, not New York. You're in the country. Loosen those ties.'

Putting on a happy face, I retrieved two coffee mugs from a cupboard disguised by mirrored doors in one wall of my office. It was not my habit to require my secretary, Helen, to serve my guests, as did most CEOs. I suppose she would have if I had asked her, but I enjoyed doing away with certain assumptions of power, instead using the casual gesture of serving guests as a symbol of my good intentions. Foreign visitors occasionally expressed genuine surprise when I served them. I didn't mind. This was my office, and this was how I operated.

Placing a prepared thermos of coffee on a table in front of my guests, I never poured the coffee. They could pour their own.

After retrieving a plate of rolls, I asked, 'Arthur, you like your coffee sweet with a little cream... right?'

'Past my coffee time, old chap,' Arthur replied. 'I'm on London time. Don't bother.'

'Something to eat for lunch then? I can have Arny prepare a sandwich.'

'No, no,' Arthur responded with his usual flippant wave of his hand.

'I appreciate you guys coming,' I said as I poured coffee into my mug. 'I would have suggested a meeting, but I thought you had enough problems to occupy your time without my dragging you out to my country office.'

Bob didn't immediately reply; instead looked to Arthur, who was studying the rolls, as if something slightly odd was wrong with them.

'I'm afraid we're not here on usual business,' Bob finally replied, sounding like a sergeant at arms.

'I see.'

'Look, John,' he continued. 'Sorry, this wasn't my idea. But since the last board meeting, we've had numerous calls from members, past and present. Well, you can imagine. No one is happy. Everything is breaking down. And then Vidu died, poisoned to death... and the London shipments got permanently lost... well, you can imagine....'

'Stolen, you mean,' I interrupted, not wanting to allow our discussion to get totally out of control. 'I think we need to assume the shipments were stolen.'

'Okay, stolen. But the point is the board feels something needs to be done.'

'Yes,' I replied, my jaw tightening. I didn't like the direction this conversation was headed.

Arthur chirped in at this juncture, his high-toned, affected English accent sounding unusually nervous. 'John, your office has been very quiet through all this. No real direction coming from Charlottesville, old chap. That's the message we keep hearing.'

I didn't respond, curious now, wondering where they were headed.

'Our clients are upset, naturally,' Arthur droned on. 'And our miners are unhappy. Everyone is asking what we're going to do.'

'Why would the miners be unhappy?' I countered. 'Their payments have not been delayed.'

'Yes, yes,' said Arthur. 'But that's not the point, is it?'

'What is the point?'

'Something needs to be done.'

'You came so we could formulate an answer for them?' I asked hopefully. 'Is that what this is about?'

'I'm afraid it has gone too far for that,' Arthur replied solemnly.

'What has gone too far?'

'Well, tell him, Bob,' Arthur exclaimed, his voice rising an extra octave.

Bob hesitated. 'Sorry, John, but we are here to tell you the board has voted an informal 'no-confidence' in your leadership. They all wish to express how grateful they are for the work you have done for the company. But now, in this time of crisis, they feel new leadership is required. They wish you to stay on as a consultant with full benefits for a period of time. In addition, you may continue to use your office suite as before, but they are asking for your resignation as the CEO and Chairman of the Board.'

BANGKOK THAILAND, SUNDAY, JANUARY 26, 1:30 P.M. LUANG

The old patriarch received constant updates.

These memos, as they were called in Western business jargon, detailed the affairs of the family. Sent from his nephew's office, this privileged information had not been withdrawn from him, not yet. His nephew, Nue, was still keeping him informed. Even though Luang was no longer in a position to exercise influence over the family's businesses, he was still considered an important insider.

Not long ago, Luang Nue had retired from his position of power, the chair at the head of a long conference table, a position he had inherited from his father. He decided it was time to enjoy what remained of his life. He had no sons. When he retired, the head of the family council, the chair of power was given to his closest living relative, his nephew, his dead brother's son.

The family business was still highly profitable at the time of his retirement, established, operating as it had for more than a hundred years. He had no reason at this time to assume this would ever change. But change it did, undermined by a company from America. Everything had gone downhill fast: jobs, money, and connections; everything that made his family respected in his homeland of Thailand. The international business of selling sapphires, the core family business, had been unceremoniously stripped from them by a young American and his company, little by little, until most of it was gone. Luang could not believe it had happened so fast. But the evidence was all around him, factories closed, men and women out of work. It had been a disaster.

Something needed to be done and His nephew Nue was doing it. But the methods he chose were all wrong as far as Luang was concerned. Violence and death were not tactics he would have employed. His nephew had other ideas.

Recently his nephew had changed course, revised his plans, began a strategy more in step with what the old patriarch might have done if he was in control. He attempted to influence matters from inside rather than violently destroy the structure of the American's company from the outside.

The old man knew his plans would take time.

He hoped his nephew had the patience to make it work.

Words from Readers

Author Richard Jan does it again with his tenth book, Casualties of War. If you like the twists and turns of CIA intrigue, a secretive "House" in Washington DC, a menacing plot hatched to blackmail the President, and romance... this book is for you. It will keep you on the edge of your seat. The main character in Richard Jan's series of books is John Van Laan, the Chairman of Gemstone International. He is always in the middle of national and international suspense. Richard Jan's style of dialogue writing is so descriptive you feel you are at a drive-in movie...its that vivid! Casualties of War is about a "House" in DC whose secret members are high-ranking officials from numerous nations who plot revenge against President Obama. If you like a roller coaster ride of mystery and suspense, you will want to read this terrific book.

- *James Haveman, Director of the Michigan Department of Community Health.*
Former Iraqi Senior Advisor for Health to the Coalition Provisional Authority.

I have read Book 1, Winds of Success, and Book 2, Living with Death by Richard Jan. These are new first-time novels, and they are two excellent adventure stories that entice you to read the others in the series (Dying to Succeed). As a reader with a PhD in English literature, one who has published reviews, one who has taught college literature courses, and one who has read countless novels over the course of years, I am impressed with the quality of these two novels. They are packed with international intrigue and displace a convincing knowledge of business in general and the gem trade in particular. And they weave an engaging plot with well-developed characters. One of the strengths of both of these novels is the attention to detail as the author takes you around the world to such places as Bangkok, Thailand, Hong Kong, New York City, the mountains of Montana, Charlottesville, Virginia, the shores of Lake Michigan, and elsewhere. He knows these places intimately: the clubs, the restaurants, the hotels, the landscapes, and the people. His main characters are fairly well-developed and creditable. The Novels also hold interest and attention by the emerging power struggle, crimes violence and sex scenes. And how all of these are played out in the context of a very successful business being brought down political forces and criminal actions. If you are looking for well written adventure novels which keep you wondering what's next and in which you develop an empathetic for the two main characters, I highly recommend these books and I plan the others in the series with eager anticipation.

- *Robert Van Dellen, Ph.D, former professor of English, November 14, 2012*

Being a long time aficionado of mysteries and thrillers, this series has all the potential to be included in the best. The storyline keeps your attention and the desire to never stop but continue reading forever is always there. This is the ultimate test of a great thriller. The series delivers.

-    *Dr. Robert Lamberts, June 26, 2011*

www.ingramcontent.com/pod-product-compliance
Lightning Source LLC
Chambersburg PA
CBHW060426310726
48977CB00001B/69